KASHMIR

ON A

KNIFE–EDGE

BY

MARTINA NICOLLS

STRATEGIC BOOK GROUP

Strategic Book Group
P.O. Box 333
Durham CT 06422
www.StrategicBookClub.com

ISBN: 978-1-60976-413-5

Printed in the United States of America

Book Design: Bonita S. Watson

ACKNOWLEDGMENTS

FOR THE PEOPLE OF KASHMIR: JEWELS IN AN
EXQUISITE LAND.

FOR MY FAMILY, FRIENDS AND FANS ACROSS THE
GLOBE WHO WANTED TO READ THIS NOVEL BEFORE
IT BEGAN, I THANK YOU FOR YOUR ENCOURAGEMENT
AND SUPPORT.

CONTENTS

PART I - MARCH 2002

Chapter 1   Impending Doom 1
Chapter 2   The Journey. 4
Chapter 3   Muzaffarabad 14
Chapter 4   A Confluence of Rivers. 18
Chapter 5   The Minister's Plan. 23
Chapter 6   The First Morning. 28
Chapter 7   Gadi's Secret. 35
Chapter 8   Tea and Vodka. 38
Chapter 9   Jorja Sees Imran 42
Chapter 10   Operation Anaconda 54
Chapter 11   Shaking 57
Chapter 12   Pins and Needles. 63
Chapter 13   Letter to a Lover 67
Chapter 14   The Complexity of Complexions 71
Chapter 15   A Godsend. 76
Chapter 16   Unrest 79
Chapter 17   Couplings 82
Chapter 18   A Knife-Edge 90

Chapter 19   The Photographer 94
Chapter 20   Stairway to Heaven. 101
Chapter 21   A Date With Destiny. 104
Chapter 22   The Intrusion. 107
Chapter 23   A Surprise Package. 112
Chapter 24   A Lesson on Latrines 116
Chapter 25   A Weekend in Islamabad. 121
Chapter 26   The Church Bombing 124
Chapter 27   An American in Pakistani Clothes 130
Chapter 28   Do Not Worry 139
Chapter 29   Pakistan Day 144
Chapter 30   Melody Queen. 149
Chapter 31   The Internet Café 156
Chapter 32   The Thrill of the Tailor's Tape 163
Chapter 33   Another Tremor. 167
Chapter 34   Purdah. 169
Chapter 35   Naked 174
Chapter 36   The Dinner Party. 177
Chapter 37   The Old Hag 182

Part II - April 2002

Chapter 38   Why the Poor Stay Poor and
              Why Osama is Still Hiding 190
Chapter 39   A Visit to the Doctor 198
Chapter 40   Mother and Son. 206
Chapter 41   Spermatization 211
Chapter 42   Loneliness. 219
Chapter 43   Literacy and Cows 225
Chapter 44   Arranged Marriages 231
Chapter 45   Marriage Proposals 239
Chapter 46   As You Wish 246
Chapter 47   A Tale of Two Houses. 249
Chapter 48   White Skin, Pink Skin. 253
Chapter 49   Osama's Eyes 256
Chapter 50   Temporary Prisoner. 264

Chapter 51   Terrorism and Taliban 274
Chapter 52   The Death of Reason. 280
Chapter 53   A Stab in the Heart 283
Chapter 54   How Many?. 289
Chapter 55   Shareef's Company. 294
Chapter 56   In Control 298
Chapter 57   The Referendum Question 301
Chapter 58   The Road Home 310

PART III – MAY 2002

Chapter 59   A Win and a Loss for Pakistan 316
Chapter 60   Increasing Tensions. 321
Chapter 61   Preparing for War 324
Chapter 62   Hopes Rise 330
Author's Notes 334

PART ONE

MARCH 2002

CHAPTER 1

IMPENDING DOOM

Tragedy was surely on its way. Beauty attracted it and death confirmed it. Jorja Himmermann had entered Muzaffarabad, the jewel and capital of Pakistan-administered Azad Kashmir, a city between two volatile conflicts. Pakistan bordered Afghanistan to the north, India to the east, Iran to the west, and the Arabian Sea to the south. In the northeast was the disputed territory of Kashmir. Pakistan and India's dispute over Kashmir had escalated and the American war against terror was at a climax in Afghanistan.

It was 2002, the International Year of the Mountain. The Pir Panjal Range of the Himalaya spread across northern Pakistan and Kashmir. The Kashmir dispute had raged since Pakistan's and India's independence from the British in 1947. Each country claimed it as a part of their territory. A rebellion during Independence, or Partition, led to the establishment of the Line of Control—a cease-fire line—that bisected the area. To the east of the line was the valley of Kashmir, Jammu and Ladakh administered by India. To the west was Azad Kashmir, which had its own government, although administered by Pakistan. Azad Kashmir was Pakistan's "Jugular Vein"—strangulation by India would be certain death.

From the Sangam Hotel, Jorja's line of sight moved from the mountain peak behind Muzaffarabad to the sprawl of the city and the river flowing through it. Two rivers—the Neelum and the Jhelum—converged below her balcony, clashing fiercely to form white surface spume that masked their turbidity. They were the lifeblood of Pakistan and Kashmir. The Jhelum River, a tributary of India's grand Indus River was Pakistan's and Kashmir's main water source, critical to their existence. This was, the Kashmiri's believed, the real reason for the relentless conflict between Pakistan and India. If India seized Azad Kashmir and cut off its river, Pakistan would be doomed. India held both Azad Kashmir and Pakistan by the throat. One squeeze would prove fatal.

After the series of terror attacks by four hijacked aircraft on the United States on September 11, 2001, the American government declared "War on Terrorism" and vowed it would hunt down al-Qaeda's leader Osama bin Laden and depose the Taliban—the protectors of terrorism. The alleged mastermind behind the attacks that killed 2,976 people in New York City, Shanksville in Pennsylvania, and the Pentagon near Washington, D.C. was last known to be living in the mountainous border regions between Pakistan and Afghanistan. Foreign assistance workers in Kashmir were evacuated. Three months later, the Indian Parliament was attacked, purportedly by Pakistani insurgents. Indian and Pakistani defense forces were at their highest state of alert since their last war in 1971.

Six months after 9/11, foreign workers had not returned, delaying the progress of Kashmiri's education assistance by the World Bank. Jorja Himmermann was deployed to Kashmir to audit the donor's funding support and to assess the impact of the interruption. It was to be a brief visit: two days.

"Fear the river," the hotel manager said quietly. "It has taken the lives of many Kashmiris because of its rocky bottom and its swiftness. It can freeze a body or pound it to death in a matter of minutes." Riyad Dilawar placed her suitcase beside the closet and opened the curtains.

"What is the name of the mountain?"

"I know of no name. It is not important because it is far away. The only thing to fear is the river. You must not go near it, especially where it joins the big river. I heard of your problem on the way here. I am sorry. You are safe now. It is my promise that the hotel staff will keep you safe. There are no bad people here, so please do not be afraid."

Jorja stared at the river. The turbulent river reflected the lives of the Kashmiris, yet it knew no political bounds. It had a sense of direction and cut its own path to freedom.

"We cannot protect you against Allah's will and the moon," he continued.

"The moon?"

"Sometimes there is a bad moon rising."

Jorja faced the manager. "Trouble?"

"Yes. Nature is not judgmental."

Riyad left Jorja to contemplate her fears. It was nature that killed her husband. It was two years since his death in a white-water rafting accident. The river was swollen, the weather was inclement, and he was under-prepared. Her therapy was work. It was only recently that she had begun dating again. Her hopes were that a three-month relationship with Denny Mazzola, who lived in Canberra—her home city in Australia—would evolve and strengthen, despite her fear of commitment.

Work made her fearless in the face of extraordinary danger. Her focus on equality and justice for all, particularly the children of the world, spurred her forward. But it did not prepare her for what happened on the way to Kashmir.

CHAPTER 2

THE JOURNEY

Chilled, thinning altitude air dampened Jorja's porcelain face. Her journey from Islamabad in northern Pakistan to Muzaffarabad in Kashmir, from capital to capital, peaked at the town of Murree. Summer holiday homes were eerily empty, jutting precariously over the precipitous mountainside. Winter wind whipped through the vacant, ghostly town. Grimy, slippery ice clung to tufts of grass along the roadside. Melting snow seeped down the valley like rain on a window pane. Water oozed across the road. A recent landslide's tumbling boulders had formed craters in the well-worn bitumen of the narrow Karakoram Highway.

It was an election year. Imran Khan's political aspirations aroused Jorja's curiosity. So too did the controversial views of the country's military leader, General Pervez Musharraf. Tension between Pakistan and India over the ownership of Kashmir added fuel to the political fire, firmly placing the countries in the international spotlight. As Jorja traveled north to Pakistan-administered Kashmir, she pondered its democratic destiny: liberation from India, accession with Pakistan, or the formation of a sovereign republic?

Her Pakistani colleague, Jamshid, denounced India's stranglehold on Kashmir. He wanted accession. He was stocky with a soft girth that hung over his tightly-belted trousers. A red tie constricted his thick neck.

Jorja's driver struggled to keep pace with the lead vehicle. Jamshid's driver was more experienced and drove instinctively on the narrow, winding route to Kashmir. The vehicles traveled at break-neck speed, reducing their pace fractionally at hairpin bends, and only slowing when they moved through townships. Villagers stared at the approaching white vans and craned their necks for a better view. She was as curious of them as they were of her. She gazed intently at their daily movements—selling wares, scrubbing laundry, sweeping leaves from doorways, and lifting caskets for the dead into flat-tray vehicles—until their presence faded into a mysterious film covering the landscape. It was a distraction from her real fear: a panic she had never known before.

Neither kidnapping, border conflict, shooting, bombing, nor full-scale nuclear war between Pakistan and India were on Jorja's mind. Something imminently more urgent, dangerous, and tragic occupied her thoughts. At bends with missing guardrails, her van veered perilously close to the edge with only millimeters to spare. Her mortal fear was that the driver would fail to negotiate a corner and send the van plunging headfirst into the foggy abyss. It was a premonition of a fall from grace, a descent into oblivion.

Jorja's breath halted momentarily at each curve. "You're driving too fast," she said as calmly as she could.

"No, no, I have a certificate," said Fadil. "I am the best driver. I must travel faster on the straight parts so that I can go slower on the bends. That's the way it is. I don't want to have an accident with a foreign woman in the car. We can't have a political incident, can we?" Her Kashmiri driver laughed.

"I guess not," she answered feebly.

"Don't worry!"

Tall, spindly trees—as gangly as the region's inhabitants—extended upward toward the cloudy sky, reaching for heaven. Recovering bodies from the inaccessible forest would surely be futile. She gripped the door handle and prayed for a safe journey's end as she'd never prayed before.

Descending from Murree to the warmer border, they entered Pakistan-administered Kashmir. "This is Azad Kashmir, madam," said the driver. "Azad means free: Free Kashmir. But it is not free. As a Kashmiri, I'm ashamed to say this."

It was the last day of February, nearing the end of winter. New buds had not yet daubed the barren trees. The emergence of a muddy, violent-flowing river, mirroring the darkness of the landscape, relieved the monotony of meandering roads. The van slowed to walking pace as it rolled cautiously over a skeletal bridge.

"We must stop soon, madam. Please have your papers ready."

Jorja held her long rectangular scarf—a dupatta—tightly around her as a flimsy form of protection, attempting to cover her blond hair. The van stopped at a ramshackle group of sheds that seemed to lean into each other for stability.

"Jamshid's car isn't stopping," she said.

"They are Pakistanis, madam. They can drive straight through the border check. Any car with foreigners must stop and present security clearances, visas, and passports. If the car doesn't stop, the police will arrest the foreigners and put them in jail. Do not worry. I will do the talking. Please pass me your papers."

She dutifully obeyed and passed the papers, handwritten in Urdu, to Fadil. "Do they need my passport to see the visa?"

"Have it ready," he advised.

A Kashmiri guard instructed the driver to stop outside a derelict hut. Three unarmed guards sitting on a bench stood and moved quickly toward the vehicle. Motioning the driver to roll down the window, the guard spoke for some time, asking questions and perusing the papers. He peered into the back of the van to speak to Jorja.

"Australian? Himmermann? Your name is Himmermann, yes?"

She smiled and nodded. "Jorja Himmermann. Himmermann is my surname, my last name," she explained. "Jorja is my first name."

"Ah, so! Why you here? What business? Are you journalist?"

"No. Not journalist. Education. Here to work in the Ministry of Education. World Bank project. In Kashmir for two days." Suddenly conscious that she was speaking in clipped English, she became embarrassed and covered her flushed cheeks with her shawl.

The guard nodded and wrote in his official ledger. He waved a piece of paper at her. "Copy?" She confirmed that it was a photocopy and held up the original as he slid the copy between the pages of his ledger. "Visa?" She handed him her passport, and he flipped through it until he found her visa. He wrote the visa number in the ledger and conversed with the driver, then motioned him forward.

"Madam, you must keep a copy with you at all times," said Fadil. "You understand? You must make another copy in Muzaffarabad in case someone wants to see it. Everything is okay, but the guard says that this is a dangerous place and very bad men are kidnapping foreigners. You must be careful." He was insistent as he edged the vehicle beside Jamshid's car waiting at the side of the road. "Get out of the car and have a stretch for a few minutes."

Jamshid and Jorja walked to the edge of the road overlooking the river while the drivers lit up cigarettes. "Beautiful, isn't it?" Jamshid said. "This is the end of Pakistan. Choudhary Rahmat Ali created the word *Pakistan* in 1933. The *P* stands for Punjab, the *A* for Northwest Frontier, also known as the Afghan Province, the *K* for Kashmir, the *S* for Sindh, and the *STAN* for Baluchistan. Others say that Pakistan means the land of the pure because *pak* is Urdu for pure, but that's disputable. Four quarters, that's how I describe my land. The Indus Valley is flat and alluvial; Sindh is mainly a desert wilderness. The Baluchistan Plateau is an arid tableland with mountains on its perimeter; and the northern highlands of the Hindu Kush near here are rugged and mountainous.

Glad of the temporary halt from the stomach-churning drive, she watched the river tumble downstream. "The river's very fast. How much further? My stomach can't take much more."

Jamshid laughed. "That's why I had a small breakfast; only one egg this morning. It's not good to have a big breakfast for this journey. Your eggs are still sitting in the stomach, eh?"

She grimaced. "They're about to come up."

"No, no. Do not worry. There are not so many bends now. The river, the Jhelum, it is from Muzaffarabad. We'll be there in about an hour," he reassured her. "*Calo*. It means let's go!"

Jorja nestled her head into the seat and closed her eyes. She thought of the lover she'd left behind in Australia. Crumpled shirts hung on Denny's lean body as if a familiar friend had thrown a brotherly arm around him. Cuffs, unbuttoned, covered his long-fingered hands. Faded jeans embraced his body. His scent was a heady mixture of basil-garnished cannelloni, bold Chianti, and sensual, sporty sex. She imagined touching his three-day stubble, his dimpled chin and his secretive smile. She imagined strok-ing his shoulder-length, wavy, chestnut-colored hair. Into his sea green eyes framed with long, dark, winking eyelashes, she probed his soul: intellectual, inspired, and unpredictable.

The driver's abusive shouts forced her out of her reverie. He was yelling and gesticulating at a fast-moving truck as it over-took him on a bend.

"Fadil! Look out! The tree! Fadil!" Instinctively, Jorja raised her arms to protect her head. The car screeched and skidded sideways as the truck's low-sounding horn vibrated in her ear. Brakes squealed. She hunched her shoulders and gripped the handle so tightly her knuckles ached. She sealed her eyes shut to brace for the inevitable impact. Fadil emitted groans and curses as he attempted to control the car. Time stretched into an end-less vortex of confusion as a soothing calmness wrapped itself around Jorja. Fadil's prayers whispered hauntingly in her mind. She was sure it was a precursor to her premonition. In the dust, she could taste the end. She knew this journey would be her last. She just knew.

A brutal thud ended the turmoil. Dust penetrated her nostrils. "Fadil?" she whispered. Jorja unhunched herself and peered around. The back-end of the upright car was embedded in a tree that had dumped an avalanche of twigs, bark, and ants over its penetrator. Debris bombarded Jorja and nicked her skin as she poked her head out of the window. Jamshid's car was nowhere in sight.

Fadil was slumped over the steering wheel. Swirls of dust had settled over the middle-aged man as he unfurled himself and beat both fists on the steering wheel. Jorja's door was sealed shut so she crawled through the rear window and helped the driver crawl through his.

He shook himself, wiping powdery earth from his dark curly hair. "Go, run! Run! Run! Kidnap!" he yelled, then muttered unintelligible phrases. Jorja's aching body was paralyzed. Her driver shouted louder and more urgently, "Run, Jorja! Now!"

Instinctively, she headed down the steep slope. Blood pumped into her head, causing it to ache more. Her shoulders ached. Her whole body throbbed with pain and tension. She flung off her dupatta, and it floated in the air, like a red sail, before landing on a bush. Her cheeks flushed and perspiration shone on her face. She ran as fast as her legs would go, down the mountain side and around the bend. To where, she did not know. To whom, she did not know. She ran to her destiny.

Sweat stung her eyes. Her vision misted as if a thin veil had masked her face. She saw movement in the distance. She stopped. A herd of goats meandered beside the roadway. She moved cautiously forward, not wanting to startle them. An irate goat herder was not what she needed right now. She blinked and saw that they weren't goats, but a group of young men, squatting on the ground at the verge of a bend. Perhaps they were road workers taking respite from their duties. They ended their conversation abruptly in mid-sentence. One stood and looked toward her. He motioned the others to stand. They did. One by one, they stood and stared. Jorja stood still and stared down at them. One of the tall men scowled and began moving up the mountain toward her, slowly and deliberately. The man's dark traditional clothes—a shalwar kameez—appeared steeped in sweat and grime. Swathes of once-white fabric were wrapped around his head to form a turban with a long loose end dangling down his face. His face was bristled, well-weathered, and rugged from years under a baking sun.

Jorja turned and scurried up the mountain. Her fitness lessened the strain, but the pace was slow. Not once did she look back. Off the main route, a track meandered toward four huts perched on a nearby ridge. Amorphous forms moved in the distance. Women, Jorja thought, and took the high road in their direction. The unmoving women stared at her. As she approached them, they began screeching and waving their arms. Jorja stopped, unsure what to do.

Panting, she walked slowly toward the women shrouded in dark clothes, their dusty faces exposed. Age had forced one woman into a stooped position. Younger, pregnant, and bare-footed women surrounded her. Their shrill screams and flailing arms made them appear more threatening than the men on the lower slope. Surely it was better to be amongst women, nurturing and caring, than potential kidnappers? Jamshid had warned her repeatedly to be careful in the aftermath of September Eleven—9/11.

Where the hell was Jamshid? An overwhelming feeling of aloneness and vulnerability enveloped her. She was not in a panic, but rather resigned to her fate. Just as Jorja turned her back on the women, their shrieks became louder, higher pitched, and more frenzied. One woman in a beige shalwar kameez grabbed her arm, twisting her body around. The woman's black eyes stared into her. Mud-smeared marks stained the skin under her eye sockets. The corpulent villager yanked Jorja with the strength of an ox and pulled her toward the group of women. Each grabbed at parts of her body, dragging her toward their village. All the while, they chattered excitedly. Jorja didn't utter a word.

Wooden shacks clustered together to form a village. Signs of everyday life littered the ground: plastic bowls of water on a concrete tile, opened sacks of rice propped against the outer walls of a building, clothes hung on rope stretched between trees, and goats roaming the area. The women forced Jorja into a dreary little room at the back of a dilapidated hut. A small open window with wooden bars admitted a stream of subdued light. Two beds abutting the walls were covered with brightly colored blankets, sheets, and pillows. The women gestured to the chairs lining two perimeter walls, prompting Jorja to sit down and wait. She wasn't optimistic about the outcome of her detention, but didn't protest. Tired and confused, she had lost the ability to speak and think clearly. She heard the twitter of birds, the babble of women, the splash of water, and the drone of a generator.

Some people fear crowds; others fear solitude. Jorja was not afraid of being alone, but she hated uncertainty. She sat on an uncomfortable, rigid wooden chair. Enticing and snug, the beds were neat with drum-tight sheets stretched over mattresses. She tested one mattress by pushing her hand deep into the rectangle and sat perched on the bed's edge. Eventually she lay down. She waited for the return of the village women. She waited and waited. She slept and slept.

Jorja awoke, unsure of the amount of time that had passed. She thought of the car smashing into the tree, of Fadil slumped behind the steering wheel, of his warning shouts for her to flee. Foolishly, she had done the worst possible thing. As a child, she had been told there was safety in numbers. She had been told never to leave the vehicle or the main road in an emergency. Jorja didn't listen to the wise advice given to her during her childhood; instead, she listened to Fadil whom she trusted. She had fled with no clear plan in mind and this had been her downfall. The choice between the group of staring men and the group of shouting women offered no encouraging alternatives. Exhausted, the women's screeches had numbed her into obedience as their powerful arms dragged her to a bleak fate. Destiny had played its hand, and it didn't seem to be an advantageous one.

She tried to open the door, but it was locked. She peered through a crack and watched as three women performed ordinary daily chores. One washed clothes while the other two, perhaps a mother and daughter, gutted a freshly-plucked chicken. She watched as their knife twisted deep into the chicken's bowels.

Jorja looked toward the small window, but it was too high and too narrow to climb through. In any event, she was not sure where she would go. She sat on the bed and contemplated her next move. A commotion from the next room interrupted her thoughts. A man's voice boomed behind the door. A chill ran up Jorja's spine. She knew, without a doubt, the women had informed the man of her capture.

A key unlocked the door and Fadil walked in, waving his hands with disgust. "What are you doing here? I tell you to get help. You run off!"

Jorja could barely look into his eyes and said sheepishly, "But I thought you said to run so I wouldn't be kidnapped. You yelled run, kidnap!"

Fadil roared with laughter. At that, a crowd congregated by the doorway. Some women pushed themselves into the room, elbowing Fadil out of the way. "I said run, get help, run, and get help, not you'll get kidnapped." He doubled up with laughter.

"Fadil, this is no laughing matter!" Jorja said as she stood and glared at him. "I *was* kidnapped. That's why I'm here in this bloody room. How did you find me?"

"Kidnapped? You weren't kidnapped. A man from the village helped me with the car. There's a dent in the backside where it crashed into the tree, but the car is okay. It was lucky that the car did not tip over. The car works. The man said his wife helped you and showed me where to find you." He howled with laughter again. Fadil faced the crowd of women squeezed in the doorway and they giggled with him as he explained the situation.

"The women say you lost your way and they helped you. They say your face looked red like a tomato. They say your hair looked bad like a mop." He laughed. "They say you looked like a lost, skinny dog with torn rags and torn skin."

Jorja had drawn blood during the accident, but had not noticed. Slashes in her long-sleeved blouse exposed a bandaged arm that suddenly throbbed with pain. The village women had dressed her wound without disturbing her sleep.

"They fixed the blood on your arm and some sores on your head," said Fadil.

An aged, hunched woman pushed through the crowd with a tray of tea. Nodding her head, she indicated for Jorja to sit down. Both Fadil and Jorja sat on the bed while the women sat on chairs. Laughter and giggles interspersed incessant chatter. The joke was clearly on Jorja, but she merely shrugged her shoulders and drank the hot, sweet tea.

The old woman took Jorja gently by the arm and led her from the room to an outside shed. Curiously, Jorja looked inside. In it was a deep hole—a toilet. Afterwards, she washed her face with a clean cloth and refreshingly cool water from a plastic basin the woman placed in the shed. She rearranged her straggly hair. When she exited the shed, the woman tenderly stroked Jorja's arm and cheek, smiling benevolently.

Jorja returned to the room on the arm of the matriarch. Fadil arose and said, "Your kidnappers are releasing you. It's time to go to Muzaffarabad."

"Yes, Fadil, it's time to go to Kashmir."

CHAPTER 3

MUZAFFARABAD

Muzaffarabad's tourism office was closed. Jamshid's car waited in the empty parking lot near a group of government offices in the suburb of Chattar. Jamshid stuck his head out of the window when Fadil stopped, and yelled, "What happened? What took so long?" Fadil dismissed the questions with a wave of his hand, stating it was time to go. Jamshid's driver assumed the front position again as they continued toward their office.

"This city was once a magnificent tourist spot," Fadil told Jorja. "It was famous for its beauty. The idea of war keeps tourists away now. The government makes it difficult for tourists, too. It takes so long to get a security clearance to enter the country. Often the government refuses the request anyway. That's life now." He shrugged. "We're on our way to the project office."

The project office was a large, cream-colored residential building halfway up a hill, in Upper Chattar, facing the center of Muzaffarabad. The road ran parallel to a sheer drop at the front of the block. Turning right, they entered the driveway and stopped within a meter of the front door.

Inside, the air was stifling and putrid. A hot, musty odor of chili and cigarettes permeated the foyer. In the center was a large dining table with six, high-backed wooden chairs, some with dirty or damp tea towels draped over them. A tiny kitchen lay ahead; the source of the heat and stench. Through a door on the right-hand side, the group entered a modest, rectangular office. Grime and dust stuck to the walls and to every surface. "It's not clean like the Islamabad office. Every time I come here I speak to the men, but they don't clean," Jamshid said embarrassed. He spoke in Urdu to two office staff, pointing to the tattered curtains, the cobwebs on the ceiling, and the black smudges on the computers. The two young men merely nodded.

Jorja's stomach growled, but the stench made her ill, dampening her appetite. She made several photocopies of the No Objection Certificate and shivered in the cold, dim room. Although wanting to open the thick curtains to let in light and warmth, she refrained from touching the soiled drapes.

Jamshid escorted Jorja up a grand U-shaped staircase to the guesthouses on the second and third floors. The upstairs windows were free of curtains, exposing a brilliant view of Muzaffarabad. Staff had cleaned the bedroom designated for her use yet its grubbiness was overpowering. Black, ground-in filth was sticky underfoot, as if the floorboards were composed of viscous tar that had dried imperfectly in tacky lumps. A square of snot-green carpet was dotted with stains and cigarette burns. The unmade single bed sat awkwardly in the middle of the room next to a small desk. The toilet in the en-suite bathroom was a low porcelain-covered hole. She pressed a button and the toilet flushed with a trickle of brown water. A hot-water cistern clung to the wall, dripping water onto the bathroom's tiled floor, green with slime.

"I stay in the Sangam Hotel when I come to Muzaffarabad," said Jamshid. "Only the local consultants working on the project stay in this office. I'll take you to the hotel if you don't want to stay here, but first I have some work to do. You can wait downstairs. The boys can get some project material for you to read. What's wrong with your arm? Why is it bandaged?"

Jorja dismissed Jamshid's questions with a wave of her hand. "It's nothing."

"Do I need to talk to Fadil about his driving?" Jamshid asked.

Jorja shook her head and descended the staircase. When Fadil signaled that it was time to leave four hours later, Jorja still hadn't eaten. Her arm ached and her eyes felt gritty with dust and tiredness. Fadil skillfully reversed out of the driveway and positioned the vehicle facing the descent to Muzaffarabad.

The Sangam Hotel was an oasis compared with the unhygienic project office. Jamshid arranged for the hotel manager, Riyad Dilawar, a tall handsome man, to show Jorja some rooms. She opted for Room 105 with a Western-style toilet, clean sheets on a standard double bed, fresh-looking carpet, a worn but large desk, and a round dining table surrounded by four upholstered chairs. The bottle-green diamond-flecked fabric matched the curtains. The bar fridge was small, old and unbalanced, but quiet. The staff had stocked it with two packets of potato crisps, two packets of peanuts, and four small soft-drink bottles. The television on a black stand nailed to the wall peered toward the bed. Disappointingly, the bathroom was shabby with a yellow-stained, chipped, bath-tub, but natural light streamed through the window.

She had chosen the double suite with two balconies because of its extraordinary views. The southern balcony overlooked the route of the morning's journey through Murree. The western balcony revealed a stunning, sole mountain peak, three thousand meters high. The peak was a thousand meters higher than Australia's largest peak, Mount Kosciusko. Polish explorer Paul Edmund de Strzelecki named it after a compatriot: *although in a foreign country, on foreign ground, but amongst a free people, who appreciate freedom and its votaries, I could not refrain from giving it the name of Mount Kosciusko.* Jorja wondered about the name of Muzaffarabad's mountain. A hundred and fifty kilometers northeast of Muzaffarabad was Nanga Parbat—Naked

Mountain—the ninth tallest peak in the world with a height of eight thousand meters.

It was nearing evening as Jorja Himmermann stood on the western balcony under a full moon. Staring upward for a long time, she compared the night sky with that of the southern hemisphere. The planets seemed upside down and it took some time for her to adjust to the position of the constellations. Familiar and constant amid the temporary confusion was the moon. She thought of full moon legends: higher incidences of insanity, homicides, and unexplained events. Coincidences of cosmic and lunar cycles triggered earthquakes, some believed, although the logic was often distorted. Nevertheless, these Western myths fascinated Jorja. Lyrics of a Creedence Clearwater Revival song lingered with her, a portent of a bad moon rising and of earthquakes and lightning. Tragedy was surely on its way.

CHAPTER 4

A CONFLUENCE OF RIVERS

The Neelum River poured through Muzaffarabad. It was the power and the glory of Kashmir, gathering rain, mud, and melting snow from the north. *Neelum* was the Urdu word for sapphire, but the river was not a sparkling iridescent blue. A murky, dull-brown flow bubbled swiftly over boulders in a shallow riverbed. The Jhelum River from India rushed westward to Muzaffarabad to meet with the Neelum where they both collided with the force of two butting rams. Merging into a single stream, the waters continued southward to Islamabad and the plains of Pakistan. Jorja wondered whether the confluence was symbolic of unification between Pakistan and India or whether India would triumph, just as it had done in naming the conjoined river the Jhelum.

The two rivers coupled to travel in one direction flowing united to its end. They were not large, nor wide, but converged uniquely, rapidly, and ruggedly at this famous point right outside her bedroom window. Riyad, the hotel manager, spoke of the locals who came sporadically to the rocky banks to pray while laundering their clothes. They would hang their sheets on twine strung across two makeshift posts that impaled the chocolate river sands. She thought of her lover, Denny. Watching the fast, muddy river, she had a deeper understanding of Denny's love of water. High in the mountains, far from the sea that surrounded Australia, it mesmerized her.

"Twelve million people live in both Pakistan and Indian Kashmir," said Jamshid as she sat down to join him in the restaurant. "There are two capitals of India-administered Kashmir. Srinagar, the City of the Sun, is the summer capital and Jammu is the winter capital. That's where the majority of Sikhs and Hindus live. There is only one capital of Azad Kashmir on the Pakistan side and that is Muzaffarabad."

"Why do you call it Azad Kashmir when this map calls it Azad Jammu Kashmir?" Spread over the table was a map of the region that Jorja had bought in Australia. They sipped tea while waiting for their meals.

"Ah yes! Most people refer to the Pakistan side as AJK, Azad Jammu Kashmir, but that's incorrect. AJK really refers to all of Kashmir, this side and the Indian side. Jammu is in the Indian side of Kashmir, not the Pakistan side here. This must be an old map. The Pakistan side is smaller and there are fewer people, maybe three million. They're mostly conservative Muslims. To the east is the forgotten Ladakh, adjoining China," Jamshid said, pointing on the map. "It's the home of the Buddhists, mainly from Tibet, but there are also some Muslims."

"Politics! It's a sensitive subject," Jamshid continued. "The Kashmiris will say one thing, the Pakistanis will say another. I'm from Karachi, and it's said that we are a fair and intelligent representation of Pakistan, so I'll tell you about Kashmir from an educated perspective. Let's not go back to the beginning. Before the beginning, we knew the end. Let us start from May 1990 when the tension between India and Pakistan reached a high point. India launched air strikes against guerrillas trapped in the Kargil region of Kashmir. For three weeks, the Indian and Pakistan armies battled across the Line of Control. The newspapers reported over a hundred people killed. The main provocation for the Indians was the presence of heavily armed freedom fighters in Kargil. The freedom fighters put the Indians under tremendous pressure causing them to retaliate against Pakistan. Everything went downhill and there was much aggression and death. Kofi Annan, the United Nations Secretary-General, called for a halt to the conflict just in time. He said the two governments were eyeball-to-eyeball and advised both of them to pull back at once in order to avert a war."

"I remember that," Jorja said, nodding and sipping her tea. It soothed her, but her hunger intensified with each mouthful. The rice arrived with an assortment of meat platters.

"Things were quiet for a while, but tensions between India and Pakistan reached ominous proportions last year," Jamshid continued as he folded the map. "We thought there'd be another war. The Indians said there were terrorists in Pakistan and Pakistan's General Musharraf didn't know how to control them. India did not trust Musharraf because he was the Army Chief during the invasion of the Kargil sector of India in 1999 and had kept the current Pakistan Prime Minister, Nawaz Sharif, uninformed."

"You would have heard all the news about the money coming into Pakistan after the September attacks in America," continued Jamshid. "America and the International Monetary Fund, and other aid agencies too, helped Pakistan by sending money so that the Pakistani rupee would not crash and affect the stock markets. Americans liked General Musharraf because he listened to them. He withdrew state sponsorship of militant Islamists which earned him a lot of praise from America and the West. Musharraf refused to cultivate a political constituency within Pakistan, although he intends to remain in power after this year's elections in October. Anyway, he concentrated on administrative reforms such as the control of mosques and religious schools—known as *madrassas*—and the reduction of corruption. The Pakistani press portrayed Musharraf as an American-backed military leader implementing an agenda influenced by India. The press was partly right. The press, and most people, think once Pakistan loses its importance to the American-led coalition waging war in Afghanistan, Pakistan's international standing will be tested again. We don't have a good international record, you know. In fact, it's regarded by most as dismal."

Scooping spoonfuls of food onto her plate, Jorja didn't wait for Jamshid to start eating. His portions were miniscule in relation to hers. Perhaps he had eaten at the office. "It'll be interesting to see whether the people support Musharraf and his allegiance to America," she said.

"Musharraf will do well in the election. He'll make sure of that. But he's a military man and I don't think Pakistan needs a strong military presence. He spent almost eighty percent of our national revenue on defense and debt repayments last year. In comparison, the Indian government spent about forty-two percent. In a television address in January, General Musharraf spoke for more than an hour but devoted only five minutes to Kashmir and relations with India. He didn't want to say any more because it's such a sensitive issue, particularly within the military. The best hope for Kashmir lies in an end to military rule in Pakistan." Jamshid was optimistic for the upcoming election. "I almost forgot to mention. We have a meeting with the minister of education at ten sharp. Now where was I? Ah, yes. Participation by all political parties in Pakistan and Kashmir in the assembly elections and a representative government may lead to meaningful talks between India and Pakistan. Peace would be possible. Don't you think so, Jorja?"

Jorja knew there were no such talks of peace in Kashmir and persistent border fighting continued between India and Pakistan at the Line of Control that lay twenty kilometers from Muzaffarabad. Also, there were no reports of full-scale border war. The talk had turned instead to the global war on terror and America's imminent raid—Operation Anaconda—in Afghanistan. Operation Anaconda was to be a brief, intense bombardment to ferret out Taliban groups that were purportedly harboring Osama bin Laden, the alleged mastermind behind the 9/11 attacks. Bin Laden was rumored to be sheltering in one of the caves in the mountainous region.

"Tell me what people know of Kashmir or Pakistan in Australia," asked Jamshid.

"They know nothing. All they know is from rumor, hearsay, and two-minute news grabs. I was advised by my aunt not to make eye contact with Pakistani men!" Looking into people's eyes was cultural. Jorja did it automatically: prolonged, uninhibited eye contact. It was the ultimate human connection. "And my uncle said not to discuss sex, religion, politics, or money because if I did, it would get me into trouble. My mother said I should dye my hair black because I'd be too conspicuous in Pakistan."

"Let me guess. They also said that there'll be a nuclear war soon in Kashmir and told you not go."

"That's exactly what they said."

"They are right. Since 9/11, the world, especially Pakistan, is a more dangerous place, Jorja, *a more dangerous place*." Jamshid leaned forward. "You could have been kidnapped this morning. Fadil told me everything. I laughed at him. It is true that I laughed when I found out, but really, in the deepest portion of my mind, I prayed to Allah for sparing you. Thank Allah that you were not kidnapped. Thank Allah that you were not killed by the car accident or by the Talibs. The men you saw by the roadside were Talibs. Fadil does not think so, but I'm sure of it. There are many Talibs here. You can never be too careful. Remember what Hemingway wrote in *The Torrents of Spring*? He wrote that *when you're traveling abroad alone, or even with your mother, you simply cannot be too careful.* I repeat, Jorja, you simply cannot be too careful. Promise me to keep safe."

"I will," Jorja obediently promised.

CHAPTER 5

THE MINISTER'S PLAN

"Now, remember our plan," said Jamshid. "The minister will be here soon for our meeting. He prefers to meet in the comfort of the Sangam Hotel. The plan is that we only stay in Muzaffarabad for two days. You are here only to assess the delays to the project and to conduct the audit. You will write the report in Islamabad where it's safe. At our meeting, we must determine the minister's expectations for the report. That is our goal for today."

Just as Jorja nodded, the minister arrived. His oil-slicked hair conjured up images of an officious Adolf Hitler. Fortunately, he did not have a mustache. Immaculately dressed in Pakistani clothes, with an expensive gold watch on his left arm, he exuded taste and style. His posture was erect, his pace purposeful. Quietly spoken, he had a well-traveled confidence and an excellent command of English. The minister was direct, however, wasting no time in expressing his disappointment at the terrorist attacks of 9/11 and frustration at the subsequent delays to the education project. The World Bank evacuated international consultants from Kashmir, but they hadn't returned. They were reluctant to do so due to the escalating border conflict and impending terrorist threats. Jorja's role was to report on the project's progress.

"Have you forgotten the teachers' manual? With respect, madam, and to you my friend Jamshid, the part of the contract relating to the teachers' manual requires another sixty working days. You must undertake the work in Muzaffarabad, not Islamabad. Curriculum experts in my office are willing to assist you, and we will have two Pakistani consultants here, too. Professor Lufti is here already and the other is on his way. It would be silly to do the work from Islamabad. How can you assist Kashmir when you are not here? We have faced that problem with the Pakistani government for so long. I want a quality product, not something conjured up many kilometers from this country. I understand that you may be concerned about terrorist threats and kidnapping, but I'll talk with the hotel staff to ensure Jorja's safety. Jorja, I heard of your unfortunate incident yesterday and I am sincerely sorry for you. It was not a welcoming experience and I apologize on behalf of the people of Kashmir. I hope your arm heals with speed and with no complications. For your safety, it would be best to stay in the hotel where your protection can be assured, and not the project office in Upper Chattar. But I cannot and will not allow the work to be done in Islamabad. That, Mr. Jamshid and Miss Jorja, is my last word."

Sixty days. Two months. No negotiations, no variations. The minister remained resolute as he smiled benignly. Jamshid agreed to his request.

Two months in Kashmir was not on Jorja's agenda. She thought of her mother's seventieth birthday reunion. She thought of her triathlon competitions. Foremost on her mind was her lover Denny. Upset at the mix-up and the additional work, she glared at Jamshid. In truth, she was furious, but she controlled her emotions in front of the minister. When she saw the minister's back disappear from the restaurant, she turned to Jamshid and looked at him fiercely. Bubbling like a volcano about to erupt, she blurted out, "What the hell were you thinking? We had a plan. What happened to our plan? What the hell were you thinking? What the hell were you thinking?" Like a broken record, she was stuck on a phrase. She didn't know how to continue.

"Now, now, Jorja. It does no good to get angry. We are gentle people. I'm glad you were wise enough not to say anything in front of the minister. It wouldn't have been good to embarrass him or me."

She huffed and took a breath, but had no time to launch into a response.

Jamshid spoke quietly. "I'm sorry, Jorja. Be calm now. We need this project to work. The teachers must be educated and the children need assistance. We cannot walk away. There is no one who can replace you. It took us time to find you. Consultants won't come to Pakistan or Kashmir now. Everyone is scared. International consultants are scared of Pakistanis. They think that we are all terrorists. We were glad when you agreed to come here. I'm certain that you will be safe in Muzaffarabad. I will ensure it. The minister will also strictly ensure it. I cannot stay, however. I leave tomorrow morning. You will have full use of the project office in Upper Chattar. Please stay. We will not be able to get anyone to do an assignment here, then there will be more delays to the project and the minister will lose face. Miss Jorja, we really need you. I need you and I beseech you to remain in Kashmir to work with the minister and to make him happy and to get the project going again."

She sighed and spoke as quietly as her host. "Jamshid, I'm in an unfair situation. You deployed me to Pakistan so quickly that you hadn't finalized my contract and scope of work. You know that. I have no contract so I can walk out now if I wish. I do have a conscience though. Can you imagine what I'm feeling?"

"Absolutely, Jorja! If I were in the same situation, I would not be pleased. I would miss my wife and children. But you have no husband and children. The project would suffer badly if you refused to work here. I will lose my job. The minister might even lose his job. The money from the World Bank will not be given to Kashmir and then Kashmiris will suffer because of it, because of you."

"That's not fair, Jamshid. It's not fair to make me feel guilty. First, I'm in an accident, then nearly kidnapped. Yesterday, I had nothing to eat since breakfast and I was holed up in that stinking office. I'll do this job, but I'll need your support from Islamabad while I'm in Kashmir." She had to resign herself swiftly to the longer stay and the isolation of Azad Kashmir. All she could think of was getting access to e-mail, because there was no e-mail capability in the hotel. "E-mail, Jamshid. And a mobile phone, Jamshid."

"Thank you so much, Jorja. I will support you. You start tomorrow. No more delays. Do not worry. You will like Kashmir. I will tell Hamid and Gadi in the project office that you must have access to e-mail. You can use Hamid's computer. We did not get you a mobile phone because we thought you'd only be in Kashmir for two days. We cannot get a phone for you, but you can get a mobile phone when you are back in Islamabad. I'll give you some project documents so you can read them this afternoon in preparation for tomorrow. You must not worry. You can arrange to visit Islamabad in a few weeks. You stay in Kashmir now and make the minister happy."

"I have no money, Jamshid. There are no automatic teller machines—ATMs—here. And stop saying 'do not worry.' It annoys me. I need to let my friends and relatives know that I'm staying longer." Her mind was in a spin. "No one is looking after my apartment. I must find someone to stay in the apartment. I need to have my rent paid. I need to ..."

"Jorja, Jorja. Do not worry. Everything will be okay. I will ask Hamid to pay you two thousand rupees until your money has been organized. You will have access to e-mail to tell your family. They will understand. The project is important. It's lucky that you brought your suitcase, isn't it? Aren't you glad you brought the vodka with you?"

Jorja had forgotten about the bottle of vodka. In Islamabad, she had applied for a liquor license at the insistence of Jamshid. Non-Muslims could procure a license, stamped in their passport, which would allow them to purchase a monthly ration of six bottles of Pakistani vodka or a crate of Pakistani beer. She chose vodka and packed a bottle for the two-day trip to Muzaffarabad, again at Jamshid's insistence. It was cold in the high altitude and he thought vodka would be warming.

CHAPTER 6

THE FIRST MORNING

On the morning of her first working day, Jorja ran the shower for an eternity, but the water remained icy. The basin water was warmer. There were no plugs so she stuffed her knickers into the drain to fill the basin for a wash.

Jamshid advised her to follow Professor Lufti's routine: work in the curriculum office in the morning until one o'clock, have lunch at the Sangam Hotel, and work in the project office until evening. Lufti had been in Muzaffarabad for six months and that was his daily practice. Another local consultant, Mahmud, would commence work on Monday. The two men and Jorja would form the team to produce a teachers' manual and low-cost teaching materials for primary school teachers in Azad Kashmir.

Jamshid departed Kashmir after breakfast, and she, reluctantly, waved him off. She waited in the hotel foyer for the driver.

The red car eventually arrived. Lufti was in the back seat and Jorja slid next to him. Tarif Gilani, the project's team leader, sat in the front where he could stretch his long legs. Both Lufti and Tarif resided in the guesthouse of the Upper Chattar office where it was considerably cheaper than the hotel.

"*Assalam alaikum*," the two men greeted her cheerfully. In the fifteen-minute drive to the curriculum office, they remarked on her clothes. Tarif appreciated Jorja's "appropriate" clothes: a pair of navy trousers with a navy knee-length long-sleeved dress and a light blue scarf draped over her head. She accepted his remarks as a compliment. As usual, she fumbled with the scarf to keep it from slipping off her hair. She had searched her bags for hairclips to secure the scarf, with no luck.

Both men were wearing the shalwar kameez, a long shirt—a kameez—with baggy cotton trousers—a shalwar. A padded, sleeveless jacket worn over the kameez kept them warm. Tarif's head was uncovered, but Lufti wore a mustard-colored knitted cap. Many Kashmiri men wore head garments, either a soft cap or a swathe of cloth wrapped around their heads, often with a rectangular length hanging down one side of their faces.

Lufti talked of his family and two daughters, Selma and Sarah. He had a distinct English accent in comparison with Tarif's incomprehensible mutter. Fortunately, Lufti sensed Jorja's difficulty and translated Tarif's enunciations into understandable English. She warmed to Lufti immediately.

"Lufti, your English is excellent. Have you been to England?"

"I studied in England, in Leeds. My language teacher was brilliant and very patient with me. Many people say that I speak like an Englishman." He raised his white eyebrows in delight.

"You do!"

Tarif departed the curriculum office after introducing Jorja to the director, Mrs. Tansoor, her assistant directors, an assortment of subject specialists, and education department staff. He preferred to work from the project office or in the nearby building that housed the minister's office. Lufti showed Jorja to the workroom in the curriculum office.

The office had no power, forcing them to work in the dark. They sat at a large wooden table with six solid, matching chairs in the middle of a small room. Two elongated windows were sealed shut and cloaked in thick, dirty-brown curtains. On the table sat a pin cushion studded with long, silver sewing pins and a desk calendar, two years out of date. Two computers were situated on desks butted against the back wall. Lufti said that one of them didn't work and the other was old. It was a stark, dark working environment.

Curriculum specialists came and went, stopping to greet Lufti and to discuss the project. Jorja shivered for four hours, listening to the wind blowing off the surrounding snowy mountains and the sound of Urdu conversations. Donning a mask of perky cheerfulness, she acknowledged everyone with a smile and a handshake. She suppressed her discomfort by planning a work schedule, making appointments, and prioritizing the reading material. Lufti made jokes to distract her from the chills and the pain of frozen fingers.

A man entered and greeted Jorja in Urdu as Lufti left in search of stationery and a gas heater. "So you are the new consultant, yes?"

"Yes, I'm replacing Dr. Waters. He's not able to return."

"Ah yes! I met Dr. Waters. It was sad when he was evacuated because of the terror attacks in America. Terrorism is a sad thing. September Eleven was very tragic, yes? Now you are here. Are you also from Australia?" He pulled up a chair and sat with his legs wide apart, smoothing his kameez over his knees with large square-fingered hands.

"Yes, but I'm not from the same area as Dr. Waters. He was from Brisbane and I'm from Canberra, the capital."

"But you are not originally from Australia, no? You do not sound like an Australian. I can understand you. Dr. Waters did not open his mouth wide to let the words out and the accent was strange. I can understand you, but you speak too fast. We call them running words. They run so fast that we can't understand them. What is the land of your birth?"

"I'm originally from England. My mother is British and my father is German."

"Mmmm, academic English. Bookish English. Lufti also has bookish English. Do you have issues?" His deep-set eyes glared at her, eager for a reaction.

"Issues? With the language?"

"No, no. Issues."

"With September Eleven?"

"No, no. Issues! We have lots of issues: sometimes five or six, sometimes ten or eleven."

"I've only just arrived. I've yet to speak with many of the subject specialists and teachers. Maybe by the end of the week I'll have some issues about the work here. I'd be happy to discuss them with you then."

He looked confused. "Issues, issues!" he said loudly, gesticulating with his large hands. "By that I mean, children. Do you have children?"

"Oh, those issues! No, I have no issues. I have no children."

"Ah, that is strange, is it not?" He placed his hands on his knees and bent forward, peering into her face, waiting for an answer.

"Not to me."

His stomach was a ball in his lap, resembling the mound of a pregnant woman. He had a prominent nose that hooked toward a wide smile. His eyes were kind, smiling, inquisitive, and as brown as his hessian shalwar kameez and tanned leather shoes. "You cannot have children? You are barren?"

"No, I'm not barren. It just hasn't happened yet." An article in yesterday's daily newspaper came to her mind: *A man was shot dead allegedly by his former brothers-in-law. Sabir Husain divorced his wife, as she was issueless. On Friday, he was sitting in his house when Nasir, Babar, and Sajjid came there and shot him dead following an exchange of hot words.*

Lufti made a timely return, empty-handed: no stationery and no heater. "You have met Rabi, I see. Rabi, you have met Miss Jorja?" he said. They nodded. He did not comment on his lack of resources.

"What is your father's name?" Rabi asked Jorja.

"My father's name is Karl."

"Jorja Karl."

"No. It's Himmermann. Jorja Himmermann. Karl is my father's first name."

"Jorja Himmermann. Good. But what is your other name?"

She was puzzled and looked toward Lufti for assistance.

"Do you have a middle name?" Lufti clarified.

"Eloise," she said and Rabi repeated the name, nodding slowly.

Addressing Jorja, Lufti said, "Rabi is a good man and very clever. He speaks English very well. He's the science specialist." They exchanged words in Urdu and laughed, embracing each other. She heard the phrase "bookish English" and Lufti nodded in agreement.

Another Kashmiri entered the room as Rabi departed. "Ah, another invader! *Salam,*" he greeted Jorja and dipped his head slightly. Her issues status was not of concern to him. He preferred to question her on her professional status. "My name is Khurshidawanossain. I have a Master of Education from AJK University. I am well traveled. I'm a distinguished scholar and well known in Kashmir. I've written many scholarly books. And what are your qualifications?" He took a seat, crossed his legs, and puffed out his chest importantly. Jorja explained that she had a Master of Science. He smiled as if impressed.

"Science? That is good. What sort of science? And what is your experience in education?"

"I studied mathematics and astronomy." He again nodded approvingly as she explained her experience in education from primary to tertiary levels.

"So, what's your experience of multi-grade teaching?"

She gave many examples. Lufti, who had been smiling at Jorja, joined the conversation on contemporary views of teaching multiple grades in one classroom. Surprisingly, Lufti's colleague shook his head, dissatisfied. A frown lined his broad forehead. Lufti defended Jorja's reputation. "Miss Jorja is very clever, Hossein. We'll work well together. Do not be afraid of that." He continued in Urdu. The stern man looked at her intently. He nodded very slowly. Satisfied, he left the room with a bow toward Lufti and Jorja. She felt as though she had been treated, not as a foreigner, but as an equal—intellectually if not maternally.

"Please don't take offense at Hossein," Lufti cautioned her. "He's wary of foreigners who tell Kashmiris how to teach in their own country. He thinks international consultants don't know much about Kashmir and are arrogant, but I assured him that you'd soon know a great deal about his country. I explained that you're not so rigid in your views and you'll listen to the experts in our education system and work in cooperation with them."

"Thank you, Lufti. What's his name? He said it so quickly."

"He is Khurshid Awan Hossein. My full name is Professor Yacoub Ali Lufti, so I'm Lufti to everyone. Your counterpart who arrives on Monday is Dr. Sajid Mohammad Mahmud and you can address him as Mahmud. It's the custom to call men by the last name and women by their first name, but not always. If you're in doubt, it's best to ask people how they wish to be addressed. Names are very important to us because our parents have chosen them carefully. They usually represent a person's character. For example, Mahmud takes his name Mohammed from the great Prophet Mohammed, may the peace and blessings of Allah be upon Him. You must call Khurshid Awan Hossein, Hossein, as that will be respectful. He's sometimes a gruff man, but his heart is good."

"I thought he used the word 'invader' when he saw me." She looked at Lufti's kind face, jovial eyes, and silvery hair. He resembled an elderly prophet: a wise man whose quietly spoken words could be trusted. Integrity could have been his middle name.

"He *did* call you an invader. He thinks anyone who's not Kashmiri is an invader. But I told him that you are different."

"How do you know this, Lufti? We've only just met," Jorja teased.

Lufti chuckled and winked at her, rubbed his eyes and re-arranged his black-rimmed glasses with his long, elegant fingers. "I'm a good judge of character because I'm old and wise.

I know already that we share the same humor and that we'll be good friends. We're almost relatives because we were both in England." He laughed. "I know people will like you and will listen to you because I know that you'll listen to them. Besides, I'm a mean Muslim man and a member of the Taliban and will beat you into submission if you don't." He roared with laughter at his joke.

Jorja laughed loudly too, so loudly that a passing man poked his head into the room scornfully.

"You loud madam!" he chastised and moved on.

Jorja covered her mouth to suppress the laughter and looked quizzically at Lufti. Without speaking, he knew her question. "No, I don't know him. But now he knows you."

They giggled to themselves. She liked Lufti. He was right; they did share a similar humor. At noon, the naked light bulb suddenly flickered and lit up the room. No one remarked on the resurgence of power.

In the Sangam Hotel restaurant at lunchtime, Jorja spread two newspapers on the table, given to her by Qaseem, the receptionist. *Dawn* announced that it was Pakistan's most widely circulated English-language newspaper. Similarly, *News International* promoted itself as the largest English and Urdu newspaper publication in Pakistan. She favored *Dawn*; the title seemed symbolic of her arrival in Pakistan.

She heard the wailing of Arabic prayers from a nearby mosque. There was no need for a watch for she knew it was 12:24. She read the daily prayer times in *Dawn*. The prayers commenced without fail at precisely the times indicated: On Friday, the first day of March, the prayer times were 5:17, 12:24, 16:27, 18:07, and 19:30.

CHAPTER 7

GADI'S SECRET

It had been cold and depressing in the darkness of the curriculum office throughout the morning. Frustration with trying to connect to the internet at the project office cast a shadow over Jorja's afternoon. She tried for two hours to connect. Tension in her shoulders grew as the overwhelming urgency to contact people increased. She wanted to relieve her disappointment with tears. Soon Lufti's light banter eased her anxiety again and, eventually, a successful connection rewarded her persistence. Denny's message was at the top of the list. She read it repeatedly. In the middle of answering his e-mail, the power failed again.

Gadi, the typist, had been sitting quietly at his computer, casting intermittent glances at Jorja.

Jorja pretended not to notice his glances, but she certainly noticed his attractive appearance. As soon as Lufti left the room, he approached her.

"Fadil told us of your misfortune on the way to Kashmir. I'm sorry for your distress."

"Thank you."

"So, you have seen the Talibs. I have many true tales of the Taliban."

"Really? Fadil doesn't think they were Talibs." Jorja waited for the electricity to resume. She was desperate to connect to the internet and with Denny.

Gadi leaned toward her. "I know a secret."

Jorja looked him in the eyes. They were kind, full of expression, and a touch of mystery. There was something special about them. "Really?"

His finger glided along the edge of the desk. Jorja suddenly shivered. She was thankful that the desk was between her and the young man. "I know where Osama bin Laden is."

"Really?"

"You could make a lot of money if you found him."

"Gadi, I'd be a dead woman if I found him."

"Then your family would get the money," he said.

Jorja was silent.

"I know what you're thinking," Gadi said.

"Really?"

"You are thinking that I should look for him. You are thinking that I should get the reward money from the Americans. But the Americans won't believe me. They will think I'm a terrorist. They would believe an Englishwoman." Gadi looked pleased with himself.

"Gadi, you forget that I'm confined to the curriculum office, the project office, and the Sangam Hotel because of security concerns. I can't wander about freely."

"Osama could be walking the streets of Muzaffarabad."

"Really?"

"Really!" Gadi's eyebrows formed arches. He smiled. "I propose that you look for him. I will help you. Then you will give me some of the reward money: a few million of the twenty-five million American dollars. Think about it. I know where he is."

"Really?"

"Really, madam! I have only your best welfare within my heart. Trust me."

Jorja looked into his eyes and, for a split second, she did trust him. But just for a split second.

CHAPTER 8

TEA AND VODKA

"Where's the curriculum office?" someone asked Jorja. Not knowing was understandable. The ministry was in the process of erecting a new building to accommodate all divisions of the expanding education department in one convenient location. Construction began two years ago and was not yet near completion. In the meantime, the curriculum office was accommodated in a dilapidated group of low-level buildings in a dusty, narrow laneway that dipped markedly and stopped close to the river. Merging with residences, mechanical garages and mattress warehouses, the signless curriculum office was inconspicuous and modest.

"North of the Lipton sign," Jorja answered. At this direction, they nodded, recognizing the general vicinity.

Muzaffarabad stretched for four kilometers through the gutter of a mountain range. The Neelum River bisected it lengthwise. A brilliant yellow Lipton Tea sign cut the city at its waist. The landmark billboard was oversized and intimidating by day. By night, floodlights splashed the glorious display with luminescence. Jorja loved the sunshiny billboard that brightened the muddy riverbank of gray concrete and galvanized iron structures. The smiling face of the Pakistani woman with her straight white teeth, shiny black hair, glowing skin, and sparkling eyes was the epitome of health and wealth. It was in extreme contrast to the people passing underneath. Below, a smaller green sign urged residents to KEEP THE CITY CLEAN as cars spewed fumes of black smoke into the air.

The Lipton Tea sign marked the center of Muzaffarabad. It was at the crossing of Bank and Neelum Roads, to the left of the bazaar and to the right of the bridge that spanned the Neelum River. Crossing the river led north to schools and houses, west to the hills of Mansehra, and south to the mosque and the Black Fort that lay in Jorja's line of sight from the balcony of her hotel room. The Black Fort was no longer a tourist site; the army had seized it to use as its base.

Merely a handful of main roads ran through Kashmir: Bank, Eidgah, Neelum, College, Fort, Airport, and Gilani Roads. The traffic kept to the left, more or less, and kicked up dust, honking continuously. The sunny Lipton woman smiled down on the traffic in full knowledge that their grimy soot would not reach her as it settled on fruit, live chickens, clothes, and chattels of the stalls. Lighting the junction at night, the billboard averted certain accidents and mishaps.

Jorja imagined the tea woman reciting the words of Sir Thomas Lipton: *Work hard, deal honestly, be enterprising, exercise careful judgment, and advertise freely, but judiciously.* With tea being the second most popular beverage in the world, Sir Lipton endeavored to corner the market. His liberal advertising was everywhere: the yellow tea label was even on a petrol tanker. Lipton Tea was certainly advertised freely, only rivaled by Nestle bottled water, the most popular beverage in the world.

Jorja was a tea drinker and the only other thing she drank on occasion was the vodka she'd brought with her. Not only did the vodka warm her during the wintry evenings, it probably saved her life. Skipping down the three steps that separated her hotel room's living area from the bedroom, she punctured the fleshy mound behind her big toe. A three-centimeter nail, rusted and coarse, had pierced the skin. Blood oozed from the wound as she wrapped a flannel around it. She telephoned reception for first-aid treatment. Qaseem sent a young man to the room to render assistance.

"Madam, blood! Blood!" He was flustered and ran from the room.

Hopping to the door, Jorja called out, but he had disappeared. In excruciating pain, she hobbled to the bed as blood dripped onto the carpet. Kashmir would drown in blood, not from an uprising, but from a helpless gored woman. Despite the relentless bloodletting and suffering, Kashmiris were still able to hold their heads high. Jorja, on the other hand, was sinking noisily into the mattress of the soft-centered bed. Miraculously, the young man returned with a large rectangular adhesive tape. She stopped groaning.

"Do you have antiseptic cream?"

"Madam?"

"Do you have something to kill germs?"

"Madam?"

"Do you have medicine?"

"Madam?"

She showed him the rusty nail.

"Bad, madam."

"Yes, very bad. Do you have medicine?"

"No medicine, madam."

Sending him to the bathroom for a clean flannel, Jorja grabbed the bottle of vodka that she'd hidden in the bedside cabinet.

"No alcohol, madam," he advised, doing his duty.

"It's medicine." She applied a liberal amount of vodka to the flannel and washed the infected area, grimacing as it stung.

"Oh, medicine! Very good, madam." He smiled with understanding and relief.

"Yes, medicine."

Jorja wiped the wound dry and applied the tape. "Have you seen the Taliban in Muzaffarabad?"

"No madam."

"Are you sure? Have you seen Osama bin Laden in Kashmir?"

The young man suddenly seemed nervous. He avoided looking at her. "It is not good to talk about the Taliban and Osama bin Laden."

"Why not?"

"Please madam, I must go. You fine now?"

"I'm fine now. Thank you for your help."

After his departure, she poured a liberal amount of vodka down her throat. It was hardly the quality of imported brands, but she felt instantly healed, inside and out.

CHAPTER 9

JORJA SEES IMRAN

The egg served with her breakfast was deliciously fresh. An abundance of poultry farms dotted the region; a random spacing of rectangular sheds on each mountainside. Acres of battery hens lived in the worst conditions imaginable with the best views in the world. Instantly, Jorja craved sautéed spring onions and crispy deep-fried pork. But there were no pigs in a Muslim country.

Four Kashmiri executives occupied a restaurant table near the French doors that led onto the patio. Outside, empty tables enjoyed the warmer weather and views of the river and undulating terrain. The view from the northern window looked upstream toward Muzaffarabad's mountain and city center. Ornate, golden silk cords tied the curtains open permanently, permitting light to enter and immerse the restaurant in brightness. Jorja enjoyed breakfast. It was a comforting way to start the day.

Lufti and Jorja worked until noon in the unlit curriculum office. There was no electricity again. There was no fuel for the back-up generator again. There was no heat again. They perused existing education reports in the dark. Several times Lufti removed his thick black-rimmed glasses and rubbed his eyes. Few people stopped by the room. As Jorja passed the director's office where three women were sipping tea while examining a map, one of them beckoned her inside.

Rima, the assistant director of curriculum, explained that many specialists were attending a week-long workshop in Karachi. She invited Jorja to lunch, with Lufti, at her house. His two daughters had arrived in Kashmir for their school holidays and were spending the morning with Rima's daughter who was on vacation from her university studies.

A rounded woman, thick at the hips, thighs, and waist, Kashmiris would say that Rima had an ideal figure. The forty-nine-year-old asked Jorja her age. "But you look ten years younger. Why do you look so young? Is it because you are skinny?"

"Maybe it's because I exercise a lot in Australia," Jorja explained.

"We don't exercise here. It's not good for women to exercise in front of men."

"Do you go for walks?" Jorja asked.

"No. When you walk, you sweat. And the face goes red. It's not good to look like that in the street in front of the people, especially in front of men."

"Exercise is very good for you," explained Jorja. "It's good for the heart and the circulation. I think I look young because I'm fit and healthy."

After much questioning about exercise and food, Rima said, "I might go for a walk on Sunday. Near my house."

Jorja said that it would be a good idea. Rima smiled, showing her straight, white teeth. Age was a strange thing in Kashmir. The young looked considerably younger than their true age, and the middle-aged looked considerably older. An eighteen-year-old looked twelve and a thirty-year-old looked sixty. In light of this, Jorja found it difficult to estimate a person's age in Kashmir.

Rima's house was situated up two flights of narrow, uneven, concrete steps on the side of a hill near the center of the city. It was small, but comfortable and inviting.

Photographs of her children covered the cracks and peeling plaster in the living room. "That is Mecca," said Rima proudly, when she caught Jorja looking at a black and white photograph. "That's where Muslims go for their spiritual pilgrimage. We call it the *hajj*. Millions of Muslims go every year. My husband goes every year. All Muslims who are physically and financially able should perform the *hajj* at least once in their lifetime. Faith, prayer, the *zakat*, the fast, and the pilgrimage; they are the Five Pillars of Islam. The pilgrimage to Mecca is part of Islamic life." Her thin lips contrasted with her full, rotund face that protruded from a velour scarf of autumnal colors. She had the air of a content person.

"*Zakat* is the giving of alms," explained Lufti. "Actually, it means to purify one's wealth by giving some to the poor. It's like your government social welfare policy in Australia, except here it's every individual Muslim's responsibility and not the government's. If you give to the poor, it means that you'll have abundant rewards in this life and in the hereafter."

Still looking at the large picture, Jorja asked Rima how long her husband stayed in Mecca.

"The pilgrimage can last for six days. We celebrate when he comes back for he has survived the *hajj*."

"Survived the *hajj*? What do you mean?"

"Many old people die in Mecca during *hajj*. Sometimes the large crowd crushes them, sometimes by heart gone, and sometimes by fire."

"Heart attack," explained Lufti. "The experience is often too much for the elderly."

"But by fire? What do you mean?" Jorja looked amazed.

"When people cook meals on the open fires, sometimes they get burns," said Rima. "The burns are bad and there are no doctors. Because of the crowds and there being nowhere to sleep, they lie in dirty places. Sometimes it is very cold and they die of flu or sickness. So it's such a wonderful thing to see people come back alive from the *hajj*." Rima noticed Jorja's eyes focus on another painting. "Ibrahim, the Prophet, may peace be upon Him, built the shrine shown in the picture. It's called the *Kaaba*. We pray five times a day." As she pointed, Jorja saw markings on her palms. Rima was adorned with *mandi*—temporary henna dye—painted in an intricate pattern on her hands. Her daughter applied the henna for a wedding they attended. From a distance, her hands seemed covered in lace gloves.

Sunlight streamed into the square room through lacy white curtains. Sofas lined three of the eggshell-colored walls. Two plush velvet sofas flanked the northern and southern walls. Underneath the front western window was another sofa. A large kitchen table hid the fourth wall. Jorja, Lufti, his two young daughters Selma and Sarah, Rima, and her daughter Melek maneuvered themselves into the high-backed wooden chairs. Rima served exotic curries, rich in taste and hot on the tongue. The pride of place in the center of the table was a traditional Kashmiri dish of meat and yoghurt, swimming in oil.

Jorja asked what the meat was. "Yes, meat," said Rima nodding.

Jorja looked at Lufti. He shrugged. Her scarf slipped off her hair during dinner so she left it around her shoulders. Melek had removed hers. Rima and the young girls kept themselves covered. Melek had lush, thick, red hair. When Jorja expressed surprise at the color, she explained the Afghan origins of her father and pointed to a photograph of him on the wall behind the table.

"That's Imran, isn't it?" Jorja noticed Imran Khan in the photograph first.

"Yes, it is. My father collected money for Imran's hospital and this is the presentation of the check. See my father's hair. It has red tones in it." Her voice was soft; her movements were graceful and elegant. In the photograph, Imran towered over her father.

"Are you taller than your father? You seem to be?" Jorja hoped she would not take offence.

"Oh yes! Everyone is taller than Papa." She giggled.

"When was the photo taken?"

"Two years ago. Imran came to Kashmir. He's a kind and benevolent man," said Melek. "My father was proud to meet him."

"He's well regarded in Australia. Everyone knows of him, mainly for his cricket success, but they're also aware of his humanitarian and political interests. They respect him in Australia. Your father was lucky to meet him."

"Yes, and he was lucky to touch Imran's hand too. It's a good photograph and deserves its place on the wall with Mecca."

Jorja took the statement to be recognition of Imran's status while she mused at the thought of touching his hand. "I know what you mean. I think every woman in Australia would have wanted to touch his hand when he was playing cricket." Jorja sighed reminiscently. "I was very surprised to see him on the plane from Lahore to Islamabad when I came to Pakistan a week ago. He's still very attractive, I think. So tall, so. . ." Her mind wandered.

Days before, at Lahore airport, underneath the rays of a waking sun, there was a long wait for the connecting domestic flight to Islamabad. The terminal was eerily quiet. A man mopped encrusted grime from the linoleum floor.

"Excuse me, is there a waiting area?" Jorja asked.

"No, madam. Very sorry. You can wait in the ladies' restroom over there." His rubber-gloved finger pointed toward a corner room.

The restroom's urine-soaked floor and two dilapidated cubicles made Jorja thankful that she had a strong bladder. She returned to the hall and sat on her suitcase.

"Are you alone? The check-in counter will not be open for a very long time, madam," said the mopping man.

"Yes, I'm alone. I'll wait here. Thank you."

"As you wish, madam."

An older man emptied ashtrays. "So sorry, madam, but tea and magazines are not available at this hour," he said as he wiped the ash with a well-used, tattered cloth, sending fumes of stale cigarettes into the air. She nodded to indicate that she understood.

The janitors, all men, cleaned around her. Some made polite comments; others merely smiled. She sensed their unease near a conspicuously unaccompanied woman. Usually a brother, an uncle or, even better, a husband, escorted a Pakistani woman in public. She had no such accessory. She felt alienated and alone.

Hours passed. A security guard approached her with hands clasped behind his back. He was stocky and potbellied. "We will have a new airport soon. The Alamo Irbil International Airport has been under construction for a long time. It was due to be finished two years ago, but now it will be ready by mid-August, in time for Independence Day. It's supposed to handle six million passengers a year. That's three times more than this one," he said proudly, puffing out his chest. "That's what the newspapers say. The facilities will be better too, madam, like a real airport with a hotel and duty-free shops and banks and restaurants. You will not have to wait like this."

"I look forward to it."

"This old airport will become a sporting complex with squash courts."

"Pakistan had excellent squash players years ago," Jorja said. "I remember the Mighty Khans: Hashim, Jahangir, and Josher. They often came to Australia and had fierce battles with Geoff Hunt."

"Fierce, but fair, madam. I regret the standard of squash in Pakistan has deteriorated. I used to play squash and am a great enthusiast of the game. I look back with nostalgia. Years ago, this country had famous players. Now, we don't even reach the semi-finals." He shook his head then broke into a broad grin. "But we still have fierce cricket matches with Australia."

"Indeed we do," Jorja laughed.

"You must have heard of Imran Khan, our famous cricketer?"

"Sure I have. I've seen him play many times. He's a legend in our country as well as yours. Many would say he's handsome as well as an articulate humanitarian and politician."

The security guard leaned toward Jorja and lowered his voice. His eyes darted sideways a few times before he said, "Let me tell you a secret. He'll be on the flight to Islamabad."

"Really?" Jorja said, smiling to indicate great appreciation at the gesture of trust.

The man nodded several times. "The sun is rising. It is dawning. The first-class check-in counter is now open, madam. May I help you with your luggage?"

"I'm traveling economy."

"Very sorry, madam." He departed to continue his patrol of the terminal.

Jorja waited. The airport filled with the bustle of impatient travelers. Like ants emerging from the woodwork, people rushed about to secure prime line positions at the economy check-in counters. They pushed and pulled their suitcases, cocooned in plastic cling-wrap, onto jerking conveyor belts as airport staff attempted to maintain order. She remained seated on her suitcase.

A young man in a crisp, white airline uniform moved from behind the first-class counter, now free of customers, and stood by her side. "Come with me, madam. I will check in your baggage."

"I'm traveling economy."

"I understand, madam. You are expecting to go to Islamabad?" His manner was impeccably polite. Diamonds embedded in a silver ring encircled his finger and dazzled in competition with the matching watch, strapped so tightly it seemed to pinch his hairy arm.

She stood and stretched. "If I expect to go, will I get there?"

"Surely, madam!" He grabbed the handle of her suitcase. "If you come with me."

She obeyed, glad that someone was taking charge. A man that knows what he's doing and does it with confidence is a man indeed, she thought. The man she was following was tall, broad-shouldered, and had an assertive stride. She conjectured about his wife, imagining a prim, pretty, intelligent woman, self-assured without being demandingly shrewish. She would have a professional job, but she would not earn more than her bread-winner. The imaginary wife would be younger and shorter than her husband. She would have the finest shalwar kameez, jewelry, and cosmetics, but not be irrational with her spending. Her neighbors would say that they were the perfect couple. Perhaps they would be secretly envious.

Jorja thought about her perfect man. She thought back to her previous partners. They certainly could not be categorized by looks as she'd dated men of varied nationalities, both dark and swarthy and fair and freckled. They'd been neither all tall nor all short. All had an engaging smile. Most were expressive communicators. All were creative, resourceful, or inventive. Most were athletic or health-conscious. All had a good sense of humor. Most could cook. In addition, all were avid readers. At present, Denny represented her ideal man: intelligent, eccentric, sensitive, athletic, and generous.

Boarding the Pakistan International Airlines plane, Jorja tripped on the top step. The tall passenger in front of her turned to offer assistance.

"Are you all right? Be careful now. Walk in front of me." Gently, his arm guided her as she passed him. As he did so, she inhaled a whiff of aromatic soap instead of the unpleasant odor of a smoker. His strikingly handsome face was instantly recognizable.

She stammered, "Thanks so much Imran. I mean, Mr. Khan. I mean ..."

"You know of me!" He seemed genuinely surprised. "You must be English."

"I'm Australian. I used to watch you play at Adelaide Oval. I met you many years ago. You signed my autograph book." They moved along the aisle, searching for their designated seats.

"Adelaide Oval is surely the most picturesque cricket ground in the world. I remember it well. In '72 the Aussies won convincingly."

"Pakistan tied the matches in '76, '83 and during your captaincy in 1990. I remember the last one because it was a very exciting game."

His smile widened. "That's correct. What a memory! There's been much water under the bridge since then. This is my seat. And yours?"

"Mine is another few rows down on the right-hand side. Thanks for your help."

"Thank you, and enjoy your stay in Pakistan."

Swooning as she slid into her seat, she considered meeting the legendary Imran Khan was her reward for the long, dreary wait in the airport terminal. "Water under the bridge," Imran had said. The phrase reminded her of Denny. Whenever he walked along a bridge, he'd lean over the railing and stare at the water's flow, surveying the trajectory of floating leaves and debris with fascination. Fountains, oceans, lakes and puddles; any formation of water attracted him like a magnet. He especially enjoyed the luxury of lingering showers. Jorja loved watching his naked body and would trace the water's path with her eyes as it flowed over his lathered form, from the moment it flattened his chestnut hair to the second it divided around his nipples and coursed toward his navel, where it would spout into the air. Side streams spilled like tributaries into his pubic curls, along his flaccid flesh and down his muscular legs. Closing his eyes, he'd sit ball-like on the floor under the shower spray, with his knees raised and his arms wrapped around them, as it cascaded like a waterfall over a smooth pale rock. Even as the water became colder, he didn't move. Eventually, he would unfold and step out of the shower, ready to begin a new day.

Jorja's name, legibly written in ink on a signboard, bobbed up and down amid the crowd. The man holding the sign was Jamshid's driver, a lean man, almost two meters in height, with a clean-shaven, square jaw. Jamshid grinned as she approached.

"Miss Jorja, I presume? Did you have a good flight? I'm Jamshid. It's so good to meet you after all the e-mails. I'm delighted that you accepted the job at such short notice." He clasped her hands in his as they exchanged greetings. The tall driver introduced himself as Noor. They walked a short distance to the car where Noor placed her luggage in the boot and threw the cardboard sign on top of it.

"It'll take less than an hour to get to Islamabad," said Jamshid, turning to her in the back seat. "Is there anything you want to know?"

"Yes. Will Imran Khan win the election in October?" She positioned herself behind the driver.

The two men laughed loudly. "Oh, no, no, no!" Jamshid replied. "He will not win. He's popular, but he will not win. Why do you ask?"

"He was on the plane from Lahore. I've been a fan of his since childhood."

"The Australians love their cricket and so do we. It's a pity you're only here for a short time. You're going to miss the New Zealand series."

"I'll be barracking for the Pakistanis. You know how much Australians dislike the Kiwis winning."

"Yes, yes. The fighting is like big brother and little brother. It's the same with India and Pakistan: such great rivalry between brothers! But you also have bitter rivalry with the English team, don't you? Australia versus the mother country! What wonderful sporting battles you have with your national relatives. At least you keep your wars on the playing field. That's not so with us." Jamshid turned his head occasionally while Noor looked at Jorja through the rear-view mirror. Jamshid's eyes protruded from their sockets and his generous lips extended over his mouth. His undersized podgy hands and stunted plump fingers made the rest of his body appear bloated.

"Imran Khan once said that cricket is a pressure game and, when it came to an India-Pakistan match, the pressure was doubled," Jorja said.

"Yes, Jorja, you're an intelligent woman, but you mustn't keep talking about Imran Khan. I'm sure you're lying when you say he was on the plane. Maybe it was someone else. Your imagination has got the better of you. There was no such sighting."

There was no such sighting Jamshid said a week ago. Melek interrupted Jorja's thoughts of her arrival into Pakistan and of Imran Khan. "Allah's luck is with you for meeting Imran. And here he is in our room. That's another sighting, isn't it? Allah is sending him to you."

"Oh, I wish!" Jorja laughed.

Lufti smiled at her. He was wearing a gray shalwar kameez with an old tweed jacket. "Melek, I rather think that Allah is sending Imran's message of peace to Miss Jorja and not Imran himself. I'm certain she didn't see him on the plane last week. It would be highly unlikely. Allah is not so benevolent as to send Miss Jorja a man like Imran. Perhaps He has another man in mind." Lufti winked at Jorja.

She had not told him of Denny and wondered what Lufti was thinking. She also wondered why Pakistanis believed that it was so unlikely that she would meet Imran. "But I *did* see Imran, Lufti. I *did*. Jamshid didn't believe me either."

"Two Pakistanis can't be wrong then. Perhaps you should stop telling people that you saw the great Khan!"

"Lufti, I *did* see Imran Khan. Anyway, what are his chances for success at the October election?"

Lufti was quick to respond. "He's well thought of but he'll not win the election. He doesn't have the votes of the masses as a politician yet. He will be vocal on a number of issues and will probably give his support to General Musharraf. People consider his party insignificant. And besides, foreign women are not allowed to vote, lest they cast a thousand votes in his direction," he teased and slapped his hand on the table.

His daughters looked at each other. The girls and Melek looked at Jorja. Rima whispered to her daughter in Urdu. Melek came to Jorja's rescue. "Lufti, you are making Miss Jorja blush. Her face is red with blood. You mustn't tease her. I must clean the table and while I'm gone you must be kind to our guest."

Lufti and Jorja grinned at each other. After lunch, they returned to the project office, and Lufti retired to his room with his daughters. Jorja worked until six o'clock, spending some time sporadically e-mailing friends in between power stoppages.

Fadil drove her back to the hotel. She entered the small bakery-cum-supermarket next door, unaccompanied, just as the power failed. Fortunately, the windows allowed sufficient light to see without strain. There were four sales clerks: one at the cake counter, one at the cigarette counter, and two in a central cashier booth. A few customers browsed the aisles, but no one seemed concerned about the loss of power. They were more interested in Jorja's presence and stared as she wandered slowly along the few aisles of mixed foods. She smiled politely at them. The goods were free of dust and lined neatly in rows in a semblance of order.

The store contained most essential items. She looked for stationery, particularly paper and pens, but there were none. She looked for hairclips, but there were none. On the counter in front of a young man, she placed hair conditioner, toothpaste, tissues, and two bars of chocolate. Diligently, he wrote the prices on a piece of paper and handed it to her, then placed the items in a plastic bag. Courteously, he instructed the foreign woman to take the paper to the cashiers. A cashier checked the calculations on a large-padded calculator, took her money, slipped it in a till under the counter, and dispensed the change with a beaming smile. The simplicity of the transaction and the customer service made Jorja briefly appreciate life without a computerized cash register and power.

CHAPTER 10

OPERATION ANACONDA

Jorja Himmermann didn't hear the bombs during the day. It would require bionic ears to hear gunfire and mortar above the noises of the city, especially the continuous hooting of car horns with their rapid staccato beeps, long drawn-out honks, and fancy air horns playing melodies. Layered over the racket of automobiles was the braying of donkeys, the shouts of storekeepers advertising their wares, the megaphonic calls to prayer, and the singing of children spilling out of schools.

Bombing raids seemed loudest after seven-thirty in the evening. Long defensive fire sounded mostly around midnight. "The guns you hear with your ears," said Rabi at the curriculum office. "Bombs you feel in the legs." Jorja's hotel room was on the first floor so it would require extensive nearby bombing to feel anything in the legs. *News International* reported the events of Operation Anaconda: *Around 400 al-Qaeda fighters have been killed in a five-day offensive by US-led forces in eastern Afghanistan, a US military spokesperson said Wednesday. Eight US servicemen, of the 950 regular and Special Forces, had been killed and around fifty wounded in intense fighting against the besieged extremists holed up in the mountains of Paktia province bordering Pakistan, US Major Brian Hilferty said. Hilferty said he did not know how many al-Qaeda and Taliban soldiers were left. At the start of the offensive, the Pentagon gave a figure of "hundreds" of hostile fighters regrouping in the Arma mountains, but local Afghan fighters put the number as high as 2,300.*

Often an Urdu newspaper was tucked under Rabi's armpit or poking out of his briefcase. His colleagues gave him the nickname, Public Informant. He had his own version of Operation Anaconda events, declaring that al-Qaeda fighters had captured and killed an American soldier, and six more died as they tried to rescue him.

Ground fighting continued in the Shahikot Valley fifty kilometers south of the Afghan provincial city, Gardez. Infantry forces edging up the sheer mountains had entered caves, finding a stash of weapons including mortars, rocket-propelled grenade rounds, and small arms, as well as foreign passports. American warplanes relentlessly bombarded al-Qaeda forces. *News International* described the bombardment as "punishing" and that it had weakened the Taliban and al-Qaeda fighters who were unable to gain reinforcements from Pakistan. Rabi said that American warplanes were only fifteen kilometers from the Pakistan border in South Waziristan. Pakistani travelers from Birmal told him that the air strikes had continued for four hours during the day.

The next day, snow swept across the mountains where the American forces were targeting the Taliban and al-Qaeda guerrillas, adding another element of unpredictability to the largest American-led battle in Afghanistan's history. The temperature dropped noticeably and Jorja shivered throughout the day that did not rise above nine degrees Celsius.

Army helicopters flew in and out of Muzaffarabad during the day resupplying the American-backed Afghan troops with food, fuel, and ammunition. Rabi translated the Urdu newspaper report for Jorja: *Commander Abdul Muteen, who has about a hundred and thirty-five fighters in the Afghan force of about eight hundred, said before the bad weather arrived possible rebel reinforcement routes had been sealed and fighters were beginning to enter tunnel systems held by the diehard Taliban and al-Qaeda fighters. "We might have killed non-combatants," he said in response to a question. "But they certainly went in there knowing what they were going into. We have no indication, we haven't seen little kids in a yard and blown it up, or women walking around and then shot." But he feared the besieged guerrillas might now try to slip away under cover of snow. "The weather may ground some US planes and these Taliban know the area very well and might try to slip through our lines and escape," he said. The US military has ordered up to three hundred extra troops, seventeen attack helicopters and several A-10 ground-attack aircraft armed with rapid-fire cannons to the battlefield to counter the rebels. US President George W. Bush, who in October launched the campaign that toppled the Taliban for harboring Osama bin Laden, blamed for the September Eleven attacks on the United States, expressed confidence in the outcome of the battle. "There's a fierce battle waging, but we're winning that battle," Bush said, adding some elements were trying to undermine the interim Afghan government to use the Central Asian nation once more as a base to launch fresh attacks on the United States.*

"Americans won't be popular if women and children are killed in the fighting," Jorja said.

"This is war, Miss Jorja, and all wars are bad. Americans aren't bad, but I think President Bush is a mad man. I think all Pakistanis will think like me. Don't you agree?"

"I don't know, Rabi. I don't know what Pakistanis think, but they should use their voice in the next election."

"The election will not represent the people. It will only represent Musharraf's intentions. That is all."

CHAPTER 11

SHAKING

An eagle skimmed the river for fish. Jorja watched it from her balcony as she dried her hair. Patchworked amongst the snow, the mountain's brown tracts looked dark and ominous.

At breakfast, the waiter asked, "Are you taking tea, madam? Are you taking toast, madam? Butter, jam?"

In Pakistan, people "take" breakfast and "take" tea; they "have" lunch and dinner. So she took tea and toast while she read yesterday's *Dawn*. She liked the regional insert dedicated to the northern areas of Pakistan and Kashmir, from Islamabad to Muzaffarabad. The language was simple and somewhat poetic: *The political authorities have destroyed poppy crop grown over thousands of acres in the far-flung mountainous area of Gabri along the Pakistani-Afghan border. The locals resisted the operation and armed tribesmen threatened the tribal security force with dire consequences if they did not abandon the anti-poppy drive. To save the situation from turning bad, some influential tribal elders persuaded the growers not to oppose the operation.*

A government advertisement for a national monument in Islamabad called for public participation: *The Government of Pakistan is desirous to construct a monument in a beautifully strategic spot in Islamabad. Selected design will be rewarded. Let us participate for an idea on the most appropriate design dedicated to the greatness of people in Pakistan.*

The waiter brought her a pot of tea with a small pewter jug of milk. It was customary in Kashmir to add milk to the teapot so that a flow of milky tea poured directly into the waiting cup. Jorja found it to be over-milked so she ordered separate tea. "Separate tea" was a pot of black tea with the milk served separately.

"My name is Awan. Muhammad Shafi Awan," he said. "I get you *lassi*?"

The salted milky-yoghurt drink filled her mouth and the Pakistani omelet curdled on her tongue. She was thankful for the mounds of toast served underneath a cloth napkin that kept the slices warm. Returning to her room, Jorja cleaned her teeth over the chipped basin. The stinking drain emitted fumes that mingled with the scents of toothpaste and *lassi*.

It was Sunday and a day of rest. The hotel staff advised Jorja not to venture outside without an escort. With an audit report to write and a cricket game televised that afternoon, she resigned herself to a day inside. She wrote a few personal letters and exercised for half an hour by running up and down the three steps to the bedroom area. A mere half an hour of stomach and leg exercises was pitiful and a token effort. She hardly broke a sweat. However, content with that, Jorja showered and worked on the audit report.

Wedding music from the hall on the mezzanine floor, directly below her room, filled the air. Jorja telephoned the reception desk for information. "Two weddings on this day," Qaseem said, explaining that there would be a wedding of two hundred and fifty people and another of a hundred and fifty people in the hotel. Shrill bells and drums sounded relentlessly and repetitively. Although she was curious to witness the wedding, Jorja didn't want to attend unaccompanied and without invitation. She moved to the balcony where there was a hint of spring sunshine. A pair of mottled brown birds was busy building a nest in the tree overhanging the balcony. The naked branches were stark against the pallid sky. Two young boys flew thin tissue-paper kites on the flat roof of a nearby house. Kite-flying was a popular pastime in Pakistan.

Three loud raps vibrated the door, announcing the newspaper, *Dawn,* being delivered. The news heralded the weekend of *Basant*—the kite-flying festival—but it was not celebratory: among seven injured in *Basant*-related accidents in various parts of the district on Sunday were three children and two women. The three children fell from the roofs of their houses while trying to catch kites in the Cantonment area and the two women in Uggoki fell from their car in an attempt to catch twine from the vehicle windows. They received severe injuries. Two men in Model Town were struck by a car as they flew their kites. All the injured were in critical condition in various hospitals across the city.

Another rap on the door interrupted her reading. Boys from the wedding party were playing an impish game of banging on hotel doors and running away. She ignored subsequent knocks and an intense banging competition ensued. It seemed as if the goal was to beat the door down. Tiring of their game, Jorja opened the door at the next round of furious knocking and glared into the surprised eyes of one of the youths who fled down the stairway in horror. The banging competition ended and the boys sought entertainment elsewhere.

By five o'clock, both weddings ceased. Never before had she appreciated peace and quiet as she did now. Thankful for the end of the reverberating music, the thumping of boys' fists on doors, and the shrill squeals of seemingly millions of children, Jorja sighed in relief.

It was quiet. The tree skimmed its branches against the railing on the western balcony. Birds flew off the tree in a flurry. Jorja turned her head away from the window and focused on the words in front of her: a letter to Denny. At last, silence. She dropped her shoulders and released the tension. The naked tree shuddered in the breeze. The birds had not returned.

She felt it first through the floor. Vibrations reverberated up her legs. She knew it was a tremor and was unperturbed. She had experienced minor quakes before and had become used to them, never expecting the worst. Concentric circles formed in the drinking water on the desk, but the glass remained still. She watched in fascination. Tremors were usually only a few seconds, but not this one. The vibrations intensified. The undulations in the drinking glass crested into miniature waves. Window panes shook and the door bolt rattled. All the while, the framed painting of a mosque banged against the wall. She held onto the desk attached to the wall and thought of running to the door, into the corridor, down the stairs, and outside into the open air. That would take a few seconds and the tremors would surely have finished before she had unbolted the door. But this quake had not abated. She realized this was a quake of sinister proportions and noted the time. It was 5:08 p.m. on the third of day of March, three days before a half moon.

Jorja felt the wall with the palm of her hand. An electric shock passed through her body. The whole room shook and creaked, rattling and moaning under the force of the fierce movements. Her body moved in rhythm. She crept steadily to the balcony and peered over the railing. Men and women had vacated the restaurant and congregated on the patio, wailing in prayer to Allah, reciting verses from the Holy Qur'an. A tearful woman beat her breast. A man dropped to the floor, in the prayer position, facing Mecca. One man rocked back and forth on his haunches while emitting a mournful sound. Another knelt beside him and comforted him by patting him on the back.

Jorja looked across the river to the symbols of safety and security: a religious mosque and a military army camp. She glanced at the river, at the sky, at the riverbank, and at the outer walls of the hotel. The shaking continued, but Jorja saw nothing telling her she was in immediate danger. Inside, she returned to the desk. She grasped the edge of the wooden tabletop and waited. The tremor was sure to pass. By sitting still, she did not feel the paralysis of dread, but more a feeling of reverence, a respectful waiting, and a deep attentiveness to forces much greater than her own. Jorja was sure that by the time she rushed out of the room, or to the door of the bathroom and the shelter of the doorframe, the quake would have stopped. And eventually it did. Two minutes must have passed. Again, there was an eerie silence. Even the wailing of the Kashmiris on the restaurant patio ceased. Knowing that they were not about to die, they finally calmed themselves.

A hotel supervisor arrived at her room to check that she was safe. "You be having shakes, madam? Shaking all over?"

"Is anyone hurt? Is there any damage to the hotel? Is Muzaffarabad okay?"

"No one is hurt in this hotel. It is not damaged. It is strong. The weddings are finished and people gone. You okay, madam? You scared?"

"I'm fine, thank you. I'm not scared."

"I was scared, madam. I was very scared. You are brave, madam."

* * *

Copies of *Dawn* and local newspapers lay open on the wooden table in the curriculum office and people huddled together to read about the earthquake. The quake measured 7.2 on the Richter scale with a depth of one hundred and ninety-five kilometers. Its epicenter was in the Hindu Kush Mountains of Afghanistan, two hundred and fifty kilometers north of Peshawar in Pakistan and about four hundred kilometers west of Muzaffarabad. The Islamic Press reported at least a hundred and fifty people killed by resulting landslides in Afghanistan's northern Samangan province, taking the death toll to over two hundred in the region. Nine hundred houses had been destroyed, five hundred of them in the provincial city of Aybak. The tremors had been widespread across Pakistan and severe in Peshawar, Parachinar, Muzaffarabad, Islamabad, Lahore, Faisalabad, Multan, Vehari, Jhelum, Quetta, and the northern areas including Gilgit and Chitral. The meteorology department in Lahore timed it at two and a quarter minutes.

Triggered by the earthquake, landslides had blocked the mountain roads from Islamabad to Muzaffarabad along the Karakoram Highway. That news worried Jorja most. The Karakoram was narrow and treacherous at best. Rain and landslides made driving suicidal. She wondered how the fragile, precarious houses had fared.

In the curriculum office, talk was rapid and breathless.

"It was fearsome, fearsome."

"Miss Jorja, we've never experienced an earthquake of such intensity before."

"Yes, yes. Ten years ago, remember. Remember the big one then?"

"No, this one was worse, much worse

"What about more earthquakes? Will they come?"

"Aftershocks? Yes, we'll get aftershocks."

"No, we won't. Not here in Kashmir. They'll only be in the Hindu Kush, not here."

"Here too. We'll have them here. Just wait and see. I am right. I am right."

"No, no, no. I cannot bear the shaking. No, no, no! No more earthquakes," screamed one woman, hitting her head with her palms as she left the room.

Their anxiety distressed Jorja. Her eyes caught Lufti's. They looked at each other amid the noise of the crowded room. He mouthed the words, "It'll be okay."

They prayed for peace and calm, this time from another source of terror: the devastation wrought by nature itself.

CHAPTER 12

PINS AND NEEDLES

Lufti bundled the newspapers into a tidy pile and replaced them with work papers, which he gathered up when Fadil arrived. Jorja collected four pages and asked Lufti for a stapler. He pointed to the pin cushion that permanently sat in the middle of the table.

"No, Lufti, I asked for the stapler," she repeated, thinking he had not heard her. He pointed again to the pin cushion. "Stapler, Lufti," she said a little louder. *Was he deaf?*

He smiled and said quietly, "That *is* the stapler."

Jorja sighed as she picked out a long silver pin and placed it neatly through the top left-hand corner, binding the pages together.

In the afternoon at the project office, Jorja had her first encounter with Dr. Sajid Mohammad Mahmud, her local counterpart from Lahore. He recounted his two-day journey in a tired, quiet voice. A tall, thin, elegant man with long fingers, he was dressed in starched Pakistani clothes with permanent creases along his baggy, beige shalwar. Lufti introduced Jorja and she approached Mahmud with her hand outstretched. Mahmud stepped backward, raised both hands and shook his head, muttering in Urdu. Her initial thought was that his hands were wet from washing. They talked briefly and he politely excused himself to retire to his room upstairs. Again, Jorja moved to shake his hand and, once more, he recoiled. She looked at Lufti, hoping for an explanation, but he was engaged in conversation with Gadi and had not noticed. From this moment, she began to have doubts about her own judgment. Baffling, contradictory actions mystified her. Whenever she did not understand something, she blamed herself. A sense of inferiority made her breathless with anxiety.

Hamid had left work for the day and Jorja slipped into his chair in front of the computer. She waited to ask Lufti for the reason behind Mahmud's reluctance to shake her hand. Was it a gender or religious issue or some other innocuous reason? Her initial impression was that he would be difficult to work with. She assumed that he objected to her presence.

Spying an actual stapler on Hamid's desk, she reached for it excitedly and exclaimed, "Oh a stapler."

"Yes, madam, a stapler," said Gadi, puzzled at her surprise. Lufti smiled and walked toward the door.

"Lufti! Lufti! Wait!"

"He cannot hear you, madam. He's going for his walk," Gadi said.

Excitement turned to dismay at finding the stapler empty. "Please, Gadi, do you have any staples?"

"Staples, madam?"

"Staples to go inside the stapler." She pointed to the open-mouthed pink stapler.

"Ah, pins, madam."

"No, no, I don't want pins. I want staples to hold the pages together. Do you understand what I want Gadi?"

"I understand madam. You want pins for the stapler."

Jorja shook her head, explaining again that she wanted staples, not pins.

"As you wish, madam." He rummaged around in a large cupboard for some time before turning to Jorja with a small cardboard box in his hand. "Madam, we have no pins for the stapler, but we have these." In his strong sinewy hand, he held a box of sewing pins. She sighed disappointedly and politely told him that it was not what she wanted. "As you wish, madam."

Jorja and Fadil drove to a stall with office supplies so she could buy envelopes and staples. They stopped at a poky, cluttered stall with goods in a scattered display on tables shrouded with what appeared to be the remains of a dust storm. She purchased twenty-five airmail envelopes. The shopkeeper brushed the dust from them, counted them twice, and beamed at her with pleasure. He asked if she wanted string to tie them together. She shook her head, and he gently placed them in her hand with great care. He did not stock staples, but was pleased to tell Jorja that he did have sewing pins. She smiled, thanked him, and declined his offer. Pins were plentiful in Kashmir.

Back in the office, Gadi asked whether she had found the staples she wanted. He knew by her grimace she was not successful. He handed documents to her and their fingers touched. Briefly.

Jorja decided that it was a deliberate action on Gadi's part. Their eyes locked together.

"I *do* know where Osama bin Laden is, madam. Trust me. Are you going to look for him? I can help you."

Fadil entered the room and Gadi returned to his desk. The driver settled on the divan with the daily Urdu newspapers. Gadi and Jorja worked in silence, not daring to look at each other.

Jorja tried to connect to the internet delaying her departure at the end of the day and this prevented Fadil from leaving at his usual time. He waited and drummed his fingers on his leg. Eventually, overcome with frustration, Jorja gave up, and grabbing her bag, she took a seat next to her driver in the red Toyota. She tensed when he reversed out of the driveway, fearing that they'd plummet down the precipice. Once the car faced the descent to the city center, Jorja instantly calmed and looked forward to the drive to the hotel. In the glove box, Fadil stowed a large English textbook. They used the travel time to and from the hotel to the project office, when they were alone, to practice English and Urdu. Whenever Jorja was quiet, Fadil prompted her to speak. "Urdu, madam, Urdu!" She would choose an English sentence from the book and he would repeat it, translate it into Urdu, and wait for her to echo the words. They would correct each other's pronunciations and laugh when they stuttered over difficult words. "*Accha, accha,*" he would say when a word or phrase was repeated flawlessly.

"Fadil, do you think Osama bin Laden is in Afghanistan?"

"No, madam, he is not in Afghanistan. He is here in Kashmir. Sometimes he travels between Pakistan and Afghanistan, but most of the time he is in Kashmir."

"How do you know this?"

"Everyone in Muzaffarabad knows this, madam."

"Did you know that there's a large reward for his capture?"

Fadil looked her in the eye and smiled, "Dead or alive?"

"I don't know. Either way, have you ever considered looking for him?"

He laughed so much that his hands shook the steering wheel.

"*Shukriya*, Fadil," Jorja said as she left the car and waved him away. He always waited until she entered the doors of the hotel or the bakery next door. Jorja browsed the shelves quickly and, empty-handed, skipped up the steps to the hotel entrance.

CHAPTER 13

LETTER TO A LOVER

The heater in her room didn't work. Water from the hot tap was icy cold. Crumpled wastepaper spilled over the rubbish bin. There was no toilet paper. The cleaners had not made the bed, neither yesterday nor today. Jorja telephoned the supervisor of cleaning, Pervaiz, who arranged housekeeping staff to attend to the room.

Leaving the cleaners to tidy her room, she dined alone in the restaurant. The menu offered a wide choice of Western and local food. The Western food consisted of steak and chips, so instead she ordered chicken *biryani*, *raita*, *pullau*, and green tea with lemon. She read Denny's e-mail printed on thin, puce paper:

Hello there!
I'm sorry you need to stay in Kashmir longer than ex-
pected. I'm sure it's very important, and there are many

positives for a lefty. It's quite some time to cover up though with all those clothes and shawls. I'd imagine that you'd want some quality liaison like never before when you get back. It'll probably be a bit cooler here by that time—which is nice. There's nothing like cold weather to get people deeply, tightly wrapped around each other: it's an aphrodisiac!

On that note and being where I am in life, I want you as a lover rather than a lifelong partner (I know what you really want is a greater, more fulfilling commitment). I really do enjoy your company. I can't offer you commitment in the longer term, but I can definitely offer you great affection and stimulation in the shorter term. Hopefully, that's enough. I wish you were here right now so I could see you tonight.

D

E-mails seemed too formal to Jorja. Jorja desperately wanted to talk to Denny and impulsively inquired at the reception desk about telephoning Australia. An explanation ensued about costs and payments. Since Jamshid was paying her hotel bills and Jorja was paying for meals and incidentals from her allowance, which she hadn't received, she had to limit her spending. The hotel manager agreed that she could put expenses on a tab and pay later, but payments for telephone calls were required immediately after the call, explained the receptionist.

"International calls are very expensive, madam."

"How expensive?"

"Excuse me, madam. I will get the book." He rifled through the pages. "Oh, madam, it is very, very expensive."

When Jorja converted rupees into Australian dollars, she gasped with horror. "You're right. I'll have to wait until I get some more money. Thank you."

"As you wish, madam. Very sorry, madam. Very sorry."

She felt even more isolated. Eventually she had the energy to write Denny a letter. Propped against the four pillows on her bed, Jorja turned on the television.

Denny Sahib,

There's nothing like cold weather to get people deep-
ly, tightly wrapped around each other: an aphrodisiac,
you wrote. Where were you five days ago when it was
so cold and rainy here? I'm glad you think that we can
be together in the short-term. I prefer that to nothing.
I'll respect that and accept what you so nicely offer. It
just seems so long until I can see you. Only a week has
passed and it seems like an eternity. You talk of positive
things: great affection and stimulation: of finding it very,
very satisfying. We're so far apart physically. I can't wait
for us to be close again.

I wanted to phone you tonight, but the hotel re-
quires payment immediately after the call and I don't
have enough money. It's outrageously expensive. I'll find
a way to call when I can. From my balcony, the moon
seems so close I can touch it. It seems to connect us in
some strange way. It seems to speak to me, or maybe it's
just listening to my thoughts and understanding them. I
follow its every movement; its waxing and its waning.

I wrote about Lufti in my e-mails and he's the only
one that really understands me. I don't know why, but we
had an instant connection and I appreciate it so much.
He's like a favorite uncle. It's comforting although it
doesn't compensate for the lack of physical closeness.
You're so much on my mental wavelength, but I need the
physical stuff too.

I thought I saw you yesterday. Fadil was driving to
the Sangam at lunchtime along a different route so he
could collect Shalam, a guy who fixes the education de-
partment computers. We passed a large congregation of
people and I was certain I saw you. I noticed the man's
hair. He had your hairstyle. Pakistani men don't have
long hair so it really stood out. When I told Fadil, he
said the man was a Talib. The Talibs have long hair and
wear black. In any case, I thought he was handsome

and intriguing. He was so different from everyone else. I guess that's what caught my eye.

I'll e-mail when I can, but it's so temperamental. I don't know how long it'll take you to get this letter—a week maybe.

Love you,
Jorja

The hotel staff had fixed the heater, but it inexplicably turned itself off. Nothing was working. Patience was to be her lesson in Pakistan. The can opener didn't open cans. The bottle opener didn't open bottles. The door to the balcony didn't open. The remote control didn't work and the television remained on one channel, merely serving as background noise in a silent room except for the babbling of the river as it rushed onward toward Islamabad.

CHAPTER 14

THE COMPLEXITY OF COMPLEXIONS

Skin color aroused Gadi's curiosity. "Madam, your colleagues at the curriculum office tell me that you open the curtains every day. Is this because you want the sun to darken your skin? I ask this because Kashmiris don't want their skin to become too dark. Why do you open the curtains?"

It was true. The view from the small windows in the curriculum office was a concrete wall that blocked natural light, but her Kashmiri colleagues preferred a dark room. On days when more sunshine than usual penetrated the room, they would close the curtains. Jorja found it disheartening. Every day she opened the thick curtains to encourage any possible rays of sunshine to enter the room. She explained to Gadi that she liked natural light and warmth. "Gadi, there would never be enough sunshine in that dark room to change the color of my skin."

Gadi said to Jorja, "Western women like men very dark, yes, like African men, or very fair like British men, but not coffee-colored like Pakistanis. They like extremes, don't they? Why is this, madam?"

"That's quite a good observation. I'm not sure why, but it's a very, very interesting observation."

"But madam, you have not said what your view is on this matter. You merely make a general statement of uncertainty." He was amazingly straightforward, direct, and perceptive.

"That's another good observation, Gadi." He was a young, intelligent man in his mid-twenties. He was frank, open, and honest. He was considerate, helpful, and respectful. Gadi was also incredibly inquisitive and probing. Jorja liked him. She liked his strong hands, shapely fingers, and clean fingernails. Every day he dressed his left hand with a ring: pewter with a large stone, sometimes amethyst, sometimes aquamarine, and sometimes tourmaline. She adored the rings and complimented him on their beauty. His favorite was aquamarine because it was the color of Jorja's eyes, he said, flattering her. Muscular and manly, he was solid with sinuous arms. It was rare to see a bare limb in Pakistan. Gadi often pushed up the sleeves of his kameez to reveal powerful arms. He had studied physical education and had taught at a school in Islamabad, although she hadn't seen him undertake any physical exercise in Muzaffarabad.

"Well, I'm not sure that I should be telling you, but since you asked, I'll give you some sort of answer. I like British men because I was born in Britain and I share their sense of humor. I like fair-skinned men because they are generally of my background or culture. I must admit that I like looking at very dark men, too. I like their physical appearance. They are generally tall and lean and athletic, and I quite like that look. See, that's it."

He showed his white teeth in a wide smile. "And coffee-colored Pakistanis? What is your view of us?"

"Mmmm. Well, I like Imran Khan very much. He's tall and sporty and well-spoken and intelligent and good-looking and worldly. He's caring and considerate and has a political view of his country and ..."

"Madam, he talks like an Englishman. He looks like an Englishman because he's not a dark coffee color. You like him because he's famous in your country."

"I like him because he's a well-educated man. He talks to all people. Yes, he's famous and is British in some of his mannerisms and he has a British wife, but I like him because he's achieved much in his life. I guess I like him, too, because he's of my generation. There are many reasons why I like him and why many women around the world like him. He has a fabulous smile too, if truth be known." Jorja giggled and Gadi joined her.

"But your talk means to me that you like Imran, but not other Pakistanis," he probed deeper, gently and humorously. "Coffee-color is not good, madam?"

"Complexion is not important, Gadi. It's a man's behavior and actions, his mind and manner and values that are important." Jorja again tried to wriggle out of any comment on Pakistani men. Generally, she thought they were heavy smokers with decayed and stained teeth; their health was often not good; they sniffed and spat; and they sometimes picked their noses. The two men in the office were exceptions to the average Pakistani. Both Hamid and Gadi were good-looking, tall, and well-mannered, with excellent teeth even though they smoked constantly. Hamid was very striking with chiseled looks. He had a prominent aquiline nose, looking exceptionally domineering and arrogant, but he was neither. "Gadi," she eventually said, "Pakistani men smoke too much."

"Ah, yes, that's true. I think Western women do not like the smoke. No, they do not like the smoke," he affirmed as if from previous experience. Gadi smoked continuously, but Hamid was the most habitual smoker of the two. They both smoked while working in the office and the ashtrays on their desks were always overflowing with butts and burnt-out matches. "Women do not like the smoke." He nodded.

Gadi shifted in his seat restlessly. "Have you given some thought to looking for Osama bin Laden, madam?"

"Not yet."

"But, madam. . ."

"Gadi, before you start that nonsense, I'm not going to hunt down Osama bin Laden just so you can get the reward. Do you know what an absurd idea it is?"

"But, madam, it's not absurd because, as you know, I know where he is. And I will help you with your task."

"Everyone in Kashmir knows where Osama is."

"I know *precisely* where he is." Their eyes locked together. Gadi nodded and a strand of hair slid over his dark eyes. He stopped typing and stood, rearranging his kameez. Picking up a pile of papers, he placed them in front of Jorja. "I've finished the notes for you and Mahmud." He remained next to Jorja's desk, counting the pages.

"Thanks, Gadi." When he didn't move, Jorja said, "Apart from the idea being idiotic, it's dangerous."

"It is very dangerous, madam. You must not mention this to anyone. You never know who could be helping the Talibs, or even Osama himself. People hear things, then tell others. Then they'll be after you. They'll kidnap you or kill you. So, you are right. It is dangerous. That's why you need my help." All the while, Gadi stared down at Jorja, watching her reaction.

"If you know everything, then you do it and claim the full reward."

"I live and work here. It would be too easy for the Talibs to find me and kill me. And, as I've said before, the Americans would never believe me."

"They won't believe me, either. I tell people that I've seen Imran Khan and no one believes me. They think I'm a silly romantic woman. Besides, it's impossible to capture bin Laden. It'd be easier to kill him, and I can't do that. Firstly, I can't kill anyone, and secondly, almost everyone looks like Osama to me. You don't know how many people here have the same beard as he does. Besides, it's said that he has an army of followers. It's ridiculous."

"But, I have an idea . . ."

Neither of them heard Fadil enter the room. "The car's ready, madam." Gadi, startled, knocked the top papers onto the floor. Fadil helped him scoop them up.

"Tell me tomorrow, Gadi," Jorja said.

Gadi reordered the pages and handed them to Jorja. "As you wish, madam." His eyes showed immense relief and his smile seemed to tell Jorja that she would not be disappointed.

CHAPTER 15

A GODSEND

After showering in the evening, Jorja left her hair loose rather than rebraiding it. Half a bottle of vodka remained in the closet, but she had a yearning for gin and tonic. Perhaps she merely longed for something she could not have. She thought of her present cravings: Australian newspapers, magazines, pasta, red wine, chocolates, a spa, her car, running, books, cinema, seafood, letters, flowers, French champagne, and music. More hedonistically, she thought of Denny: showering together, smelling him, tasting champagne on his lips, kissing his stomach, looking into his eyes, hearing his breath, touching the small of his back, feeling the sensation of him licking her, feeling him inside her, and feeling him withdraw.

Continual popping noises reminded her of firecrackers. Penny bangers. The din sounded as if it were from the west, perhaps from

Afghanistan. Heavier, duller noises of mortar thudded in the distance, sporadic but persistent. From the balcony she saw no movement at the army base. Hotel staff hadn't telephoned Jorja to notify her of anything or to appease her, so she wasn't excessively concerned. She convinced herself that it was the sound of a distant American-led attack on the Taliban in Afghanistan, borne by fresh spring winds from the west.

Watching a Harrison Ford movie on television, Jorja wrote to Denny, reassuring him that she would be evacuated rapidly if border fighting escalated. She had registered her presence in Pakistan with the Australian High Commission when she arrived in Islamabad. In Muzaffarabad, the army base across the river was equipped with helicopters. Jamshid had contingency plans. Naturally, he had also told her not to worry.

Instead of getting into bed naked, she remained dressed and lay on top of the bed covers. She was not scared, merely prepared. It was nearly midnight and the bombing continued. The remote control was working again so she clicked between BBC and CNN news. Reports told of Taliban troops in Afghanistan encountering heavy fighting from American forces during Operation Anaconda. The Americans were regrouping across the border in Pakistan. Grateful to receive global news, and comforted, she undressed and snuggled into the tight sheets that formed a protective sheath around her.

The sound of the river woke Jorja at three o'clock. She turned on the reading light and reread the print-out of Denny's latest e-mail:

> *Hello there!*
> *Sorry I didn't get back to you yesterday. I really wanted to respond, but I was here at work until eleven at night preparing for today's press releases. I'm delighted you accepted my lover option. To be honest, I think we fit together extremely well in that respect, so I think we're always going to be lovers despite what we discussed. I think we satisfy each other immensely. We*

*both have work demands that make commitment diffi-
cult. I think our compromise as lovers and friends will
work out just fine.*

*I really want you right here, right now. So what's the
verdict? When are you expected to get back? Hope to
hear from you soon.*

D

Jorja longed to be with Denny: to hear his voice, to see his
eyes, to touch his skin, to taste every part of him, and to smell
his body. Nothing excited her more than the smell of sex on a
man. She could lay in his carnal aroma for eternity, as arousing to her as the aroma of fresh-mown grass and seaspray on a
wintry day.

She swapped his e-mail for the daily newspaper. Bad
weather was hampering Operation Anaconda: *Winter conditions
in the high mountains near Gardez were limiting air strikes by
US warplanes to satellite-guided bombs and preventing AC-130
flying gunships from using 105mm cannon and 40mm machine
guns against entrenched guerrillas. Other defense officials said
the harsh winter was keeping US attack helicopters temporarily
out of the battle. Rumsfeld appeared on television to back away
from a prediction made on Thursday that a week-long assault by
more than 2,000 US-led troops on hundreds of guerrillas might
be over as early as this weekend. He expressed confidence that it
could end in days. "It looked to me like it would be days, meaning seven, eight, ten as opposed to weeks or months," he said.
With the battle in its seventh day, the US military said a large
number of al-Qaeda fighters were killed in overnight battles and
routes used by reinforcements were being cut. Operation Anaconda was initially expected to conclude this weekend. But the
larger than expected number of al-Qaeda fighters, the intensity
of the clashes, the determination of the fighters, who are mostly
non-Afghans, and the large quantity of weapons and supplies at
their disposal make that date too optimistic, the sources said.*

The bad weather was a godsend.

CHAPTER 16

UNREST

Gadi wasn't in the office. She wondered whether his intentions were to kill or capture Osama bin Laden. *How did he know where the terrorist leader was hiding? What did he expect from her?*

Jorja witnessed the first hint of unrest in Muzaffarabad as Fadil drove her to the hotel at lunchtime. Lufti had stayed at the curriculum office so she traveled alone with Fadil. A throng of people forced him to slow to a near halt. An angry mass of anti-Indian demonstrators had congregated in the streets, most belonging to Islami Jamiat Tulaba. Some of them stuffed rags into tires and lit them in their path: the acrid smoke spiraled high into the air. Others carried sticks to stoke the fires or to beat them against metal creating a thumping noise in unison with their chanting. It was deafening. Police moved toward the main dissenters.

A group of whooping men branched out of the general crowd forming a smaller demonstration, eddying on the side of the main throng. The men waved automatic rifles and pistols in the air. The glottal cries of the few women present—somewhat like hiccoughing—pulsed rhythmically and painfully against Jorja's eardrums.

A youth draped a Kashmiri separatist flag around his shoulders like a cape. The national flag of Pakistan had a vertical white band on a third of the left-hand side and the remaining two-thirds was dark green with a white crescent moon and a five-pointed star in the center. The white represented the minority religions and the dark-green represented the Muslim majority. The crescent represented progress. The five-rayed star depicted light and knowledge. Pakistani's, proud of their flag, displayed it on cars, government buildings, and houses. The Kashmiri flag incorporated the Pakistani crescent and star in the upper right-hand corner, with a block of orange in the left-hand corner. These split the flag in half with the lower section consisting of white and green horizontal stripes. A Kashmiri separatist waved an unofficial flag of fifteen green and yellow alternating horizontal stripes with a canton of plain yellow. The flag fluttered in the slight breeze.

One youth flew the separatist flag and with each step, he strutted and swaggered, the whole demonstration a celebration of rebellion. He thrust his weapon in the air with each shout of defiance, his cockiness nothing more than a display of puberty at its peak.

Activists of Islami Jamiat Tulaba were protesting an attack on two colleagues in February by the People's Students' Federation, a youth group within the local university. PSF members had pushed two men off their motorcycles, beaten them, and shot them while fleeing. One of them received two bullets in his right leg and a dagger wound in the buttocks, while the other had minor wounds. Both were hospitalized. Islami Jamiat Tulaba demanded that the authorities arrest and punish the attackers. Tension between the groups had been brewing since the attack and escalated a month ago when the student group organized a musical show in the university auditorium. Islami Jamiat Tulaba opposed the show, declaring that revenge would be forthcoming. The activists responded by rallying on Eidgah Road before entering the university. Marching in noisy demonstration along the streets of Muzaffarabad, they stopped at Bank Road where the leaders spoke out in anger.

In unison with the ululations, menacing young men thrashed metal containers and garbage bin lids with sticks. Fadil's vehicle barely made headway in the dense crowd. Two stocky men moved toward the vehicle seizing the opportunity to continue their protest in front of a foreigner. The acrid smoke from the burning tires hit the windscreen, obscuring their view. Sticks struck the car. Police moved forward in anticipation of trouble although they did not intervene, requesting that the protestors move the burning tires from the main street. The police remained close by, reticent to take action for fear of exacerbating the situation. The crowd continued beating the vehicle, more to increase the noise and confusion than to inflict damage, so Jorja believed. Fadil tried to reverse, but couldn't. The crowd became increasingly vocal, chanting in time to their incessant drumming and thrashing. Jorja remained quiet, but alert. A cricket bat thudded against the windscreen in front of Fadil, miraculously not cracking the glass. *Whack! Whack!* Twice it smacked close to Fadil's face. He muttered in Urdu, accelerated slightly while turning the steering wheel, and diverted them away from the incident through side streets and over the bridge to the other side of the river.

"Fadil, what were the men yelling into the car?" Jorja asked when they had distanced themselves from the scene.

"You do not worry what they say, madam. It is best that you do not know." She did not query him further.

CHAPTER 17

COUPLINGS

All was not lost. Jorja remained realistic, but hopeful, as she read Denny's e-mail. They both had similar needs and feelings. He was, perhaps, more apprehensive about the loss of independence and less guilty about his own selfishness. It was more that they had differing definitions and interpretations of what it meant to be in a relationship, but they both had the same notion of commitment. Jorja responded to his e-mail:

Denny, hon!
I've settled on short e-mails and long letters. The power is just too erratic here. Everything's going well on the project. Mahmud and I work well together—no problems. He's just quiet, that's all. I must admit, he's very

industrious and thorough. I still don't know why he didn't shake my hand when we first met, but it appears to have nothing to do with our working relationship. Lufti and Mahmud are great to work with. I'd love to go for a walk with them. They go every day at five o'clock, but Lufti said Mahmud prefers just the company of men when he exercises. I can understand that.

I'm hoping to call you when I go to Islamabad. I'll let you know when. Then we can talk—intimately, I hope.

Much love, Jorja

It was a wintry Saturday. The temperature never exceeded seven degrees. Snow fell on the Himalaya. The skies darkened from slate to indigo. The snow covered Muzaffarabad like a coarse wool blanket. At the curriculum office, there was neither power nor fuel for the back-up generator, as usual. Staff sat in the frosty, depressing room. They weren't the only ones: *Around 20,000 residents of seventeen villages in Bajwat have been without electricity for the last three months. In a special meeting here on Wednesday, residents of Kachhi Maand union council adopted a resolution urging the Gepco chairperson to restore electricity supply without any delay. The participants said that due to heavy Indian shelling on these villages, the supply of electricity was disrupted. Since then, no effort has yet been made by the Gepco authorities to restore power supply. Due to the non-availability of electricity, residents of these border areas have been forced to live in the open and Indian forces often hit these villages, they added. Also, Abdul Kaliq Samejo, a washer man, was brought to Ghotki Hospital in a precarious condition after having been allegedly burnt by Wapta staff after he failed to grease their palm regarding the settlement of his electricity bill.*

Mahmud left early to catch a public wagon to Islamabad where he was staying for three days for medical tests, and Lufti had a meeting in another office on the eastern side of the city, leaving Jorja alone in the arctic room. Raja entered to practice his English.

"I am so sorry for you being alone," he said. He was small and thin with a kind face and soft, sympathetic voice.

"Lufti won't be long, an hour maybe."

"No, no," he chose his words carefully. "I mean, I am sorry for you being alone in the hotel with none of your own people to talk to. People need their own kind for company. You think so, Miss Jorja?" Raja seemed genuinely empathetic.

"I do miss the company of my own people, but I'm lucky that I have friends here too, like Lufti and Mahmud."

"No, no. It's not the same. You must have your own people to laugh with, to be understanding your mind. You are the only foreigner in Azad Kashmir."

"Maybe there are other foreigners in other hotels?"

"No, there are no other foreigners. Sangam Hotel is the best in Muzaffarabad and foreigners stay there. Everyone knows if a new foreigner is in town. There are no others. You are alone in Muzaffarabad. You not married, Miss Jorja?" He frowned.

"I'm not married."

"You live alone? It's not good to live alone. Man is a social being. Man needs company. I think so and all Kashmiris think so. Why are you not married? You are very beautiful and very intelligent. Is your husband dead?"

"I have friends."

"It's not the same, Miss Jorja. Friends are not the same as a married partner. I feel very sad for you. I pray to Allah that you not be alone." He was insistent.

"It's better to have company, I agree, but I have a special male friend."

"Does he live with his parents?"

"No, he lives alone."

"Why does he live alone? I do not understand."

"It's different in Australia. We don't have the same extended family system that you have here. Many people live by themselves in my country." Jorja fiddled with the old desk calendar on the table, turning the months over and over.

"That is a sad thing. It's important for a man to seek the company of a woman and to live together. It's nature. It's not good for man and woman to be apart. A man and a woman must be together. This coupling is Allah's will. That's why man and woman are here on this earth. This coupling is essential for a happy life. I'm sad that you are not coupled with a man. This is a very, very sad thing."

"Please don't be sad for me. Living alone is very common in Australia. We don't have the same view of permanent relationships that exists in this country. It's not such a sad thing for me."

"You do not want coupling with a man?"

"Well, yes I do, but it's not that simple."

"It *is* simple. Why do you complicate things? A man and woman must be coupled. There must be a mutual link of great affection."

Great affection: the exact words in Denny's e-mail. Jorja wondered whether they were a coupling. It was an unusually appropriate word. A pang of emptiness and loneliness coursed through her. At this point in her life, she seemed to be in between interpretations: Raja's definition of coupling and Western society's interpretation. In the East, relationships seemed so permanent. In the West, they seemed so transient. Yet both seemed desirable. In the most unlikely spaces, in the strangest of situations, and in the remotest places, people discovered themselves. Or rather, they discovered parts of themselves. Charlie Chaplin, the comedian, said that space is good for the soul, and Jorja had connected with his sentiments. For Jorja, it represented not merely physical space, but mental space, especially in relationships. But just as she had decided that she preferred a permanent relationship, Denny entered her life and offered her a temporary one. It appeared to be a reasonable compromise: the step between nothing and commitment.

Raja, the English specialist, spoke of his family living in a village half an hour's drive to the north of Muzaffarabad, close to the Line of Control. He offered to take Jorja there when the fighting stopped. Indians across the river had shot many of the villagers, including children, during border fighting. Raja lived in Muzaffarabad to be close to work. Due to the conflict, he did not return to his village regularly. This struck Jorja as strange, particularly as Raja thought it was important for a man and a woman to be together, yet he was away from his wife for long periods. Jorja questioned him on this.

"My wife comes into Muzaffarabad often to sell eggs and chickens and to buy food. We see each other many times, and I have this photograph of her with me." He took out a worn photograph from his wallet. The cloaked woman had a weatherworn face with deep-set eyes.

"She's beautiful," Jorja said tactfully and he nodded. Longing for a photograph of Denny, she was worried that her memory of him, like colors in the sun, would fade. Some of his features remained very clear in her mind: his wavy dark hair, mesmerizing green eyes, rounded buttocks, and strong calves. She recalled his hands and slight mannerisms, like the way he tilted his head when he was thinking. She had to concentrate hard to remember his lips, ears, and arms.

"But Raja, if it is dangerous for you to travel back to your village, why do you let your wife travel into town?" Jorja asked.

"Women with eggs can travel more easily than men, like me, with books. It's just the way it is." Raja continued talking about his wife. "I remember the first photograph of her when our parents arranged our marriage. I knew that it was a good coupling. There was a knowing that I would be in love with her for all time in the deepest way. I knew that love would be our future, and it is." It was the first time Jorja met a man who admitted to being totally in love. "I don't understand why you are not coupled with your man friend." He resumed the interrogation. "You both like each other, yes?"

"We have not known each other very long, only a few months. People in the West have long courtships."

"This I don't understand. Why do you have long courtships?"

"So that we can be sure that we'll be in a long marriage with someone we love if we choose to marry."

"I knew from a photograph. Why does it take Western people so long? I think Western people move from person to person and do not love the one selected by Allah. Western people want too many people before they say that someone is their true love. They are greedy. They do not want one person. Why is this?"

"I don't know." Jorja lowered her gaze.

"But you know about yourself. Why do you not want your man friend?"

"We have to both want each other."

"Why does he not want you?"

"I have no idea," she lied.

"If you are not true loves then why are you together?"

"We like each other very much."

"If you like each other very much then why are you not marriaged?"

"Married, Raja, the word is married. Will you stop asking me so many questions? I can't answer them. Everything is different in the West. That's all I can say. We don't have arranged marriages. We have long courtships. Western people want everything to be right in a relationship. They aren't in a hurry to marry. Western relationships are based on love and not on convenience," she said agitatedly. "Pretty much, anyway," she added in a lower voice. Unnerved, Jorja moved restlessly on the chair, banging her leg against the table, causing a sharp pain.

"No, I think that's not right. My marriage is about love, not convenience. I think that Western relationships are all about sex. They look for sex and not coupling or great affection."

"Maybe."

"Western people should be coupled because then they would not have to look for sex. The sex would be there all the time, with each other, and then there would be no frustration. Western people are too frustrated, too blocked up from not releasing their emotions. That is the problem with the West. They do not stay and be fulfilled with one person."

"You could be right, Raja. There are many things wrong with the West."

"I pray to Allah that you will not be alone."

"Thank you, Raja. I hope Allah doesn't get too frustrated in His quest to find me someone."

"Allah is kind. You think He forgets you. He does not. I will pray to Allah so that He services you very quickly and gives you what you want."

"Raja, are there Talibs in your village?"

"Not in the village, but nearby. Yes, of course. The Taliban are everywhere in these parts."

"And Osama bin Laden? Where is he?"

"He is in western Pakistan. Why do you ask?"

"I'm looking for him."

Raja laughed loudly. "You, a foreign woman, are looking for Osama bin Laden, the greatest terrorist of all time? I think you are telling me lies."

"If I *were* looking for him, would I find him near Muzaffarabad?"

"Of course not! I said he was in western Pakistan. What would you do if you found him? Hold his hand and say 'come with me?' You are a very funny woman." He laughed at the thought.

Lufti entered the room, apologizing for being late. "The driver is waiting. Are you ready to go back to the hotel? *Calo!* Thank you, Raja. It's kind of you to converse with Miss Jorja."

As they left the room, Jorja turned to farewell Raja and saw him close his eyes in prayer. He swayed back and forth gently. He was quick to seek help for her. Lufti hurried her along and she obeyed.

In the evening, Pervaiz brought a dictionary with him when he came to supervise the cleaning staff in Jorja's room. As they made the bed, he commenced reciting words from the beginning of the alphabet. He knew the meaning of most words although he had difficulty with some pronunciations. He taught Jorja some Urdu words. She noticed more cleaning staff than usual. They came and went. Perhaps they wanted to see Pervaiz practice his English, she thought.

"Why are there so many cleaners today, Pervaiz? Some days I can't get anyone to clean the room and today everyone is cleaning it. Why can't they clean the room when I'm at work?"

"Oh, I'm very sorry, madam. They clean the room at night when you are here so that you can see that they do it to your satisfaction. Remember when you complained that the room was dirty?"

"No one had cleaned the room for days. I wasn't complaining. Well, maybe I was. So why are there so many today?"

"They don't come to clean the room." He smiled. "They come to see you."

"Me? They've seen me before."

"No, madam. They come to see your hair. It's not braided, as usual. They have not seen long, silky hair like yours. It's very, very blond. They like it very much. Mohammad told everyone that he sees your hair down and they all come to look."

The telephone rang. "Would you like me to answer the phone, madam?" When she nodded, he politely answered, then turned to her. "It's Minister Nasim."

It was late and she wondered why he called. "I *am* eating," she said forcefully into the receiver. "Sometimes I buy food from the store next door."

The minister wasn't pleased. He demanded that Jorja eat in the restaurant. "You can ask the cook for anything, but you must eat," he said. "You are too skinny. Kashmiri women like food and eat well." He asked if she wanted anything. Jorja needed nothing.

"Alcohol, you need alcohol?"

Again, she said no thank you and he insisted that if she needed *anything* he could arrange it. *Anything? What if she wanted to find Osama bin Laden? Could he arrange that? Surely not!* She declined his request and replaced the receiver. She looked around at the clean room and at Pervaiz.

Clapping his hands, he cleared the room of cleaning staff. As he stood by the door, he said, "I like your hair too, madam. Why aren't you married?"

"Shoo!" Jorja demanded, with a smile. Pervaiz grinned and shut the door behind him.

CHAPTER 18

A KNIFE-EDGE

The red velvet armchair was no ordinary chair. It was a special chair earmarked for Jorja, the special foreign guest at the official opening of a weeklong workshop for education managers, conducted by Kadir. A small and shabby room in the Hotel Riverina was adorned with red plush curtains, cloth-covered tables with name tags lined in neat rows, and a stage area bedecked with a row of sofas. Muslim prayers opened the inaugural workshop, sung to the audience, followed by official speeches; all in Urdu with a mixture of English phrases. The minister of education greeted Jorja warmly and asked if she had been eating. She assured him she was, to which he smiled and replied that he would check with the hotel manager periodically.

At lunchtime, she returned to the Sangam Hotel for a Russian salad of tomato, apple, banana, grape, guava, and hard-boiled eggs. Awan, the waiter, thought that eating a salad as a main dish was highly unusual.

"You not eating food, madam?' asked Awan.

"Yes, this is food."

He shook his head, disgusted. "This is not food. This is salad, madam."

"This will do nicely, thank you," she smiled. Perhaps the manager and the minister also thought she wasn't eating because she didn't consume the expected meat, vegetables, and rice every day.

No longer required at the workshop, she spent the afternoon in the project office with Mahmud. They worked together on a section of the teachers' manual, discussing suitable timetable examples. The selection pleased him, and she placed them near Gadi's computer for Gadi or Hamid to type while Mahmud went for his daily walk.

Climbing the stairs to the roof, she watched Mahmud and Lufti walk up the mountain along the goat track. Mahmud wrapped a muddy brown shawl over his shoulders. The two men linked hands, and she listened to their muted conversation until the wind carried the words north. She walked the perimeter of the roof, hearing rousing cheers from the neighboring building. Previously, when Jorja asked her colleagues about the house next door, Hamid said it was a *madrassa* for young boys learning the Qur'an; Lufti said the youth were from the local university's People's Students' Federation; and Gadi said they were Talibs or al-Qaeda trainees chanting war cries.

Jorja stood at the edge of the roof, peering into the adjacent faded pink building. With curtains drawn to cover the windows, she could see no students, no university scholars, and no al-Qaeda trainees. She couldn't see anyone, but the cheers continued, sounding like footballers cheering a goal.

Jorja clambered down a rusted ladder clinging to the side of the project office. It led to a ledge with a boardwalk that joined the two buildings. *Who had placed it there? Why?* On the neighboring building was an identical ladder, providing access to its roof.

Jorja looked around. No one was in sight. Nimble-footed in her flat loafers, she crossed the plank and ascended the ladder. Standing on the pink roof, she realized what a stupid idea it was. If there were students or university scholars inside, she'd be viewed as nosey and intrusive. If there were al-Qaeda trainees inside, she'd be in trouble. She still couldn't see anything. Examining the roof for openings, vents, skylights, or any other opening to peer through, she was consumed with concentration and a single-minded focus. She didn't hear the Talib approaching her.

A heavy hand dropped onto her shoulder, making her jump with fright. She twisted around and looked into the charcoal eyes of a bearded young man, bristling with anger. Shiny, black hair skimmed his shoulders and protruded from his dark turban. Towering over her, he removed a knife from his waist, blade glinting, and stood, legs wide apart, as if demanding an explanation.

"I … I …I'm looking for my cat," Jorja lied. "It's small and little and furry and, well, it looks like a cat."

The man's black-whiskered face remained stern. The exquisitely crafted bone handle of the knife, a kerambit, blended into the palm of his hand. His index finger slipped into the handle's circular hole. The curved, white-hot blade, like a tiger's claw, could disembowel a body with one swift stroke, ripping out every organ. Raked across a throat, it could slice it neatly with one powerful slashing action. He wasn't menacing it in front of her, but merely displaying it, demonstrating that he was prepared for a violent end.

The solid weight of his hand on her shoulder immobilized her. Fat, firm fingers clawed into her skin. In her nervousness, Jorja resorted to mime. Her hands outlined an animal, while she meowed apprehensively.

The man released his thick hand from her shoulder. He ran his broad thumb over the knife-edge. It nicked his skin and a bead of scarlet blood formed, fat on his greasy thumb. Lifting it to his lips, he sucked the droplet gently, never diverting his hostile eyes from Jorja's.

Jorja did not look away. She continued emitting cat noises. Dropping to her knees, her cat-like motions seemed demeaning, but it was her last resort. She lifted her head to look at the giant menacingly above her.

The man nodded and began scouting the roof for a cat. The kerambit stayed snug in his hand. Jorja joined him. The two of them meowed and purred around the roof, along the gutters, around the ventilation stacks, peering over the side of the building toward the garden.

"Ah so! Ah so!" the Talib shouted as he hitched the knife onto a hook at the top of his shalwar and pounced on a shivering, skinny cat huddled near a grate. "Ah so!" Stroking the stunned animal, he beckoned Jorja, who rushed toward the Talib, ingratiating herself.

She had never seen the cat before, but she took it gently from the large hands of its rescuer, holding it to her chest.

The thick-set man escorted her to the ladder, descended first, assisted Jorja, and watched as she carefully crossed the boardwalk to the project office.

Waving to the Talib, Jorja shouted her gratitude. He smiled and returned the wave.

Jorja did not like cats, especially mangy ones. As soon as she was inside her office building, she dropped the cat in disgust. It shrieked and ran under a table. Jorja soaped her hands and scrubbed them raw. She was convinced that Gadi was right. The building next door was a Taliban training center. She was certain of it.

CHAPTER 19

THE PHOTOGRAPHER

Instead of facing the balcony, Jorja sat at a different table for her evening meal, looking toward the restaurant entrance.

Hurriedly, a man with short, stocky legs pushed through the restaurant doors, leaving them swinging in his wake. Tapping the pockets of his khaki cargo pants, he seemed to be looking for his wallet or reassuring himself he had his room key. He looked up, saw Jorja, and stopped instantly with his mouth agape.

"My God! Do you speak English? Are you English?"

"Australian."

"No kidding! Crikey! Can I sit with you? Would you like company? I presume you're alone? Are you waiting for someone? Can I sit with you? The name's Arthur. Arthur King. Seriously, that's my name. What the hell are you doing here?" He shook his head, took a seat, and proceeded to empty the contents of his pockets onto the table. He had pockets everywhere: in his cargo pants and in his flak jacket. He looked like a fly fisherman without wading boots.

"Been fishing?" Jorja asked.

"What?"

"It looks like you've been fishing. Good trout in this region."

"Eh?" Out of his pockets spilled keys, coins, rupees, notebook, and wallet. More followed: cigarettes, pens, and chewing gum. "Eh what? What the hell are you doing here? You're a woman. I can't believe what I'm seeing."

"Jorja. My name's Jorja." She looked at him in amusement. A King Arthur he wasn't. He looked more like a nuggetty leprechaun. The minister entered the restaurant, waved to Jorja and smiled. He was conducting a daily check of her food intake.

"You've ordered?" asked the leprechaun. "Where's the menu? I'll have er. . . I'll have er . . ."

Awan, smiling, had been loitering by the table since Arthur walked in. Jorja ordered in Urdu while Arthur scanned the menu and fossicked in his pockets for his glasses. She turned to Arthur, "No, no, not that. Too oily. No, this one. Do you like spicy food? No? Then this. I've already ordered for you. So you're not a fisherman?"

"Photographer," he said, as he continued emptying his pockets. His sun-spotted hands darted in and out of the deep hollows, fossicking for treasures. "I'm looking for my business card. I can't find it. I must've left it in the room. BBC. I work for the BBC. I've been taking photographs all afternoon. Who are you? How long have you been here? You speak Urdu? What am I eating? What are you doing here? You're a woman for God's sake. Mind if I smoke? Do you smoke? Would you like one?" Again, his hands tapped his pocket-covered body, feeling for cigarettes.

"On the table," she said, pointing to the squashed blue packet.

"What the hell are you doing here? A woman here! In Kashmir! I was told that all the foreigners had been evacuated and no-one was here. It's a war zone out there!" He frisked himself once more and said in frustration, "Hell, I can't find my business card. Here's a roll of film. I thought I used all of them. That can go back." He returned it to the pocket in the right hand side of his trousers, pulled it out and put it on the table with the other paraphernalia. "Who are you? I'm starving. I haven't eaten all day. I left Islamabad at six this morning. What a hell of a drive to get here. I haven't stopped all day. Straight here, two minutes in the hotel, and then out photographing. I hired a driver in Islamabad. When I arrived, I arranged a meeting with the public relations officer in the army. Nice fellow. He went with me on the photo shoot. If you're out taking photos, stay away from three things: women in purdah, bridges, and donkeys."

"Donkeys?"

"I'm lost if I know why. I had one more shot on a roll of film and aimed the camera at a donkey when the army man stopped me, telling me it was forbidden. Protocol, he said. I'll give you his contact details because they come in handy. In case there's trouble. Just call him and he'll get you out of here. Swear he will. Now, where did I put his details?" He reached for his wallet and took all papers and cards out, put them back, stood up, and frisked himself. He was forever frisking. "I've got his name somewhere. On a piece of paper. You never know when you'll need it. I'll find it and give it to you. I think I left it in my room."

At this point, Jorja laughed. She had been amused since he walked in asking a million questions, never pausing long enough for her to answer. Always three steps ahead, click, click click, onto the next shot, the next thought.

"What a laugh you've got, woman! It's loud," he said, which made her laugh louder. "It's good to laugh, eh? What the hell are you doing here? I never expected to see a woman here. I never expected to see another foreigner, let alone a woman. I won't bring my wife here." He picked up the cigarette packet, withdrew a long, thin cigarette, and fumbled around the table for his lighter. As he lit up, he said, "Wait, and let me take a puff. God I needed that. Who the hell are you? What the shit are you …?" He drew another prolonged puff on the cigarette.

"Are they French cigarettes?"

"My wife's French. Not that that explains the French cigarettes. Well, I suppose it does. I've been smoking them ever since I met her. We met in Cairo. Been together ever since. I usually take her with me, but not here. Not in a Muslim country. Not anymore. Used to. She used to come with me. Too many restrictions nowadays. Too many men staring at her. They make her feel uncomfortable so she just stays in the hotel room. Not much fun for her. She liked Saudi Arabia in the early days. Not now. Too much ... Who the hell are you? ... Why are you here? How did you know they were French cigarettes? You look French. You could be French. Are you French? French Australian?"

"Make room for the food, Arthur. Move your things up that end of the table. Hey, let me help." Jorja swept his paraphernalia to one end of the table. "I'm naturalized Australian. I was born in the Midlands to a British mother and a German father. I'm here to assist a World Bank education project. I've been here for three weeks with another few weeks before I return home. Are you originally English?"

"No, no. I'm a true blue Aussie. I was born in Darwin. I've been working for the Brits for thirty years, so I guess I've picked up their accent." He coughed, a hacking cough, and his wrinkled face shuddered. The smoke from the cigarette billowed over the food. "World Bank, eh? Is there a photo in that? Schools or something? I can't believe someone would send a woman here, education project or not. You're brave. How frigging brave. Food's good. What's this? They couldn't have found a woman with blonder hair and bluer eyes. What were they thinking? You've got a shawl I see. If I were you, I'd be wearing the full burqa that covers everything but the eyes. Jeez, look at your white skin." He laughed.

"I ordered the best, since you're paying." Jorja smiled. "That's chicken," she said, answering one of his questions. "There's lots of chicken in Muzaffarabad. Fresh chicken." She had found a wishbone. It snapped in her fingers before she could make a wish. "I wear the dupatta to cover my hair. It's too much of a beacon otherwise. I was only going to be here for two days, but there's work to do and I agreed to do it. It's relatively safe here. Besides, I have a driver and the hotel guys look after me. People stare of course, but they're just curious. Some of the young boys get a bit excited, but I cover up my face if they get too frisky. You know what I mean."

"Young boys! Hell, *I'm* getting frisky looking at you. Those horny, repressed, testosterone-filled, hormonal jumping beans would be thinking beyond frisky. Pardon me, but let's get real here. You're so gorgeous and a helluva temptation to them. All of them, not just the young ones. I'm seventy-one and I could have the hots for you easy enough."

The thought of the short, stumpy leprechaun fly-fisherman taking his clothes off made her squeal with laughter. "Hey, I'm not that desperate. Not yet anyway. Seventy-one? Heck, you don't look a day over eighty!" she roared with laughter.

"Yeah, it's a pity I left my condoms back in the hotel in Islamabad." He laughed. "Hey, seriously, have you got condoms? You'd better get some. How can a young beautiful woman like you go without sex for more than a day? Better get a truck load of the things."

"I don't plan to be doing anything like that. There's no one that takes my fancy here and I'd be stupid to anyway. The whole of Muzaffarabad knows exactly what I'm doing."

"What about a randy American? A young foreigner could tempt you, I bet. I wish I were twenty years younger. Forty years younger." He ate in between puffs of his cigarette.

"It appears that there are no other foreigners here. You're the only one I've seen in three weeks. And look around. There's no one else in the restaurant. I'm alone most of the time. I usually have my choice of tables every night. There are not a whole lot of people to get excited over. Now tell me about your travels. I love a good travel story. I bet you've got a thousand."

"Make it twenty thousand. Where do you want to start? In Vietnam, Cambodia, India, Saudi Arabia? What about Cuba, Chad … or Libya?"

"No, no. Start with Cairo. Tell me about Cairo and how you met your wife."

"Ah yes, that's the best one. How astute. French women are so sexy. I was a horny bastard back then, I must admit. I took one look at Jeanne and fell in lust with her black eyes, black hair, and her perky, champagne-glass breasts. Beautiful. Don't know what she saw in me. Maybe I was taller then." As he broke into a long laugh, he reached for another cigarette. The laugh became a relentless cough.

After the languid dinner, Jorja returned to her room and had a cold shower to rid herself of the smell of smoke. She wrote a letter to Denny and prepared for bed as the telephone rang.

It was the receptionist Qaseem. "I see you with a foreign man like you and I am happy that you talk your language together. I see you laugh and I think you are very, very happy. You are happy now, madam?"

"Yes, thank you, Qaseem. I'm very happy now."

"I'm so sorry that he leaves tomorrow. I tell you when another countryman comes to the hotel. I tell you so that you can talk together and be happy."

She thanked him. The telephone rang again. It was the minister. "Hello Miss Jorja. I saw you eating in the restaurant tonight. I checked that you were eating well. I saw you with a gentleman and did not want to disturb you. I brought some alcohol with me, but I will give it to you another time, if you wish it. I'll call into the hotel tomorrow evening."

"Before you go, minister, there's something I'd like to ask you."

"Anything, Miss Jorja. I'm at your service."

"Donkeys. I'd like to know why Kashmiris don't like donkeys being photographed." She explained Arthur's situation.

The minister laughed. "You can ask me anything and you want to know about donkeys. Here's the secret. They are often the means for smuggling goods, particularly alcohol, into the country. People buy the contraband from the donkey's owner. Your photographer friend must have come across an enterprising alcohol merchant. Miss Jorja, I can tell you that you don't need to look for donkeys and their owners. You just ask me if you want alcohol."

* * *

Surrounding Arthur was a smoke haze from his roll-your-own cigarettes. Ignoring the smoke, Jorja joined him for breakfast.

"Donkeys and alcohol! Ha! If I'd known I could have bargained for a bottle or two. Thanks for telling me about that. How interesting!" Coughing and spluttering, he continued puffing on his death stick.

They took a photograph of each other. Arthur used his expensive BBC camera while Jorja used a cheap automatic that jammed, rendering it totally useless. Telling jokes on his way to the foyer, he whistled for his driver, who appeared promptly. Jorja couldn't have wished for a more jovial companion. With a mischievous wink, like a leprechaun, Arthur vanished. She had enjoyed his companionship but, right now, she fancied a younger man, easier on the eye, and a non-smoker. Closing her eyes, Jorja made another wish.

CHAPTER 20

STAIRWAY TO HEAVEN

Jamshid arrived in Muzaffarabad the next day, unannounced. Jorja asked whether he brought a mobile phone for her and some money, but he had neither. Jamshid ignored her complaints and merely shrugged his shoulders.

Accompanying Jamshid was Wasim, his superior, a short man with large lips and an even larger smile. Jamshid suggested a walk to the bazaar. The terrain was flat for the first two kilometers until they reached the bazaar that weaved up and down and in and out of a labyrinth of streets. Beggars with appalling deformities sat cross-legged on tea-colored hessian mats strewn on the filthy ground, limbs crushed and distorted, bones protruding from rags. Amid the masses of market stalls overflowing with food, spices, knick-knacks, carpets, mats, woodcarvings, shoes, jewelry, books, and shawls, the ever-present odor of rotting food, perspiration, and urine permeated the air. The smells of the market, enticing and foul, accompanied the three travelers through each winding passageway. Plucked chickens hung on hooks while feathers floating in the air rained over everyone, making the marketers sneeze. In a pool of bloodied water near the chicken-seller's stall floated more of the sodden plumage. The city was stained with the mess of living.

Everywhere they walked, people stared. Intrigued with what Jorja was doing and buying, the marketers gazed curiously. Jamshid apologized for her lack of privacy. She didn't notice that much. She was too captivated by the system of stairs throughout the bazaar. The steps had long treads and short treads, and high risers and short risers, with no logical construction. She decided that Kashmiris needed guidance in building stairways.

"Why can't Kashmiris build proper steps?" she complained as they stopped to allow Wasim to gain his breath. Wasim was too exhausted to answer. "You wouldn't be so puffed if they built proper steps. See, here the steps are too high and there the riser is very low. It's not an even, gentle step up or down, therefore you're working your body too hard."

"No, Miss Jorja, he's not fit like you and me. We go for walks and Wasim does not," explained Jamshid. "Anyway, all the steps in Pakistan and Kashmir look like this."

Not convinced, Jorja continued, "Steps consist of risers and treads. A riser is the elevation of the step and the tread is the part that we put our foot on, Jamshid. A riser of less than a hundred and fifty millimeters is more of a trip than a step, and anything greater than two hundred and twenty-five millimeters is a bit of a challenge. It's too high. The tread should be as wide as practicable, but never less than two hundred and fifty millimeters. Personally, I like a minimum tread of three hundred millimeters, although four hundred and fifty millimeters is much more comfortable for most people. These are all different sizes. There's no uniformity, Jamshid."

"As you wish, Miss Jorja."

He was not interested in her theory of step construction. Nevertheless, she continued, "When designing steps, Jamshid, it's important to ensure that the dimensions of treads and risers are regular. Large flights of steps, like these in the bazaar, can benefit by the inclusion of extended treads. We call them landings. They provide a safe resting stop for non-mountaineers amongst us, like Wasim. Because there are no landings, poor Wasim has to rest against the wall with everyone rushing past him. It isn't safe to stop here."

Wasim had partially regained his breath. "I had to stop. I'm going to die of a heart attack if we continue. You walk too fast up the stairs. I can't keep up with you. Why do you know so much about steps? I've never heard anyone talk so much about stupid steps."

"I'm a mathematician, Wasim. The construction of steps is applied mathematics. You could do with a handrail, Wasim."

"I could do with a new heart," he said as he placed his hand across his thumping chest. "A mathematician is no good to me, I need a surgeon."

"Let's continue and find something to drink," offered Jamshid.

The deftly-played guitar refrains of Led Zeppelin's *Stairway to Heaven* filtered through the humid air. Turning into a narrow lane, Jorja spied a teenage boy leaning against a wall with a cheap guitar resting on his knee over his long, mushroom-colored kameez. Tossing some rupees on the ground next to him, she listened to him play. The wiry youth lifted his head and looked at her. Strands of loose black hair fell across his dark eyes. He smiled as she winked.

CHAPTER 21

A DATE WITH DESTINY

In the evening, Jorja dined with Jamshid, Wasim, the minister, the minister's deputy, Tarif, and Shareef. Shareef Zardini was a businessman from Islamabad and Jamshid's friend. Two of the gentlemen had been to Australia and were imitating the Australian accent in a comic fashion. The minister's deputy whispered in Urdu, but Jorja heard "Kings Cross," as they guffawed loudly. She told them that she knew of the red-light district, and he finished the tale in English of a sex worker's proposal.

The minister and his deputy left with Tarif, the project's team leader. Wasim retired early to his room, presumably exhausted from climbing the stairs in the market. Jamshid, Shareef, and Jorja were in Shareef's room. Jamshid was arranging a marriage partner for him and they discussed the progress. He had recommended a beautiful, modern, educated woman with the distinction of having royal relatives, albeit of English heritage. Shareef had visited her workplace but had been too shy to speak to her. Unsure whether Jamshid should proceed to present his credentials to her parents, Shareef was dithering. A vote was taken and it was agreed by all that "nothing ventured was nothing gained."

Shareef remained in Muzaffarabad for an additional night while Jamshid and Wasim returned to Islamabad. The telephone rang and Jorja expected it to be the minister. It was Shareef requesting her company for dinner. "In my room," he added.

Four rooms along the corridor, she knocked and, with his mobile phone attached to his ear, Shareef welcomed her inside. Finishing his conversation, he rang the restaurant and ordered a variety of platters while she admired the view from his balcony. It faced north and she looked upstream to the city center—speckled with glistening streetlights—and to the mountain peak beyond.

"What's the name of the mountain?'

"Pirchinassi, I think. I believe it's about thirty-two kilometers away. Devotees of Saint Pirchinassi pay homage at the Shrine. There are other Shrines too, if you want to take a look sometime."

Inside, she gazed about the room. It was considerably smaller than hers, confining the cigarette odor to a condensed area. Shareef lit up another cigarette as he motioned her to sit at the table, situated close to the door. He flung the cigarette packet onto the bed where it collided into keys, a can of spray deodorant, and a hairbrush. Loosening his tie and removing his jacket, he took a seat opposite Jorja. She was beginning to think that this was not a good idea.

They discussed work and life in general. Nothing memorable was said, nor implied. Shareef was polite and amicable, apologizing when his mobile phone rang, but always answering it. Relaxed, he ordered a bottle of red wine. The waiter came in and out of the room. He didn't seem suspicious or offended to see a foreign woman with Shareef. It was as if they were in Australia: two colleagues having a meal. Jorja relaxed and enjoyed his company. The waiter opened the bottle and let the wine breathe. When he arrived with food, he poured the wine to fill three-quarters of the glass.

Shareef swapped the cigarettes for a thick cigar. For Jorja, there was a delightful, if perverse, satisfaction in watching him pucker his lips around the fat cigar. He leaned toward her. "Jorja, you're such a dear friend. I've enjoyed this evening immensely. Will you. . .?" The shrill ringing of his phone distracted him. "Mummy, hello! Yes, yes, very well. I'm in Muzaffarabad. No, I'm leaving early in the morning. I'll be back in Islamabad by mid morning, lunchtime at the latest. Yes, yes, of course Jamshid is arranging everything. One minute; can you wait a minute, dear mummy?" He indicated to Jorja that it would be a long conversation. She stood to leave, and he pulled her gently toward him, kissed her on the cheek, and said he'd see her soon, *Insh Allah*, in Islamabad.

Conjecturing that Shareef's demeanor was a prelude to something more romantic, Jorja wondered about the outcome. But not for long. It was too easy to fall into Denny's familiar embrace. That night her heart belonged to Denny.

CHAPTER 22

THE INTRUSION

The curriculum office had electricity. It was the first time that it remained on for the entire morning. Spring had arrived. It was twenty-three degrees Celsius. The snow on the mountain was melting, revealing squares of brown earth.

In the afternoon, Jorja prepared papers in the project office in readiness for a meeting the next day. Mahmud sat beside her at the computer, and they worked together compiling the text. They worked well like this and, satisfied with their work, Mahmud went for his daily walk at five o'clock with Lufti. He was diabetic and maintained his health with exercise.

Jorja tried for two hours to log onto the internet. Overcome with impotence and fury, she directed her outrage at no one in particular and everyone in general. In her loudest voice, she screamed, "I love Kashmir!" as she flung off her dupatta and rested her head in her hands. She felt cut off from the rest of the world. Only Gadi was in the office, sitting at his computer in the furthest corner of the elongated room.

He looked at her, smiling. "Yes, I know madam. You love Kashmir very much."

"I meant it sarcastically, Gadi. Why can't the blessed internet connection work? It's driving me crazy. I'm going crazy!"

"The internet does that to foreigners. They always go crazy. You are more patient than most."

"I am?" She was surprised.

"Yes, but you are also louder than most."

"Thank you, Gadi," she said in a sarcastic tone. "In Australia, people think I'm very quiet and soft spoken." She felt the need to defend herself.

"It's true that you do not speak as much as others. It's true that you do not yell at us and tell us what to do. But it's true that when you laugh, you laugh loud! When you are frustrated, you are loud! I can't understand why you do not yell at us when you are frustrated like other foreigners do. You just yell into the air. Then you laugh." Again, Gadi spoke forthrightly. "I hear you laugh with Lufti and you are very loud with him. You make him loud too."

Fadil entered the room and asked if Jorja was well. He had heard the scream. He asked if she was ready to return to the hotel. Fadil waited patiently for her and again, she had kept him at work longer than his finishing time. She was thankful that she was going to Islamabad on the weekend where the office computers and the power were more reliable. Lufti had given up completely on the e-mail system in Upper Chattar and no longer tried to connect. He asked Jorja to download material for him while she was in Islamabad. The list from Lufti and Mahmud was increasing each day. Stuffing her documents into her bag, Jorja entered the car and sat next to Fadil. Gadi accompanied them so that he could visit a friend in the city.

At the Sangam Hotel, Gadi stepped from the car and opened the door for Jorja. "I'll accompany Jorja to her room," he told Fadil.

Jorja was about to protest, but Gadi's strong arm was already wrapped around hers, leading her toward the foyer. Inside, she whispered her objection.

"Madam Jorja, I just wanted to have a word with you in private. I can arrange for you to visit a village. Near the village is the area where Osama bin Laden often frequents. As you can appreciate, he does not remain long in one place. He is always on the move so that nobody knows of his hiding place. But, as I have told you before, I know where to find him."

"Gadi, this is absurd. Let me go."

"As you wish, madam. I will always be at your service. Always."

"Gadi?"

"Yes, madam?"

"The pink building next door to the project office ..."

"Yes, madam?"

"Who are the people in there?"

"It's best to stay away from the building, madam. The people keep to themselves and you should, too. I've told you that before."

"But you said there were al-Qaeda or Taliban trainees in the building. Is that true or were you joking?"

"I always tell the truth, madam. And I tell you, truthfully, to stay away from the building."

"Is Osama bin Laden in there?"

"Madam, that is nonsense. As I have said before, I know where to find him. Would you like me to?"

"No!" Jorja raced to the first floor and unlocked the door to her room. A lanky, young man stood beside the bed, startled, but motionless. Jorja was unsure whether he was a cleaner or a supervisor. His uncombed hair contrasted with his well-pressed black trousers and starched, white shirt. The stranger's presence made Jorja uneasy. She had not seen him in the hotel before. They both remained still. Looking him in the eye, Jorja motioned him toward the open doorway. Following her hand signal, he lowered his gaze as he passed her and left the room. Neither of them uttered a word.

Bolting the door, she checked the doors to the two balconies. She found the entrance to the southern balcony unlocked. She presumed the youth had entered via the balcony, unseen, effortlessly, and opportunistically.

The sun had disappeared, bringing about a chill in the room. The heater didn't respond when Jorja turned it on. No amount of banging on it would make it work. She telephoned reception to report the stranger and the heater. Pervaiz, the cleaning supervisor, was rostered on the reception desk while Qaseem was on leave. He asked many questions about the intruder to determine if staff might know his identity. He resolved to inform the manager before turning his attention to the heater.

"Are you cold, madam?"

"Yes, I'm very cold."

"Why are you cold?"

"Because the heater is not on."

"But it's not cold for the heater to be on, madam."

"It's cold to me. Please may I have it fixed?"

"As you wish. Just wait, madam."

When Pervaiz arrived, the radiator bar began to glow. "Oh, it's working now, Pervaiz. It wasn't a minute ago."

"I turned it on from the work room. We can fix it from there," he explained.

"I don't understand."

"We turn the power off sometimes. Not all the power, just the heaters. It saves money. Don't worry. When you want the heater on, just ring reception and we'll fix it. Ring reception about anything, madam. You were very wise to inform us about the intruder. He is not a cleaner. In fact, he is not an employee of the hotel. He is a stranger, madam. I will arrange for someone to check the locks on your balcony doors regularly, madam. Can you help me with English again?"

After reciting words from his English dictionary, he opened a sporting magazine and read the names of Australian cricketers. "McGrath," he enunciated.

"It's pronounced Magrar," Jorja corrected. "The *t* and the *h* are silent."

He repeated the name and said another. "Worg." He pointed to the word, 'Waugh'.

"It's pronounced Wor. Steve Wor. The *g* and the *h* are silent," she emphasized.

"Madam, why are there so many silent letters in English? What is their purpose? Why are they there when they should not be there? I think it's very strange indeed."

She agreed with him. They continued with Urdu translations. She could ask someone's name, how old they were, whether they were married, and accept or decline a marriage proposal. Pervaiz said that these were the important sentences for a woman to know. "They may be important for a woman, but I have a more important sentence to learn. How do you say in Urdu: 'my heater is not working'?"

Pervaiz smirked and said, *"mera heater kam nahi kera ha hai."*

Jorja practiced it several times before Pervaiz was satisfied with the pronunciation of each word.

"Madam, do you know why Muslim men are allowed four wives? The first wife is for his parents. The second is for himself. The third is for socializing and the fourth is for his neighbors." He laughed.

Jorja joined in, not fully understanding the humor. Nevertheless, it was comical to see Pervaiz tell the joke.

"Oh madam, I nearly forgot," he said excitedly. "I have something for you." He placed his hand deep into his Western trousers and pulled out a silver toy ring. With a grin, he knelt on the floor, took her left hand and proposed, *"tum mujhe shadi karon ge? Kya ap?* Do you understand me?"

She replied, pushing the ring further along her finger, *"hame tumse shadi karon ge."*

"Oh, very good, madam. You have learned Urdu very well. I'm your teacher and you are my teacher. Very, very good, madam." They laughed together and as she bolted the door after he left, Jorja could hear him bellow, "I will tell everyone that we are engaged," as he laughed loudly down the stairs.

CHAPTER 23

A SURPRISE PACKAGE

The tinfoil moon shimmered. Stars blinked in Morse code, piloting the way for night travelers. *Star Wars* appeared on television, and the distant sounds of border fighting seemed to beat time with the battle for the empire.

Standing on the balcony in the nightlight, Jorja looked at the mosque across the river. It was a low, elegant building with green minarets and ornamental roofing. Three colored lights had been recently attached to the roofing, resembling decorations on a Christmas tree. The loud speaker, placed at the northeast corner of the roof, called people to prayer five times a day and they would sit outside on mats placed on the ground. The site of the mosque was prime land on the edge of the riverbank with views of the converging rivers and next to the army barracks with a path joining the two structures. A man on a rickety wooden ladder was white-washing the mosque's chimney. Another was digging a trench in the garden, while three others raked the ground.

An old man at the river's edge carried a metal basin by its handles. He washed his clothes, pounding them on rocks and draping them over large boulders to dry. Another man was sitting, contemplating. Jorja could see a man holding a black briefcase. He stood further along the western side of the bank in the distance. He opened it, took papers and documents from it, ripped them into pieces, and tossed them into the river. The racing stream transported the papers to the meeting point of the two rivers where the tumbling, crashing waves churned them as if in a washing machine. The river's spume spat out the confetti further down the river and continued its rapid journey to Islamabad.

The telephone rang. Pervaiz called Jorja to the reception area. "Parcels, madam. They are from London. Please pay two hundred and fifty rupees to receive them." He handed her two large packages from Australia, not England. The parcels were from her triathlon teammates: two sisters, Kate and Kora. As she rushed up the stairs, she looked at the postage marks and noted that they took ten days to reach Kashmir; six days to get to Karachi and four days to travel from Karachi to Muzaffarabad.

Jorja had e-mailed a request for hairclips to hold her dupatta in place. She ripped the padded parcels apart and rifled through individually wrapped chocolates, tubes of facial masks, fruit-scented soap, an Australian magazine, and packets of moist towelettes. Pushing them aside, she was relieved to find a clutch of hairclips. She rushed to the mirror and fidgeted with her scarf until she was content that, at last, it would remain firmly on her head. In frustration, she had often tied the scarf into a knot underneath her chin. She looked like a Russian peasant woman rather than an elegant Kashmiri. It was a mystery to her how the dupatta rarely slipped from a Kashmiri woman's head.

A recollection of seeing chocolates in the parcels surged through her like an electric shock. Chocolates, lots of chocolates! Stuffing the confectionary, misshapen from heat, into her mouth, she read Kora's message: *I hope you enjoy the party balloons!* A collection of colorful condoms fell into her hands. She giggled to herself and contemplated blowing them up as balloons in the coming weeks to celebrate her departure. She raised the dewberry soap to her nose and inhaled its sweetness, a welcome change from the Tibet Deluxe hotel soap.

Clutching the magazine, Jorja descended the stairs to the restaurant. She watched two workmen building an extension to the hotel. The wood and bamboo scaffolding bent precariously as they moved across the beams. They seemed neither nervous nor aware of any threat of an impending accident. Calling to each other amid puffs of smoke, their cigarettes hung just as precariously on their lips.

The weather was changeable and Jorja shivered in the evening's cool winds blowing into the open patio doorway. In two days she would brave the winding Karakoram Highway on her way to Islamabad and prayed for a journey without landslides, fog or rain-soaked, slippery bitumen.

"You are happy with parcel, madam?" said Awan. "You have book with Western pictures?"

"Yes, it's a magazine from Australia." It was tabloid press, but she had never been so thrilled to read the trashy movie news and local gossip. "I will try Kashmiri tea this evening, Awan, with Kashmiri kebabs and plain rice. Thank you."

"You like Kashmiri kebabs. *Raita*"?

"Oh yes, don't forget the *raita*." The spice-filled kebabs were delightfully hot and sinus cleansing. The *raita*—yoghurt dressing—added a refreshing mint taste to the meal, making it Jorja's favorite. She had not tried Kashmiri tea before. The dusky, milky-pink brew poured into the cup. An aroma of almond filled her nostrils and the nutty texture crunched on her tongue. It seemed more like a meal than a beverage. Kashmiri tea—*numkeen chai*—contained salt, coconut, almond, cardamom, and green tea that brewed into a dusty pink color.

She sipped the tea while staring through the window with a northern view. The glass reflected a blond with a crooked nose and small blue eyes. She shifted in her chair and the face disappeared. Raising a hand to her cheek, the skin felt flaky and dry. It was as though she had aged ten years in ten minutes. Jorja found it distressing.

CHAPTER 24

A LESSON ON LATRINES

Latrines and ablutions were everyday issues in Kashmir. During breakfast, Jorja met a young Dutchman who worked in refugee camps for *Medecins Sans Frontieres*—Doctors without Borders—inspecting latrines and assessing water sanitation.

There was an Afghan refugee camp in a valley on the outer edge of the city that Jorja passed on her way to village schools. A tall fence topped with a spiral of barbed concertina wire enclosed the entire camp. Concertina wire was the nastiest of all wires. Studded with small blades, nearly as sharp as razors, it could slash through skin like a knife through runny cheese. No trees stood inside the fence, nor was there any grass: just dirt, rock, mud, and half a dozen large corrugated-iron buildings.

Dr. Dirk Andriessen, smooth-skinned and sandy-haired, described a family of fifteen living in a small tent in one of the camps.

Relief agencies provided canvas tents, but most were cruder, made from tree branches, twine, and heavy-duty plastic sheeting. Part of the doctor's role was to notify refugees of the current political situation, as they had been without news for several months or even years. His directive was to inform them to pack their possessions and return home. Many Afghans had begun to cross the border, despite continued bombing by American troops, but there were still thousands in refugee camps in the region. He was also to impart the skills of cleanliness and hygiene that they may have forgotten during four years of displacement.

"So what do you do when you inspect the latrines?" Jorja was genuinely curious.

"You don't really want to know, do you?"

She pleaded with him to talk to her, to tell her something, anything, of his daily routine.

"Latrines are different in different places. It's important to understand the habits and cultural beliefs of the local people and involve them in the planning, construction, and use of the latrines. Muslims have rules covering such things as how a person must carry water to wash himself after defecating, acceptable places where one can defecate, and other personal details about performing daily ablutions. I ask the health workers to design basic pit latrines that are odorless and easy to clean, economical to produce, and are acceptable to most refugees."

"What about the tough weather conditions here with the altitude of the mountains? Does that make a difference to the design of the latrines?" She was intrigued.

"We've been trying to develop a latrine that will work during the monsoon season when the water levels are at their highest, but which is still affordable and accepted by the refugees. A few years ago, when the first Afghan refugees came to this area, we installed some experimental water-seal latrines. We recommended the installation of six-ring, one-slab latrines, but in a number of the refugee camps, where the water rose to high levels relative to the norm, they didn't work. We made some modifications to the six-ring structure with a pipe running from the top ring to the edge of the camp that discharged the floodwaters into the hoar, in theory anyway. Throughout the monsoon period, the water levels in this area were relatively low and the normal six-ring latrines didn't have any overflow problems so the effectiveness of the pipe latrine couldn't be determined. We'll monitor the latrines again this coming monsoon season. I won't be back, but one of my colleagues will come and check them. He'll work with some local doctors from the World Health Organization here in Muzaffarabad." Dirk was spooning mounds of instant coffee into his cup. "Sorry to bore you with all of this."

"No, don't be sorry, I'll talk to anybody at the moment about anything. It's just so good to see another foreigner."

"It's funny that *we* are the foreigners. It seems a strange word. Anyway we tried some compost latrines too, if you really want to know."

"I do. Tell me more," Jorja urged. She just wanted to hear a European voice.

"Well, the refugees didn't like them too much at first. I don't think they were prepared to pay attention to maintenance, but then they found them to be less smelly with less flies than the traditional pit latrines. On the social side, there was often a preference for the sitting position while defecating, and the lack of smells or flies was an attraction. Compost latrines often overcome technical problems such as if the terrain is unsuitable for pit latrines, particularly if there's a high water table or collapsing sandy soil. Compost latrines also require minimal space and are associated with low or no emptying costs. Anything here that is cheap is well accepted."

"Who empties them?"

"The refugees have to be taught to look after the latrines themselves. Each time the latrine is used, they need to add ash to the feces, and close the lid. They can add soil, garden and kitchen waste daily if they want to. They need to keep the toilets clean and this isn't always done. Users need to ensure that urine is disposed of separately to feces. There's a separate urine collector, but sometimes it gets clogged with ash and needs to be kept clean and emptied regularly."

"Every day?"

"God, no." He laughed. "The chamber needs to be emptied about every six months and the urine container should be emptied weekly. Once a year we recommend that they change to an alternate chamber. The joint pipe from the urine collector can occasionally disconnect itself, which means that the system won't work properly. The system needs to be inspected regularly and that's part of what we do when we visit."

"Why would you use compost latrines though instead of pit latrines, apart from less smell?"

"They save water," he said, as he scraped the last of the omelet from his plate. "And the hygiene is better. They last longer too. But they have to be inspected more often. Some people think this is a good thing because it means we come here regularly, and therefore check people's general health at the same time. Others say that the cost in getting us here negates the savings made in installing the compost latrines. There's a cultural barrier though as the refugees don't like the sight of the feces."

"Well, who does?" They both laughed. "That's enough toilet talk. I have to get to work, where I don't use the toilet. I wait until I get back to the hotel."

"I do, too, except if I have to pee," he said. "I don't like using the latrines to shit so I hold on even if I stay overnight. Now we both know we shouldn't deliberately stop ourselves from shitting, but our bodies seem to hold on quite well. Mine does anyway. Yours would be working overtime if you can't pee or shit."

"Yep, it's working overtime," she agreed, as they left the restaurant. From there, they went their separate ways.

Jorja's mind was on urinating and defecating as Fadil drove her to the curriculum office. She noticed several Kashmiri men urinating in the gutters of the crowded streets. They urinated discreetly. They didn't stand as Western men did, preferring to squat close to the gutter. The baggy shalwar allowed them to extract their digit without exposing it to the view of passersby. It seemed to be a natural phenomenon for it did not attract attention. People near the urinaters continued their usual business and activities, not pausing in conversation at all. Occasionally, if those urinating noticed that Jorja was in the car, they would follow her gaze to see if she was watching them. Mostly she was.

In the project office, she connected to the internet briefly before the power cut out. There was no e-mail from Denny. She hadn't sent him one for days and she felt a strange disconnection.

In the evening, Jorja assumed her usual post on the balcony. The mosque had another colored light. The count was now four: red, green, yellow, and blue. They shone across the river end of the garden and lit up the newly dug earth. She wasn't sure why they had erected the colored lights, but she liked them.

CHAPTER 25

A WEEKEND IN ISLAMABAD

It was Kadir's last day in Muzaffarabad. Tarif, Kadir, and Jorja planned to leave for Islamabad at midday. The workshop Kadir conducted seemed to take forever to conclude, due to endless speeches. While Jorja waited in the project office, she spoke in Urdu to Gadi and Hamid. Gadi kept a strange watch over Jorja, anxiously hoping he could speak with her privately about the hunt for Osama bin Laden. Jorja remained close to Hamid's desk.

She read the newspapers. Kidnapping seemed prevalent. Kidnappers, usually members of the family or known acquaintances, abducted college students for ransom. The list of abductions was long and contained advertised pleas by parents for the safe return of their children. Newspapers published car license-plate numbers whenever there was a car accident, with the full names of all victims and offenders. There were also many reported deaths, under the "Transition" column: accidents, suicides, murders, and natural deaths.

Suicides were also common. They included wives without issues, children who had argued with their parents about money allowances, and men with financial problems. More people committed suicide in Kashmir than elsewhere in Pakistan. Within the past week, there were five suicide deaths and three attempts. Hamid said that suicides were due to the border tensions and fighting. "The fighting everyday and the many deaths are generating a negative effect on the human mind. It makes people angry, and they feel useless and depressed. Suicide comes from depression, especially here in Kashmir. My friend's father is a doctor and he says depression and anxiety are so common now that it's difficult to cope with the number of patients. People go to the pharmacy, buy their own drugs, and take too many on purpose. They attempt suicide at night and doctors can't get to them because of curfew. This causes a delay in bringing them to hospital and they ultimately die. It's very tragic."

"They buy drugs without a prescription from the doctor?"

"Yes, madam. There is no drug control in Kashmir and any person can get any drug anywhere, anytime. The medical shops operate without any control from any proper agency. The government department of drug control is non-functional."

It was rare for people to report unnatural deaths to the police and hence the numbers cited in newspapers were significantly lower than actual figures. If they did report unnatural deaths, they were seldom officially registered. Registered cases had to be followed-up to determine the cause of death and to find the perpetrator. This generated a lot of work for the under-staffed police stations. The incidences investigated usually resulted in court cases. Twenty thousand cases were pending in Islamabad alone.

Tarif, Kadir, and Jorja left the project office at four o'clock and arrived in Islamabad three hours later. Jorja was looking forward to staying at the office guesthouse with access to computers and the internet, but it was full. Jamshid had given the bedrooms to local consultants. Unfortunately, Jamshid asked her to reside, by herself, in a small hotel called the Decent Lodge, some distance from the office. The bathroom was better than the one at the Sangam Hotel, and thankfully so, because the rest of the room was pitifully inferior. Two coat hangers, a desk the size of a pair of manila folders, and two seedy stained sofas were the highlights of the cheap, shabby room. A frayed sheet covered the mattress of a single bed. Over the sheet lay two thin, abrasive, acrylic blankets.

With no access to e-mail in the evening, she couldn't contact Denny, adding to her irritation. It was three days in a row, or maybe more, since she had e-mailed him. Jorja felt ill. The office staff would not be working in the morning because it was Sunday, so at least she'd have unlimited access to the computer. That was some consolation.

She crawled into bed. The blanket was itchy. Incessant barking kept her awake until two o'clock. She thought of Lufti's phrase, "not a dog barked." He used it often when speaking of controversial conversations that, in reality, caused minimal sensationalism. It was similar in intent to the Western phrase, "no one batted an eyelid." She said the phrase aloud, "Not a dog barked." But this was not the case. Every dog barked; every dog in Islamabad. She was tired, but she was more tired of the lack of communication and the restrictions placed upon her. She detested not being in control of her day. She still didn't have any money. Rocking rhythmically to comfort herself, she couldn't dispel the images in her head of dogs copulating. A canine howl was the last sound she heard.

CHAPTER 26

THE CHURCH BOMBING

The shower pelted Jorja with hot water. It was heaven after a fitful night. Miraculously, it seemed to soften her skin, parched and wrinkled from the drying climate and hard water of Muzaffarabad. She was in Islamabad and glad about that.

The city of Islamabad had no axis or center. Each sector, built around a commercial center, had a letter and number designation, such as F-7, with quarters numbered clockwise, such as F-7/1 in the southwest corner, F-7/2 in the northwest corner, and so on. The Orwellian coordinates also had names, but were known, more commonly, by their markets: Aabpara and Civic Center in southwest G-6; Super Market in F-6; Jinnah in F-7; and Ayub Market in F-8. Between the F and G sectors was a commercial belt, the Blue Area. The new capital of Pakistan was largely a government city, housing central administration functions. Amid this orderliness were the embassies and consulates, reserves and parks, schools and museums, churches and mosques.

It was a Sunday and a lazy day for Jamshid and Jorja. Jorja checked her e-mail and searched the internet for information requested by Lufti and Mahmud.

Jamshid's mobile telephone rang. "*Ji, ji.*" Breaking into agitated English, he uttered, "Oh my goodness. Was anyone hurt? Where are you? No, no, I'll ring him. I hope everyone is fine. Yes, we'll be seeing Anthony shortly. Bye."

Jorja looked at him for an account of the telephone call. Explosions had ripped through a Protestant international church in Islamabad, a church used by foreigners due to its proximity to the embassies. Insurgents had thrown grenades into the building killing two Americans. Jamshid didn't know much more.

They left the office to visit Anthony Parker, an Australian, at his palatial white-bricked home where he lived with his wife, Jane, and their two children. Anthony was at a school fete when security police intercepted him and advised him to return home as quickly as possible. Security organizations were on full alert for all embassy and foreign staff.

As they sat on the lush lawns at his heavily secured home, drinking ice-cold Australian beer, Anthony, well connected socially and politically, updated Jorja on the Kashmiri conflict. He told of a situation near Muzaffarabad a few days ago. An Indian plane flew over the Line of Control into Pakistan-administered Azad Kashmir. When the pilot realized his error, he U-turned swiftly and headed toward his homeland. Indian military personnel on the ground, seeing an oncoming plane from Azad Kashmir and not recognizing it as one of their own, fired upon it, hit its broadside, and almost shot it down, nearly causing a major political incident in the process and an escalation of border fighting. The media never reported the incident.

"How's the project going, Jorja?" Anthony asked, as he poured another beer. "If it's progressing anything like the ones I hear about, it's slow going. Right? Implementation is not an Urdu word." He was in shorts; attire he did not wear outside the perimeter of his residence. It was a rare sight in Pakistan. His wife dressed elegantly in a simple dress of pink shot-silk. Her tanned glow contrasted with Anthony's color-less skin. They kept themselves fit by walking, like Jamshid, in the Margalla Hills nearby.

Christa and Stephano, friends of the Australian couple and employees of the Swiss embassy, arrived in a distressed state. Jane ushered their two children inside where a nanny tended to them. Five people were killed in the morning's bomb attack, including an American diplomat's wife and daughter. The cur-rent count of injured was forty-one. Christa and Stephano had come from the hospital where they comforted a Swiss woman struck by shrapnel.

"It was horrific. Ambrila is fine now, but quite shocked, of course. We'll see her again on our way home. A lovely woman she is, about thirty-five, and a dear friend." Christa spoke with un-wiped tears that she allowed to stream down her face. "There were lots of police at the hospital. It seems there were eighty to a hundred and fifty people in the church including families of diplomats. The church is in the Diplomatic Enclave, near the American and Chinese embassies."

"It happened just before eleven this morning," said Stephano as his wife caught her breath. "The police think that there were two attackers who entered the church and hurled hand grenades. After the first explosion, Ambrila lay on the floor. That probably saved her. She saw a person in his thirties wearing a black shirt who may have been one of the attackers. When she stood up there were blood-soaked people around her. How ghastly for her."

Jane intervened. "You two should go home and rest."

"No, no, we're fine. We'd rather be here, and besides, the children wanted to play with yours. They were so looking for-ward to it. Let them play while we have a few drinks and some-thing to eat," said Stephano.

"Sure. That's fine. I've prepared some hot cross buns. I know it's not Easter yet, but I thought we'd make this an early celebration. We can have them after the food. The cook's made some light snacks."

"Just what we need, Jane darling," said Christa. Jane signaled to the cook to serve the food while Anthony positioned chairs around the low table.

"Any more news?" asked Anthony.

"Well, a security official I spoke to said that at least ten or twelve grenades were thrown," said Stephano. "Another policeman said that it was six and three exploded. And another policeman said that there were four and two went off. Apparently, they were Russian-made grenades. Ambrila can't remember whether there were two or three explosions because there was so much confusion and noise. Most of the damage occurred when the window panes shattered. There was broken glass and splintered wood all over the floor," continued Stephano.

"A policeman was on duty outside the church, but the attackers entered from the side doors. They escaped on foot, but probably arrived on motorbikes," added Christa.

"I've got a list of those killed and injured," Stephano said, as he pulled out a white sheet from his back pocket. "The death toll includes two Americans, two Pakistanis and an Afghan. The two American women were the wife and daughter of diplomat Milton Green. I didn't know them, did you?" Anthony expressed his condolences. "Of the two Pakistani victims, one woman was an employee of the American Embassy, and the other victim, a male, has not been identified. The Afghan national was Anwar Baizar, son of Ali Baba, a resident of Islamabad. Relatives are yet to claim the unidentified person so he could be one of the attackers. That's what we know at present, except for the injured so far. The injured include fourteen Pakistanis, nine Americans, three Britons, five Iranians, one Iraqi, one Afghan, one Swiss, three Sri Lankans, one Canadian, one Australian, one Ethiopian, one German, and a man whose nationality is unknown. The Afghan national apparently escaped from the hospital bed and is now a key witness to the attack. The injured are at Shifa International Hospital or the Federal Government Services Hospital."

"Who's the Australian? Do you know? Have you got a name?" asked Anthony.

"Yes, Stainly. He's sixty. That's all I know."

"Where is he?"

"At Shifa. It doesn't state his condition."

"I'll go and see him tonight. I'll see if he's still there and make sure he's okay. What of Milton Green? Where's he?"

"He's at the Federal Government Services Hospital. That's the Polyclinic. Do you know it?" Anthony nodded. "There's also some other American embassy staff injured. Some are at the Polyclinic and others are at PIMS, the Pakistan Institute of Medical Sciences. We might check on them too, but we know that the American Ambassador has visited them."

"So there have been no arrests?" asked Jamshid.

"No arrests. One policeman told me that investigations are in progress at a pace. They were his words: 'at a pace'."

It was, in many ways, a normal Sunday. If it weren't for the talk of the church bombing and the presence of security guards in the driveway, they could have been in Australia.

* * *

Jorja e-mailed Denny about the bombing. Jamshid and Jorja discussed extending her stay in Muzaffarabad for a further five months to complete more work on the project. She had mixed emotions about it. In truth, she wanted to be home, not because of the bombing, but because she missed Denny. She e-mailed him again:

I hope I didn't scare you earlier about the bombing. I really am fine. Jamshid said the minister called him and wants me to stay another five months—apparently to train more teachers. The minister didn't mention it to me. Jamshid has only just told me. I think it's ridiculous. Jamshid said he'd talk to his boss, Wasim. I'm not sure whether I have a say in this. There's too much pressure from the minister in Kashmir and they're placing the burden on my shoulders. It sucks!

The bombing here has shaken up the Westerners and security has been stepped up. Islamabad is generally the safest city in Pakistan, so it's really scared the foreigners. I'm not scared, but I'll remain alert.

I really miss you. I miss your green eyes and fair skin. I miss looking at your long, chestnut hair, which I adore. I love it when you tie it back in a ponytail. You don't see that in Pakistan!

It's time for dinner. I'm eating here with Jamshid before the driver takes me back to the Decent Lodge. I'll e-mail you again tomorrow. Hopefully Wasim will make a decision soon. Maybe I can telephone you. I haven't mentioned phone calls to Jamshid yet. I must go now—pity.

Jorja

CHAPTER 27

AN AMERICAN IN
PAKISTANI CLOTHES

Jamshid annoyed Jorja. The cook, Abassi, had prepared a meal of fish with a curry sauce. He was preparing dessert when Jamshid announced that Jorja would be returning to Muzaffarabad in the morning. She was under the impression she was staying an extra day.

"Hell, Jamshid, when am I going to get paid? And do my banking? And buy some stationary and clothes and . . ."

"And what?"

"And do women's things! I was supposed to have two days in Islamabad, not one! Most of the shops were closed today and we spent the day at Anthony's. You distinctly said

130

that after a month in Kashmir, I could have a weekend here. A full weekend, Jamshid."

"Don't worry. Our accountant has put money into your Australian bank. You can go to the ATM in the Blue Area and withdraw money. It'll give you rupees. Then you can stop at the supermarket before you go back to Kashmir. It will be done, don't worry."

"That's pathetic, Jamshid. I wanted to get an Urdu dictionary and some more clothes. I was hoping to get a shalwar kameez or two. It's warming up a bit and I need some lighter clothes."

"You don't need more clothes now. You can wait until next time to get some."

"And when will that be?" she had raised her voice.

"Whenever you wish."

"And has Wasim made a decision yet about my stay?"

"Not yet. He was in Karachi and I could not talk to him today."

"Tell him to do the job himself!"

"Now, Jorja. You don't mean that. You're tired and upset. I'll ask Noor to drive you back to the Decent Lodge. Noor will pick you up at nine o'clock in the morning and take you to the bank. He knows where it is. Then you can go to *Mr. Books* to buy a dictionary. It's near here, so he'll bring you back to the office, and you can change to Fadil's car to go to Muzaffarabad. I will arrange everything."

"Hell, Jamshid. I'm tired of you arranging things for me. You have no bloody idea! Tell Noor I'm ready now." She gathered up her bag and some papers, most of which were for Lufti and Mahmud. Two hot cross buns, carefully wrapped, courtesy of Jane, jutted out of her bag. She had forgotten that they were there. Noor was washing the car when she ran outside. Jamshid was behind her giving him orders. She sat in the front seat and slammed the door. Noor hurriedly moved the hose and opened the large wrought-iron gates. As they drove out, the security guard closed the gates behind them.

"You cross, madam?" Noor looked concerned.

"I'm very cross. I want to spend more time in Islamabad, but I must go back to Muzaffarabad tomorrow."

"Very sorry, madam." He locked the doors. The streets were dark with few cars. Noor overtook a lanky man on a rickety bicycle, his Pakistani robes fluttering against his body. Several groups of military police congregated at intersections. Jorja heard the chirping of cicadas.

In the morning, Jorja hastily packed and waited in the foyer of the Decent Lodge for Noor. He arrived on time and drove to the Blue Area where he parked next to the ATM machine. An armed guard, big and burly, stood beside it. The ATM instructions were in Urdu and English making the transaction simple and quick. *Hell! A withdrawal limit!* She hadn't telephoned Denny, and she didn't know how long it would be until she'd be back in Islamabad. She still wouldn't have enough money to telephone Denny regularly. The withdrawal limit might only be enough for one telephone call. She sighed and returned to the car.

"Are you fine, madam?"

"I am fine, Noor. Can you take me to *Mr. Books* now? Thanks."

"Sunglasses, madam? Would you like to buy sunglasses? Lovely sunglasses! Protect your eyes, madam, and buy sunglasses." A teenage boy raised a plastic bag of sunglasses toward the window.

She hadn't seen any Pakistanis wearing sunglasses. "No thank you. I have some." Noor drove away and she muttered, "In Australia."

Noor laughed. "You're funny, madam."

Noor accompanied Jorja into *Mr. Books*. It was a corner bookstore with an impressive selection of stationary, magazines, and maps, including books written in English. She found an Urdu-English dictionary, not of high quality, but it would suffice. Noor collected stationary and assisted with her purchases.

"Noor, can I purchase a mobile phone in one of these shops?"

"Not here, madam, and Mr. Jamshid said I must have you back in the office in five minutes."

Jorja emitted a low growl that attracted the attention of shoppers. Noor took a step backward as the angry foreigner strode toward the car and slammed the door.

At the office, while Jamshid was allotting drivers their duties, she rushed to the computer. The electricity and internet connection were reliable and, within a few minutes, she saw an e-mail from Denny, printed it and dashed to the car. Almost making herself sick, she read it several times during the long, treacherous drive back to the altitude of Muzaffarabad:

> *Hi there.*
> *I'll send a consolidated response to your e-mails. Sorry to short-change you on the number of replies I send, but hopefully my responses are quality if not quantity.*
> *I send you my apologies for not writing on Friday. The day got away from me. Work stuff, you know. But also, my rightist capitalist tendencies have led me into the shops again. I've been spending up a storm. Two expensive business shirts and a tie, and some really exotic sunglasses. . .*

"Oh, toss it! Damn! Shit!"

"Madam, you are not well?"

"Sorry Fadil. I've just realized that I've left clothes in the wardrobe at the Decent Lodge. I was in such a hurry to pack that I damn well forgot most of my clothes. I've hardly got anything as it is."

"Very sorry, madam."

Putting the drama behind her, Jorja continued reading Denny's e-mail:

> *Well, regarding the situation over there now—I got your e-mails and it seems as if you're safe and well. But before that, I had seen footage on the news, none of which seemed very good, and left me unexcited about having a friend and lover over there now. But what you do is important and I suppose someone needs to do it. You are very brave.*
> *Regarding your possible extended stay, I guess you have to wait and see what your boss says. I'm a hundred percent*

with you. I think what you're doing over there is significant (including actually going over there in the first place).

I was nervous just watching the news footage. I believe you when you say you're safe, but things can escalate rapidly and get out of control in that kind of environment. Having said that, I'm sure you'd be back on the first plane if you were in danger.

Look forward to hearing from you,

D

* * *

Jorja had Denny's e-mail in her hand as she stood at the balcony looking up at Muzaffarabad's mountain. Wispy mists obscured part of the peak. *Was it safer to climb the mountain laden with snow or to have the hardness of the brown earth underfoot? Was the feeling of confidence and familiarity with the environment a positive factor or did it blind a person to the pitfalls? Did uncertainty guarantee a sharpness of mind and thus a greater awareness of the environment?* It seemed to Jorja that the surer the foothold in the upward mountain climb, the more likelihood of being in danger of missing a crucial grip.

"Hey there! Hey there! You up there!"

An American voice startled her. She looked down to the restaurant patio where a tall, dark Pakistani was standing, waving excitedly at her.

"What nationality are you? American? I'm American. Come down and have lunch with us."

Her stomach didn't feel like a meal after the drive along the Karakoram Highway, but she politely accepted his offer and darted down the stairs to the restaurant. Seated at the table was his wife, Neelum. The tall man was even taller than she had first noticed. He also looked darker against the fresh whiteness of his shalwar kameez. The clothes of Pakistanis were always a dull shade of cream or gray, never white, and never starched. This man wore the whitest, most starched shalwar kameez she'd ever seen. He introduced himself as Mohammad.

"Mother-fucking hot, isn't it? So you're not American. An Australian, eh? Probably just as well in these times. It's not a good time to be an American. That's why I'm wearing my Pakistani clothes. I've got such a mother-fucking American accent that I don't want to draw attention to myself while I'm here."

His wife smiled as she sipped tea. Jorja asked her if she was staying in the hotel.

"She doesn't speak English. She's from this region so we're staying with Neelum's parents. I've brought her here to rest. She's just miscarried and I want her to have a rest with her family."

Jorja leaned forward toward Neelum as the waiter brought more food and tea. "I'm sorry to hear that. Was it your first child?"

"She doesn't speak English. Yes, it was our first child. We've been trying to have a baby for ages. We'll keep trying though. She had the best doctors in America and now she'll have the best rest, away from the pollution and noise of Washington, D.C. That's where we're from. It's better here because the air is clean and pure."

Neelum wore a red embroidered shalwar kameez with a contrasting dupatta that draped neatly around her beautiful face. She looked considerably younger than her husband, but her large brown eyes were sunken into darkened baggy folds, making her look even more doleful. Whenever Jorja looked at her, she smiled demurely.

"I like your shalwar kameez. It has unusual embroidery; very detailed," said Jorja. Mohammad's wife had not eaten much of her rice. She preferred to sip tea and water.

"She made it herself. She's very clever like that. She makes most of her clothes. She cooks well, too. She's a wonderful wife. But she doesn't like America much. We come back to Pakistan and Kashmir as often as possible. I was born in Lahore. I worry now about how the Pakistanis feel about mother-fucking Americans. I'm really all-American now, but I try not to be American when I'm here in Pakistan. I don't want to be kidnapped like Daniel Pearl." He spoke between gulps of rice and chicken korma that he pushed down his gullet with a spoon as if to assist its long journey down his excessively thin frame.

"Are you a journalist in Washington then?"

"I work in Washington. I have a business in Pakistan. It's a clothing business. Making Scottish clothes, you know, like kilts and stuff."

"Kilts? There's a demand for them here?"

He laughed. "There's no demand here. The demand is global. Big mother-fucking business. No shit. But I'm scared. Mother-fucking scared. I was in Washington on 9/11 and had just passed the Pentagon when the fucking thing blew apart. I didn't know at first that a plane had dived into it. Fuck, it was some scene, man. We arrived here last night. Yesterday, I was in Islamabad when the mother-fucking church bomb went off. Two streets away from the Protestant church, I was. My friends were in that hellhole. I'm mother-fucking scared, man. Take a look at this." He pulled a leather wallet from the pocket of his kameez that had previously added depth to his left breast. He slowly extracted a business card. It was conservative white with blue print. Jorja expected it to announce his business venture, but as she looked at it, she felt a sickness in her throat. She was confused at what she saw and looked more closely at the typeset. It read *Wall Street Journal* with its Washington address. Underneath were the words *Daniel S Pearl*. In blue biro, hand-written, was scribbled a telephone number across the spare whiteness of the card.

Her head was spinning with questions. Mohammad noticed her surprise and confusion. "I knew Daniel. I knew him. I mother-fucking knew him. He gave me his card. Be careful. I mother-fucking . . ." The waiter arrived to remove the plates of half-eaten food. It distracted Jorja. Mohammad retrieved the business card and returned it to his wallet. "Must go," he said urgently as he unraveled his tall body to stand erect. "*Calo* Neelum!" She stood obediently and picked up her handbag. He grabbed Jorja's hand, strongly shaking it. "It's been nice to have met you. We have to be going now. Perhaps we'll have lunch some time. Be careful. Be very careful here and trust no one." He swiftly led his wife through the restaurant and out of the hotel.

His departure was sudden, leaving Jorja no time to question his connection to Daniel Pearl. It was a mystery to her and it left her feeling decidedly uncomfortable.

Daniel Pearl was a Wall Street journalist kidnapped in January while in Karachi. The kidnappers, calling themselves The National Movement for the Restoration of Pakistani Sovereignty, initially claimed that Pearl was a CIA agent—from America's Central Intelligence Agency. Later they claimed that he was working for Mossad, the Israeli intelligence agency.

Members of the Movement demanded the release of all Pakistanis held by the United States because of the war on terrorism. Other demands included more access to lawyers for Pakistanis taken into custody in America since 9/11; the release of Abdul Salam Zaeef, former Taliban ambassador to Pakistan; and the transfer to Pakistan of American-built F-16s held up after Islamabad's May 1998 nuclear tests. The Movement also warned American journalists in Pakistan to leave the country within three days or they'd be targeted. Pearl's wife, a French citizen and journalist, was pregnant with the couple's first child. She said a pregnancy-related illness prevented her from joining her husband, as she usually did, at the interview he was attending the night he had been kidnapped.

In February, the Pakistan interior minister announced there had been an arrest in connection with Pearl. The police identified the suspect as Sheikh Mubarik Ali Gilani, the head of a fundamentalist Islamic group Pearl had intended to interview. Pearl was on his way to see Gilani, the leader of the Jamaat ul-Fuqra group, when he was taken. Pearl wanted to ask Gilani about contacts his group supposedly had with Richard Reid, the accused "shoe bomber" in the United States, and the al-Qaeda terrorist network. Khalid Khwaja, who described himself as a friend of the sheikh, told CNN that he had no arrangements with Pearl. He said Pearl's kidnappers had nothing to do with Jammat ul-Fuqra. In addition, Khwaja denied that ul-Fuqra had anything to do with Reid.

In the third week of February, CNN confirmed the slaying of Daniel Pearl by his abductors. The Federal Bureau of Investigation—the

FBI—and Pakistani officials said they had received videotape containing "indisputable" confirmation that the thirty-eight-year-old journalist had been killed. The American government condemned the murder as "an outrage." The *Wall Street Journal* called it "an act of barbarianism."

Leaving the restaurant, Jorja saw Pervaiz and Qaseem. Mentioning Mohammad to them, they nodded in acknowledgement.

"He comes here sometimes. His wife's family lives in Muzaffarabad. Don't worry about him," said Pervaiz.

"He is, he is, how do you say it?" Qaseem struggled with the English language.

Simultaneously, Jorja said "exaggerator" and Pervaiz said "liar."

Qaseem laughed at them. "No, no. Those words are not what I am thinking. Mohammad says words that might be true, but might not be true." Qaseem paused. "I remember the word now. It is show-off. Yes, that's the word. Show-off."

CHAPTER 28

DO NOT WORRY

The week depressed and frustrated Jorja. Jamshid and Wasim couldn't make a decision between them and aggravatingly told Jorja to "Just wait" and "Do not worry."

Fortunately, the minister was busy with other matters. This meant that he applied no pressure on Jorja to stay longer in Kashmir. She had made it absolutely clear to Jamshid that she wanted to go home after the teachers' manual and workshops were completed. Lufti and Mahmud comforted Jorja as they discussed the possibility of her extended stay. Both were of the opinion that the decision should be Jorja's, and it was unreasonable for anyone to exert their influence.

When she was alone in the curriculum office's workroom, Raja entered. "Lufti has told me you might be staying longer. Five months longer, he said. Would that be so, Miss Jorja?"

"It's a difficult decision for me to make. The minister would like me to provide training to managers and teachers although I'd prefer to go home after this assignment. It's not that I don't want to be in Kashmir, you understand, but I have other things to consider."

"Such as your man friend?"

She was embarrassed. "Yes."

"There is no hesitation to be made. You must be with your loved one. A relationship is more important than work. I would like you to stay in Kashmir, but being with a loved one is very, very important."

"Well, it's not like we've been in a long relationship, but. . ."

"But, it will never be a long relationship if you spend a long time in Kashmir. That is what you are thinking, yes?"

"You are so right. You know me well now, so well that. . ."

"I finish your sentences." They both smiled. Lufti entered the room and Raja departed, saying, "I will pray for you, Miss Jorja."

"What was that about?" Lufti asked as he wiped his glasses.

"We were just talking about my possible extended stay, that's all."

"And what did our friend Raja recommend?" Lufti always sat opposite Jorja, facing the door. Mahmud usually sat next to her, but he was meeting with the science specialist.

"Raja said that I should go home. He said ...oh it doesn't matter."

"You want to say something?"

"Lufti, I have a friend at home. We aren't really in a relation-ship, but . . ."

"Ah, say no more. Your decision is made."

She looked at him and he nodded. "But the minister . . ."

"The minister is not the one to decide," he said firmly. "I came to say that Fadil is ready. Kurshid will drive Mahmud home. *Calo*!"

Jamshid, the mediator and messenger, telephoned Jorja. He had been in contact with the minister and Wasim. They had debated the advantages and disadvantages of her extension.

Emotions were the key to Jamshid's argument, emotions that focused on guilt.

Jorja voiced her exasperation. "I can't stay anyway, Jamshid, even if I wanted to. My visa will run out soon and, I suppose, so will the No Objection Certificate into Kashmir."

"That can easily be fixed, Jorja. Do not worry. We can arrange to extend the visa when you next come to Islamabad. It'll only take two days. Let's not argue anymore now. Just wait and everything will turn out fine."

"Sure, Jamshid! Oh, by the way, can you please call the Decent Lodge and arrange to pick up the clothes I left in the wardrobe? I was in such a rush that I completely forgot them."

"Do not worry, Jorja. I will see to it."

To ease her stress, she wrote an e-mail to Denny.

Dennis, honey!

No one has made a firm decision yet on my extended stay. Clearly, Jamshid and Wasim want to please the minister. The minister himself has been unusually quiet and I haven't seen him at all this week. Of course, it makes sense to continue and wrap up the project. Teacher training would complete the project and it'll then have met all of its objectives. I can understand that. It makes sense for me to stay on because of the difficulty in finding another consultant, but I miss you terribly and want to come home.

It's difficult to convince Jamshid and Wasim. They can't understand the reasoning behind my urge to go home. Lufti, Mahmud, and the curriculum guys are definitely on my side and can't see why Jamshid is pressuring me so much. They understand my reasoning without me having to explain it. That's the strangeness of it all and I'm in the middle.

Hey, I haven't heard from you—it's been days. I know you're busy, but I really need a few words from you— even one sentence would be wonderful!

Jorja

"There's an e-mail from your man friend?" Lufti asked. Mahmud would never consider asking such a question.

"No, not yet. I was just writing one to him. Jamshid and I are still arguing. Have you seen the minister this week?"

"He's been busy. The education minister is here having talks with him."

"What do you mean? He *is* the education minister."

"He's the minister of education for Kashmir only. Pakistan's minister of education is here. Have you met her yet?" Jorja shook her head. "The Kashmiri minister has autonomy, but many resources are shared with Pakistan. They're probably talking about revisions to the curriculum and the upcoming workshops in Karachi. I think Rima should attend. I don't think he has the budget to send people all the way to Karachi for a week at a time, but at least Rima should go."

"I'm not that interested in his worries. I have enough of my own. I was just wondering why he hasn't been annoying me. Jamshid said the minister rings him daily."

"Good for you. Let Jamshid handle it. Don't worry for now. The weekend is here so enjoy it while you can."

"If I let Jamshid handle it, he'll cock it up for sure."

Lufti laughed. "Cock it up! I haven't heard that expression before. I take that to mean he'll make a mess of things. Well, that you can count on! I'm off for my walk. Go home early. I'll get Fadil for you."

The telephone rang and Lufti answered it, spoke for a few minutes, and then hung up. "That was Jamshid. He wanted me to pass on a message to you. Your clothes weren't in the wardrobe at the Decent Lodge. The hotel cleaner didn't find any clothes."

With her eyes raised to heaven, Jorja said "What twat! I left them in the wardrobe. I hardly have any clothes, Lufti. Oh well, no point telling you."

"Jorja, you're in the wars today. I'll arrange for Rima to help you buy some clothes from the market. Jamshid has arranged your pay, I hope." When she nodded, he said, "Now, go home."

"Yes, soon, I need a stapler. I think Gadi has one in his drawer. Where's Gadi?"

Lufti answered, "He can't be far, but you can get it from his drawer."

Jorja opened the wooden drawer and rummaged around. Her hand slid deep into the rear and felt the coldness of metal. She pulled out the object and dropped it on the desk, screaming. "Lufti, what's this? What's this?" It was a kerambit—a hooked knife—the exact likeness of the one carried by the Talib next door. The Damascan steel glinted as the knife came to rest.

Lufti laughed. "Don't worry about that. Everyone has one. You can buy one at the bazaar. Surely, you've seen one before?"

"I *have* seen one before, but not at the bazaar. I saw a Talib with one."

"Ah, here we go again with your lies and nonsense. You do have a wonderful imagination, Jorja. You see Imran, you see Talibs, and you see Talibs with knives. What will it be next? Put the knife back in the drawer." Jorja obeyed Lufti and watched him leave the room.

Fadil was pleased to leave work early. Gadi wasn't available to help him reverse out of the driveway so Lufti obliged. It was policy that someone assist the drivers to ensure that they negotiated the precipice safely.

She mentioned the hazard to Fadil and asked his opinion. He merely laughed and said, "The precipice isn't going to get any wider, Madam Jorja. Do not worry."

CHAPTER 29

PAKISTAN DAY

A tremendous boom tore Jorja from her semi-conscious sleep. Morning prayers, chanted in Arabic, usually woke her in the morning. At half past five on Saturday the twenty-third of March, she woke to the sound of a deafening explosion. As her feet touched the floor, another thunderous boom shook the room, rocking it with each explosion.

The balcony was always the first place she went in the event of strange noises. She looked toward the mosque and the army camp. In the grounds of the army barracks, a distinct red glow appeared as another boom sounded. The gunfire emanated from the large, black-metal cannon, partially shrouded by bushes. Another boom and another resounded from its circular mouth. It was a mystery to her as the explosions continued.

She telephoned reception, her other source of information.
"Pakistan Day, madam. Do not worry. It is just Pakistan Day."

Awoken to a twenty-one-gun salute, Jorja experienced Pakistan Day for the first time, celebrating the founding father of Pakistan, Mr. Muhammad Ali Jinnah. It was a public holiday as Pakistanis rejoiced in their freedom from India. The whole of Pakistan was free, except Azad Kashmir. During lunch, hotel staff educated Jorja on the meaning of their national day.

In the time of pre-partition India, before 1947, Jinnah, a brilliant lawyer, rose to the forefront of the struggle for a Muslim nation as India negotiated its independence from Britain. He was Muslim and proud of his ancestral heritage. He had a dream. The dream was a simple one: that Hindus and Muslims had a right to two separate nations within the subcontinent and were entitled to self-determination. The dream, steeped in ideologies and political rhetoric, gained many enemies at Jinnah's insistence of a separate Muslim state. The last viceroy of India under British rule, Lord Mountbatten, referred to him as a "lunatic," an "evil genius," and a "bastard."

Early in his political career, Jinnah was chiefly concerned with achieving independence for a unified India. Increasingly, however, he worried that British oppression would be replaced by Hindu oppression and continued subjugation of India's Muslim minority. In 1919, Jinnah turned his focus to Muslim interests. Over the next two decades, he became determined to continue the vocal ideas of Muslim poet-philosopher Muhammad Iqbal that Indian Muslims would someday have their own nation.

Iqbal, in his famous Allahabad address in 1930, began the dream. Jinnah made it a reality. By the late thirties, Jinnah, who had become leader of the Muslim League, convinced that a partition of India along religious lines was the only way to preserve Muslim political power, continued Iqbal's dream. The demand for a separate nation for Muslims was primarily the result of religious nationalism, not of racial, linguistic, or territorial nationalism. In 1940, the Muslim League adopted the Lahore Resolution calling for separate autonomous states in majority-Muslim areas of northeastern and eastern India.

Iqbal's dream of a Muslim nationhood was at the macro level. Jinnah's expression of Iqbal's dream was at the micro level. Iqbal's visions were ideological; Jinnah's were grounded in realities. Iqbal provided the intellectual justification while Jinnah provided the political and territorial justification. The two addresses complemented each other and together they presented a composite and integrated concept of Muslim Nationhood that constituted the cornerstone of the Pakistani demand.

Even so, the micro approach brought the concept within the realms of ordinary people. It helped establish emotional rapport between them and Jinnah's leadership. This enabled the Muslim League, despite all odds, to sweep the polls in the 1945-46 general elections, taking seventy-five percent of the popular vote and eighty-five percent of Muslim seats. Jinnah's approach had helped to make Muslim Nationhood a political reality that was difficult to ignore in any future constitutional settlement of the Indian problem.

Jinnah had listed five factors warranting the recognition of a Muslim Nationhood and the establishment of a Muslim state. In an address to the nation, he elucidated some of these factors, saying that Hindus and Muslims belonged to two different religious philosophies, social customs, and civilizations based mainly on conflicting ideas and conceptions. They had different heroes, he said. Very often, the hero of one was a foe of the other and, likewise, their victories and defeats overlapped.

Jinnah's ideal concept of Pakistan was a call for an indivisible Pakistani Nationhood. All inhabitants, of all races, colors, or religions were to be fully-fledged citizens with equal rights, equal privileges, and equal obligations. While this seemed to oppose his views of Muslim Nationhood, he argued that the notion of full citizenship for all, for Muslims and non-Muslims, was in harmony with the Islamic pluralist tradition.

In 1946, violence between Hindus and Muslims broke out after Jinnah called for demonstrations opposing an interim Indian government in which Muslim power would be compromised. In the first weeks, the uprising had caused more than three thousand deaths. Against the rising tide of ethnic unrest, Jinnah demanded partition of India. Britain, eager to make a clean break with India, finally relented and Pakistan was born.

Jinnah, however, did not live to see the development of his fledging country. He died of tuberculosis just thirteen months after the formation of Pakistan. Some said that tuberculosis was a slum disease and that officials recorded his death as heart failure. Nevertheless, people agreed that Mohammad Ali Jinnah had significantly altered the course of history, modified the map of the world, and created a nation-state. To Pakistanis, Jinnah was revered, and became known as *Quaid-e-Azam*—Great Leader. He was their Washington, their de Gaulle, and their Churchill.

Islam came to provide the overarching set of values that constituted the ideologies of Pakistan, the source of public morality, social philosophy, and ethos. For Pakistan, the Objectives Resolution in 1949, an integral part of the Constitution, ensured these ideologies. The Objectives Resolution recognized, not the followers of a particular faith, but the people irrespective of their faith. Mian Iftikharuddin, the foremost spokesman of the Left during Pakistan's formative years from 1947 to 1958 described the concept of Islamic Democracy saying no one need object to the word "Islamic" because the words "Roman Law" and "British Parliamentary System" and so many other terms were used without shame. However, he believed that there had to be an Islamic Constitution. He publicly stated that, had Pakistan given the world a proper Islamic Constitution, a fine ideology, and a new way of achieving real democracy, it would have performed a great task.

Jorja posed the question to Sajid, a part-time student of politics, "Do you think Pakistan is an Islamic democracy now?"

"Ah, that dream has yet to be realized. Democracy in Pakistan is a difficult thing. The wealthy people of Pakistan have kept the poor people poor. They have prevented the formation of a strong middle class that is essential to a democratic order. Isn't that so, madam?"

"Well, I've certainly noticed the big divide between rich and poor in Pakistan. There are many rich people in Pakistan and there are many poor people, but there's a very small proportion of the middle class. In Australia, we have small proportions of rich and poor, and a very large middle class. The middle class keeps the country going. And yes, we are a democracy, so you may be right, Sajid."

He smiled and Qaseem nodded. Sajid continued, "Any alternative would bring disorder and anarchy because the rich would certainly protest in large numbers. Any change in the class structure of the political and bureaucratic order is unthinkable. No government in Pakistan can function without the approval and help of the upper class, and no one has the strength and the political will to cast them aside. It seems that the class that made the creation of Pakistan possible in the first place has been jealously, and so far successfully, guarding its status to the detriment of true democracy."

It seemed that Sajid was right.

CHAPTER 30

MELODY QUEEN

Lufti and Mahmud had surrendered to their frustrations with the internet. Jorja had all but given up the temperamental connection at the project office just as Sajid came to her technological and emotional rescue.

"There's an internet club near the hotel, madam," he explained when Jorja told him of her communication troubles. "I will walk you there when I finish my duties. Meet me at the reception desk in one hour."

Sajid was punctual and delighted to accompany her a hundred meters to the Internet Café—a misnomer since food and beverages were not available. It was more of a confinement, a shoddy square space, where, in all impossibility, the internet remained incredibly more reliable than in any other place in Kashmir.

Jorja entered a glass door and took one step to the counter. Sajid explained to the manager that she wished to use a computer and negotiated a local fee for her. Sajid assured Jorja the manager was a caring man. Harish escorted her to one of four computers in a sardine-tin-sized cubicle. The internet worked immediately and for this, she was happy. Sajid, pleased that all was well, left the café. Fifteen minutes had elapsed when a pre-pubescent face peered over the cubicle.

"Very sorry, very sorry. My humblest apologies, madam. I thought you were my friend Mohammad. May I ask where you are from and why you are here?" He spoke in clipped, rounded English.

"I'm from Australia and I'm in the Internet Café because my work office has many problems connecting to the internet. Here it appears to be very reliable."

"Oh yes indeed, madam. It's extremely reliable here. My cousin, who is most skilled in the internet, runs it. He did not learn at college. No, he did not. He learned it by himself. But I did not mean to ask what you are doing in the Internet Café. I meant to ask what you are doing in Muzaffarabad. I have not seen a foreign woman for a long time, madam. I am most surprised."

"Thank you. I'm here as a consultant for the World Bank education project. I'll be here for another month or so."

"Oh, that is a very long time. I think that we should be friends. I will be your friend and you can ask me to do anything for you. You must be staying at the Sangam Hotel. That is the only respectable hotel in Kashmir for women. Foreigners stay there. Am I correct, madam?"

"You are correct."

"I'm always correct. May I sit in the chair next to you?" Jorja agreed and he entered the booth and shook her hand. "My name is Jahmal. Jahmal Arif Malik. I'm very pleased to meet you. May I ask your name?"

"My name is Jorja. Jorja Eloise Himmermann."

He dressed immaculately. Tucked into Lee Cooper blue jeans was a maroon Calvin Klein shirt that looked exceedingly smart and expensive for a place such as Muzaffarabad. His face was marginally fuller than his thin frame. Deep-set eyes appeared under bushy eyebrows and his hair was perfectly trimmed.

"Madam Jorja, do you need some assistance with the internet?" Jorja indicated that she did not need any assistance. "I see that you are e-mailing a letter to a friend. Is it a friend in Australia? Oh, I'm reading some very naughty words. It's to your husband, yes? I will let you finish the e-mail to your husband and I'll be back soon to offer you my assistance. Is that okay, madam Jorja?"

Embarrassed, she nodded and finished her e-mail to Denny.

Jahmal returned and again shook her hand. "You have finished your very secret letter? I introduced myself at a very unfortunate time for you and I apologize. Your husband is a lucky man. You are very beautiful. What's your husband's name?"

"I'm not married. The letter was to a male friend. His name is Denny."

"I cannot believe that an attractive woman like you is not married. I am thinking that you have been married and that your husband is killed."

Jorja wanted to say that a cricket ball to the heart had slain her husband. That would impress most Pakistanis. However, she could not lie. Her husband had, in fact, died while white water rafting in New Zealand. She thought it best not to mention his death. Instead, she lied and said she had no such dead husband, no husband at all.

"Oh, that's a tragedy," Jahmal said. "No husband at all is very bad, but at least you have a man friend. I will call him Mr. D. I'm not married. I'm yet too young to be married, but in any case, I will never be married."

Jorja was intrigued to know the reason, as she thought it was the desired state of all Pakistanis.

"Please madam Jorja; first of all I'm *not* a Pakistani. I'm a Kashmiri. I will never marry because my heart has been captured by a woman I cannot have. I love her very much and there'll never be anyone else for me. I will love her forever. She's my world, my inspiration, my dearest love."

"You are so young to have a girlfriend," she said. He looked twelve.

"I am eighteen and a college boy," he answered, puffing out his sunken chest.

"Why can't you be with your girlfriend? Is she in another country?"

"No, no. She is not. She died three years ago. It was a tragedy for me. It was a tragedy for the whole country. I miss her very much, but I listen to her every day. I will sing one of her songs for you." He erupted into an operatic song with such intensity that Jorja felt quite embarrassed. He was in love with a Pakistani songstress. "Did you like my singing? I'm such a *great* singer. I practice every day singing the Melody Queen's songs. Have you heard of Noor Jehan, the Melody Queen?"

Jorja shook her head.

"She is the most exquisite singer and actress. Maybe you have seen her in movies? In old movies, you must have seen her. You could not miss her most beautiful face. I will show you a picture of her."

Expecting Jahmal to fetch a picture from his pocket, he took the mouse and clicked several times until the website of Noor Jehan appeared. She was a puffy-faced, elderly woman overladen with colorful make-up.

"She is old!" Jorja said surprised.

"She died at the age of eighty. Age is nothing to me. I love her for her beauty and for her most melodious voice. She had the voice of an angel."

"How old are you again?"

"I'm a college boy and I'm eighteen years old. I'll be going to university in England after my exams. I know I look very skinny and very young. Everyone thinks I'm younger than my real age. I will get muscles one day and look manly. I know in my heart that Noor Jehan loved me. We never met, but she liked singers and I'm an excellent singer. I won a competition. I'll be a singer too one day, like Noor Jehan. Let me educate you on Pakistan's most famous singer."

This he did with the passionate dedication and knowledge of an ardent fan. "She was a child prodigy," he said. "Do you know what a child prodigy is?" Jorja said she did. "She was unique. At five, she could reproduce the style of most leading singers of the subcontinent. At the age of five, I tell you. She began her singing career at the age of seven. Her name was Baby Noor Jehan. She became Madam Noor Jehan and earned the title of Melody Queen. She was Pakistan's most popular personality. At ten, she was singing *Bas bas wey dholna.* It was a big hit. At fourteen, she made a movie called *Khandan.* It was long ago in 1942. She fell in love with the director, Syed Shaukat Hussain Rizvi, a handsome man from Calcutta. Their love was full of passion and very, very full of hate. They had three children and they were always fighting. It was in the newspapers all the time. It was a, how do you say, a tumatous marriage."

"Tumultuous," she corrected. His animation and enthusiasm made her smile.

"It was that. They eventually made peace with each other. She was not a tall person. In movies, sometimes they raised her on bricks so that she would look taller. She was very, very good-looking with an irresistible charm. The Westerners would call her sexy. I thought she was sexy."

It seemed odd to Jorja that an eighteen-year-old Muslim boy would use that word.

"I think that you have seen her because she did Indian movies in Bollywood. Have you heard of Bollywood? I think you have." Jorja moved her head in acknowledgment. "She made movies in Pakistan too. She was the first woman director of films in Pakistan. That was with *Chan We* in 1951. She did not stop singing. Do you believe me when I say that she practiced singing sometimes for up to twelve hours a day? This is true. She divorced her first husband, but she could divorce because she was famous and that is what famous actresses did. She married again to Ejaz Durrani and had three more children. She loved children. But Ejaz did not want Madam Noor Jehan to continue acting so he demanded that she stop. He did not want her on the screen and she did what her husband said. She was a good wife. He allowed her to keep singing but not acting, and she sang for all of her life. Sometimes she recorded five or six songs a day. She had the energy of a young person. Nobody knows the exact number of songs she recorded in her lifetime. It is very, very many. Some people say it is more than ten thousand. The Ministry of Culture must find out how many and keep all the recordings in a safe place for history. That is the wish of the people of Pakistan. The Melody Queen is a gift from Allah. I will love her forever."

"I'm sure that when you're ready to marry, you'll meet a nice girl of your age," Jorja assured him.

"Do not tease me, madam Jorja. Age is nothing to me. A girl of my age will never be as beautiful or as talented as my first love, my only love. Age is nothing to Kashmiri men and to Pakistani men. The father of Pakistan, Mr. Jinnah, believed that too. His true love was older than he was by fifteen years. He married his true love and she was a loyal wife. Age is no barrier to love. Do you know of Mr. Jinnah?"

"Yes, I read about Mr. Jinnah in *Dawn* on Pakistan Day. There was some very interesting information about him. The newspaper made no reference to his wife though."

"Oh, yes, it was a famous love affair. In Pakistan, it's not unusual for a man to love an older woman and his parents can arrange a marriage if his prospects are good and he is a worthy man. Women usually marry young, but sometimes a husband dies, and then she can take another husband. The husband can be any age of course. This is allowed. It's not a bad thing to marry again as Catholics believe. Islam is a fair religion to everyone, especially women with dead husbands. In the West, I think the women like older men?"

"Usually, yes."

"How old is Mr. D? How old are you?"

"He's younger than me."

"Oh, that is good. You are a wise woman. But you didn't answer me when I asked your age."

"Guess."

"I think to myself that you are twenty-five or thirty. It's good for an older woman like you to have a younger man because you look young. A younger man will keep you happy." He looked at her watch. "Oh, is that the time? I must go. Are you staying here or may I walk you back to the hotel? You must not walk alone. Is your driver picking you up? You have a driver, yes?"

"I have a driver although it's his day off today. A man from the hotel walked me here. I can walk back on my own. It's not far."

Jahmal admonished her for thinking of walking alone. "I must walk you back. It's dangerous to walk on your own. I would stay with you in the Internet Café, but I must study for my exams. I'll arrange to meet you again here. We are friends now, yes?" They probably were. Jahmal escorted her to the hotel, only a hundred meters along the dusty road.

The earth moved for the second time in the International Year of the Mountain, occurring three weeks after the earthquake of the third of March. The recent quake registered six on the Richter scale. Again, it hit the Hindu Kush range in Afghanistan, resulting in many casualties. Again, the Sangam Hotel remained stable.

CHAPTER 31

THE INTERNET CAFÉ

The manager afforded Jorja preferential treatment at the Internet Café. Jorja went every day. Whenever she arrived, the manager ordered someone out of a cubicle to accommodate her. It was a seedy-looking place, but the computers were clean and the cafe was most probably the only place in Azad Kashmir, and all of Pakistan, where smoking was prohibited.

Mostly Jorja was engrossed in sending e-mails, but sometimes she would hear sniggers and laughter as young boys congregated in a booth to drool over pornographic websites. Once she heard the slapping of a hand on a prepubescent penis until its owner fell from the chair and landed sprawled in the cramped cubicle. She giggled quietly to herself at the mental image of his antics. The manager, Harish, disciplined the boys by separating them or expelling them from the premises. Their childish pranks were harmless and never created any conflict, and they always obeyed Harish as if he were their father.

Young boys embraced each other, often holding hands and displaying physical affection. Lufti and Jorja discussed this one afternoon when she commented that most Western men, especially Australians, were averse to physical contact with other men in public.

"Young men hold hands with each other, but not with young girls. Young girls hold hands with each other, but not with young boys. That's the way it is in Pakistan. That's friendship and we do not have a problem with people of the same gender holding hands. It is very normal and natural. Homosexuality, on the other hand, is against the law in Pakistan and the penalties are harsh, often with long jail terms and public whippings. It's also against Muslim beliefs and families deal with it severely. It's not common here in Pakistan. I don't know the numbers, but I'm sure it would be low. Besides, how do you count them? Homosexuality is not a threat here, at least not in relation to AIDS. Most reported cases of AIDS transmission in Pakistan are amongst heterosexuals or from contaminated blood."

"Really?"

"Oh yes. The first reported HIV positive case was in Lahore in 1987 and since then it has increased, but mostly in men who have lived or traveled abroad. Some of these men infected their wives, who, in a small number of cases, passed the infection to their children. During the Nineties people with HIV or AIDS were sex workers, injecting drug users, long-route truck drivers, and prison inmates. This year, there were about two thousand reported cases, although the World Health Organization estimates the number to be more like seventy thousand, which is still only one percent of the adult population. I don't think it's that high although I don't really know these things. I just know what I read."

"But do Pakistanis know about HIV and AIDS and that it can be transmitted by unsafe sex? Do they talk about it? Are there any education programs about it?"

"Despite the low literacy rate, awareness levels of HIV and AIDS are gradually increasing, although often misguided. In an AIDS awareness campaign on television last year, the overall awareness level for both rural and urban people was seventy-seven percent. That means they know it's a dangerous disease with no cure, but most people think they won't contract it.Condom use for disease prevention is very low."

"Is there open commercial sex here in Pakistan? Do the sex workers use condoms?"

"You ask me like I'm an expert on this." He laughed. "Commercial sex may be widespread in major cities, particularly in Karachi and Lahore. I read that there are sixty-two thousand female sex workers in Karachi and twenty-six thousand in Lahore. The number of male sex workers in Lahore alone is around a hundred and eighty-eight thousand and, by all reports, very few use condoms. Some men have sex with *chavas*—college boys."

"But Lufti, you just said—oh, never mind." Her voice trailed away as Lufti hurried toward Mahmud.

When Jorja met Jahmal at the Internet Cafe, she couldn't help thinking of Lufti's comment about college boys.

"Madam Jorja, I hope you don't mind me asking, but can you please tell me the meaning of some naughty words?" Jahmal asked. His big brown eyes blinked innocently.

"Naughty words, what naughty words?"

"Well, I noticed that you were writing to your man friend Mr. D about sex words. I know what they mean. I know what cock is and . . ."

"Okay, okay, I get your drift. What's your point, young man?" she said, trying to deter him from the topic.

"What is it when two girls like each other very much?"

"Friendship," Jorja said tersely.

"Madam Jorja, you tease me. I'm most anxious to be educated in the way of sex, love, and relationships. Soon I'll be a man and I need to know these things."

"You said you weren't going to have a relationship with anyone because you loved only the Melody Queen."

"But madam Jorja, when I go to England I will not know what to do when a girl asks me to sex her." He looked seriously concerned about this. "If a girl asks to be sexed then I must sex her. Girls are so forward in England and I will not know what to do."

"Jahmal, firstly, it is highly unlikely that a girl will ask you for sex, and if one did, it doesn't mean that you have to do it. Likewise, if you want it and a girl says no, then you must respect that. Besides, if you're Muslim you're expected to wait until you're married, aren't you?"

"Yes, madam Jorja, you are right. It's not permissible to have sex with girlfriends before marriage. I think it might be okay to sex an English girl, but only if she asks me to sex her." His frown was extreme and he became quite agitated. Jahmal seemed to turn life into a trial, wallowing in insecurities, doubts, and fear of the unknown.

"Jahmal, I'm sure that you won't have to worry about it for a long time. You'll be going to England to study. You must study hard because your parents will be paying a lot of money for you to attend university. You won't have time to chase young girls."

"I would be most respectful of English girls. I am very, very respectful of all women. It's just that I'm an Aquarian and I'm sensitive to these things because I want to do the right thing. What star sign are you?" His bushy eyebrows lifted in a high arch to express curiosity.

"I'm a Leo. I'm surprised that you know of astrology. I thought your destiny was Allah's will?"

"Astrology is *not* destiny, madam Jorja," he said emphatically. "Nothing happens by itself. Allah made the stars, so astrology is almost the will of Allah anyway. Allah leads us to our decisions and our destiny: astrology only chooses the timing. There is a right time for everything. Isn't that so, madam Jorja?"

"Ah yes, timing, Jahmal. That's the very philosophy you should apply in England when you're there. There is a right time for everything. There's a time to study and a time to chase girls."

He was genuinely relieved and his frown disappeared. It was as if the world was suddenly a less complex place. "Ancient spiritual wisdom teaches us to rise above our problems," he said. "Yes, I must do as I believe. You are so right, madam Jorja."

Jorja played along with his newfound excitement. "We're encouraged to emulate the lotus flower that blooms most beautifully above the muddy water even though its roots are embedded in the mire. We too should blossom and go beyond our earthly concerns even though we may never fully free ourselves from them," she said, smothering a smile.

"Oh madam Jorja, you're so wise," Jahmal said in wide-eyed wonder. At this point, she broke into a long laugh. "You laugh loud, madam. I see that you are teasing me again. I like you very much." He joined in the laughter. "Come, I will show you something on the internet."

As he grabbed the mouse and began clicking, Jorja said, "It's not pornography, is it?"

"Oh no, madam Jorja. I could show you some sex sites if you wish," he said helpfully.

"No, no. What do you want to show me?"

"Here it is. I've found a very funny webpage on astrology. This page is about Leos like you. It says that Leos don't carry grudges because they prefer to party all the time. It says that Leo's talk very loud."

"I *don't* talk very loud," she defended herself.

"Madam Jorja, you may not talk very loud, but you laugh loud." They giggled together as he read more. "It is written that the Leo's search for romance can be very expensive and very unsatisfying. It says marriage for the Leo is like playing Russian roulette with a slight twist. I don't know what that means." He clicked onto the Aquarius webpage. "Oh, it says Aquarians have an opinion about everything. Of course we do, and I think that is a good thing. It says Aquarians often drink like a fish. That is silly because I do not drink much, and I don't drink alcohol. Lovemaking is simply another way of making new friends and inquisitive Aquarians may be interested in pornography, it says.

They are also absent-minded, interested only in themselves, and lack confidence."

"And so, Jahmal, is that really you?"

He looked shocked. "Madam Jorja, I do not have girlfriends so I do not do lovemaking. I think I'm not very confident so the webpage is correct, don't you think madam Jorja? And pornography? Well, because we're friends, I can tell you the truth. I like looking at pornography on the internet." He smiled sheepishly at her.

"Really!" she smiled.

"Yes, really. But, you know madam Jorja, all the boys like pornography and they aren't all Aquarians! What star sign is Mr. D?"

"Aquarius," she said, looking at Jahmal. She could see his eyes light up.

"Really?"

"Really! Tell me, Jahmal, do you think Osama bin Laden is here in Kashmir?"

"Oh yes, of course, madam. He is hiding here, but the Americans will not find him. They think he is hiding in Peshawar or in Afghanistan."

"How do you know he's here?" Jorja looked into his boyish face.

"Everyone knows this. There are many Talibs here so Osama must be here too because the Talibs are his protectors. The Taliban are hiding here because there are many caves in the mountains. Western people would get lost and die due to lack of food, or because of the cold. They do not know where to look for Mr. bin Laden."

"Would you know where to look for Osama?"

"No, not yet, but it would not take me long to ask someone and find out. I am an intelligent boy, yes I am, and I could easily learn of his whereabouts. I know what he looks like too. Everyone knows what he looks like."

"Why don't you find him, tell the authorities, and get a big reward?"

"I do not want to die, madam Jorja. Whoever finds Osama bin Laden will die by his hand, or by the hand of his allies. He has many allies, madam. He has an army of men who will fight for him, fight to get him back if someone took him, and fight to kill those who betray him. I tell you this, madam, he has a very big, very fierce, very gun-happy army. They would love to shoot and kill foreigners, especially Americans. I tell you this, because I know this."

"What if I wanted to look for him to collect the reward? What would you say then?"

"I would say that you are teasing me again. I would be right, madam Jorja, wouldn't I? You would be teasing me?"

"Yes, I would be teasing you."

"I knew this."

Jahmal offered to walk her back to the hotel. They stood at the side of the dusty road, the hotel in view, waiting for the traffic to pass. A group of teenage boys gathered nearby, and seeing Jahmal, called out in Urdu. They laughed and made suggestive hand signals.

"Do you know them, Jahmal?" Jorja asked as they hurriedly crossed the street.

"They are boys from my college. Big fuckers they are. Do not be friends with them. They are just big fuckers." Surprised at his language, she asked what he meant, in case she had heard incorrectly or had misconstrued him. "They sex girls. They are not nice boys. They are not good Muslims. All of them sex girls. They are big fuckers. Because I am with you, they are teasing me. They are jealous. They think I'm sexing you."

"Well, just tell them that you are," she joked.

He put a hand to his open mouth. "Oh madam Jorja!" When he saw her large smile, he said, "Oh madam Jorja, you're teasing me again." They both shrieked with laughter.

After seeing Jorja safely into the hotel, Jahmal swaggered off toward the big fuckers.

CHAPTER 32

THE THRILL OF THE TAILOR'S TAPE

Jorja needed new clothes. She lost a dupatta on the road to Muzaffarabad and tore the sleeves of her dress in the car accident—and that was her first day. She had since ripped a dress on a chair and snagged a long-sleeved sweater on the ragged plastered walls. A pair of socks was threadbare at the heels, and the lace on a pair of knickers had frayed. And she had left a pile of clothes in the Decent Lodge in Islamabad. Now her wardrobe consisted of one pair of trousers and a long black skirt.

Rima accompanied Jorja to a cluster of dress stalls opposite the Combined Military Hospital. The assistant director of curriculum held her elbow and whispered. "We will get you

163

Pakistani clothes, but first we must get you a proper brassiere." She placed a large hand over Jorja's left breast and said, "Your brassiere is too thin."

In a cramped store, cluttered with cardboard packets of brassieres and underwear, a full-bodied woman with a cheery smile asked Jorja for her bra size. The shopkeeper displayed a range of floral well-padded brassieres.

"Goodness me," gasped Jorja, "they are thick aren't they?" Both women smiled approvingly. "Aren't there any lacy ones?"

"Of course there are, but they are very expensive and are for married women who can afford them. You need decent underwear," said Rima.

Jorja bought two pairs of "decent" brassieres with matching "decent" underpants. Rima urged her into a curtained cubicle to put on a newly purchased bra before their shopping expedition. Rima then guided Jorja into a dress shop. "Let's look at these Pakistani clothes."

Every shalwar Jorja saw resembled clown's pants with folds of material hanging below the crotch. After some joking, Rima understood. She nodded and took Jorja by the hand, leading her to a material shop. "We'll have a shalwar kameez made for you, then you can ask for pajama pants to be tailor-made. The tailor will make straight Western pajama pants for you. Some modern women in Lahore wear straight pants. I know the style you want."

The manager of the material store, Mr. Hamad, invited the women to sit and take tea while choosing from an infinite selection of fabrics. The counter was almost the length of the store, some eighteen meters long. A golden brown roll of material thudded onto the counter. "Shalwar," Mr. Hamad said. A matching cream roll was next as he called out, "kameez." Lastly, there was a contrasting design, to which he added, "dupatta." He pushed them to one side. He flung a roll of blue material on the counter, a patterned roll, and a contrasting roll. As the three cylinders thudded in front of Jorja, he called out "Shalwar, kameez, dupatta," pointing to the fabric that would be best matched to each garment. He again pushed them aside. Hues of red were next. "Shalwar, kameez, dupatta." Ream after ream of fabric was presented in a flurry of colors, designs, and textures. "Shalwar, kameez, dupatta." Again: "shalwar, kameez, dupatta." All the while, Rima and Jorja sipped their tea, nodding their approval or wrinkling their noses doubtfully. Rima suggested cotton and Mr. Hamad displayed an extensive collection of colors.

They made a selection of fabrics for three suits. Mr. Hamad smiled and indicated that he would take the material upstairs to the tailor. Rima took Jorja by the hand again and led her up a set of stairs into a stream of racks with finished tailor-made suits.

The tailor did not speak a great deal of English, but this did not seem to matter. Jorja merely had to point to a design for the kameez: scalloped neck, round neck, v-neck, rolled neck, collared neck and so on. The dupatta was simply a long strip of material. The difficulty arose with the design of the shalwar. The tailor asked whether Jorja preferred elastic at the waistline or material drawstring ties to secure the pants. She requested elastic. "Good, finished," he said. "Now measure."

"Wait, wait," she said, looking at Rima. "I don't want clown pants, remember."

"Ah yes, yes. No clown pants." Rima laughed. "Pajama pants. I'll tell him." The two women pointed to the straight-legged pants Jorja was wearing, saying "Pajama pants, pajama pants."

"Yes, pajama pants. I make pajama pants. Now measure." The tailor approached Jorja with a long, white tape measure. "Shoulders," he said as he deftly placed the tape across the back of her shoulders. The tape did not touch Jorja's clothing. "Down," he said and he placed the tape from the back of her neck to the desired length of the kameez. The tape did not touch her body. "Arms," he said, measuring her for short-sleeved summer suits. Again, the tape did not touch any part of her body or clothing. The tailor faced her and ordered her to hold her arms beyond her side. "Front," he said as he raised his tape measure to her chest.

Swiftly, he placed the white strip around Jorja's upper body and it skimmed the tip of her chest. As the measuring tape slid across her breasts, it seemed as if the motion had slowed to a surreal sensation. She felt the tape suggestively touch the small mounds held upright with her new excessively-padded bra. It hid her womanly attributes. No curves, no mounds, and no nipples: her breasts were cosseted, bound, and concealed from any man's view. As the tape slithered over her breasts, a pleasant arousing sensation coursed through her entire body: momentarily, of course. Nevertheless, it was enough to feel a rush of exhilaration followed by a warm inner glow of contentment. Jorja silently sighed.

"Pajamas," he declared next.

Jorja looked at Rima as if to ask whether he was about to measure her inside leg. There was no time for pondering as he skillfully held the tape down the outside of her trouser leg.

"Finished," he said, and it was all over in a matter of seconds. All the while, he had been scribbling the measurements on a small white notepad. "One week, madam. Maybe less."

By the time they finished shopping, it was nearly eight o'clock. Fadil had worked overtime and she apologized for this. Brushing the apology aside, he said he had spent the time with a friend who owned a stall nearby. To express her thanks, Jorja bought fabric for Rima and Fadil's wife and they extended their profuse gratitude.

CHAPTER 33

ANOTHER TREMOR

Jorja didn't linger over her evening meal as usual. After eating a small portion of salad and two Kashmiri kebabs, she retired early to her room. Sleep came easily.

At two o'clock in the morning, Jorja was shaken awake. A third tremor had struck the region with a lesser force than the earlier ones, but with a greater degree of devastation. With no power, she hurriedly dressed in the dark. Rushing to the balcony, she looked to see any movement in the city. The moon, the size of a silver dollar, caught her eye. Everything was still. Carrying her slippers, she ran downstairs to reception, and found Qaseem there alone. He pointed to her bare feet with a shudder so she threw the slippers on the floor and pushed her feet into them, saying, "Sorry, sorry."

"You'll be safe here, madam. We are seeing the damage now." Hotel staff, including the manager, shone flashlights around the walls and ceilings. Jorja remained in the lobby with a handful of guests. Ten minutes later Riyad declared everything safe. Only the tarpaulin canopies from some windows on the western side had fallen off and one of the windows had shattered.

Riyad moved a television into the restaurant during breakfast so that guests could watch news of the earthquake. The news was in Urdu, but as the guests departed, Awan switched the channel to the BBC.

The quake measured a moderate 5.2, striking four hundred kilometers northwest of Peshawar in Afghanistan. However, the devastation was immense, killing up to three thousand people and leaving twenty thousand homeless. United Nations helicopters and planes were already in the region searching for landmines and were able to provide immediate assistance. Aerial surveillance by the United Nations a hundred and seventy-five kilometers north of Kabul showed six villages reduced to rubble.

The Afghan interim leader, Mr. Hamid Karzai, declared a national day of mourning. Flags were at half-mast across the country and at the Afghan embassies and consulates around the world.

CHAPTER 34

PURDAH

Jorja's new shalwar kameez caused significant attention. The director of curriculum, Mrs. Tansoor, invited her to morning tea with the two female assistant directors, Rima and Nighat. "Rima has told me of your shopping adventure. Thank you for wearing Pakistani clothes. We truly appreciate it," she said, with an approving nod.

Nighat added, "The purdah means a lot to us. It's a very respectful practice for women to wear the purdah. As you know, purdah is the Muslim custom of concealment; wearing a veil or clothing that covers a woman's body." She had initially kept her dupatta drawn across her lower face, but today her face was fully visible with only her hair covered.

Even though men dressed conservatively in Pakistan revealing neither bare arms nor bare legs, the women's purdah drew the most attention from the Western world. Purdah was the practice of covering the shoulders and hair with a shawl, or the body with an abaya or djellaba, exposing the face. In the extreme, a burqa cloaked the whole body and face with a mesh aperture in front of the eyes. The shawl covering the hair had many local names, such as the dupatta in Pakistan. Jorja ventured to say, "Some people in the West say that purdah is a sign of male chauvinism and that it keeps women submissive and powerless."

Rima laughed while Nighat and the director looked at each other with a smile. "Oh no, no, no! That's not the case. Look at us three. We are senior women in the education department. Is that a sign of submission? No, we are very modern women with modern ideas and we wear the purdah because it honors our religion and also because it's liberating," Rima said, as she nudged Nighat. "That's true, isn't it?"

Nighat nodded emphatically.

"But why do you say it's liberating when you hide your beauty and womanhood?"

Nighat became bolder and answered, "A woman's honor is in her veil. When we wear the purdah, everyone respects us. Men respect us. You will find too that men will respect you more in your new Pakistani clothes." Again, the women nodded. "We are judged as individuals and not judged for our beauty," she said.

Mrs. Tansoor explained, "Miss Jorja, in the West, the women try very hard to be beautiful. They do many things to change the face, yes?" Jorja nodded. "Here, physical beauty is not important. People respect us for our inner beauty and our minds. As you can see, the three of us are extremely intelligent, yes?" Jorja agreed. "By covering ourselves, we are not seen as sex objects that can be dominated. We are honored as women. Our husbands exalt us and always treat us reverently and kindly. We are on a higher level than men are. That's why they look up to us and revere us."

"But," Jorja protested quietly, "some people think that it segregates women from men, that it hides women from society, like being in a jail. It's seen as a burden, as a form of imprisonment." She waited for a reaction.

Rima touched her arm softly, "Miss Jorja. Do we look sad from imprisonment? Does society hide us? No, we are at the peak of society in our culture. We earn money and we can spend it as we wish. Our husbands like this extra money. It's good for our families. My daughter, Melek, is a modern woman learning mathematics at university and she continues to wear the purdah too. Remember her? You met her. It's not just something that older women wear. Women wear it because they want to wear it. We are strong, independent women and we wear the purdah proudly," she said, nodding to verify her statement. "Some women wear more covering, such as the burqa or face veils, but it is their choice or it is the custom of their faith in their own country or region. Some modern women in Lahore and Islamabad do not wear the dupatta over their head, but wear it across their shoulders. They reveal their hair. That is their choice. We are more traditional here in Kashmir." She grinned. "There are Muslim countries that are conservative and traditional, and there are Muslim countries that are moderate and liberal. As you can see, there are many interpretations of the purdah."

"But I've heard that even Muslim women have cosmetic surgery."

"Every woman has the right to interpret beauty in their own way. Inner beauty, outer beauty, god-given or enhanced, it is still the choice of each woman, Miss Jorja."

"The clothes feel comfortable on you, yes?" asked Nighat.

"They are very comfortable," Jorja said as Mahmud and Lufti entered the room to take tea, bringing with them plates of biscuits and samosa.

"Oh yes, Pakistani clothes. Jorja wears Pakistani clothes now," said Lufti. "You must stand up and show us." Jorja stood proudly and twirled twice. "Very beautiful," he said.

Mahmud seemed not to look in her direction, glancing at the ground and around the room. He seemed offended by her bare arms, so Jorja hid them behind her back. It amazed her when he said, "The clothes look very beautiful on your body," in his shy, reserved way. That was an enormous compliment from him and the first sign of reverence. Jorja glanced at the women who nodded and smiled as if to say, "we told you so."

"Straight pants," said Rima, pointing to them and explaining to the men. "Pajama pants. Loose kameez," she pointed to the overskirt. "Comfortable. Looks good, yes? Miss Jorja looks good, yes?"

Jorja pointed to each item as she said, "Shalwar ... kameez ... dupatta. I prefer straight pants, not those pants." She pointed to Rima's clothes.

The women laughed at her straight pants. "She wears Western version of Pakistani clothes. Pajama pants." Rima rearranged Jorja's dupatta, showing her how to wrap it around her head and shoulders.

"Modern version," Lufti defended Jorja. "I see modern women in Lahore wearing straight pants like that. And I see Lahori women wearing modern kameez with short sleeves like Jorja is wearing."

"Very modern, yes," said Nighat. "We can tease her for wearing straight pants and short sleeves. She does not mind. Jorja is very modern. Modern pants and modern sleeves."

"Khan suit," joked Lufti.

"Clown suit? No, mine is modern," Jorja said. "It's not a clown suit. Rima's wearing clown pants. Mine are straight pants, pajama pants."

"No, no, no." Lufti threw his head back in raucous laughter. "Not clown suit. I said Khan suit. Like Imran Khan. You Westerners call the Pakistani clothes Khan suits because Imran wears them and Imran is the only Pakistani most Westerners know."

The laughter continued for some time before Rima composed herself. "No, no. Khan suit is man's words for the clothes. Only men wear a Khan suit. Look at Miss Jorja. Modern colors," she said. "Blue is good, yes?"

"Blue suits you," ventured Mahmud.

Lufti continued to jest. "Did you know that the shalwar kameez came to the subcontinent with the Central Asian invaders? Invaders do bring some good ideas to Pakistan." It was a personal joke.

"Oh yes, the sari was the dress of smart women until quite recently in Pakistan," said Mrs. Tansoor seriously. "We wore the shalwar kameez as work clothes and the sari for formal occasions. In the Eighties, we started to wear the shalwar kameez as party dresses, but with more embroidery and lace."

"Party dresses. Miss Jorja likes party dresses. She wanted to buy all party dresses," Rima teased as she recalled the shopping spree. "In every shop she said, 'I like this one,' but it was a party dress, not a work dress." Everyone laughed again.

Mahmud was suddenly serious. "Lashkar-e-Jabbar, the fighter group, is demanding women in rural Kashmir wear the full burqa outside their homes or they will have acid thrown in their face."

"Most women are ignoring the demands, but they're still covering their heads with a scarf, but not the burqa," said Mrs. Tansoor. "Choice of clothes should be left to the individual."

Rima and Nighat agreed. "Covering their face or wearing a black cloak is no measure of a woman's morality. Our traditional clothes are decent enough," said Rima. "We will resent coercion."

"Throwing acid or defacing anyone is sinful," said Mahmud. "Islam is not a barbaric religion."

CHAPTER 35

NAKED

Rima invited Jorja to her place for dinner because her daughter, Melek, was home from university. Melek prepared a variety of dishes for Jorja to taste. As she poured Kashmiri tea into a fine china teacup, Jorja served herself a thin pancake sprinkled with poppy seeds.

After she cleared away the food, Melek entered the room with a shoebox. "Who taught you to tie your hair that way, madam Jorja?"

"My mother braided my hair when I was young. I learned from her."

"It also looks Kashmiri, but not the color. I like your new Pakistani clothes, but …"

"Did your mother tell you that she helped me buy the material?"

"Yes, but ..." Jorja looked at her. Melek turned to her mother for assistance.

"You're naked, Miss Jorja. That's what Melek wants to say. You're naked."

Jorja looked inquisitively at Melek and she explained. "In Kashmir, women wear jewelry. You do not wear jewelry, only earrings. It looks naked to us. It doesn't look attractive. I'd like you to accept a small gift from me. Please choose some bracelets to match your new clothes." She handed Jorja the shoebox. There were bracelets of all colors neatly sorted into their respective shades tied together with colored ribbon. Loose bracelets lay underneath the rolls of color and she chose a thin red bracelet.

"No, no. Do not choose only one bracelet. Choose one color, but many bracelets. See how I wear many bracelets on my arm. Like this," she said, as she ran her fingers over her bracelets. "Please, they are not expensive. You can buy these anywhere in Kashmir. Please choose a color."

Jorja chose red. Melek handed her a string of blue bracelets and a bolt of green. Jorja looked at Rima for guidance. She nodded and smiled. Rima was wearing two gold bracelets, three gold rings, and three golden necklaces. Her earrings were large golden orbs.

Squeezing her wrist into a swathe of ruby bracelets, they jangled across Jorja's arm. Melek, feeling considerably more confident and at ease with the foreign woman, rearranged Jorja's dupatta. "You fiddle with it too much, madam Jorja. Here, just do this and throw the rest over your shoulder."

"Where do you put the hairclips?" asked Jorja. Melek looked confused. "The hairclips to hold the dupatta in place," Jorja explained. "These." She took out two yellow hairclips from her purse.

Melek laughed. "We don't wear hairclips on the dupatta. How silly. If you wear the dupatta properly you will not need hairclips." Jorja, suddenly, seemed to have an excess of hairclips. "How silly," Melek repeated.

Jorja practiced wearing the dupatta, sometimes wrapped tightly around her and sometimes thrown casually across her chest, letting the two elongated ends fall freely down her back, a style that felt elegant and graceful. Going to the toilet became an exercise in skill and patience, for it entailed hitching the kameez up, pulling the shalwar down, and at the same time, keeping the dupatta from trailing into the toilet. Unfortunately, she frequently forgot to lift the ends of the dupatta up into her lap and had to retrieve the soggy material out of the toilet bowl. She invariably teetered precariously between sophistication and awkwardness.

CHAPTER 36

THE DINNER PARTY

Mahmud never sat next to Jorja in the car. She assumed that Lufti sat beside her deliberately because he enjoyed their conversations for the fifteen minute drive to the curriculum office. This was not so. Lufti and Jorja had been speaking candidly one day about the dynamics of their working trio when Mahmud was absent.

"Jorja, have you noticed that I always sit between you and Mahmud in the car?"

She was surprised he mentioned it. "Why, yes!"

"It's because Mahmud requested it. He's a quiet man and doesn't like to be physically close to women. He's like that."

"Oh, Lufti, I thought you sat next to me because you liked me." She smiled. "I think you're wrong anyway because Mahmud sits next to me in the office. We work side by side especially in

177

the project office. I sit at the computer and type because I'm fast and Mahmud sits next to me as we prepare the teachers' manual together. We work all the time like that. So, you see, he doesn't mind sitting beside me at all."

"Ah, that may be so, but in the car I'm always piggy in the middle." He laughed. "When Mahmud is working with you, he doesn't mind being close to you. He won't sit next to you when you're not working, such as in the car or even at morning tea. You'll see, Jorja. You'll see. He doesn't want to touch a woman because he remains respectful to his wife. He doesn't mind working with women, but he doesn't want anyone to misread his intentions. He has strictly honorable intentions. That's the reason he didn't shake your hand when you first met him. You thought I didn't notice, but old Lufti notices everything."

"So you *did* notice. You sly fox! I'm glad you told me. He gets on well with you, Lufti. You two always go for walks. I don't see much of Tarif, either. He's quiet too."

"Yes, Tarif keeps to himself. He stays in his room in the evening and doesn't socialize with Mahmud and me. He goes back to Islamabad every Saturday too, so we don't see him on Sunday. He said he'll be staying in Muzaffarabad this weekend."

"Perhaps we can do some socializing this weekend, Lufti Sahib," she suggested in an affectedly formal tone. "What do you think? Any ideas?"

"That would be a grand idea, Jorja Sahiba. What about a dinner party?"

"Glorious, old wise one. At my establishment. At my invitation. And at my expense."

"That would be most grand. Saturday night at seven?"

"Perfect. Wear your best shalwar kameez."

"And you."

* * *

An e-mail arrived from Denny, concerned about the earthquake.

Babe,

Are you safe? I heard about the earthquake in Afghanistan near the Pakistan border. The news said Pakistan felt the shocks too. I know you must have felt them. I hope you're okay.

Sorry for not writing earlier. I was in Sydney for a week and so awfully busy. I didn't have a moment to myself.

Still no word I guess about you staying longer. Maybe they won't decide until you've finished your current assignment.

It seems so dangerous to me. What with the fighting, the bombings, and the earthquakes, I just don't know how you cope. I'm a mess and I'm here in Australia. I just can't cope knowing that you might be in danger. I've never left the country before. The only time I've traveled was when I came to Australia on the boat as a young boy. That hardly counts. I'm not a seasoned traveler like you. And you know that I'm not very social. I'm the archetypical introvert.

Write me when you can. I have heaps of e-mails from you. So glad you found the Internet Café. It sounds very reliable. Keep writing, but you know I'm a crap correspondent. And work is so hectic. My computer at home is on the blink—completely stuffed—so I only have access to the one at work now. I know it's going to frustrate the hell out of you because you're such a prolific writer of e-mails and I'm the world's worst. So sorry, babe, but keep me informed and I'll try to write.

D

Denny's social insecurities showed in his e-mail and Jorja felt powerless to do anything about them. She needed to speak to him so she e-mailed that she would contact him as soon as she could. Confidence wasn't his forte and Jorja was losing hers.

Four uniformed Pakistani Intelligence Agency men appeared at the project office and the hotel, enquiring after Jorja's safety. Hamid reassured her it was routine. With the restrictions imposed upon her, and the strain of loneliness, a dinner party seemed a wonderful idea. Jorja's first bath, in preparation for her outing, was relaxing and enjoyable. Covering the drain with electrician's tape was not ideal, but at least it stopped the water from draining out too quickly.

When Lufti, Mahmud, Tarif, Shalam—a young computer expert—and Jorja gathered in the Sangam Hotel at a restaurant table near the window, they vowed not to discuss work. All other topics were permissible. The hotel waiters were pleased Jorja had company, and they were most attentive to her guests all evening.

Tarif, a gentle giant, was exceedingly reserved and withdrawn, choosing to spend many hours in his room in the Upper Chattar project office where he lived during the week. He drove to his Islamabad home on the weekends. He had bought himself a portable television and a radio and seemed comfortable in his self-imposed exile. His conversation was always about work and never personal. His focus was solely on the management of the project, which he performed with diligence and painstaking detail. Rarely did he join Lufti and Jorja in the curriculum office, preferring an office in the Ministry of Education. At the dinner party, he was relaxed and talkative. He was, surprisingly, rather comical as he told tales of visiting New Zealand and America.

In New York, Tarif was at a friend's house until late into the evening and returned to his hotel on foot. People had warned him of thefts and muggings, and that every three seconds in the city a person was murdered. They advised him to be cautious. Following this advice, he was alert to dangers in the darkness and hastened to return to his hotel nearby. As he was crossing a busy road, he noticed another man and thought he'd run up to him so they could walk together. Tarif believed in the safety of numbers. The man saw Tarif running toward him and began to run. Both men were running scared: one to avoid being alone and the other to avoid being attacked. The more Tarif tried to catch the man, the faster the man ran from him. Tarif was a tall, imposing Pakistani with a rough and rugged exterior. Having only three front teeth did nothing to diminish his somewhat fierce and brutish appearance. The dinner guests roared with laughter at the vision of Tarif running terrified down the road with an even more frightened New Yorker fleeing from him.

The dinner party ended at a reasonable hour. Lufti whispered to Jorja on the way out how much they appreciated it. "Well done, Jorja. Don't be alarmed at the early night. It's polite not to overstay our welcome. You understand."

Feeling satisfied and elated at the party's success she vowed to repeat it regularly. In her room, she rang reception to book a call to Australia.

"It's very expensive, madam, and you must pay at the end of the call."

"Yes, I'm aware of this. You explained it to me last time, Qaseem. Please book the call."

"As you wish, madam. I will call and when it is successful, I will ring you. Please put the phone down."

She waited. Excitedly, she danced around the room in her new shalwar kameez, thrilled with the prospect of speaking to Denny. She waited. An hour later, she rang reception to remind Qaseem of the call.

"So sorry, madam, but I'm not getting a line. Shall I keep trying?"

"Yes please. Do try again."

Jorja waited. After another hour, she again asked Qaseem about the progress.

"Same, madam. No line. So sorry."

"I'll try another night then. Goodnight, Qaseem."

"As you wish, madam."

The lack of communication distanced her from Denny more than she had thought possible. She washed away the tears of frustration and despair before crawling into bed with notepaper, but she was too despondent to write.

CHAPTER 37

THE OLD HAG

CNN news announced the death of the Queen Mother on Easter Sunday. The grand matriarch of Windsor was not only the last British empress, but also the supreme grandmother. Jorja's thoughts turned to her mother, having her seventieth birthday in a few weeks. Easter always reminded her of her mother. The "moving feast" occurred from early to mid-April. This year, it was early.

Jorja arranged a shopping trip to the bazaar with Jahmal. Jahmal's father was pleased his son was receiving extra English tuition through their association and granted permission. The college boy, rather annoyingly, provided a running commentary on everything they saw on the way. "This is the bridge that crosses the river; this is a government building; this is a school for girls; this is a building that belongs to the university; this is a dentist shop; this is where my father worked in 1980." They approached the radio station and her young guide insisted they visit. He addressed the guard at the entrance to seek permission for Jorja to enter the production studios.

"You journalist?" questioned the guard. She assured him that she was not.

Patiently, they waited in the guard's cabin while he telephoned higher authorities. A man approached the cabin in a gray Western suit. As he shook Jahmal's hand, he said, "And how does a man as young as you marry a foreign woman?"

Jorja and Jahmal looked at each other and chuckled. "He's not my husband. He's my chaperone," said Jorja.

After the tour, they spent an hour shopping at the bazaar. Jahmal hailed a colorful Suzuki-taxi—a motorbike with three wheels and a closed-in compartment that barely accommodated two thin people. It was a cheap form of transport, but a deafening one, for its motor chugged raucously as it spewed black smoke from its exhaust.

Leaving her purchases at the Sangam Hotel, Jorja walked the hundred meters to the Internet Café, accompanied by Jahmal. Jahmal chatted to his cousin while she e-mailed Denny.

> *Denny darls,*
> *I tried to call you last night, but no luck. Apparently, the receptionist couldn't get a line out. Or into Australia. I don't know which. I forgot to ask. I so wanted to talk to you. No decision yet. Jamshid, Wasim, and the minister have all been strangely quiet. I don't want to say anything lest I stir the pot.*
> *The big dinner party last night was fabulous. I enjoyed it so much. The fellows were in fine form and so entertaining. Even quiet Tarif was full of jokes and banter. I've never seen him like that. He's normally an extremely shy man and he always returns to Islamabad on the weekends. Lufti says he's building a house. I don't know how he can travel on that dreadful road every weekend.*

I hate it. It makes me ill.

 Enough of that. I wanted to call to say I miss you. If I have to stay longer, I'll ask for a short holiday first before starting the five months or whatever. Perhaps we can meet in Singapore. The airport is brilliant—you'll have no problem getting around. And Singapore is a great place—you'll like it. It's great for shopping and you'll be able to buy as many shirts as you like.

 Anyway, I wanted you to know that there are options. I'll let you know more when I hear of anything. In the meantime, assume that I'll be home soon.

Much love,
Jorja

Jahmal left the Internet Cafe before Jorja had finished, apologizing profusely for not being available to walk her back to the hotel. He disliked Jorja to be unaccompanied, but on this day, he had a migraine that, he said, often occurred after shopping in the bazaar.

Jorja darted across the street and quickly approached the building adjacent to the hotel. People mingled on the narrow walkway, some waited to cross the road, some talked to friends, and others strolled in the opposite direction toward the center of Muzaffarabad. She avoided bumping into a young man and was startled when she felt a tight hold on each arm. An old woman stared at her as she dug her bony fingers into Jorja's arms. Jorja looked her straight in the eyes. They were red, not from crying, but from infection. Pus pooled in each corner. Brown wrinkles folded across her face, the texture of a worn leather handbag. Thick ropes of mucus had run down her nostrils and dried in white streaks that attracted flies. Like a ragged monk, her undernourished body was shrouded in hessian Pakistani garb full of gaping holes. She would not let go. "*Nehe, nehe*," Jorja said firmly, but the old woman's fingers dug deeper into her skin. She clung as hard as she could. "*Nehe, nehe*," Jorja repeated louder, emphasizing each syllable sharply. The old woman's grip was fierce and unrelenting. Her emaciated limbs belied her brute strength. She twisted Jorja's kameez at the shoulder. It tightened across her body almost wrenching her arm from its socket. *Could this shriveled, sunken-cheeked old beggar really be so strong?* Paralysis pinched Jorja's throat shut. No one came to her rescue. It was as if everyone feared being sucked into a vortex of crime and recrimination.

With a nod of her head, the hag beckoned to someone behind Jorja. Powerless to free herself from the grip of one person, the thought of an accomplice was terrifying. A small lane between the buildings led to the riverbank. *Would her disappearance be this simple: two strong, deft assailants forcing her out of sight of the main road into an alleyway?* Looking in the reflection of a window, Jorja could see behind her. A scrawny middle-aged man, possibly her son, was approaching them with a slow, deliberate saunter that drew no attention. The woman's grip tightened. The man was soon by Jorja's side, his erratic breathing in her ear. Adding his strong grip, he shoved the two women effortlessly into the alleyway. Strewn with litter and reeking in the warmth of the sun, its fumes made Jorja giddy and nauseous. Another push and they'd be half-way down the lane, away from the bustle of the crowded street.

While Jorja's body stiffened and refused to move, her brain churned furiously trying to process what was happening. *Would she be held for ransom? Or would someone find her slaughtered on a pile of rat-infested rubbish, decomposing in the heat?* Warm, slimy moisture seeped into her shoes. Strangely, calmness coursed through her as she looked at the mound of garbage near her feet. The beggar woman wore no shoes. Her narrow, bare feet were calloused and pocked with sores. This was Jorja's cue: her "now or never" moment that she had learned from the Oprah Winfrey Show. Jorja stamped on the hag's foot with her thin leather shoe: not so much with force as with defiance. The old woman let go with a scream, startling her accomplice, who released his grip. Seizing her chance, Jorja fled to the hotel where she collided with Riyad. She pointed behind her, without looking, and spat out a few words. He didn't listen to the full account before ordering Qaseem to assist Jorja while he rushed toward the two assailants.

Qaseem escorted Jorja up the flight of stairs and unlocked her door, apologizing abundantly for not coming to her aid in the street. He left Jorja in the privacy of her room.

Astonishingly enough, it happened quickly. Shocked by her attackers' intentions, Jorja's body trembled. The effrontery of being ambushed in broad daylight, amid a sea of people, had shaken her more than she expected. Admonishing herself for her carelessness and for not calling out for assistance, she paced the room in an effort to remain calm. She vowed never to mention the assault to Jahmal, knowing he would feel the weight of guilt for a long time.

Jorja's left arm throbbed painfully. In the mirror, she saw small, black bruises forming perfect fingerprints on her arms. The appearance of her hair distracted her. She felt its coarseness. It was brittle and as dry as straw. The shock had seemingly sapped the energy and life from her body, from her legs, and from her hair. She cut a centimeter off the length and trimmed the hair free from her eyes. Before coming to Pakistan, she had lightened it to a shade above natural to give it a healthy glow. The darkened roots were now beginning to show, not obviously, but conspicuous to her.

She rearranged her kameez, wrapped a dupatta around herself, and ambled downstairs to the lobby. She hesitated at the door as Qaseem opened it. He assured Jorja that the beggar woman had gone, escaping capture.

"Are you fine?" Qaseem asked.

"Are you fine?" Riyad asked.

Jorja told both of them that she was fine. Qaseem accompanied her to the adjacent supermarket and held open the door to the odor of freshly baked bread. He returned to the hotel and left her to find blond hair dye.

In Pakistan, fair hair was not the norm. Knowing her mission would not be easy, Jorja thought of waiting until she returned to

Islamabad, but impatience triumphed. She found a limited range of hair dyes to choose from, most of which were on shelves behind the counter and out of reach. The salesman was exceedingly patient. After looking at several bottles, packages, and sachets, he said, "Madam, black is very popular. Perhaps you can use black like the Kashmiris."

"That's my last option." She laughed as he rummaged through the shelves. He eventually found a "very light blond" and tactfully said that it would be perfect for her. As she leafed through the rupee notes for payment, her left hand shook.

Back at the hotel, the shock of the assault remained as she applied the hair color and conditioner. Her hands trembled, her body trembled, but more than that, her left shoulder ached as she strained to lift her arm. It wasn't long before her hair became silky tresses again. Somehow, the transformation comforted her.

If a beggar woman could whisk her into oblivion, swiftly and silently, the thought of hunting Osama bin Laden seemed even more ludicrous. Fleetingly, the thought was tempting but insane. No wonder no individual was hunting the most wanted person on earth. In six months, the American defense force, with all the intelligence and equipment at hand, had no success in capturing him. *If everyone in Kashmir seemed to know where Osama was, why was he eluding the Americans?*

Feeling calmer, Jorja ate chocolate while watching reports on the death of the Queen Mother. The royal demise and Jorja's ordeal made it difficult to celebrate Easter. Half-heartedly, Jorja poured a small vodka and toasted her escape from what may have been an attempted kidnapping, or at the very least, an unpleasant assault and robbery. In her mind, Jorja trivialized the day's event and the consequences it may have had. Denial made her calmer. She raked her fingers through her hair, stroking the softness, combing composure and serenity through to her soul.

PART TWO

APRIL 2002

CHAPTER 38

WHY THE POOR STAY POOR AND WHY OSAMA IS STILL HIDING

The minister paid Jorja an unexpected visit. If he had come to inspect her eating habits, he made no mention of it. In any case, she had dined satisfactorily on kebabs and rice. Instead, he seized a chair and asked if he could join her for tea. On this occasion, he resembled an undertaker: admirably tailored in funereal black. Black suited him. An affable smile, full of perfect teeth, lit his face. Some people would have considered him handsome. The minister cleared his throat and placed his hands on the table, where his gold watch gleamed under the ceiling lights. Occasionally, he turned his gold ring around his finger.

"A session on poverty has just finished in the conference room, and I was hoping you'd be here in the restaurant. Sometimes these events are so dreary. It's a mere formality that I attend. This time, however, the information was rather interesting." He was a willing talker and, having nothing to do, Jorja was a willing listener. "I think it began in the early Fifties," he said, "when a large number of developing countries got their independence, including Pakistan in 1947. I don't make the distinction between Pakistan and Kashmir, even though I'm Kashmiri. I'll talk in generalities, if you don't mind." His English was clear and understandable with a hint of a colonial upbringing. "Most of the developing countries failed to start an indigenous process of development. Almost all of them equated modernization with rapid industrialization. They ignored their historical and cultural differences and began to imitate the West. I hope what I say doesn't offend you."

He smiled and continued. "Consequently, they got the sequence of the development process wrong. In Pakistan, and elsewhere, there were probably five major flaws in the development strategy," he conjectured pensively, counting them on his long slender fingers. "The first was industrial development without adequate agricultural development; the second was large-scale industry without prior development of small-scale industry; third was urbanization outpacing industrialization; the fourth was the services were growing faster than the productive base of agriculture and industry, and lastly the population growth raced ahead of employment growth. I think that's it really, in a proverbial nutshell." He was confident of his analysis, and proud but also wistful. "When you've been living in a poverty-stricken country for much of your life as I have, you tend to form strong opinions. It's become a study of mine, I guess. I've mentioned some large flaws, but we have other failures, too. We tried to adopt the welfare state model, you know, free education, free health service, free rural water supply, free sanitation, all of those things that you probably take for granted in Australia. We tried to adopt the model without having a broad-based taxation system like Western countries or huge natural resources like Kuwait and Brunei. Because of the lack of vision and poor implementation, the government didn't deliver the services and scarce resources were wasted. Consultants, engineers, contractors, and bureaucrats skimmed off a major portion of the resources. As you've probably noticed, some people, particularly Kashmiris, who I think are not as corrupt as the Pakistanis and who are far poorer, do not like consultants advising them on how best to make use of their resources. There is some bitterness. Anyway, the government no doubt delivered some services, but it created a dependency syndrome. In spite of our failure to improve the social indicators, we didn't learn the lesson that you can't run a welfare system with borrowed money."

His insights were thought provoking and his mellifluous voice soothed Jorja.

"We involved the state in almost all activities, although it had neither the capacity nor the resources to perform the jobs," he said. "At the same time, instead of devolving authority to the lowest level, we placed heavy reliance on an overcentralized bureaucracy. It was a multi-layered, underpaid, overstaffed, ineffective, and corrupt bureaucracy, and it kept on expanding exponentially. By its very nature it was *status quo* oriented, slow-moving, and stifling the initiative of the people." When the waiter arrived, the minister nodded and lifted two fingers.

"So you see," he continued. "Most poverty alleviation schemes seldom reached the needy in Pakistan. I know that's a fact in Kashmir. The schemes were hijacked by the upper classes who wanted to keep the poor in eternal poverty."

"But what do we do about it now?"

"I have many ideas on *that* subject. Let's see." He reclined in his chair, took a deep breath, and stretched his shoulders. "What can we learn from past experiences? Well now! How can you expect to reduce poverty by launching a few projects while all other macro policies continue to increase poverty? So, don't treat the alleviation of poverty as a sector. That's number one. Number two would be not to start grandiose projects to help the poor. They never work. Start small, I'd say. Scale-up and mainstream gradually. Can I think of a third?" He grinned. "My number three would be not to believe that massive foreign aid can lead to poverty reduction. The International Monetary Fund and the World Bank are not the solution. Actually, they are part of the problem. The thrust of their strategy lies in the obligation upon the aid-receiving countries, like Pakistan and Kashmir, to align their own economic policies with the requirements of the World Bank. Dependence on aid-giving agencies has created a new type of poverty, I think, and in many cases, it has resulted in a destabilization of societies. Sustainable development is only possible with local resources that are participatory and low in cost. I don't know what your beliefs are, but I've given mine."

"So you don't think this project in Kashmir is benefiting the children? We might be working at the ministry level and with teachers, but the ultimate beneficiaries are the children."

"Don't get me wrong. There are great benefits for children's education, but I think that at times there's too much influence by the donors and international consultants. What do they know of Kashmir and its people and problems? What do they really know? How about you giving a suggestion for lessons learned?" Tea for two arrived.

Jorja pondered his questions for a while and said, "A lesson would be not to believe that people are ignorant of what's happening around them. Perhaps some consultants forget that local people have a vast knowledge of the region and what works for them."

The minister laughed. "Well done! What was that? Number four? My number five would be not to use soft projects and subsidies to solve social problems. They won't be sustainable in the long-term. If properly targeted and effectively monitored, subsidies can be effective in specific projects, but normally groups other than the target groups consume the subsidies. I don't believe non-government organizations can replace the government. They can, at best, quicken the process of social mobilization and can mediate between the state and the poor, and perhaps carry out research to find low-cost solutions and implement pilot projects, but the ultimate responsibility rests with the state. The state cannot abdicate responsibility. That's number six. Do you have a number seven while I think of something?"

"You mentioned that the upper classes are stifling progress and keeping others poor, but I think that the poor may be sabotaging their own future."

"Elaborate, if you will."

"I think that there's widespread frustration over the gap between the rich and the poor in this country. Poor people are angry at the inequitable distribution of resources, but they don't organize themselves into a unified sector. Without unity, they are resistant to change and progress. They don't have the strength of unity, integration, and cohesion on their side."

"It's possible," said the minister, sipping his tea. Black patent-leather shoes jutted out below his trousers. "That's number seven," he continued. "I think the current community-based projects make people participate in government projects, but I believe it should be the reverse. Government should support what the people are doing. We need to recognize that poor people do have assets, but they don't usually have formal title. In rural areas, the land they till, the place where they live, the tools they use, and the cattle they own, can't be transformed into capital because of a lack of title. Similarly, over thirty-five percent of our urban population lives in *kachchi abadis*—squatter settlements—but in most cases, they don't own that land legally. This is a huge resource, but because poor people rarely have formal title, they can't use the assets as collateral to raise cash."

"Pakistan seems to be an over-regulated country to me," Jorja added.

"Mmm, true! Government not only regulates, but also tries to control most of the business and trade activities. Whether it's purchase of land from the government or starting a new business, it may take years. The cost and burden of this over-regulation makes most businesses uncompetitive and difficult to run. Conventional methods to eradicate poverty won't work. But, I admit, the government can't do everything. It has neither the capacity nor the resources to do so. In Pakistan, the problem is neither shortage of funds nor lack of skilled manpower. The main issue is poor governance and poor management. People don't expect much from the government. What people want and need are low-cost, easy-to-implement, sustainable projects that can solve their basic problems." He leaned back again and yawned.

"You make it sound so simple and logical," she said.

"Yes, but it's not so, is it? Did you see the paper today? *Dawn*, I think. There was an article on the Asian Development Bank's support to Pakistan after September Eleven. In fact, the Bank's support came after Pakistan declared its backing for America's war on terror. Pakistan has a big opportunity now to achieve sustained growth and reduce poverty. For now, the Asian Development Bank predicts economic growth of about five percent to June 2003 after an expansion of two-and-a-half percent this year. But we did have a severe drought and falling exports then. The Bank said that if the government continues to follow sound macro-economic policies and implement planned economic and governance reforms it could, fairly quickly, achieve sustainable growth and poverty reduction. But the corollary is that Pakistan would remain caught between low growth and high poverty if it failed to implement the reforms. I think if increased aid postpones the necessary reforms and macro-economic developments, as happened in the Eighties, Pakistan will be unable to break out of the existing vicious cycle of low growth and rising poverty. Anyway, the Bank said it planned to fund about a billion dollars in aid to Pakistan this year. I suppose that's a good thing."

"To change the subject completely, can I ask you something that many people are asking me?"

"Of course, Jorja, you can ask me anything."

"It's about Osama bin Laden." She looked into the minister's eyes and he did not flinch, so she continued. "The Americans are offering a big reward for anyone who can find him, dead or alive, so why doesn't the Kashmiri government send a posse out to look for him?"

The minister smiled. "Firstly, governments are not expected to harbor terrorists and should, at all times, ensure that their citizens and those of the world are safe. We would not need the incentive of a reward to look for him."

"Do you think Kashmiris are actually hiding him, helping him to elude the Americans?"

"With a statement like that, you could start another war!" He laughed. "But I promise not to tell anyone what you said. Besides, perhaps it is the Afghans who are hiding bin Laden? That is the rumor, not that I accept it. I suppose it won't be long before he is found, since the Americans have troops in the border regions."

"Is anyone looking for Osama besides the American government?"

"Individuals, you mean? Or political groups? Who knows? I don't know anything, nor do I waste my time thinking about such preposterous thoughts. I have my hands full with the education portfolio."

"Hypothetically though, where would you look for him? In western Pakistan or in the mountains of Afghanistan or in Kashmir?"

"Hypothetically, I would start in Kashmir. I think he was in Peshawar, and I think he was in Afghanistan where the Americans are looking for him now, but he could be in Kashmir now. No one seems to consider looking here. We, the Kashmiri government, are not hiding him, if that is what you are hinting, but if his whereabouts are known, then I am certain that he will be detained. But, as I say, no one really knows where he is."

"Except every Kashmiri!"

"But this is all hypothetical, isn't it Jorja?"

"If anyone was looking for him, and found him, they'd be the heroes of the world? Something to think about, isn't it?"

He laughed. "Let's leave it in the hands of the diplomats of the world and the American government, with our assistance. I'm sure the Americans have the resources to find anyone they choose. You and I cannot solve the world's problems in one night, Jorja. Firstly, poverty, and now, terrorism. Goodness, aren't we above our status tonight? What makes you think that we can overcome terrorism over a cup of tea?"

"Over a cup of tea in Kashmir."

After a gap in the conversation, the minister said, "I admit to feeling tired. I must leave you to ponder the issues for yourself. Thank you very much for allowing me to take tea with you. I'll fix the bill." He smirked to himself as he sauntered to the door. "Oh, Jorja," he called out. "Don't do anything foolish now!"

"Me?"

He stopped by the door. "We had an incident when we evacuated the Westerners from the region after September Eleven. A young woman—British I think—hid in the mountains because she didn't want to be evacuated."

"Why?"

"I guess she didn't want to go home. But she was found and she eventually left the region. Promise me you won't do anything stupid like that."

"Like what?"

"Like hiding in the mountains to look for Osama bin Laden."

Jorja laughed. "Not me. I want to go home."

"Home? Er. . .er. . .er," he stuttered. "Er. . . home, yes, of course." The door swung three times before clicking shut.

CHAPTER 39

A VISIT TO THE DOCTOR

Jorja had few contraceptive pills left; it was time to see a doctor. While she waited for Fadil one morning, she asked Riyad to arrange an appointment for her to see a woman doctor.

"Are you sick?" He expressed concern. Riyad was casually dressed in a tartan shirt with breast pockets and navy corduroy trousers. Flecks of ginger dusted his treacle-colored hair.

"No, no, I've just got a sore throat."

"I'll make the appointment for tomorrow morning at nine o'clock. Wait here tomorrow, madam."

Promptly at nine o'clock, Jorja arrived in the foyer. She waited and waited. Riyad didn't appear. Perhaps he had forgotten. She waited. Eventually she asked Qaseem at reception if he knew where the manager was, but he didn't know. Half an hour later, after receiving a phone call, Qaseem called to her and announced that the manager was busy.

"I have to see a doctor this morning, Qaseem. The manager was to arrange for me to see a doctor."

"No doctor here, madam. No doctor in the hotel. You see doctor at two o'clock."

"No, no, I wish to see a doctor now. Please can you arrange for me to see a woman doctor *now*?"

"You sick, madam?

"Sore throat."

Fadil arrived to take Jorja to work. "Are you better?" She told him that she hadn't been to the doctor yet. They convinced Qaseem to telephone a doctor. He picked up the telephone receiver, spoke to someone briefly, and issued instructions to Fadil on how to get to the doctor's clinic. Fadil assured Jorja that he knew where to go.

The imposing whitewashed clinic was behind the Combined Military Hospital in the northeastern corner of the city. Fadil avoided exposed tree roots in the driveway and stopped close to a red brick wall. He suggested that Jorja wait in the car while he confirmed that it was the correct location. Returning, he said confidently, "No problem. You follow me." Jorja followed him up a flight of concrete stairs to a long narrow corridor, devoid of light. Fadil stopped outside the third door on the left. "You go in. I'll wait at the car."

Six men occupied rigid chairs around the perimeter of the square room. The doctor's generous oak table, to the right of the room, took advantage of the window view. Behind the table sat a slim, middle-aged man, speaking in Urdu into the telephone. He didn't acknowledge Jorja. Surprisingly, Riyad was also in the room. He sat opposite the door and smiled when she entered. She returned his smile.

A gentleman showed her to a chair. "You take seat, madam. You take tea?"

"No, thank you. I'm here to see the doctor."

"You take seat," he said and removed a cup and saucer from a cupboard near the door. He poured tea into a green porcelain cup rimmed with gold. The cup appeared new, free of stains, faded patterns, and hairline cracks.

Men wandered in and out of the room, sitting, drinking tea, smiling, and talking in earnest about Iraq. A prominent-looking man entered. He kissed and hugged his way down the line of men, all bobbing up from their seats for the embrace. He commented that some Iraqis were irreligious men who didn't obey the Qur'an. Everybody nodded. "Really, it's true. They have no regard for Allah at all."

Someone added that it was due to Iraq's violent history. "What sort of Muslim brother is this Saddam Hussein? He's not our brother if he commits violence."

"Bah! It's not the way of all Iraqis," said another in their defense. "It's only Hussein and his henchmen. Although the Mongols in the time of Genghis Khan slaughtered people at an unprecedented rate to create terror, they never tortured, mutilated, or maimed their foe, as Hussein appears to have done. The Mongol army did in two years what the European Crusaders from the West and the Seljuk Turks from the East failed to do in two centuries. The Mongols conquered the heart of the Arab world: Baghdad. Why can't anyone bring Hussein, the Baghdad Brute, to his knees?"

Another man mentioned Jews. "Arabs are pure at heart, but Jews are different because of their religion, you see. Jews kill their own prophets. This is known." The men nodded.

A thin man said, "Be thankful to Allah that there are no Jews in Kashmir."

The men nodded, except for one sitting by the window. "The Jews are all in the Indian side of Kashmir."

"We could do with Israeli tourists that visit the graves of Jesus Christ and the Egyptian Prophet Moses, may peace be upon them. The graves are in Indian Kashmir. If the graves were here in Muzaffarabad, their tourist dollars would add to our economy. We should be praying to Allah to send us Jews."

Another scoffed, "There is no proof of the graves of Jesus Christ and Prophet Moses, peace be upon them. There's no proof at all. People have been looking, but as far as I know no one has found anything."

Riyad added, "I've heard that it is true. Just because they have not been found, it does not mean they are not there. Zaithanchungi is convinced all Mizos are descendants of the Menashe. The Menashe are the ones the Assyrians enslaved and kept in Assyria when Jerusalem fell. They are said to have traveled to Afghanistan and maybe even Mongolia via Kashmir and Tibet. I think there are plenty of Jews in Indian Kashmir and maybe even here too."

The Mongol expert said, "The Mongols are still in Karakorum. Khubilai Khan, the grandson of Genghis, built the Forbidden City and it was the city of the world. There were Muslim leaders, Catholic and Buddhist priests, Indian mystics, and Jewish rabbis. There were Tibetans, Armenians, Khitans, Tajiks, Arabs, Uighurs, Tanguts, Turks, Persians, and Europeans. The city of the world was a success because it was the city of trade. If people trade, they do not fight. There is a lesson there for everyone."

The man by the window said, "Jews and Arabs will always fight."

The defender of Iraqis spoke again. "Bah! It's not just the Jews that kill. Men kill men all over the world. Someone tried to kill the Pope. Bah! What is all this talk of killing?" The men nodded again. "We do not need to fear Jews, Hindus or whatever. It is the heteroclites that cause the problems in the world."

"Those heteroclites," the men said in unison, nodding vigorously.

"Yes, they aren't team men, are they, the heteroclites? Talking of team men, the important question now is—will Shoaib Akhtar be ready for Stephen Fleming in May?"

The group broke into peals of laughter. "The New Zealand cricketers should beware of Inzamam-ul-Haq. He's in fine form, and so is Imran Nazir. The Gaddafi Stadium in Lahore will be a batter's paradise for us, you'll see. We'll win easily. . ."

Jorja sat on a chair backed against the wall and sipped her tea. She smiled. The men smiled and nodded. She waited for the doctor to finish his telephone call. He was not in a hurry. She waited for the men to finish their tea. They were not in a hurry. No one was making the slightest effort to leave the room. She waited. She wanted to interrupt, but it was difficult to do so. A kind of narcotic emerged from their talk. The room became infused with the soothing murmur of their vowels and soft consonants. Although their conversation never seemed to be going anywhere at all, it also seemed as if it would go on forever. Their talk was a combination of English and Urdu out of politeness to Jorja. Their voices, deep and low, continued, but she heard less and less. "The way up and the way down are one and the same," she heard. "One and the same, one and the same," the men repeated.

"We need peace between our countries. That is what is needed in the whole world."

"No, we need more than peace. We need equality and justice."

"Yes, yes, equality and justice," the men chorused. Seeing her sleepily unresponsiveness, they continued in their native language.

Jorja stared at the jade-colored china cup. It mutated slowly into the green flag of Islam as her mind numbed. She thought of Yusef Islam's song about a peace train, when he was known as Cat Stevens. The lyrics played in her head. She felt as if she was out on the edge of darkness longing for the peace train to take her home to Denny so she could look into his green eyes again. She finished her tea. The doctor finished his telephone call. He smiled and apologized in English. He was a nondescript Pakistani of medium height and stature with no prominent features. Pakistanis always had an outstanding feature or two: the nose, the teeth, the hair, the build. The doctor did not. He poured himself a cup of tea.

"May I talk to the doctor?" Jorja addressed the men.

"Yes," they responded in unison. No one moved. She stood up, picked up her chair, and placed it as close to the doctor as she could. She looked across at Riyad. He smiled.

"My name is Jorja," she said directly to the doctor. "I have a sore throat." Her throat was fine, but as she had told Riyad she had a sore throat, she thought she ought to begin with that complaint. Without touching her, the doctor asked a few questions. He nodded whenever she answered.

"I will send some tablets to the hotel. You are staying at the Sangam Hotel, I presume." Jorja nodded. "They're good American tablets. I've just been to America."

She was nervous about this. "Are you an actual doctor?"

"Yes, I'm a doctor. My name is Dr. Khurshid. I'm a dermatologist and tropical diseases doctor. I'll arrange for my driver to take the tablets to your hotel."

"Thank you." She looked at Riyad. He was drinking tea. The men seemed engrossed in conversation. She drew closer to the doctor. "Could you please write me a prescription for the contraceptive pill?"

"No," he answered instantly, abruptly.

"No?"

"No," was his firm response.

"Oh! Is there anyone in Muzaffarabad, Islamabad or anywhere in the whole of Pakistan who could write me a prescription for the contraceptive pill?" She was a little concerned.

"No."

"No?" She shifted in her chair trying to think of another question. "Can I ask why? Do you not have the contraceptive pill in Pakistan? Are single women not permitted to purchase the contraceptive pill?"

"Yes, you are permitted to have the pill." He smiled.

"Then why won't you write a prescription for me? Is it because you're not a general practitioner?"

"Oh no! I've not written one for many years. That's not the reason though. You don't need a prescription. You can just go to the medicine shop. You can get as many as you wish."

"As many as I wish? As many packets as I wish? No limit? No prescription?"

"We don't write prescriptions for many things. You can just go to the medicine shop and ask. There'll be many packets. We don't use such things here, not to the extent that the Westerners do anyway."

"Perhaps then you can advise which brand to get." She mentioned the brand she'd been using. He made a short telephone call.

"I've spoken to a person in a medicine shop. He says that the shop has plenty of tablets. The cost is two hundred and thirty-seven rupees per packet for one month's supply. You can ask for as many as you wish." He wrote the brand on a piece of paper and handed it to Jorja. Embossed in gold on the paper were Dr. Kurshid's name and credentials.

"Thank you. So you *are* a doctor."

"Oh yes, I'm a doctor. This is the office of the World Health Organization. I work for them now. I don't practice medicine as such any more. The gentleman nearest to you works for the World Health Organization also. And the man at the computer is doing a report for me."

"And the rest?"

He laughed. "They are taking tea."

"Really? Thank you so much for your help."

"Just call me if you need anything. I can help you with anything medical. Just call. I'll send the throat tablets to the hotel. Take one a day."

"Thank you." She rose to leave.

Riyad looked toward her. "Are you better, madam?"

"Yes, thank you. I'm better."

He smiled. Everyone smiled and nodded.

"You don't need to leave so quickly. Stay and have another cup of tea. It's polite to talk awhile," said the doctor. Jorja asked him about his work. "I'm not a practicing doctor as I said, but I volunteer at the Combined Military Hospital in my spare time. Just during this time of crisis because of the many casualties and injuries. The hospital is short-staffed."

"On my way to the hotel each day from north of the Lipton sign I hear the ambulances. There must be a great number of cases to attend to."

"Many, too many. A villager sustained severe injuries during the border shelling yesterday. He was a young man, about twenty-five years of age from Khariyal village, the Charwa sector of the Sialkot boundary. He was sitting in the courtyard of his house when the bullets hit him. In a precarious condition, he was, when the ambulance men admitted him. The fighting continues in Chlumb, Joriyaan, Bajwat, Charwa, and Akhnor sectors, the rural areas. It disrupts the sowing of the sunflower and watermelon crops. An eleven-year-old boy was killed, and his two brothers were seriously wounded by a landmine that exploded under their feet. The three of them tripped off the explosive device hidden under dirt while grazing sheep in Panjilu village, some ten kilometers from Banihal. The brothers are in a critical condition. And someone decapitated an abducted government employee in Shopyan. It's terrible at the moment," he continued, needing to talk. "The foreign troops set fire to a hundred and eighty-three houses and shops in different regions of Kashmir, mainly on the Indian side, but all in border towns. The police keep arresting people, but it does no good. They say they've arrested almost seven thousand civilians in thirteen years since 1989, but the atrocities haven't stopped. I don't know what can be done to stop this. I do my part to help, but it's not enough. It's a small part."

CHAPTER 40

MOTHER AND SON

Everybody wanted to be Jorja's friend.

Called to the minister's office to update him on the progress of the project, Jorja arrived promptly at the designated time. A male assistant ushered her into the room and said, "Just wait, madam." And she did. She waited while the minister signed papers. She waited while he spoke to two women about textbooks. She waited while he conferred with an older man about finances. She waited until it was her turn.

The possibility of staying longer in Kashmir didn't arise and she didn't ask. It was a brief meeting. The minister telephoned Fadil to collect Jorja, and she waited. Pacing the corridor relieved her boredom. A striking woman with auburn hair poking out of her dupatta asked if she needed assistance. Her shalwar kameez was of good quality in shades of green. Gold jewelry rattled opulently with every turn of her wrist and each movement of her head. Explaining that the minister had telephoned her driver, Jorja resumed pacing.

"My name is Mrs. Kaliq. Just wait, madam," she said, pointing to a chair. "I'm sure he'll be here shortly."

Fadil was prompt. "Back to the curriculum office, madam?"

"No, Fadil. I'd like to go to the Internet Café near the Sangam."

"It's not good to go to those places. Only men go there. Young men and silly boys."

"That's fine. They know me. If you wish, you can wait in the Internet Café or you can go back to the project office and I'll walk to the hotel when I'm finished."

"I'll wait with you, madam."

"Thank you, Fadil. You're so kind." Jorja read Denny's e-mail.

> *Babe,*
>
> *I know you're trying to come up with options to please me, but let's wait until we have a decision on your extension. Why are they taking so long? Have you heard anything at all?*
>
> *Glad that the dinner party went well. What a great idea to have it in the restaurant—so simple and non-threatening. I bet you were the life of the party. Which of the new clothes did you wear? Did you wear the blue one that Mahmud likes or your favorite red one? I like red or pink on you. You didn't have a pink one made, did you? I remember the first time you came to my place. You wore your faded blue denim jeans with the pink top. It really suited you. I'll never forget it. I can't wait to see you in your Pakistani clothes though.*
>
> *Must fly now. It's late. I worked again until eleven last night and want to get away earlier tonight.*
>
> *Till next time,*
>
> *D*

Jorja e-mailed Denny:

Den,

I told you yesterday I was going to the doctor. All is okay and I managed to get what I wanted. Fadil drove me to the pharmacy straight after the doctor's visit.

I met with the minister a few nights ago and this morning. He asked about the progress of the project—very formal, he was—quite unlike his usual self. No friendliness at all. I'm not sure what's happening and I didn't ask. It didn't seem an appropriate time to question him. He made no mention of me staying longer.

I think maybe Jamshid and the minister have had words. I haven't called Jamshid for some time and he seems to be ignoring me. It's just as well too as our conversations were getting quite frustrating.

I think we can assume now that I'm coming home as soon as I've finished this assignment. Not long now, honey! See you soon,

Jorja

The next day a clerk entered the curriculum office, delivering a note from Mrs. Kaliq. She requested that Jorja join her and her son at the Sangam Hotel in the evening for dinner "as her friend." Although Jorja had only met the woman for two minutes, she sent back a message of acceptance.

Hasibur, Mrs. Kaliq's son, was a slim, good-looking boy with exceptional manners. He took the role as lead spokesperson. They met in the hotel lobby, and he directed them to a restaurant table overlooking the river. Hasibur ordered food and drinks and gave polite instructions to the waiters on how to serve them as well as making suggestions on the timing of courses. Jorja was impressed. Mrs. Kaliq spoke little, except to talk of her son. He introduced himself as an army medic, newly administered to the service. Articulately, he described the physical intensity of military service and the mental concentration of medical studies. At twenty-three years of age, he was in the process of a marriage arrangement. He expressed his pleasure with his parent's choice of bride-to-be.

Mrs. Kaliq was clearly proud of her son, her only child. When they finished the meal, her husband appeared by the table and announced that his meeting had concluded and that their driver was waiting. He introduced himself as Mr. Kaliq, Attorney-at-Law, and shook Jorja's hand firmly. While Mrs. Kaliq was auburn-haired with golden skin and her son had bitter chocolate-colored hair with a nut-brown complexion, Mr. Kaliq was the darkest of the three. His hair, bushy eyebrows, and mustache, were as dark and as shiny as coal. Solid with square shoulders, his presence was megalithic. He wore a white shalwar kameez with panache, topping it with a flamboyant black and white hounds-tooth sleeveless jacket. They were a handsome family.

* * *

Jorja remarked to Lufti on the aristocratic look of the Kaliq family. He advised her not to trust Mr. Kaliq. "I've heard stories, Jorja—stories of his infidelity. I've never met him, but I hear that he's a man of ill character when it comes to women. He's a … a … a sleaze ball, as you Westerners might say." Lufti clicked his tongue when Jorja mentioned that she thought Mr. and Mrs. Kaliq just wanted to be friends. "No, no, Jorja. There's no such thing as friendship in Pakistan without it meaning something else." Jorja protested, saying that he was too suspicious, too doubting, and too mistrustful. "Trust me, Jorja, the word 'friends' may not be as you think. Trust me. You will see." He smiled knowingly.

Friendship in Pakistan was a strange concept to Jorja. Everybody wanted to be her friend for various reasons: her friendship gave them status in the community because she was a foreigner; it was an opportunity to ask for money; perhaps she would provide sponsorship so that they could live in Australia; or it was an avenue to seek funds for investment into their son's or daughter's education abroad. Often they asked Jorja to purchase a four-wheel drive or a laptop computer from project funds for their relatives. Mostly they assumed she was eminently wealthy and would assist them with their financial problems. It was difficult to determine true friendship in a society as poor as Kashmir.

CHAPTER 41

SPERMATIZATION

Mr. Kaliq's forceful knock on her door almost unhinged it. As Jorja opened it, he bounded into the room and sat cross-legged on a chair next to the bed. A string of religious beads dangled from his hand, delicately crafted from jade. Jorja was too stunned to protest.

"I've just been to the mosque for *salat*," he said. "Muslims practice *salat* five times a day, so I went to the mosque before I came here. *Salat* is our ritual prayers. Islam means 'turning to God' and that implies that we must turn to prayer when we're called. The word 'religion' means to bind together and Islam is our binding faith." Placing his hand on his chest, he attempted to regulate his breathing, strained from rushing up the stairs to the room.

From his pocket, he retrieved a small book, *What a Muslim is required to know about his religion*. "This is for you. I'd like

you to have it. It's a very informative book. It instructs you when
and how to pray."

As he cleared his throat and recited Arabic verses from the
Qur'an, Jorja leafed through the book. It was better for a woman
to pray in her own home, but men should go to the mosque to pray
in company, it said. A man must cover his genitals when he enters
a mosque. It mentioned rituals and bathing before praying, for example: *In case of a spermatize resulting from a man's sexual inter-
course with his wife, or from any other cause, a full bath is to be
maintained before prayers. If no spermatize has taken place, but a
smell is pumped out of his body, or any substance seen coming out
of his urine stream; or anus; or direct touch of penis or vagina—no
full bath is necessary, but ablution should be carried out.*

"Spermatize" was a new word to Jorja.

"So," he said finishing his prayers, "we are friends, yes?"

"I guess so," she said cautiously. Generally, the phrase pref-
aced a request for money. "Thank you for the gift. I appreciate it
very much. It will teach me many new things."

"You are most welcome, but I did not come solely to present
you with this book. I'm here to offer my services to you. You are
alone in Kashmir and I ask you now if you would like a fucking
relationship?"

"A what?" Her eyebrows arched toward her hair.

"A fucking relationship. You and me. I can arrange it," he
cleared his throat with a long-winded "mmm" noise.

"You're married. Your religion frowns on this, yes? No religion supports adultery," she answered calmly.

"You are right in a small way, but I have asked Mrs. Kaliq
and she says I can have a fucking relationship with a foreign
woman. She knows this will bring great status upon me. Allah
is a benevolent God and He will grant me permission to service
you. He'll see I'm a good man for thinking of the welfare and
the desires of a foreign woman who is far from her homeland."

"Really?" Jorja stifled a laugh. "I'm sure Allah is benevolent.
However, we're not going to have any sort of relationship," she
said as she shook her head. "How old are you?" She was merely

curious. He looked sixty and, given the propensity in Kashmir for death by heart attack, the thought had crossed her mind he could die during paroxysms of excitement. The life expectancy of Kashmiris was forty, and Mr. Kaliq was probably living on borrowed time, although in reality he looked as strong as an ox.

"I'm fifty-and-a-half years old, but I'm exceptionally healthy and am able to have a fucking relationship."

"I bet you are. I just don't want you to drop dead of a heart attack right now."

He calmly said, "Life and death were created by Allah. Mmmm." He cleared his throat again. "Good and evil are challenges to test our faith."

"Then your faith will be strongly tested tonight and you're sure to cark it," she muttered, more to herself than to Mr. Kaliq. Raising her voice, she said, "Let me just say that I don't intend to have a relationship with the fifty-and-a-half year old man sitting in front of me. Now, next week, or ever."

"You do not like penises? Mmmmm," he said as he cleared his throat.

"What?"

"You like your own sex?"

"Well, when you're alone, your own sex is the best sex," she said, thinking he was referring to masturbation.

"I mean you are a Lesbonese?"

"A Lesbonese? I think I'm not understanding you," she answered mockingly.

"I mean you like a fucking relationship with a woman and not a man. If so, I'm not sure that I can arrange a woman for you. I don't know where to find one, but I can ask Mrs. Kaliq to find a woman for you."

"You mean, am I a lesbian? No, I'm not. I like penises. But not yours."

"That's good you like penises. It's good you are not a thesbian. If you're worried that I'll put a river in you, you don't need to be. I practice considerable restraint. It will be a tantric fucking relationship."

"It's interesting that a respected lawyer and a married Muslim man who has just been to the mosque wants to have Hindu sex with a woman to whom he's not married. Can you see how I would find this interesting?"

"Yes, because Western women are interested in sex with married men." He was serious.

"*Oh no we're not,*" Jorja said emphatically.

"I think Western women have a high sexual appetite and have a fucking relationship with everyone. They have regular sex because it's not good to block the flow of desire. Muslims know this too. Within Islam, women have formal rights to sexual satisfaction in marriage, and the denial of such satisfaction constitutes grounds for divorce. By contrast, Christianity is silent on women's sexual satisfaction within marriage. Mmmmmm," he cleared his throat again.

"Is that so?"

"It is so. Men have desires. So do women. The Qur'an says that Muslims should balance the needs of the body with the needs of the soul and the material needs with the spiritual needs. That's why Allah said a man could have four wives to fulfill his desires. I'm happy with one wife because she is modern when I say that I want to have a relationship with another woman. Allah says that everyone experiences the temptation of the flesh and that we have freedom of choice to accept or refuse temptation. Allah challenges our choice only according to our ability to handle the challenge. Allah desires to ease our lives and not make our lives hard. Allah is benevolent. With every difficulty comes relief. He punishes no one atoning for past sins. He waives punishment if others force Muslims to perform acts that are contrary to their beliefs because they have no other choice. I will assure Allah I can handle the challenge of having a relationship with you."

"Good for you, but we will not be having a relationship. I've made a decision and Allah thinks that the decision is good."

"Mmmm," the throat cleansing continued. "It's Allah's will that we met. When I first saw you in the car, I knew I had to meet you. When Mrs. Kaliq told me she saw you in the Ministry of Education,

I asked her to arrange dinner with you and Hasibur so I could meet you. Therefore, it's Allah's will I'm here with you at seven o'clock on this day to ask you for a relationship. That is the wish of Allah. It's predestined. It's our fate and destiny. Mmmmm."

"Really? It seems you've contrived to meet me, not that it was Allah's will. Allah brings to you many interesting cases in your legal practice, doesn't He?" They nodded together. "But you don't always win the cases, do you?" He agreed. "So, you see, it's your destiny to have these cases presented to you and it's your destiny to fail in some of these cases."

"Ah, you are a clever woman. That's why I like you." He smiled. "Mmmmm. That's true. It is my destiny not to win every case. It's a similar situation with you, yes? I cannot win you."

"Yes, I'm glad you understand. I shall tell Mrs. Kaliq we've decided not to have a sexual relationship."

"No, no," he said quickly. "I will tell her. You can be assured of that."

"I'm sure you will." She smiled.

Praying quietly to himself while fondling his religious beads, Mr. Kaliq broke his concentration by clearing his throat. "Mmmmm. You would like a kissing relationship?"

Persistence was his forte. Negotiation was his means of persuasion: start with high expectations before moving onto the lesser option. Jorja pursed her lips to stifle a smile. "A kissing relationship?"

"Like this," he pounced and covered her closed lips with his, balancing one hand on the bed where she was sitting and the other in the air. His hands never touched her. The suction was fierce, like a love bite on tender flesh. Returning to the chair, he asked. "You like kissing relationship?"

"No," she said firmly, as she waited for her numb lips to recover.

"No, you do not like kissing?"

"Yes, I like kissing, but not with you. There'll be no sexual relationship and there'll be no kissing relationship. I'd be very pleased if you left now. Shall I say it in Urdu?"

He laughed. "Oh no, I understand your English very well, but I cannot understand why you don't want a kissing relationship with me. However, it's your wish. I am most respectful of your decision. Please call me if you change your mind. I must return to my practice now."

"I'll see you to the door, yes?"

As he stood to leave, he negotiated once more. "Would you like to have a weekend with me in Islamabad? No fucking relationship, no kissing relationship. We just stay in the same hotel, in the same room?"

Opening the door, Jorja said. "Good try. Mrs. Kaliq will like that one when I tell her. Shall I tell her the answer or can you guess it?"

"I'm very good at guessing games, so you do not need to speak to Mrs. Kaliq." He always referred to his wife as Mrs. Kaliq. Jorja didn't know her first name, nor did she know Mr. Kaliq's first name. "Would you like to go for a drive with me tomorrow night? My driver will take us to the park that overlooks Muzaffarabad. It's very beautiful at night."

"Guess again. You can bring Mrs. Kaliq with you next time you visit. It'd be lovely to have dinner with both of you, yes?"

"No, no. Mmmmm. It's not a good idea," he mumbled as he left the room. Jorja could hear him clearing his throat loudly as he descended the stairs. In the bathroom, she surveyed her tingling lips and was surprised to see a swollen pout. She splashed cold water over her mouth then ran to the telephone.

"Qaseem, can you please connect me to the project office? Wait, wait. Before you do, why didn't you telephone me when Mr. Kaliq arrived? You know you should announce visitors so I can meet them in the restaurant. No one is to come directly to my room. You call me when the minister comes to visit, so why did you let Mr. Kaliq come to my room?"

"But madam, Mr. Kaliq is a lawman. He is a good man and a person of status in Muzaffarabad," he said, defending himself. It was true Mr. Kaliq enjoyed a position of privilege that made him seem untouchable.

"The minister is a person of status too. It doesn't matter who they are, they must not come to my room without my consent. Even Jahmal meets me in the foyer or restaurant first, and he's just a boy. Enough of that now, can you connect me to the project office please? I wish to speak to Lufti."

"Yes, madam, as you wish." Qaseem hung up. Seconds later the telephone rang.

"May I speak to Lufti please? Is Lufti there?" Lufti took some time to reach the telephone. "Lufti, Lufti, you were right about Mr. Kaliq. He *is* a sleaze ball." Jorja fell on the bed as they laughed stridently at the events she related.

"So you and Mr. Kaliq are no longer 'friends'?" Lufti laughed. He was a confidant, a friend with whom she could have a raucous laugh. His patience, understanding, and his uncritical acceptance of her stirred her heart. Jorja felt an extraordinarily strong bond of fellowship, of true friendship, with Lufti. They enjoyed this diversion. Mr. Kaliq's indiscretion was their secret.

"Lufti, can we go to the park on the hill one night. I hear it's very beautiful."

"It is indeed very beautiful because you can see the whole of Muzaffarabad and you cannot tell where the lights of the city end and the stars begin. Let us go tomorrow evening."

* * *

Fadil drove skillfully and slowly along the narrow dirt road to the crest of a hill and parked underneath a leafless dead tree. Lufti guided Jorja to a bench and they sat close together, appreciating the beauty of their surroundings. Fadil disappeared into the darkness. In the serenity of the evening, under a canopy of stars, Jorja and her wise companion discussed the meaning of life, their role in the Universe, and their predictions for the future of Kashmir.

When a gust of wind sprayed them with dust, they hurried toward the vehicle. Fadil turned on the headlights to light their way. The reversing vehicle cast its beams along the ridge of the hill, exposing a couple dashing for shelter. Jorja recognized the man instantly. It was Mr. Kaliq. Jorja focused her sight on the woman, but the blurred shape was unrecognizable, except that it was young, tall, slim, and female. There was no doubt that it was not his wife.

Jorja looked at Lufti, but he was looking at Mr. Kaliq. There was nothing that escaped Lufti's attention. Lufti smiled at Jorja, and in his silence, they both knew what the other was thinking. Mr. Kaliq's indiscretion was their secret.

CHAPTER 42

LONELINESS

The monotony of life in a hotel room made Jorja curious about the river's occupants. From the balcony, she could see a man tapping a donkey on its rear to move it along the pebbly bank. The river reflected the sky. Usually it was steel-gray, but on this sunshiny morning, the sky and the river were duck-egg blue. For the first time, she walked to the riverbank at the lower level of the hotel.

Sitting on a boulder, she spun a flat stone over the water, watching it plop three times before drowning. Her movement disturbed the glossy green frogs. Across the river, at the army barracks, two soldiers patrolled the thin, dirt path that led to the water's edge. They had slung their arms around each other's shoulders and were laughing and talking intimately. Jorja was too far away to make out their conversation, but snippets reached her eardrums. Someone's mother was a source of amusement, it seemed. She felt calm and serene watching the bubbling, gurgling fateful river—the fatal river.

"Madam, madam!" Awan was calling, beckoning her to the patio of the restaurant. "Madam, quick, please come quickly." His skinny arms were waving in alarm. Reluctantly, she obeyed.

"What is it, Awan?" Qaseem and Riyad arrived to investigate the commotion. Awan was gesticulating agitatedly to Riyad.

"Awan does not want you to sit by the river, madam," explained Riyad. "It's dangerous."

"Very, very dangerous," interrupted Awan. He appeared worried and angry.

"But why, Riyad?"

The manager continued. "I've told you before how dangerous the river is. Many people have drowned it in. Besides, a madman could take you away, or worse, throw you into the river. You should never sit there again. Always stay in the hotel. Why don't you sit on the patio?"

"But I was right by the hotel. I wasn't walking anywhere." Jorja defended her actions.

"Madam, our staff cannot see you there. We cannot keep an eye on you, and that is our duty. Please be so kind as to not do it again. I will ask Awan to make you some tea and you can sit here."

"Yes, I make tea for you."

"Thanks Awan. I'll take tea in my room."

"As you wish, madam."

The men dispersed as she walked despondently through the French doors, and through the restaurant, before continuing to her room.

* * *

April 7, 2002
Denny,
It'll be a waning half moon tonight. That means it'll soon be invisible and neither of us will see it.

Today is the start of daylight saving for the first time in an Islamic country. Most people are against it because they think that it'll disrupt their prayer sessions. You know, like the farmers in Australia thought it'd disrupt the cows' milking routines. It's all very controversial and topical. In Australia, daylight saving has finished, so instead of a six-hour difference, there's now only a four-hour difference between us. That makes me feel somehow closer to you.

It's raining. It's been raining since lunchtime. The day began with clear skies and beautiful weather. I was sitting at the riverbank, but Awan called me inside, to protect me from the dangers of the river, and kidnapping, and murder! It was useless to argue with him. Since then, there have been growls of thunder—rolling, rumbling thunder. It's a Sunday, a lonely Sunday.

There's a wedding in the hotel. Thousands of children are yelling and screeching with excitement. The family let off three or four marriage bombs. They scared the hell out of me. In the rural areas, they fire pistols into the air, but that's not allowed in the city. I rang reception to find out what the noise was. "Marriage bombs, madam," Qaseem said. There have been many weddings in the hotel, but this was the first with marriage bombs. I was a little unprepared, to say the least.

I tried to arrange a telephone call to you. It seems that every time Qaseem tries, there's no line. This time he got a line, but you weren't home. Your answering machine was on. I'll try again soon. . .

Later: Qaseem keeps trying to call you, but can't get a line out. I've asked him to keep trying. I'm lonely and long for the sound of your voice.

Later: Denny I'm so glad you were home. It was so, so good to hear you. I'd forgotten how wonderful your voice sounded. Sorry the line went dead. Apparently it does that after ten minutes. When I queried Qaseem, he said that there was a time limit. I wish he'd told me beforehand. It's probably just as well because the call cost me a bucketful of rupees. I've just been downstairs to pay.

I've hardly any money left now, after having the Pakistani suits made (the shalwar kameez), paying for my hotel meals for the past month, and the phone call to you. I'll arrange to go to Islamabad as soon as I can—hopefully for longer than a day!

I'm so sorry I hadn't phoned before—it's been such a hassle with money and then no phone lines. And I still don't have a mobile phone. I'm glad I persisted today. My heart jumped with excitement when I realized you were on the line, but when I finally heard your voice, I didn't know what to say. I wanted to say so much, but said very little. Fortunately, you talked a lot, which is quite unlike you. All the while, it was thundering so loud I could barely hear you.

I had to speak to you. I felt such a pang when I thought I saw you the other day. Whenever I see anyone with long hair, which Gadi says are the Talibs, I think of you. I miss you so much. Mr. Kaliq's sex proposal made me think of you too. I was bursting to tell you, so I'm glad you thought it was funny. And what do you make of his tryst in the park in the dark? What a sleaze, eh? I'll e-mail more about it later. In fact, this will all sound familiar because you would have already heard it from me and read about it in a few e-mails before you ever get this letter. But you know I like to write.

Now I'll answer some of your questions. Yes, I want to come home. It's a long time without you. It's a long time without the normal routines of eating, shopping, and working. Sometimes Gadi and Hamid talk as if I'm definitely staying another five months—they said Jamshid told them. No one has spoken to me about it—not Jamshid, Wasim, or even the minister. It's so unsettling.

I can hear someone coughing and coughing and coughing. There always seems to be someone with a bronchial infection, coughing up phlegm. Spluttering, sniffing, and wiping their noses on their shirtsleeves is so common here. Too much smoking, I guess. The men smoke everywhere: at work and in restaurants. During meals they cough, sniff, pick their noses (with their finger right up there), and even spit. It really is foul, but no one bats an eyelid here.

The internet hardly ever works at the project office. There are 152 million people in Pakistan and I swear that they all use the internet at the same time. At the project office, I have to dial in—it takes ages to connect— sometimes two hours. At the Internet Cafe, it's a different situation. The manager connects the computers when the shop opens in the morning and they remain connected all day. The only problem is the power failing, but that happens rarely this side of the Lipton sign.

The memory of your voice will get me through this week. Next weekend I hope to go to Islamabad. I'll try to call you from there.

I'm thinking of you so much—heaps and heaps.

Love, Jorja

Sunshine appeared soon after Jorja finished the letter. Since the death of her husband, Jorja had the notion that another committed relationship—staying with someone permanently in one permanent place—would end her sense of freedom. She strived to accept that one would not necessarily preclude the other. Robert Frost wrote freedom was in being bold. For Jorja, freedom lay in being able to love and to be loved.

Longing to venture outside, she contemplated her isolation. She had thought that the loss of her husband paralyzed her from venturing into another relationship, but she was beginning to realize that restlessness and rootlessness had pervaded her life. Nomadic, a gypsy wanderer, she had continually moved from city to city, country to country. Newton's law was part of her reality:

a body in motion tended to stay in motion until a force altered its course. She was a body in motion. And Einstein had said there was no global center for observing the world and any point in it was as good as any other. That was also her truth. Only now was she contemplating staying in one place. Therein lay a fundamental problem: to reconcile her need for movement with her present urge to settle, to nest, and to find her own sense of place. The telephone call to Denny triggered an attack of homesickness, an urge to return to a fixed point. *Was it a present urge or had it been a subconscious and suppressed desire that was now surfacing? Had Kashmir become a catalyst exposing her true feelings? Perhaps the Kashmiri's innate sense of belonging to their land and their family was influencing her emotions. Had family migration fractured her sense of place, of where she called home, causing her to be the eternal seeker?* Whenever she was in Australia her thoughts drifted to exotic lands, and when abroad, her thoughts were of Australia.

Since childhood, she had a recurring dream.

She drives along a road bounded on the left by a mountain and on the right by the ocean. Before her is a town and, within it, a feeling of belonging. She's driving home to an ancient fishing village with cobblestone streets and narrow alleyways. The landscape rises and dips, making the two entrances to her house on different levels. The front door is at ground level at the base of a small ascent, while the side entrance is on the first floor. Ethereal with spacious rooms, the bay windows overlook the sea. Transparent white curtains flutter in the salty breeze as she ambles over squeaky floorboards. The place has a sense of stability and permanence. There is a knowing, each time she awakens from this dream, that her place of belonging is not Australia.

Living in Australia, she had a fear its remoteness from the world was an exile. Yet its isolation had provided Australians with a land free from war and hostility. But Australia was not independent; it was not free. The 1999 referendum to determine whether Australia would become a republic was overturned. The Queen of England continued to reign over Australia. Australia, like Kashmir, was not free from the ties of the past.

CHAPTER 43

LITERACY AND COWS

Jorja's speech began nervously. It was impromptu, at Lufti's request. "Use Urdish," he whispered as he guided her to the podium. "Urdish" was Lufti's word for her mixture of Urdu and English. Instead of feeling comforted, she felt ill.

The principal of a nearby secondary school permitted them to use the hall for a workshop on the development of low-cost teaching materials. The large hall dwarfed Jorja, and she feared that her voice would not carry more than the first ten rows. Teachers, supervisors, and administrators sat on rickety child-sized wooden chairs on an uneven concrete floor. Her voice dissipated through the large open windows, their flimsy white curtains fluttering in the breeze. In the blinding sunshine, children laughed and chattered on their way to their classrooms. Relieved, she finished by thanking Mahmud and Lufti. Unexpectedly, the audience stood in unison and applauded loudly.

Halia, a school inspector, clapped enthusiastically and continued long after the applause finished. She wore a black abaya that covered her clothes and a hijab that covered her entire face. Befriending Jorja, Halia frequently tugged at her shalwar kameez, seemingly craving reassurance and attention. In a low voice, Halia declared her dislike of Pakistan, and Islamabad in particular. She disliked its irreverence toward education, brought about, she said, because of its over-abundance of schools, unlike Kashmir. The sector, F-8, led Islamabad in the category of "most schools in one place." The institutions included hundreds of kindergartens and three undergraduate course-approved universities. The cadet colleges of Petaro and Hasanbdal were sizeable, equaling at least two sectors of Islamabad. Smaller cadet colleges operated from individual houses.

In Kashmir, that was not the case. Most primary schools were in remote and isolated mountainous regions with substandard buildings, often without the shelter of a roof. Schools rarely had blackboards, and often there was no seating, no teaching aids, and minimal textbooks. Children sat on the dusty ground or on concrete slabs. The stark difference in the quality of Islamabad's school buildings with those of Muzaffarabad was obvious. The quality of education was, however, debatable. Halia insisted that Azad Kashmir, although poorer than Pakistan, had a better standard of education, evident in its higher literacy levels.

Islamabad had the Education for All office, but with only fifty-two percent of primary-school-aged children participating in education, this was a statement of intent and not a reflection of reality. The demand for access to basic education was ever increasing, but the government could not satisfy public demand. Private schools attempted to meet the demand, but there was little control over standards and quality. Private English Medium Schools were mainly concentrated in the urban and semi-urban areas where they could charge higher fees. Resources available to the Government of Pakistan remained seriously constrained and so, in the late Eighties, it initiated policies to attract international donor funding. The government provided special financial incentives to non-government organizations that could offer functional literacy, secondary education, and technical and vocational education for females in the underdeveloped and rural areas.

Despite a decade of efforts toward education, Pakistan's literacy rate was the lowest amongst the most populous countries. The percentage of girls attending school was lowest in Baluchistan, which was understandable since it was the most undeveloped province due to tribal systems and decades of a stigmatized education for girls. The highest participation rate for girls was in Punjab, the largest province. Incremental increases in funding over the previous ten years had produced a minimal increase in literacy rates across the country, particularly amongst girls. Halia and Jorja discussed this with Rabi, the science specialist.

"Aid agencies had unrealistic targets. That was the problem, Miss Jorja," Rabi said. "There was too much attention on building schools. In Pakistan, they thought if students had schools to go to, then the participation rate would increase, and so would the literacy rate. It didn't happen. There were schools, but no money to supply teachers. It was folly. I like that English word. Folly! The government closed most of the new schools because there were no teachers, especially in rural areas. The government didn't provide any more money. If schools had teachers, they were under so much stress and pressure that the absentee rate was high. There were too many students to teach. One teacher had to teach a hundred and ninety students. Folly, yes?"

"It's a similar situation in Kashmir, but the quality of education is better," Halia said. "In villages, we recruit tribal elders. They aren't qualified, but they are keen to help. There's no money to train them. We try to get to rural schools to provide training, but it's a slow process. What is Kashmir's literacy rate now compared with Pakistan, Rabi? The figures have just come out in a report last month."

"I'll tell you," said Rabi. "I have the new UNESCO report with me." From his well-used briefcase, he pulled out a wad of

papers and rifled through them. "Here it is. It says that there are
fifty million illiterate people above the age of ten in Pakistan.
Most of them are women. The report says that in 1951, the literacy rate in Pakistan was sixteen percent and it had climbed to
forty-nine percent by 2001."

"Does the report mention Kashmir?" asked Halia.

"Of course not! This is a Pakistani report, but we know that
the literacy rate in Kashmir is sixty percent. The higher rate is
because of donor agency projects in education. We're lucky in
Kashmir because we can control the funding. Less corruption
produces more education."

"The students I've spoken to think education is very important because it'll help them get a job," Jorja said. "Are there jobs
available?"

"We have an extremely high unemployment rate," said
Rabi. "Most students will leave Kashmir and look for work
in Pakistan."

Raja embraced Rabi who had raised himself to greet his colleague. "We're talking of serious things here, education and literacy. Have you come to join us?"

"Yes, I'll sit awhile, but let's talk of something just as important." He slapped Rabi on the back playfully. They were like
schoolboys, continually touching each other affectionately, albeit sometimes boisterously.

"What's that Raja?" Jorja asked. "You aren't going to ask me
about relationships again, are you?"

"Oh no, no." He laughed. "But I'm still praying for you. No,
I want to talk about Australian cows."

"Oh, no!" said Rabi, as he shook his head. "Cows are his
favorite topic with every foreigner he sees. Fortunately, he
doesn't see many."

Jorja looked curiously at the two men. Halia excused herself and moved to another group. The large hall was divided
into sections. One third was arranged with a lectern and rows
of chairs. Two-thirds of the hall was arranged so that groups of
teachers could make low-cost instructional materials around

large rectangular tables. Groupings of chairs were scattered about and easels with art paper were erected for demonstration purposes.

"I'm inquisitive about cows because I want to know how to increase the production of milk in Kashmiri cows," Raja explained. "It confuses me why I can't get mine to produce more milk. There's nothing sinister in my curiosity, but Rabi thinks I talk of cows too often."

"He does," Rabi said. "Anyone would think he had a herd of them, but he has only two!" As an afterthought, he added, "Although I suppose that's two more than I have."

"Let me be serious now," said Raja. "Kashmiri cows only produce, on average, two liters of milk a day. Most small-acre farmers only have one cow and two liters is not enough for their children's needs. I have four children and four liters is usually enough for my family, but sometimes it isn't."

"So you buy milk then?" Jorja asked. "I don't think I've seen fresh milk for sale. In the bakery next door to the hotel there's only long-life milk or powdered milk."

"That's right. There's not enough fresh milk here. That's my point. And that's my problem. It's a big problem in Kashmir. Literacy is a problem for the mind, but milk is a problem for the body. We need healthy bodies to make a healthy mind. All Kashmiris buy powdered milk, except perhaps the wealthy people who might buy it fresh from a farmer. Yes, that's our problem. My dilemma is how to get an Australian cow to Kashmir!"

"Miss Jorja" said Rabi, "Raja wants an Australian cow. Can you arrange for one to be sent to him?" He laughed loudly. "Just one Australian cow. Then he will be very happy."

"Australian cows are fat and healthy. They produce a lot of milk. Yes, all I want is an Australian cow, *Insh Allah*!"

"You're not asking for much," she remarked. "I'll see what I can do! But for now, let's check on the workshop participants. They need your expert advice."

Halia accompanied Jorja again as she moved amongst the workshop groups. By day's end, Halia had removed part of her veil to reveal her eyes, ringed with shadowy circles. Dry skin flaked around her nose and forehead, giving her an overall older appearance, but Jorja knew she was probably not as old as her face portrayed.

CHAPTER 44

ARRANGED MARRIAGES

Friendship and marriage dominated conversations amongst women in Kashmir. During the workshop on the development of teaching materials, Jorja's conversations with Halia and two young female teachers were no exception.

Ghazala, one of the young teachers, could have been beautiful, but her drooping facial features resembled a dejected hound dog. Like the eyes of most Kashmiri women, she had baggy folds of skin, from sleeplessness, lack of nutrition, or perhaps from worry. As she spoke, she seemed to turn memories into torture, wallowing in regret, resentment, or nostalgia. Hers was a sad life supporting a large family of brothers and sisters. Her parents were hopeful that she would marry her uncle, but Ghazala was resisting, although Jorja had the feeling that Ghazala was somewhat resigned to her fate. "*Insh Allah,* it will not be so. I don't wish to marry her," she said, confusing genders. During the tea breaks, she would stoop round-shouldered over her cup of steaming tea, as if she were trying to draw strength from its fumes.

Waresha was taller, livelier, and more optimistic about life. Regal-looking in a lacy black dupatta, she allowed it to slip onto her shoulders. Her black-rimmed glasses added a touch of seriousness to her demeanor.

Both women had long black hair. Ghazala's lacked life and frizzed into split ends while Waresha's shone healthily. Both women had fulfilled their ambitions to become teachers and were enrolled in legal courses at university. Ghazala studied to please her father, whereas Waresha had a genuine love of learning. They both sought marriage: Ghazala to escape the rigid rules of her family and Waresha to share the joys of life with a soul mate.

Jorja jokingly said that she was waiting for Imran when they questioned why she was not married with children.

"Miss Jorja, Imran is married," said Ghazala.

"Yes, but he can have four wives."

"But Jemima is English and she will not allow it."

"Imran is Muslim," added Waresha.

"Being Muslim makes no difference to me. If two people love each other enough to marry, then they'll make sacrifices," Jorja stated.

"Yes, that's true," they both agreed.

"Miss Jorja," added Ghazala, "If you met a Muslim man, would you consider marrying him? Would you change your religion?"

"We'd discuss it. I imagine I would be willing to make the sacrifice for love. The word sacrifice is from the phrase *sacer facere*, to rise up in a single act from the profane world of greed and fear into the serene dimension of the sacred and to transfigure one's whole life in one moment."

"Oh Miss Jorja, that's beautiful. You are so wise and yet not married. Haven't your parents found anyone for you?" Waresha queried.

Jorja replied light-heartedly, "Would the marriage have to be arranged by my parents?"

"It is preferable, yes. If your parents are not in Pakistan, another reputable person could arrange the marriage. It would be respectful of you if you followed the courtship and marriage rules of the Muslim faith. I could help you to find someone, but usually a senior male relative organizes everything. What about Lufti? He could assist you if you asked him," said Waresha.

"Can I choose my own man?"

"You can suggest someone and Lufti can check his references."

"References?"

Waresha explained. "Lufti would need to check whether your potential husband has money and can afford to keep you. And whether he's in good health, and whether he wishes to marry you. Parents or delegates discuss these factors amongst themselves first. The woman's father or delegate makes the first approach to a man's family and it's his duty to ask many questions to determine suitability. It's important that the man be of equal status or higher. Lufti should look for a doctor or lawyer for you, Miss Jorja. Lufti must also check the man's family for a history of insanity, criminal records, and any undesirable behavior. It's done discreetly so that there's no direct insult or humiliation on the man or his family. Then you can speak to the man to see whether he likes similar things. He may want to know whether you expect to work or to be a housewife."

"Yes," added Ghazala, "and he may want to know if you will live with his family or whether both of you will live with your family. In this case, he may want to stay in Pakistan. If he has a brother, the brother and his wife might live with you too. I'm sure he'll allow you to see your family in Australia, so don't worry about that. The educated men are quite modern now. All of his family members are usually required to agree for him to marry you, but because you are a rich foreign woman, I think they'll agree. Don't you think so, Waresha?"

"*Ji*. I think they'll like you, Miss Jorja. You don't need to worry."

"What if the man doesn't want to marry me?"

"The man will tell Lufti and Lufti will tell you politely. Then Lufti will find another man for you. If the man likes you, we will all help to arrange an engagement ceremony and a wedding. You'll look beautiful in a gold embroidered dupatta and lots of gold jewelry," said Ghazala. The two women giggled and Jorja joined them.

"A young woman gains confidence in marriage and is always happy," said Waresha.

"Really? I don't think I need more confidence." Jorja laughed. Lufti looked toward the raucous laughter and smiled. "But what if the marriage doesn't make the woman happy? What happens then?"

"That doesn't happen much with educated people," said Waresha. "I know a twenty-year-old who married a computer analyst ten years older than her. He wanted her to go to America where he was working. When she went to America to live with him, his American girlfriend was also living in the same house. She didn't like that."

"Who didn't like it, the American girlfriend or the Pakistani woman?" Jorja was curious.

The women laughed. "Both of them probably hated it, but I was referring to my Pakistani friend." Waresha became more serious, adding, "It wouldn't have been good to divorce. Our culture does not like divorce or separation. If Vashti had come home to Pakistan, dishonor might fall upon his parents, I mean her parents. Vashti had no choice, but to accept the situation. She still had a good life in America and could buy many nice things. She should consider herself lucky she only shared her husband with one woman and not other wives or family members in the same house. She's lucky, I tell her. I always tell her not to complain."

"Are arranged marriages still very common here?"

"Oh, yes," said Ghazala. "About ninety-five percent of marriages are arranged, don't you think so Waresha?" Waresha nodded. "Do you want Lufti to find you a good husband if you stay here?"

"If I were looking for a husband, I think Lufti would do an excellent job because he knows me very well. He would look for someone I like."

"Good," said Waresha. "It would be very successful because Lufti would only want the very best for you. You'll love the man

Lufti chooses because real love comes from a properly arranged union between two individuals carefully selected for each other."

Arranged marriages in Pakistan had adjusted to liberal Islam. Previously, to preserve an unmarried woman's purity, her most valuable asset, the prospective bride and groom were not permitted to see or speak to each other. Middle-class women could reject suitors favored by their parents, but this freedom came with a price. Some women, after having rejected many suitors found themselves in their late thirties, alone and outcast. Yesterday's newspaper reported one such situation: *According to details, one Muhammad Iqbal proposed one Fatima, but she refused. In a rush of blood, Iqbal and his accomplices shot dead Fatima.*

Waresha suggested that Lufti might need to advertise for a man, in Jorja's case, because she was not well known in the community. "Advertising in the newspaper is quite an acceptable way to find you a prospective husband." Jorja had seen an advertisement in the local paper: *By the grace of almighty Allah, we are happy to announce that we can provide proposals according to your desire (inland/abroad) from any age, class and caste. Please call for matrimonial proposal list and avoid mismatching.*

Ghazala changed the topic and asked, "Will Denny not marry you?"

"Oh no, we're just special friends. I haven't known him long, and we're not in a committed relationship. It's just a special friendship."

"He should marry you because you're very nice. We like you very much. How could a man not like you too?"

"Great question, Ghazala. How could anyone not like me?" After much laughter, they continued the discussion about the English curriculum for primary students. Eventually, the conversation returned to relationships.

"I hope you two realize I was just joking about Lufti arranging a marriage for me. I'll be back in Australia soon and I'll take my chances there. Are your parents arranging a marriage for you Waresha?"

"I've rejected two men already," she said. "My parents are talking to the parents of another man now. It's not considered good to wait too long because I'm twenty-four. I must decide soon."

"What about the man who is rejected? That mustn't be good for him?"

"No, it's not," said Waresha. "The parents of the man would not be happy to know that a woman has rejected their son. Everyone will know and the parents will lose face amongst their friends. People will then ask questions about his desirability. I always ask my father to find out how many times a man has been rejected." The women looked at each other and nodded in agreement. "An unmarried daughter brings shame too upon her parents. It'll be a burden to the parents if their daughter is not married."

"So are you under pressure to get married?"

Waresha answered, "Yes, of course. I must decide soon. It's my responsibility not to delay too much. I'm lucky that my skin is not very dark. Parents with dark-skinned daughters have difficulty arranging a marriage for their daughters. Ghazala and I are lucky."

"Rima and the other women at the curriculum office said that looks weren't important in Kashmir, so why is being dark such a bad thing?"

"Miss Jorja, Rima is an older woman and looks were not important in her day. Ghazala and I are young and modern and we think about our looks. Nowadays many of us have the possibility of marrying men who have been overseas to study and they prefer women with lighter skin. Our husbands may wish us to live in another country, such as America or England, so we think about how Western society perceives our looks. But, of course, looks are not the main thing that Kashmiri men desire. They want a woman who'll have children and a family, will care for them, and perhaps work."

Jorja merely mused aloud a line from Richard Brinsley Sheridan's poem of love: "Whatever her complexion, I vow I don't care; if brown it is lasting, more pleasant if fair."

"Exactly!" the women said in unison.

"Girls, you've heard of Osama bin Laden, haven't you?"

They nodded. "I hope you are not suggesting that one of us marries him," said Waresha. "He is married with many wives and many children, but he is not considered a desirable husband because he is a terrorist."

"Well, it seems that even terrorists marry. But I'm not concerned with that. I was wondering whether you had ever seen him, in real life. Do you think he's handsome?"

The young women looked at each other. They both shook their heads. "Of course not," said Waresha. "How silly of you to think that! He's not handsome, he's too old. And we certainly have not seen him. He's in Afghanistan where the Americans are looking for him on a secret mission."

"It's not secret," said Jorja. "It's Operation Anaconda. It's in all the newspapers. Do the newspapers speak the truth? Is Osama bin Laden really in Afghanistan or is that a decoy by the Americans? Perhaps Osama is in Kashmir? Some people think so. Do you really think he's old? He's not very old."

They glanced at each other again. "Excuse me, Miss Jorja, but I think you are going a little crazy in the head. Osama bin Laden is definitely in Afghanistan. The papers say so. And he must be at least seventy," said Waresha. Osama bin Laden, by all accounts, was forty-five years of age.

"At least seventy," repeated Ghazala.

"No, no, he's much younger than that," Jorja persisted.

"At least seventy," the women chorused.

In addition to working as a secondary-school teacher, Ghazala was also studying law at her father's request. In a quiet moment, when Ghazala and Jorja were alone, she touched the foreign woman on the arm and pleaded, "Miss Jorja, you must help me. You are my friend and friends help each other. Please, please find me a job overseas so I can escape this country."

"Don't you wish to join your father's law firm?"

"I love my father, but working together may be difficult. That is not the main reason why I want to leave Kashmir. As you know, my parents want me to marry my uncle and I do not. This is a sad, sad tragedy. I don't like her very much. Please believe me. She is a bad man, a bad uncle. She always tells me what to do. She is a bully. I don't want to marry her." The worry lines appeared on Ghazala's face as her dupatta fell from her hair.

CHAPTER 45

MARRIAGE PROPOSALS

Men proposed quickly in Kashmir.

Pervaiz had proposed while teaching Jorja Urdu, as a test of her comprehension. It was a joke they enjoyed together. Her second marriage proposal came from a hotel cleaner. She had returned early from the workshop on how to make teaching materials, cold and shivering. It was three o'clock. She ran up the stairway to her room, rubbing her arms to warm them. Running through the room to find cozy clothes, she flung off her scarf and it caught the end of the unmade bed. Staff had not cleaned the room. She sighed disappointedly. The knock on the door irritated her. The cleaner had arrived to clean her room.

Carefully, he picked up her scarf and draped it over a chair, smoothing the fabric delicately. He made the bed slowly while she shivered near the two-bar heater. One bar didn't work. A cold mountain wind stirred the white curtains. She wanted to put on warm clothes. Instead, she waited impatiently for the cleaner to finish. He resembled a prepubescent ten-year-old with apple cheeks and swollen lips.

"You beautiful, madam," he said softly.

"Thank you." She spread the newspaper across the heavy wooden desk and sat down.

"You like massage, madam?"

"No, thank you." She did not look at him.

He moved behind the chair and again asked if Jorja wanted a massage.

"No, thank you," she said more firmly. "The bed looks nicely made. Now please clean the bathroom."

The cleaner removed the slate-colored, thinning towels from the handrails and moved toward her. "I am liking you so much and want to marry you." He dumped the towels on the end of the bed and placed his small hands on her shoulders, making massaging movements. "I give you massage, madam?"

Jorja stood up, slammed the newspaper closed, picked up the towels, and thrust them firmly into his chest. "I will call the manager if you say that again. You have not cleaned the bathroom, have you?"

He muttered embarrassed apologies and scuttled out of the room.

Qaseem telephoned to inform Jorja that the minister was in the foyer. Jorja and the minister took afternoon tea in the hotel's restaurant. They discussed the progress of the workshop and arrangements for two more, another in Muzaffarabad and one in Mirpur. He urged her to stay in Kashmir for eight more months to conduct teacher training, classroom research, conclude the project, and write three reports. Eight more months! It seemed like a never-ending assignment. Jorja proposed that there should be a variety of consultants and trainers with fresh ideas, diversity, and a range of experiences. He insisted that sourcing and mobilizing consultants would take too long and he argued for continuity. The minister had a point.

Ghazala entered the restaurant. "Sorry, Jorja, for troubling you. Qaseem said you were in the restaurant. Hello minister, I need a brief minute with Jorja."

The minister nodded, pulled a piece of paper from his jacket, and perused it.

Ghazala continued. "Miss Jorja, you must help me. I need money for my father." She pleaded with Jorja. "My father, a government lawyer, has been fired from his job. Please, please Miss Jorja, can you provide me with money so that my father can establish his own law business?" The request was equivalent to Jorja's annual salary. "It's even harder for me to support my family now that my father has lost his job. I need money to buy a new business for my father. Please think about it and let me know how much you can pay. Let me know soon, please, please. I also need money to buy my friend a mobile phone. You can get one in Islamabad at the market next time you go. Please! You are my friend, my very best friend!"

"Let's not talk about it now. Everything will work itself out." Jorja reassured her that, in time, she would overcome all obstacles.

"Thank you so much, Miss Jorja. I know you will consider my needs." Ghazala tightened her dupatta around her hair and left.

"I'm sorry, but I couldn't help hearing," said the minister. "The decision to help the young lady is yours, but let me offer you some advice." Jorja nodded. "It's not wise to succumb to every person's request whether they are your friend or not. Some people don't help themselves in life. They ask too much of others. I hope I haven't offended you."

"No, no. I appreciate your advice." Providing Ghazala with financial support was not Jorja's preferred option. Privately, she hoped that Ghazala would not raise the subject again.

"Now, let us discuss your next assignments," continued the minister.

Jahmal came to Jorja's rescue. He rushed into the restaurant, talking rapidly and breathlessly, as he waved his arms in the air. "Madam Jorja! Madam Jorja! My parents want to meet with you. Yes, they really do. They have invited you to our home.

You must come soon. We'll arrange it soon. You must say yes."
Jahmal's shrill voice annoyed the minister, a calm man in comparison, who promptly bid them goodbye and left the restaurant.
The college boy, who had been jumping jerkily from one foot to
the other, took a seat and composed himself.

"Walk me to the Internet Café and I'll give you an answer
there," Jorja said.

"But madam Jorja, it's late in the afternoon and you should
not be there at this hour. This is when the big fuckers go there."

"Please. I'll be very brief. Less than half an hour. I didn't go
to the project office today because of the workshop and I want
to e-mail Denny."

"Oh, Mr. D. Yes, that's important. Come, let us go now.
Quick! *Calo!*"

Jahmal stood over Jorja while she wrote an e-mail to Denny:

> *D*
>
> *I must be quick. Jahmal is panting like a puppy.
> He's out of breath from dashing to the Internet Cafe
> from the Sangam. He has to hurry home, but I needed
> him to accompany me here. Lots of big fuckers here and
> I feel safer with Jahmal (weeny though he is, he's better
> than nothing!!).*
>
> *I've just had afternoon tea with the minister. He's
> talking about me being here for another eight months
> now, not five! Where did all of this come from? Jamshid
> hasn't mentioned anything to me. I'll try to call him to-
> night to resolve this issue. It's getting beyond a joke.*
>
> *Must fly—I'll e-mail you again soon,*
>
> > *Jorja*

"We can go now, Jahmal," said Jorja. Clutching her dupatta
firmly around her head, they dashed back to the hotel. As she
passed the reception desk, a man approached her.

"Excuse me, Miss. May I introduce myself? I'm Ali Khan
from Lahore. I'm staying in this hotel. The hotel attendants

mentioned you are involved in education. May I take some time to tell you about the schools I have in Lahore? I'm a district superintendent." He did so, and after some time they moved to the seats in the foyer to continue the discussion. Jahmal sat glued to Jorja's side.

"Here, let me write my name and telephone number on this paper. If you come to Lahore, it would be my honor to show you the schools. You can stay in my sister's residence."

Looking at the white notepaper, Jorja said to the gentleman, "So you're another Khan from Lahore? People call the famous Imran Khan the Lion of Lahore."

He laughed. "He's my cousin."

"Really?"

"So true!" He stood to leave. "Sorry to have taken so much of your valuable time." As he extended his hand, Jorja took it with both hands in a grateful handshake. "Oh, goodness me! You shake hands like a Pakistani! I can call you sister!"

Jahmal escorted Jorja to her room. "Thanks Jahmal, you can go now."

"But madam Jorja, you have not given me an answer yet."

"About what?"

"Dinner at my house, remember?"

When she agreed to his parents' request, Jahmal beamed with satisfaction. He had succeeded in his task. "Jahmal, it's late. Shouldn't you be going now?"

"Please don't worry. My father is nearby and his car is still outside the hotel. I have a few minutes. You look very beautiful tonight. I love you very much."

"More than the Melody Queen?"

"Most certainly," Jahmal insisted. "You are so beautiful that I wish to arrange a marriage with you. I will suggest it to my parents. They'll arrange everything. Please don't worry about my family's consent. They won't object to the arrangement. Please don't worry about my age. The father of our nation, Mr. Jinnah, married a much older woman, as you know. It's the practice in this country. I'll love you, respect you, and bring you much happiness, forever and forever. I'll let my father know, yes?" he urged, whelp-like. Flattery flowed forth and slipped off his tongue like a slobbering puppy. His thick, bushy eyebrows danced on his animated face and his long eyelashes flickered flirtatiously.

"What about having ice-cream instead?" Jorja suggested. Jahmal dropped his shoulders in resignation and accepted the rejection gracefully.

"Do they have chocolate? Now that we are not going to be married, I can tell you a very big, big secret because we're friends, yes?" Jorja nodded. "I'm not sure whether I can sex anyone really, you know. And do you know why? A tragedy has fallen upon me, madam Jorja?" Jorja was about to protest, but Jahmal continued. "I have a bent penis, you know. It's not straight like the big fuckers. I have seen their penises and mine is not like theirs. But they have not seen mine. Can you tell me why my penis is bent?"

She winced. "See a doctor, Jahmal," she urged. "I'm not a medical specialist." Jorja telephoned the restaurant to order ice-cream.

"I'm too embarrassed to see a doctor. This is a personal tragedy," he frowned. His bushy eyebrows came together and formed a long streak across his forehead.

"I can't believe this, Jahmal. You're too embarrassed to see a doctor, but you're not too embarrassed to talk to a foreign woman about your penis. It doesn't make sense to me. Go straight to your doctor," Jorja implored. "Jahmal, they don't have chocolate, only vanilla." Into the telephone, she said, "Vanilla will do. Two please."

"Madam Jorja, you don't understand. I tell you this tragedy because you're my friend. My doctor is a family doctor and he's not my friend. He'll tell my father. Then I'll be disgraced and shamed. I'll have no choice but to commit suicide because of my bent penis."

"Jahmal, there's no point committing suicide because of a bent dick. I've read it affects a significant number of men. I just haven't heard of someone so young being afflicted with such a problem. Find a different doctor. In fact, I know one. I'll ask Riyad, the hotel manager, to get you a doctor." Jorja worried about his distress.

"That is most kind of you, but Muzaffarabad is a small city. I'm very well known here, madam Jorja. The doctor will tell my father and then everyone in the whole of Muzaffarabad will know, even the big fuckers. I tell you the tragedy will become bigger, and I'll have to leave here forever if you do not permit me to commit suicide."

"You can always see a doctor in England in September. They'll have good doctors and they'll keep your problem confidential. I'm sure they can help you."

"Oh, madam Jorja, you're so wise. I've had a bent penis for a very long time, since I was born, and now I'll have it straightened in England. My tragedy will be over." He beamed excitedly, just as the ice cream arrived. His excitement was short-lived. Seated at the round table, he placed a mounded spoon of ice-cream into his mouth and recoiled painfully.

"Jahmal, now what's wrong?"

"I've just had a big thought, madam Jorja. In England, my personal tragedy will be over, but my money tragedy will surely begin. The English doctors will charge big pounds for such a treatment. How will I be able to afford it?" His face was an actor's study in emotion.

"Jahmal, let's take one problem at a time. Wait until you get to England. Allah may find a solution just when you need it. Let's not worry about that now."

His face lifted again. "Madam Jorja, you are right. The Prophet Mohammed, may the peace and blessings of Allah be upon Him, will provide an answer, *Insh Allah*."

"*Insh Allah!*"

CHAPTER 46

AS YOU WISH

A transformation had taken place. At the commencement of the workshop, Halia was shrouded in a black burqa, wearing black gloves. Not a glimpse of skin was visible, except her eyes. After three days, on the last day of the workshop, Halia took both of Jorja's hands in her exposed ones, brought them to her lips, and kissed them, repeatedly expressing her gratitude. Uncloaked, she wore a tan shalwar kameez with a matching orange dupatta that draped loosely around her shoulders. With her hair coiled into a bun, she seemed crowned with a practical self-assurance that softened her weather-worn face. Hyacinth fragrance, emanating from her hair, wafted around Jorja, making her want to draw even closer to Halia. It was the familiarity of the scent—the scent of her grandmother— that attracted Jorja to the school inspector. She was proud of Halia's achievements and in awe of her personal metamorphosis. A lump clotted in her throat and, for a moment, she thought she would cry with happiness.

Fadil drove Lufti and Jorja, silent from weariness and elation, to the heights of Upper Chattar. Exhausted, Lufti retired to his room.

"Gadi, can you please get Jamshid on the phone for me while I try to connect to the internet?"

"As you wish, madam." Gadi spoke briefly in Urdu on the telephone. "Madam, Mr. Jamshid says he's busy now."

"Tell him that the minister wants me to stay in Muzaffarabad for eight months."

"Mr. Jamshid says it is as the minister wishes, madam."

"Tell him that I'm coming to Islamabad next weekend."

"Mr. Jamshid says, as you wish, madam."

"Tell him that I'll be in Islamabad for more than a day."

"Mr. Jamshid says, as you wish, madam."

"Tell him that I'll be staying in the bedroom upstairs and not in the Decent Lodge."

"Mr. Jamshid says, as you wish, madam."

"Tell him that he needs to arrange a visa extension if I'm to stay longer in Kashmir."

"Mr. Jamshid says he will arrange it, as you wish, madam."

"Tell him I'm going to be angry with him when I get there."

"Mr. Jamshid says he will have some beer for you."

"As if that's going to make me feel better."

"Can I put the telephone down now, madam?"

"As you wish, Gadi."

An e-mail from Denny arrived:

> *Babe*
> *I can't believe that the minister can expect so much from you. What is Jamshid doing? Can you telephone me sometime? When are you going to Islamabad? I don't know what to write now. When you've spoken to Jamshid, let me know. Are we going to get a proper decision soon? Hell, it's frustrating enough for me, I*

feel so sorry for you. How on earth are you coping? Stay well, babe.

Denny

Gadi approached the desk and leaned over the computer, toward Jorja. "Not now, Gadi. I don't want to hear another word about your secret and how you know where to find Mr. bin Laden."

"But, madam."

"*Not* now, Gadi."

"As you wish, madam."

CHAPTER 47

A TALE OF TWO HOUSES

Jahmal and his father, Iftikar, arrived at the hotel lobby in the evening. Jahmal gave Qaseem details of his name, address, telephone number, a list of dinner attendees, and Jorja's estimated time of return. He did so without hesitation, saying it was for safety reasons. "The hotel staff should trust no one, not even me!" Jahmal emphasized.

Their home, a grand residence at the top of a hill, had magnificent views. The city of Muzaffarabad was a carpet of sporadic lights in the inky darkness. Slate tiles formed the path to the front door through an arch of fragrant climbing roses. Red budded roses dotted the dark green foliage, looking like beckoning pouted lips. Proudly, Jahmal escorted Jorja through the arch, along the stepping stones and into the double wooden doors. Pastel-colored plastic flowers and a lava lamp, reminiscent of the Seventies, were the showpieces of the front room. A wall picture, plugged into an electric socket, depicted a lifelike waterfall amid a luscious rainforest.

The dining room overlooked an illuminated rooftop balcony. Surrounding a rectangular table of immense proportions were chairs, stools, and benches padded with cushions. Within seconds, the room teemed with sisters, aunts, uncles, cousins, parents, and grandparents. A mixture of sweet and spicy foods spread across the table in a close-knit weave of bowls, platters, trays, and baskets. Women of the household served the food. Jahmal's older sister spooned mounds onto Jorja's plate ensuring that it was never empty: servings of spices and chick peas, fruit salad, shammi kebabs with rice and raisins, sweet cakes, and finally potatoes boiled in broth with sliced tomatoes. Spicy and sweet courses sat next to each other in an undifferentiated medley of tastes that confused Jorja's palate.

After dinner, Jahmal and Jorja sat in the ornamental front room with his sister, flicking through the pages of photograph albums while sipping Kashmiri tea. He showed her letters of acceptance from an English university. "This is the university that I'll attend in September. See the seal. It's a prestigious university, don't you know. My father is very proud, but also very upset, as he cannot afford it. He was a policeman and now he's the director of public lands. It's a good job in the government, but he has many people to feed. He must look after his brothers and his brothers' wives and all of their children. My sisters will go to university too, but maybe not in England. My father is wondering where the money will come from. You understand don't you madam Jorja, because you are my friend?"

"Yes, I understand." It was, under the circumstances, the worst possible thing to say.

Jahmal took advantage of Jorja's acknowledgment. "You will sponsor me and pay for my university study? I know you will because we're friends. That's what friends do."

To extract herself swiftly from the situation, she emphasized that she *wasn't* sponsoring his education in England. She watched his chest deflate and his whole body slump in desolation.

"Oh, that is too bad. My father will be disappointed. I will have to tell him carefully. Yes, indeed; very carefully."

The two rejections—one of marriage and one of sponsorship—had clearly deflated his ego. Nevertheless, he bore the rejections without malice.

Jahmal accompanied his father as he returned Jorja to the Sangam Hotel. Iftikar traveled via the Red Fort built in the seventeenth century to defend the city against invaders. The moon cast the abandoned stronghold in ominous shadows as it stood in defiance of violent floodwaters, earthquakes, and the depredation of time. Iftikar sighted his mechanic beside the road and stopped the car to greet him. Still in his grease-stained overalls, the mechanic invited them to take tea in his home, despite the lateness of the evening. Jorja had already out-stayed her estimated time of return and hoped the hotel staff would not be concerned about her safety.

The laneway to the mechanic's home was too narrow for the car to enter so they followed him on foot along a rat-infested, waterlogged, moonlit path as if he were the Pied Piper of Hamlin. A story of dismay or defeat etched the laneway in a collection of cubed, mud-brick homes. Poor, but not desperate, the mechanic possessed a city residence that protected him from the weather.

The dwelling had no entry porch. They stepped directly into the cavernous living room with a concrete floor and two beds. In the villages nearby, a room like this of three-and-a-half square meters would hold eight or more family members. The mechanic's home contrasted starkly with Iftikar's opulent manor.

A calendar, a colored poster of fruit, and a clock hung on the walls. The floor sloped at a great angle, and the walls had gaping cracks near the ceiling. The mechanic fetched several bolster-cushions, plumped them up, and placed them on the beds to convert them into couches. He was exceptionally house-proud. His wife, a nurse at the Combined Military Hospital, brought tea and homemade biscuits into the room and placed the refreshments on a low, ornately carved, wooden table. The couple did not speak much English, nevertheless their hospitality was overwhelming. Jorja felt relaxed, lounging comfortably against the downy cushions.

Jorja heard running water and asked Jahmal if one of their children was in the back room. He politely answered, "No, Allah has not gifted them with children. He has blessed them in other ways." Jorja left it at that.

CHAPTER 48

WHITE SKIN, PINK SKIN

Unexpectedly, Jahmal arrived at the Sangam Hotel the next day, as Jorja lunched on the patio in the sunshine. Breaking into agitated conversation, he shrieked, "Madam Jorja, madam Jorja, do not sit in the sun. It's not good for your skin. It's turning pink already. Put your dupatta on quickly. Quickly, I tell you!" Obediently, she lifted her dupatta from her shoulders and placed it over her blond hair. Jahmal rearranged it to his satisfaction. He continued insistently, "That's better. Never, *never* sit outside with naked skin! Your skin will burn, madam Jorja. I tell you, your skin will burn. It's already bright red," he remonstrated. He didn't have to tell her twice.

Jahmal was right, of course. Jorja's defense was that she needed to feel the sun's warmth on her skin. She had failed to notice that the heat had prickled her sensitive skin and had formed pink blotches on her arms.

"Madam Jorja, look! Your arms are marked with strange shapes. A short-sleeved kameez may be modern, but it's not protecting you from the sun. It's too late to save you. I'm so sorry, madam Jorja."

Conscious of people's stares, Jorja covered her diseased-looking arms. *Did her face have the same disfigurement?* "And what can I do for you, Jahmal?"

"Nothing, madam Jorja. I was in the vicinity and wondered if you needed to go to the Internet Café. Do you wish that I accompany you?"

She had intended to go to the project office rather than the Internet Café.

"As you wish, madam Jorja. I will call again tomorrow to see you. But please, madam Jorja, be careful with your skin. I think you need me to remind you, yes? You need a man to look after you. You don't look after yourself properly. I hope Mr. D tells you to look after yourself. I hope so, yes I do." He continued muttering, as he walked through the restaurant toward the foyer. Less than ten seconds later, he returned. "Madam Jorja, I've been thinking. I cannot leave you here sitting outside. It's my duty to tell you to come inside so you're not sitting in the sun. It would be irresponsible of me, I tell you. Please, madam Jorja, I'll help you move your tea inside."

Dutifully, Jorja stood up. Jahmal had already called for assistance from the waiter to resettle her at a table near the window, out of the sun. Content, he went on his way.

A rustling of clothes broke the silence. Ghazala appeared behind Jorja. Finding her requests for money awkward and embarrassing, Jorja dreaded the possibility of another. Fortunately, Ghazala bore good news. Her father had commenced a legal business with a friend. He had also acceded to his daughter's wish not to be forced to marry her uncle. The family agreed to pursue an arranged marriage with a younger man in the legal profession. Greatly relieved, Ghazala's anguish dissipated.

Her demands for money were now for a wedding dress, of the best quality, honeymoon costs, and a mobile telephone for her soon-to-be husband.

A fourth quake struck that night. It was Friday, the twelfth day of April, under a perilous new moon. The tremor was mild in comparison with the previous three quakes, but left the region in fear.

CHAPTER 49

OSAMA'S EYES

Jorja sensed it was an ominous morning. She rarely took breakfast in her room. On this morning, she sat at the round table close to the southern balcony she seldom used, with a view beyond the Kashmir border to Murree and Islamabad. Even with the warmer weather, the mountains still showed traces of snow and ice. Looming larger were the nearby hills of Upper Chattar where the grand white, red-roofed project office, barely visible, perched above a ravine.

Pouring "separate" tea into the stained china cup, she breathed in its fragrant fumes. Three slices of toast, wrapped in a beige cloth to trap their warmth, sat on a chipped plate. As she unfolded the soft cloth, pellets of mice droppings clung to the cotton fibers. Droppings dislodged and landed on the warm, golden bread. Nauseated, she set the toast aside.

She rang the restaurant. "Do you have fruit this morning?"

"Madam, we only have pomegranate; juicy, red pomegranate." The fleshy fruit, with its sweet and bitter flavors, was the only one said to have grown in the underworld where souls of the dead ate it in order to be reborn. The Greek goddess, Persephone, having swallowed its seeds, was destined to remain for part of each year in the land of the dead as a bride of Hades. Considering it an omen, Jorja declined.

The minister had permitted her to travel to a region outside the city, a considerable distance from the Line of Control and the dangers of border fighting. Fadil arrived promptly, and as requested, brought Jorja a paper bag of mandarins which she ate during the drive to the country.

In contrast to the ash-colored city, the countryside was verdant and full of new scents. The sky seemed bluer and purer than in the metropolis. Inhaling deeply, she considered herself lucky to be in the mountainous air, surrounded by emerald-green fields.

A farmer offered her a seat on a log and poured her a glass of water. He didn't drink in Jorja's presence, nor did he sit down, but she saw him place one hand on his lower back, as if trying to ease discomfort or pain. She stood in solidarity with her companion. Her excuse, she told him, was that she had been sitting too long in the car during the drive to his village and he nodded to indicate that he understood. He was small, less than five feet, with a concave chest and hollow torso. Periodically, he scratched himself under his armpits. Pointing with a bony finger, he showed Jorja the local school, a small and crumbling mud-brick box. Boys, about a dozen of them, sat on the concrete floor inside. Outside, five girls sat on the dirt close to the doorway. She asked where the teacher was but was told he was sick. Jorja was not surprised. In a larger village nearby with ninety-two children on the register, one of the two teachers was absent. "Sick?" Jorja queried a mother with an ailing face. "No, one works for the first six months, the other works for the second six months." They both collected full pay.

"But this school is supposed to be a two-teacher school," Jorja remarked.

"Yes, we have two teachers," the mother said. Kashmir's people, not yet disillusioned and embittered, remained confident that their teachers did their best. Optimistically, they expected positive changes and one day, there would be, at the very least, two teachers working at the school simultaneously. "Wheels of change turn slowly," the woman reminded Jorja.

The farmer led her around his plot of land. She could smell the chickens before she saw them. Manure, soiled hay, and rotting vegetables created an odor that overpowered the fresh scent of the fields. It was not a place that set her free. Freedom from Muzaffarabad's woes did not permeate the countryside. Chained by stark poverty, the villagers knew only the remoteness and inaccessibility of a harsh land. Nature was heedless of people's suffering.

On her return to Muzaffarabad, Jorja avoided Gadi for almost a week to prevent him from pestering her to hunt down Osama bin Laden. However, he informed her by telephone that she was to visit another village school. He had made all the necessary arrangements and had, as required, gained the approval of the minister. Gadi had determined that no additional security was required since the school was, as with her previous village visit, in the opposite direction from the Line of Control that separated Pakistan-administered Kashmir from Indian Kashmir. The village school was northwest toward Afghanistan, and too insignificant to be marked on any local map. Gadi's pencil sketch provided Fadil with directions. Fadil showed Jorja the roughly-drawn map before departing, but it made no sense to her; they were merely lines and crosses on a scrap of paper.

The school was in a rugged area where the vehicle struggled to reach an outcrop with a few huts. Jorja and Fadil abandoned the vehicle and walked for an hour up the mountainside to the inaccessible village. Fadil, acclimatized to the thinning air, strode silently forward, but Jorja needed two brief rest stops. It was the call of the children that encouraged her to climb the last hundred meters.

The school was a cavernously dark tent that accommodated five children: four boys and one girl. The teacher, an untrained tribal elder, priest, farmer, medic, and butter churner stooped double to enter, and sat cross-legged on goatskins as he spoke quietly to his guests and his students. Their black eyes were on Jorja. The girl cuddled close to the foreign woman, snuggling underneath her armpit.

"These are my children," said Zohair, the teacher, "except the little girl. She is the daughter of my sister. My wife bore the four boys before she died in the cold. It was a bad winter like this one. There are more children in this village and in those surrounding us, but they don't come to school often. Once, two boys came for some days. They had no shoes for the long journey so they stopped coming. I have the register in one of these boxes." The man pointed to vegetable boxes at the back of the school tent. "I could find out when they came to school, but it was not this year." He explained that when he churns the butter, he teaches children how to make soft, salty butter, how to count to a hundred, how to recognize the seasons, how to know a good wind from a bad wind, when to pick the berries, and how many hours makes a day and a night. He wore a silver watch and tapped it to show Jorja it worked. "I teach the time and how to add hours and subtract hours and how to add seconds and subtract seconds."

Before they returned to the car, Fadil and the teacher lit cigarettes and spoke in their common language. The children, on Zohair's instruction, led Jorja further up the goat track to drink from a natural spring. The water was icy and she shrieked in shock. The children laughed. To demonstrate their resilience, they splashed their faces with hand-cupped water from the ground well, leaving it to form ice pearls on their brows. Crouching to imitate them, Jorja felt a presence, a shadow forming over her.

"Ayman, Ayman," a man called out. As Jorja stood, the man stopped abruptly, stabbing his cane into the ground and holding up a hand to stem the movements of the two men behind him.

Jorja recognized the beard first, then the black arched eyebrows, the thick-lipped mouth, and lastly, the eyes of the leading man. Hiding her surprise and fear, she wiped her hands on her dupatta, and chatted inanely about the weather while holding out her hand in friendship. Osama bin Laden shook her hand gently. The men behind him scowled. Jorja continued to talk, not expecting a reply, merely to mask her nervousness. She scooped the young girl to her side, and in English, spoke of the tented school, the lack of textbooks, the lack of teachers, the remoteness of the village, and anything else that entered her head. The men remained silent.

Nervously, she said, "Oh, I'm so sorry. I only speak a little Urdu. *Mujay afsoshai, er, er, mai siraf thori see Urdu bolta houn."*

The children spoke excitedly in their language and the three men smiled, looked at each other, and around the countryside as if looking for a lost dog. Osama bin Laden motioned his minders to sit on a rock. They did, although stiffly, as if on a knife-edge.

The leader seemed relaxed. His dark turban contrasted starkly with his sallow skin. A charcoal-colored jacket covered his striped white and brown kameez. Matching trousers tucked into brown army-type boots were of thick cotton. Waving flies away, his hands appeared feminine and frail with long, slender fingers. He smiled the whole time.

"*Chai?*" he offered. "Tea?" Without orders, one of his henchmen fossicked in a backpack for a metal can and cups. The other deftly made a mound of dry twigs and lit a fire. The first man ordered a boy to fill the can with spring water while he opened a tinfoil envelop of dried tea leaves. The aroma was overpowering. Before Jorja answered, the men had established a tea-making procedure to envy. They crouched by the fire, made a tripod from stones, and placed the can on top.

Osama untucked his shalwar from of his boots and rolled them up over his knees, exposing finely structured legs, resembling those of a gazelle. He smiled at Jorja who was still standing, paralyzed, eyeing the three men in amazement. The children pulled at her arms, motioning her to sit on the grass near the camp-fire. The men spoke in Arabic, softly, in almost a whisper. Osama handed Jorja a metal cup of brewed steaming tea.

"*Shukriya.* Thank you. It's fabulous," she enthused. "This tea is amazing! I don't think I've ever tasted such flavorsome tea. It's just what I needed."

The men smiled and the children giggled.

They passed time looking at each other, smiling, drinking tea, and admiring the mountainside. No conversation was attempted. Jorja was careful not to stare at the greatest terrorist of all time in case he suspected she knew his secret. Simultaneously, she did not want to avoid his attention, and as a compromise she looked at him sporadically, always with a warm, appreciative smile. One of the henchmen, a head taller than Osama bin Laden, offered Jorja the aromatic tea leaves to inhale. She found some barley sugar, neatly wrapped in clear cellophane, in her shoulder bag and handed them to each man in her tea party. They nodded their thanks, sucked on the sweets and looked around at the countryside.

"*Bihar*. Spring, the season of spring," she said. The men nodded. "*Khubsurat*. Beautiful."

"*Khubsurat, bahut khubsurat*," whispered Osama bin Laden. "*Bahut hara.*"

"Very green, yes, very green indeed," iterated Jorja. The men nodded their heads, sipped their tea, and grinned.

Fadil's shouts called Jorja to leave her companions. "*Mauf keejay,* excuse me," Jorja uttered as she stood to leave. She handed back the empty silver-tinned mug to the tall henchman. As he clasped the mug, he pulled her by the arm gently toward him. Close by his side, Jorja caught a waft of cigar smoke, perfumed and sweet, almost intoxicating.

He swirled the tea leaves with a slight motion and they peered into the bottom of the mug. "*Dil*," he said. He looked at Jorja. "*Qalb*," he said in Arabic.

"Oh yes, it is. I see it. A heart," she confirmed. He nodded slowly. Fadil shouted again, and Jorja turned her head toward the noise. "I must go."

She ran down the mountainside. As she approached the school, she almost knocked over Zohair who was churning butter. She shook his hand and started the long walk down the mountain to the car with Fadil at her side. Jorja darted a glance upward to the outcrop of rocks. The children were skipping down the slope. In the distance, three straight-backed forms moved along the western ridge. She breathed a sigh of relief, but also of exhilaration. She had seen *the* man. She had seen the man everyone despised. If only she had done something more than just drink tea. She thought tea drinking was not an exciting tale to tell, but soon shrugged off the disappointment and replaced it with a smirk of satisfaction. She had seen *the* man, the most hated man on earth, and *survived*. A weight lifted from her shoulder and she felt as if she could float away.

* * *

Jorja's mind was in a spin. She wanted desperately to talk to someone. *Who would believe her? Who, in their right mind, would believe her?*

"Qaseem, can you put me through to the project office, to Lufti, thanks," she requested.

Two minutes later, Lufti was puffing into the telephone. "Jorja, I've just returned from my walk with Mahmud and I'm rather tired. I think the warmer weather is tiring me out. Did you enjoy your visit to the village school today? Are you packed ready for Islamabad tomorrow?"

Jorja didn't hear him. "Lufti, Lufti, I *saw* him. I saw *him*."

"Ah so, you saw Imran Khan again, did you?"

"No, no. I saw Osama."

"Osama who?"

"Osama bin Laden. Stop being silly, Lufti. You know whom I mean. I saw Osama bin Laden at the village today, on the mountainside."

"Ha, Jorja, you're the one being silly. What was he wearing?"

"He was wearing a dark turban and ..."

The Professor interrupted her. "I was joking, Jorja. I don't want to know what he was wearing. You're being silly. First Imran, then the Talibs with knives, and now Osama bin Mu-hammad bin 'Awad bin Laden, if you want to know his full name. You'll get yourself into trouble telling lies like that. What a story-teller you are."

"But Lufti, I'm telling the truth. I *did* see him. And I *spoke* to him. He offered me tea. I don't think he knew I knew who he was. He was rather polite, just like any other man. Honestly! And his eyes were quite mesmerizing. Really! If I didn't know who he was, I would say they were quite mysterious, Lufti. But of course I knew who he was and so I know there is evil in his eyes."

"Bah! Terrorists don't have mysterious eyes. What nonsense!"

"But Lufti. Please believe me. I *did* see him. He called one of his men, Ayman. That's his deputy, Ayman al-Zawahiri. I'm sure of it."

"He was with his army was he?"

"No, of course not! He was with two men."

"And they called him Osama, did they?"

"No, of course not!"

"Did he have a beard?"

"Of course!"

"Ah, it was probably Peter Bergen with a beard."

"Who?"

"Peter Bergen! Don't you watch CNN? Peter Bergen, the terrorist analyst, the Pakistan expert. Everyone knows Peter Bergen."

"Lufti, it wasn't Peter whoever, it was Osama bin Laden, the most wanted terrorist in the whole world."

"Sure. You think you see famous people. Just as you said you saw Imran, the greatest cricketer in the whole world. You do exaggerate. Your mind is much too vivid. Have a cup of tea and lie down. Did Mahmud tell you that we have had our contract extended for a month to assist you with the workshops in Muzaffarabad and Mirpur? In May we'll be gone."

"Great! I'm so excited. You're extended and I'm going to Islamabad tomorrow. Woohoo! For a date with Imran! Just kidding!" Her mind wandered. *Whom would she tell next about Osama bin Laden? Authorities? Which authorities? Newspapers? She could notify Dawn. That seemed like a good idea.* "Lufti, are you there?"

Before she heard the click of the receiver, she heard the click of Lufti's tongue, and a guttural "Bah!"

CHAPTER 50

TEMPORARY PRISONER

In mid-April Jorja thanked President Ayub Khan for Islamabad. Ayub Khan had hopes for a permanent capital city to reflect the cultures, traditions, aspirations, and dreams of the diverse groups that constituted the newly established Pakistani nation. Karachi, Pakistan's largest city and only port proved unsatisfactory as a capital because of its distance from many parts of the country and its debilitating, hot climate. Khan considered it prudent to build a new capital in a location easily accessible from the remotest corner of the country. In view of Islamic ideology, he recommended the Federal capital be located closer to the Muslim areas of Central Asia and in close proximity to the fraternal people of Iran, Afghanistan, Saudi Arabia, and Turkey. He constituted a commission in 1958 entrusted with the task of selecting a suitable site with particular emphasis on climate, logistics, military requirements, aesthetics, and natural beauty.

The commission chose northeast Rawalpindi, the headquarters of the Pakistan army. Construction began in 1961 and the first residents moved into Islamabad two years later.

A Greek firm, Doxiadis Associates, drew up a master plan for the new capital. The design for the city was triangular, based on a grid system, with its apex toward the surrounding hills. Islamabad nestled against the backdrop of the Margalla Hills at the northern end of the Pothowar Plateau. Wide tree-lined streets, sizeable houses, elegant public buildings, and well-organized shopping centers distinguished the capital from other Pakistani cities. Divided into eight zones, Islamabad catered for the community's basic needs: administrative, diplomatic, residential, educational, industrial, commercial, rural, and leisure. It reminded Jorja of Australia's national capital, Canberra. There were many similarities: roundabouts, government buildings, and wide streets with limited traffic. Both cities were clean, neat, prim, and proper.

Crowds, traffic delays, and narrow lanes were rare in Islamabad. Rows of flame trees, jacaranda, and hibiscus shaded the walkways and separated them from the vehicles. Roses, jasmine, and bougainvillea filled the parks and scenic lookouts above the city. The city appeared peaceful and ignorant of the multitude of soldiers in it. Khaki tents and Kalashnikov assault rifles were evidence that Pakistan was a military nation.

"Every country owns an army, but in Pakistan, the army owns the country," said Noor, the Islamabad driver. Soldiers, positioned at various checkpoints, maintained security by stopping cars at random. They always waved Noor through. "You have white skin, madam. That's why the soldiers do not stop me." He smiled and added, "I like driving you around."

Jamshid arranged for Jorja to stay at the office in a bedroom upstairs. His assistant had begun the visa process by obtaining a form, but Jamshid had done nothing with it. Early the next day, Jorja reluctantly took the matter into her own hands. Her visa was due to expire and she required the extension in order to conduct the remaining workshops, regardless of whether she was staying in Kashmir for further assignments. Noor waited in the oppressive heat of the car while she disappeared into a camera shop to obtain visa photos.

Noor drove her to a cluster of government buildings and waited. An official-looking person ordered Jorja to wait in the women's restroom when she asked him for directions to the visa office. Jorja protested. "I don't need the bathroom. I need the visa office." He pointed to a room nearby on the ground floor.

The visa office was open for two hours a day, four days a week. Visa aspirants queued in four dysfunctional lines on the outside of the building behind glass service windows. There was no shade. There was no movement. Two government officials sat in the room amid a chaotic pile of papers, working slowly, methodically. Jorja was the only woman in the queue. Her white face turned pink in the extreme heat. Finally, she reached the glass window. "You journalist?" the officer bellowed.

"No, I'm not a journalist. I'm an education consultant working for the World Bank."

"Next line," he said. Standing up for privileges in Pakistan caused confusion, lots of attention, or laughter. In this case, it attracted much attention, but no one came to Jorja's aid. "Next line," he said again gruffly. It was futile to protest. Moving to the end of the adjacent queue, she waited. On the glass window, a shabby notice read "Journalists and Cleaners." Certain that she was in the wrong queue, she asked a young man in front of her, who shrugged his shoulders and mumbled, "Just wait, madam."

In the line she had vacated stood a young Afghan soldier applying for a student visa. He was hoping, after studying in Pakistan, he would aid his country again, just as he had during his time in the Afghan army. Jorja asked if he and his men had distinguished themselves by any particular heroics. He shook his head, saying that everybody had played the same part. This time he would return with skills to assist in the rehabilitation and reconstruction process.

"What did you want to do when you were fighting in the army? Did you want to be an architect or a builder then?"

"I only say I wanted to live."

She persisted. "And then? You wanted to live to do what?"

"So I could get married and breed soldiers. Now there is no need for soldiers. Instead of soldiers, I will breed to rebuild the population. I'll do my part to help my country."

Again, Jorja reached the head of the queue. The same official that would not serve her earlier was looking at her again. "Papers?" She handed him a passport, photographs, and visa form. "Come back next week."

"Excuse me. My visa expires in five days. Will a new one be ready in time?"

"Ready in two days. Come back in two days."

"Thank you. Thank you so much." She thought it wise to ingratiate herself with government officials in Pakistan.

An hour had elapsed and Noor was surprised Jorja had taken so long. "Why didn't you push to the front of the line? Women can do that. Next time, I'll go with you."

Jamshid wasn't in the office when she returned. His assistant, Minhas, explained that Jamshid was in Peshawar and would be away for a few days.

"What? What do you mean? Why didn't he mention it last night over dinner? He's avoiding me, isn't he?" No one answered. With two workshops to arrange, she had much work to do. She telephoned Lufti to allocate tasks and responsibilities. As usual, he told Jorja not to worry.

Denny hadn't answered her e-mails over the weekend, which meant that he hadn't been working. It also meant he hadn't repaired his home computer. The lack of communication was frustrating. It was Monday and she hadn't received an e-mail from her lover. She attempted to telephone him, but couldn't get a line no matter how many times she tried. Minhas tried, too, with no luck. E-mails were her only lifeline home.

Two days later, Jorja returned to the visa office. Noor had to collect a parcel and couldn't accompany her. She was disappointed. She queued in the sun. This time she shielded her face from the burning rays with her dupatta. When she reached the glass window, the officious man said, "No madam, papers not here. Go to Immigration Office." When Noor returned to the car, she explained the situation.

"The Immigration Office is a long way. I hope it's open, madam."

Luckily, it was open. A kinder man in the Immigration Office explained that Azad Kashmir was not part of Pakistan but considered to be a region with its own government offices. Jorja's papers had been sent to the Muzaffarabad office where her visa was to be issued, not the Islamabad office.

"And my passport? Do you have my passport? I need it to get back into Azad Kashmir."

"No madam. Your passport is not here. It's with your visa papers that have been sent to Muzaffarabad."

Her heart sank. She couldn't travel to Muzaffarabad without presenting her passport to the Kashmiri border guards. This fact seemed not to permeate into the mind of the simple government official. She was too hot and weary to explain. She had no option but to return to Muzaffarabad the next day without a passport.

Jorja telephoned Jamshid who said he was too busy to assist and advised her not to worry. All evening she tried to telephone Denny, again with no luck. Instead, she e-mailed telling him of her confusion, frustration, and annoyance. As she did, an e-mail from her sister announced the death of her uncle, her mother's youngest brother. Billy Craddock was holidaying in Mumbai, and on his last day, while he was at the airport, he collapsed from heart failure. No amount of aid could revive him. His Indian wife, Serani, was by his side, distraught and helpless. Jimmy, the eldest of their four adult children, along with Serani's family, was assisting with the transport of the body back to England. Jorja put her head on the desk and wept silently.

Minhas was persistent in his efforts to connect Jorja with her mother. Eventually he had a telephone line, but Betty Craddock-Himmermann was already on an international flight. Minhas wept with Jorja. They sat on the upstairs balcony drinking tea to commiserate her loss.

* * *

At the Pakistan-Kashmir checkpoint, the barrier was insignificant. Only two soldiers were present. Several more soldiers rushed out of a small building when the car stopped.

"Passport," a guard requested. She explained, in a combination of Urdu and English, and with the aid of Fadil, the reason for not having a passport. Far from anyone who knew her face, she shivered in the heat. To the guard, she detailed her intention to extend the visa so that she could stay longer in his beloved country and help the people of Azad Kashmir.

"You journalist?" the guard yelled.

"No." She felt decidedly uneasy.

"Out of car, madam. Out of car, now." Four soldiers escorted Jorja to a dank, stark, rectangular room. Shafts of sunlight streamed from a narrow window highlighting the dust particles in the air. A soldier ordered her to sit in an upright wooden chair. Fadil followed, talking in Urdu and waving his arms wildly, all to no avail. He did not leave Jorja's side.

She was uncomfortable about finding herself taken prisoner and it made her adopt a stiffly formal tone. "Please sir, I have been to Kashmir many times. I am extending my visa, but the Immigration Office in Islamabad sent my passport to Muzaffarabad, so I don't have it with me."

No matter how many times she repeated the situation, the head guard continued his request for a passport. "Madam, no passport. Prisoner till we see passport." His stance was aggressive, with legs apart and his hands on his waist, forcing his jacket open and his stomach forward. Jorja swore she could see the bone handle and the concave blade of a kerambit knife in the pocket of his trousers.

Fadil pleaded with the officers for Jorja's release while she rummaged through her handbag. She didn't know what she expected to find in the oversized bag, but she had to do something.

"Madam must have visa to enter Kashmir. Must see visa," Fadil explained again. "You have copy of visa?"

She explained that the visa stamp was in her passport. Fadil signaled for Jorja to keep silent. He did an extraordinary amount of talking. The soldiers in turn, sat down, stood up, paced back and forth, left the room for a cigarette, and returned to see whether Jorja had found a copy of the visa. Fadil was temporarily quiet. The soldiers talked amongst themselves.

Desperately, frantically, Jorja searched her handbag again for any sign of a photocopy or a visa number written on a scrap of paper. Piece by piece, she examined each document in the dimming light. Fadil, exasperated, demanded he also search her handbag. Jorja passed items to him and he turned them over, looking officiously at them. She was not sure that he knew what he was looking for, but he was helpful and it passed the time.

"Madam, this copy!" Fadil exclaimed.

"No, that's a copy of my No Objection Certificate. It's not a copy of the visa entry. The soldiers want to see my visa." She continued searching.

"Madam, please look. It is the visa copy," Fadil insisted. "It's sticky to the other paper."

"Fadil, I've no idea what you're saying. I'll keep looking."

"Madam, please look. Please look."

"I *am* looking!" she said, raising her voice.

"No, madam. Please look *here*. It's sticky. How do you say? Two papers, not one paper." He waved the document in front of Jorja and pulled one sheet of paper away from the other. Her eyes opened in excitement. With a page in each hand, Fadil smiled, and wafted them close to her face. "Please look, please look." One was a copy of her No Objection Certificate and the other was a copy of the visa stamp in her passport. "Should I tell the soldiers?" Fadil asked with great pleasure.

"Yes please, Fadil. Tell everyone."

Fadil jumped up and exclaimed excitedly to the guards, who lazily perused the document and gave it to the head guard. The head guard read the document carefully and, in turn, showed each of the three officers. A teenage-looking boy copied the visa number into an official ledger. Fadil and Jorja waited for someone to speak.

The head guard nodded, folded the paper, and handed it to Jorja. "You no prisoner now, madam. You take tea?" He called for the young officer to make a pot of tea. Jorja had lost track of time. An hour may have elapsed. Maybe two. Fadil told them politely they should be on their way, and they left the darkened, stale room for the freshness of the mountain air. The guard escorted them to the car. "Madam, you must carry passport with visa. This is a very dangerous place. You understand, madam?"

"I understand, officer."

* * *

The Muzaffarabad Immigration Office could not process Jorja's visa. To do so, an official Kashmiri seal was required. They did not have an official seal. The seal was lost and they had yet to manufacture a new one. For the past six months, all Kashmiri visa requests had been processed in Islamabad.

"How many requests?" Jorja asked.

"None," he answered sheepishly.

"But, but the officer in Islamabad said ..."

Both Fadil and Hamid stopped Jorja from talking further. Hamid spoke for her. In Urdu, he asked for her documents. "Madam," explained Hamid, "they've mailed your papers and passport back to the Islamabad Immigration Office. You'll need to go back to Islamabad. You understand, madam?"

"But I have to be at the workshops in Kashmir and ..." Tired, she didn't have the energy to explain. "It doesn't matter. I understand, Hamid." She sighed in frustration, not in the least bit impressed. She kept her thoughts to herself. "Hamid, where's Gadi?"

"On leave, madam. He's visiting relatives."

Jorja suspected Gadi was purposely not at work. Perhaps he did not want to see her or, more likely, he did not want Jorja to see him. *Did he deliberately plan for her to meet Osama? Did he know Osama was in the remote village and that she would come eyeball to eyeball with the most wanted man in the world? Had he planned it? Had he known Zohair, the teacher, would instruct his children to take Jorja to the natural spring? Did Zohair and Gadi know that Osama would be at the spring? Or was the meeting just a stroke of luck? If the meeting was planned, what if Osama had harmed her? Was Gadi avoiding her so that he would not have to answer her questions? Was the passport extension delay deliberate? Did someone not want Jorja to enter Kashmir?*

Jorja's giddy brain imagined someone was conspiring to thwart the progress of her visa. Someone or some organization did not want her to remain in Kashmir and Pakistan. *Surely, Gadi would want her to remain? He would want her to tell authorities of her sighting of Osama bin Laden. He would want part of the reward. But maybe he wanted her to tell authorities from a distance, from the safety of Australia.* She was confused. She had no idea what to do next.

* * *

"Madam, Mr. Kaliq is in the foyer. Shall I send him to your room?"

"Is Mrs. Kaliq with him, Qaseem?"

"No madam, he is alone."

"Then you may tell Mr. Kaliq that I have declined to see him."

"But madam, but madam, he's an Attorney-at-Law. He's an important man. You will meet him in the restaurant for tea, yes?"

"Qaseem, thank you for notifying me of his presence, but I decline to meet him in my room or in the restaurant for tea."

"As you wish, madam."

Jorja stood on the western balcony under an oppressive night sky, looking at the river: the great comforter. Despite people's warnings that it was dangerous and deadly, she found it mysterious, intriguing, and beguiling. The sound of the river comforted her and she felt at peace. She stared at the tinted lights adorning the roof of the mosque on the opposite bank. Their reflections dotted the murky water as it streamed fervently toward Islamabad. The river sprinted to its destiny, razing boulders and rubble in its path.

The television was on. A movie was in its dying stages. She could hear the theme music when the credits rolled down the screen. It was Peter Gabriel's song, *Don't Give Up*, with Kate Bush.

CHAPTER 51

TERRORISM AND THE TALIBAN

Awan was optimistic. "You will get visa, madam, because I don't want you to go back to Australia. You must stay here in Kashmir. I'll be sad if you go."

"Pakistanis are slow, but you will get a new visa," said Pervaiz reassuringly.

"Pervaiz, whatever happened to that young cleaner? The small, skinny one?" Jorja recalled his diminutive hands on her shoulders making pathetic massaging movements.

"You do not know, madam?"

"No. What happened?"

Pervaiz looked at Awan. "He, well, he … he confessed."

"Confessed? Confessed to what?"

"He told everyone, even the manager, that he was rude to you. He said that you hadn't reported it because you were too kind, but he confessed. Then the manager sacked him. He's gone." Awan nodded. "Yes, he's gone."

"I'm sorry. I didn't want him to lose his job."

"No matter. He has another now. He's working at the Riverina Hotel. He did a bad thing and shouldn't have been disrespectful. It's best that he's not here." Jorja stepped sideways to open the restaurant doors but Pervaiz stopped her. "So sorry, but you cannot take lunch in the restaurant today. Men are having a seminar in the room," he said.

"What group are they?"

"Taliban," said Pervaiz.

"You're just trying to cheer me up." She smiled at him. Awan and Pervaiz looked at each other and laughed.

"Taliban, Taliban, Taliban. Osama bin Laden is here. He's hiding here in Kashmir, in the Sangam Hotel," said Pervaiz.

They roared with laughter, and Jorja joined them. She wondered if they knew her secret. Surely it was coincidental teasing.

Awan, without speaking, took a mandarin from his trouser pocket and put it in her hand. A whiff of its aroma reached her nostrils and her mouth watered in anticipation. Savoring each mouthful, she ordered room service and continued talking to the staff in the foyer. Jahmal entered the hotel. "Madam Jorja, why are you not at lunch. You are not eating!"

"Taliban are eating in the restaurant," explained Pervaiz. Jahmal was stunned and questioned Pervaiz in Urdu, then smiled.

"Madam Jorja," said Jahmal, "Pervaiz wants to know what the difference is between a terrorist and an extremist? What is your opinion?"

"Why do you ask, Pervaiz?"

"I'm curious. We discussed it in our study class. Some people think that the words only apply to Arabs and Pakistanis and all Muslims. I'm curious about what you think. What is your definition?"

"I haven't given it much thought."

"Think now," urged Pervaiz.

"Well, I think a terrorist is someone who commits violence against a race or religious group, rather than at a specific individual.

The terrorist doesn't necessarily know anyone in the group because he or she aims the violence at a representative group. Do you understand what I mean?"

"Yes, but terrorism is not only to hurt people. Like 9/11. That was to hit American symbols of power, like the Pentagon. Whether there were people in the buildings or nearby didn't matter," said Pervaiz.

Jahmal added, "But if a person kills a group of people in their own country, is it terrorism or is terrorism only when the person kills people in another country?"

"Well," Jorja answered, "at the moment it creates more attention when another country is involved. If, say, a person targets a school in their own country, it's rarely called an act of terrorism by the press. Is it?"

"I don't know. All I know is if an American kills a group of people, the media don't call him a terrorist. If a Muslim kills people, he is called a terrorist. And now people say all Muslims are terrorists."

She tried to explain. "If an individual or a small group of people commit terrorism, it's a minority group. Westerners know it's a minority group. It doesn't imply that all members of that race or religion, or even all members in the one group, are terrorists. Terrorists represent a small minority of fanatical individuals. It's those small groups, and their actions, that constitute terrorism. I think terrorist acts are part of a larger phenomenon of politically inspired violence and, at times, the distinction between the two can become difficult to understand. 'One man's terrorist is another man's freedom fighter' is an English phrase we use to express what I mean."

Jahmal shook his head in disagreement. "Terrorism is a word used too much now. People don't know what it means." Sajid had joined them. Riyad was close by.

"What I'm saying is that terrorism always involves killing. It always involves a murderous intent, but usually on a larger scale than one individual." Jorja tried to clarify her thoughts.

"That's called war." Pervaiz laughed.

"Okay, let me narrow it down. Terrorism is about violence toward innocent civilians."

"That's still called war," said Pervaiz, Awan, and Jahmal in unison.

Jorja tried again. "Terrorism is non-military violence toward innocent civilians by a small fanatical group of people."

"She forgot about the destruction of buildings." Jahmal punched Pervaiz playfully on the arm; both men laughing at Jorja's expense.

Fumbling in frustration for words, she said, "If a country sends bombers to destroy the communications or water system or any other civilian infrastructure of another country, this might be an act of terrorism. On the other hand, if a country sends bombers to attack military airfields of its enemy then that would be a state military action, such as war."

"Innocent people could still be killed, so it's all terrorism, if that's your definition. All killing is terrorism. Muslims are against killing. It's in the Qur'an. Muslims are not terrorists," said Riyad.

"True. Muslims aren't terrorists," she said. "Terrorists can be from any country or religion. They could be Christians. There's usually a political reason behind a terrorist's actions though. I think the media focus on al-Qaeda, Afghanistan, and Osama bin Laden makes it appear that Muslims are the perpetrators as a whole, but we know that's not the case. Terrorists are a minority group," she insisted.

"I don't like your definition of terrorism, madam Jorja. I'm not satisfied," said Sajid, the part-time political science student.

"What's your definition then?" Jorja asked him.

"I don't have one."

"What's an extremist then?" said Pervaiz smiling.

"I don't suppose you're going to like my definition, but I think an extremist has extreme views of the general population, but his or her actions don't necessarily include violence. An extremist could be pronouncing his views through the media. It might stir up violence, but the act of violence may or may not be perpetrated by the extremist."

Riyad shook his head. Awan, Sajid, and Pervaiz shrugged their shoulders.

Riyad spoke first. "Violent or extremist Islamists use the word 'jihad,' but at their own danger. They upset all the peoples of the earth and, first of all, traditional Islamists. Those who commit violent jihad are in opposition to Islam. Extremists have misinterpreted the Islamic concept of jihad intentionally. Jihad doesn't mean holy war. Its true meaning is a personal or individual 'struggle.' Islamists must struggle to defend their faith and ideals or even their own inner turmoil. Jihad, the fight against others, is not part of our religion and this is what the Muslim terrorists are doing. They are not us and we are not them. We should let everyone know that those Islamists who cause intolerance or violence will never be our heroes."

Pervaiz disagreed. "But they are heroes to the Taliban. Osama bin Laden is their hero. And he is the hero of Pakistanis who don't understand or aren't educated."

"He is *not* a hero to true Islamists," Riyad said firmly. "Osama bin Laden and his call for a jihad, or holy war, against the United States was denounced by all our leaders of the largest mosques in America. Our leaders denounced America fighting against the Taliban."

"How could the Muslim leaders in America denounce armed forces against the Taliban when there are Afghans against the Taliban? This is hypocrisy," Pervaiz argued.

"Our Islamist leaders don't want civilian Afghans killed, that's why," argued Riyad.

"Muslim fundamentalism means that Islamic leaders face a choice between moderation and militancy. That's where Musharraf is a hypocrite. Pakistan is a moderate Muslim country, but we have a military dictatorship," said Pervaiz.

Jahmal interrupted when the argument became more intense. "We are Muslim brothers. When we close our hearts to others, our eyes are closed to the beauty of humanity. The message of Islam, Judaism, Christianity, and all other religions is one of love. Everyone should have love for all other people."

"Yes, he's right," said Riyad. "Who are we to deprive someone of our love just because he is of a different color or speaks a different language or is born in a different country or prays to a different interpretation of Allah? The Taliban is, in many ways, a reflection of the present state of the Muslim *Ummah*: lots of beards and turbans but little wisdom and guidance. We must always remember that Islam is a benevolent religion. It is a balanced way of life. We are horrified by the atrocity of 9/11, and we must reclaim our faith from those Islamists that have so violently taken it away. For us, Islam and the West are not incompatible. Allah is the One Creator. The Qur'an says there must be peace and not war; any war, not even jihad. Islam is a tolerant faith."

"Madam Jorja's lunch is ready," said a kitchen-hand.

"Awan, please take it to madam's room," ordered Riyad.

As Awan and Jorja headed upstairs, he asked, "Will you stay in Muzaffarabad tomorrow, madam?"

"Yes Awan, I'll be here tomorrow to help Lufti and Mahmud and then I must return to Islamabad to arrange my visa extension. I don't want to be in Pakistan illegally."

"Will you be back for the workshop?"

"I hope so, but I need the visa to get back into Kashmir."

CHAPTER 52

THE DEATH OF REASON

Uncertainty was never pleasant for Jorja. As she packed for the trip to Islamabad, Lufti telephoned to reassure her that he would conduct the two workshops with Mahmud. She could join them later.

"Jorja, your assignment is nearly over. If you get the visa and decide to stay in Kashmir then you can come back any time. Don't hurry back just for the workshops. If I don't see you again, I pray we keep in touch. You have been a special person here and a special friend to me. But let's not say goodbye just yet. I'll see you again. I *will* see you again. Kashmir will see you again. *Insh Allah!*"

"Insh Allah!"

Jorja heard a commotion by the river. From the western balcony she leaned forward to watch the huddle of men at the water's edge. The men strained and pulled on a large object, fishing it out of the water. Screams and wails pierced the air and men beat their chests in anguish and distress. They had retrieved the purple-blue bloated body of a man, mangled from the force of unforgiving boulders.

Jorja rushed downstairs and through the side door to the river, almost slipping on the loose gravel. Riyad seized her by the waist before she collided into the huddle of men.

"Please go inside, madam Jorja. Please!" He called for Awan to remove her from the area. Awan gripped her by the arm.

"What happened? Did he slip into the water?" Jorja demanded to know, breaking free of Awan's grasp and moving closer to the corpse lying on the pebbled bank. On the body's fat, bruised hand, criss-crossed with shallow cuts, was a familiar pewter and aquamarine ring. She almost fainted. Silently and slowly, she stepped backward. Awan put his arm around her shoulder. Riyad guided both of them swiftly up the bank and inside the hotel.

Safe in her hotel room, she stared silently from her balcony, watching the men shroud the blue-cold corpse. Awan and Sajid appeared with a tray of tea.

"Madam, please drink," said Awan. "Why do you watch? It is too tragic to see."

"Madam, please don't upset yourself. It happens often," comforted Sajid.

"But how?"

"The man must have slipped. People can't swim and the water takes their breath away."

"But Sajid, the man was Gadi from my office. He was a virile man, very strong and physically fit. I don't believe he slipped. What was he doing there, anyway?"

"I do not know of the man, madam, but many people come to pray. It is like a holy place because of the rivers meeting, the confluence of the rivers. It is famous and very, very sacred. I'm sure it was an accident, madam."

"Sajid, I've never seen Gadi by the river before. I refuse to believe it was an accident. It can't possibly be." She touched him on the arm and whispered, "Am I safe, Sajid?"

Awan fidgeted. "Please drink, madam. Tea is good for your nerves."

"Yes, Awan is right, madam. You must drink because it will calm you."

"Sajid, am I safe?"

"Yes, madam. You are safe inside, away from the water. You are safe. Are you packed for your journey tomorrow morning? Do you need help?"

"I meant. . . it doesn't matter." Her shoulders felt like dead weight and her eyes fluttered with tiredness. "I'm all packed and ready. Tonight I'll go to bed early. I'm very tired and upset."

"As you wish, madam." Sajid and Awan left the room.

The river bank was quiet, and Jorja detected no movement. Gadi's body had been removed. He was gone. Forever. Jorja lay on the bed and sobbed noisily, convulsing with deep gulps of breath. Fully clothed, she sobbed herself into a state of utter weariness and sleep.

CHAPTER 53

A STAB IN THE HEART

It was the nineteenth day of April; the day Jorja's visa expired. She was in Islamabad.

"Jamshid, I still don't have a visa! How can you talk of me staying?"

"You worry too much. You can stay here without a visa. Pakistan is not like Australia."

"I can't get into Kashmir without it. I won't be able to work in Kashmir. I won't stay in Pakistan any longer because I do not want to be here illegally. I don't want to end up in a Pakistani jail." Without a visa, she would certainly be imprisoned. Perhaps, Jorja thought, she could tell authorities about her sighting of Osama bin Laden, and they would overlook her illegal status. *But where was Osama bin Laden now?* Surely Osama, his deputy Ayman al-Zawahiri, and the rest of his henchmen, had long left the region and traveled north to Afghanistan or the western mountainous regions of Pakistan. It made no difference where the terrorist and his army were. No one would believe she had seen him. No one would believe a foreign woman without a visa.

"That won't happen, Jorja. You exaggerate!"

"And pigs might fly. Here's my decision. I go home. You, Wasim, and the minister will work out a contract and a scope of work for the next assignment, and I'll consider it from my home in Australia. It's not that I don't want to stay in Kashmir or Pakistan, but originally I was to be here for only two days. Five days maximum. Three days in Pakistan. Two days in Kashmir. And the possibility of doing some work for a few weeks in Islamabad. Do you understand? Already, it's been more than two months. Now it could be another five or even eight months, which would make a total of ten months or more away from home. I live alone, Jamshid. A short time away can be arranged with not much fuss, but a longer stay requires planning."

"What planning, Jorja? You have no family or children."

"That's my point, Jamshid. I have no family near me who can look after the house at short notice. Sure I have friends, but it's polite to make arrangements with them first."

"What arrangements?"

"I need someone to stay in my house and pay my mortgage. I must arrange things such as banking, the car, mail, and other bills. Tell me, Jamshid, would you stay away from your country and your family for so long at short notice, especially when your family thinks you'll only be away for a short time?"

"Of course not!"

"Then I can't either. I'm going home."

Minhas entered Jamshid's office. "I have the man on the telephone, Mr. Jamshid. He said he'd be willing to work in Kashmir."

"What's that? What's going on?"

"Thank you. I'll take the call," Jamshid told Minhas.

"What's happening? Tell me what's happening, Jamshid? I'm not leaving this office until you explain what's happening."

Jamshid rubbed his bushy eyebrows. "I'm arranging for someone to do the job in Kashmir. The minister knows this man and asked me to contact him. He's a Pakistani living in America. Let me take the call." Speaking in Urdu, he was on the telephone for some time, taking notes and scribbling. Replacing the receiver he said, "It's arranged. You can go home. I'll ask Minhas to make the arrangements."

"Woohoo!" Jorja screamed, raising her arms in the air. "Fabulous, brilliant, wonderful! Thank you, Jamshid."

He smiled and nodded. Elated, Jorja raced to the spare computer near Minhas's desk. Connecting to the internet immediately, an e-mail from Denny stood out amongst the others.

> *Jorja*
>
> *Just a short e-mail and not one you want to see, but there's no other way to contact you to say this nicely. I don't even know if you're in Islamabad or Muzaffarabad or somewhere in between. I have met someone and I want to be with her.*
>
> *Having a lover in a dangerous place is stressful for me. I see the news every day and the situation seems to get worse in Pakistan. I need to have someone near me every day. The uncertainty of whether you're going to stay there for another five months, or eight months, or whatever is hard for me to take. It's hard to carry on a relationship like this.*
>
> *I'm not expecting you to be pleasant about this. I know it's not what you need or want to hear right now. Sorry, Jorja.*
>
> *Denny*

Denny's words were like a knife-jab to the heart. Dumbfounded, she could find no meaning in Denny's e-mail. Motionless, she stared at the words. Distressed and overwhelmed, she yearned for peace of mind.

"*Djawa*, Miss Jorja?" Abassi, the cook, asked.

"I don't feel like coffee at the moment. May I have *chai* instead, please?"

"Of course, Miss Jorja. You look sad. You should not worry. Allah looks after you. You will get the visa. And Allah still looks after Gadi. He will go to the ever-after."

"Abassi, is it possible for two people to truly understand each other?" she asked without expecting a response.

"Of course, Miss Jorja, and when it happens, love becomes possible. Love is the best remedy for anxiety and loneliness. That is what you need now, yes?"

"Maybe."

"Love must be mutual," he continued. "With it is feelings of care, affection, and warmth, and a knowing of each other's minds. Spiritually, you are one. Jalal-ud-din Rumi, the great Islamic poet, said that anyone who does not love is like a fish without water or a bird without wings. He said, through love, thorns are turned to roses, sickness becomes health, anger becomes gentleness, and ugliness becomes beauty."

"Is there a cold beer in the fridge, Abassi? I feel like a drink."

"Get drunk on love, said Rumi, because love is all there is. That is what Rumi said. Get drunk on love, not alcohol."

"It's easier to find alcohol. Well, in Australia, anyway." She laughed feebly.

"Stay in Pakistan. You belong here. You will get the visa and then you can stay here. Do not worry about your visa. Let us walk to the shops. You'd like a walk to the shops, yes?" Abassi knew Jorja liked to walk. The first time she requested that he accompany her, he was perplexed, but merely answered, "As you wish, madam." The shops were a short seven-minute walk away and he asked, "Why do you walk? Why don't you ask the driver to take you in the car? That's what the driver does. Noor is here to take you in the car so you don't have to walk." Jorja answered that it was exercise. On the journey home, he again asked. "Why do you walk? I cannot understand why you walk, but I will walk with you, as you wish." Once, when Abassi was buying vegetables, Jorja walked alone to the shops in the misty, warm rain. As she left the shopping area to walk home, Noor had come to fetch her. He beckoned her to get into the car, and as she did so, he admonished her severely for walking alone in the rain. "You will be kidnapped or, even worse, you will get a bad cold and die, then I will be in trouble."

"Yes, let's go for a walk Abassi." It was a humid afternoon, and Jorja was thankful for the time alone with the cook. He was seventy-three-years-old, thin and wiry, kind and thoughtful.

At the ice-cream parlor, Abassi insisted that he buy her a mango-flavored soft cone. They sat outside on a low brick wall. "We must not eat too many sweet foods, Miss Jorja, but it is okay to have a little ice-cream. We have too much diabetes in Pakistan. It's not good. Did you see the *Move for Health* campaign on television? Pakistanis must do more exercise it says."

"That's why I like to walk to the shops."

"But you are not Pakistani," he said.

She had seen the campaign. Non-communicable diseases like diabetes, chronic hepatitis, hypertension, stroke, and heart failure were on the rise in Pakistan. About two million deaths every year were attributable to physical inactivity. The sedentary lifestyle of the Pakistanis also increased their risk of colon and breast cancer, high blood pressure, lipid disorders, osteoporosis, depression, and anxiety.

The ice-cream made her feel better. It was nearing summer, and the days were becoming hotter. The temperature, even at night, was warm, especially if the air was still. People sought coolness and relief by strolling through the shopping mall or sitting on the lawns near the stores. Young people congregated outside a chicken take-away restaurant or ice-cream stall. Abassi and Jorja sat on a low brick wall, facing the bustle of late night shoppers. They talked for a long time and eventually ambled home under a near full moon. Clattering beside them was a cyclist, aged and worn, like his bicycle. In his white shalwar kameez, he cast a ghostly image under the moonlight.

While Jorja lounged on the divan in the dining-cum-living room, watching television, Abassi tiptoed in and offered her a cup of tea. "No thanks. Can you cut hair, Abassi?" Contemplating the question momentarily, he nodded, and said it was probably an easy task. He left the room to collect the necessary hairdressing tools. Armed with a comb, scissors, and a bowl of water, he instructed Jorja to sit at the dining table. He dipped the comb into the bowl of water, slid it through the hair shrouding her forehead, and proceeded to cut.

"There! It's done! Do you feel better, Miss Jorja? You should not worry about your visa. You will get your visa tomorrow."

The next day, Jorja did not get her visa. Somehow, somewhere, someone had misplaced her visa papers. The official returned her passport and asked her to wait another week for the visa documents to be processed. "You wait, madam," said the immigration officer.

She waited. She waited for approval of the visa extension. She also waited for some inspiration on how to answer Denny's e-mail.

Denny had another lover. Denny had another lover. She endured misfortune bravely, but loneliness made it harder. She was the lover on the wrong side. She was the lover left behind.

CHAPTER 54

HOW MANY?

Jorja waited in Islamabad. She could not go to Kashmir to conduct the workshops without a visa. The workshop material was prepared. Lufti, Mahmud, and Jorja had worked tirelessly to produce PowerPoint slides, presentations, papers, and agendas. Mahmud reassured her that he would finalize the manual. "You must not worry, Jorja. You must wait for the visa," he said through the telephone. Her visa had expired, but this did not seem to worry anybody except Jorja. Perhaps the Pakistan or the Kashmiri government had wanted it this way. They had discovered how much she knew and wanted her out of the country, out of the way. She was sure of it. Perhaps that's why Gadi was killed. He was getting too close to finding Osama bin Laden.

Jorja's muscles ached and she felt fatigue throughout her entire body. Her uncle's death, Gadi's death, and Denny's separation had all sapped her of energy. She felt alone in the world. Jamshid and Minhas had business in Peshawar. Abassi was her only companion in Islamabad, with the exception of Noor, the security guard and the cleaner.

The cleaner, Shouket Ali, was responsible for washing and ironing clothes, as well as cleaning the office and guesthouse. This he did with great diligence; often too much diligence. Jorja's underwear was disappearing. Maybe she had miscounted. *How many pairs of knickers did she bring to Pakistan?* Shouket Ali was ironing her shalwar kameez. He hung the kameez carefully on a plastic clothes hanger and draped the shalwar over another. Jorja offered to take her clothes to her room upstairs while he continued ironing. As she collected them, Shouket Ali ironed her microfiber brassiere. Two large charcoal marks stained both cups, perforating them with miniature holes, rendering the brassiere unusable. A matching pair of knickers, shriveled from the heat of the iron, lay at the end of the ironing board. She picked up the knickers and bra, politely thanked Shouket Ali, returned to her room, and threw them into the waste-paper bin.

Abassi entered her room where she was working on a report. The small desk overlooked the front garden and street. The passing pedestrians often distracted her.

"Will you take a walk now, Miss Jorja, or will you take tea?"

She opted for a walk to the shops. Abassi fetched his walking sandals from his residence, a closet-sized room at the end of the driveway, and returned to her room. "I'm ready, Miss Jorja."

The hot and humid weather caused her feet to swell and the perspiration resulted in friction with her leather shoes. "Abassi, I need to go to the pharmacy to buy Band-Aids."

"As you wish, Miss Jorja." At the pharmacy, he said, "You can go to the counter, Miss Jorja."

She asked a young man for Band-Aids.

"Please, madam?"

"I would like Band-Aids. Sticky plasters for my sore feet."

"Yes, I understand now. How many, madam?" said the round-faced man behind the serving counter.

"A small box will do."

"How many, madam?"

She wasn't sure what he meant. "One box."

"How many, madam?" he asked again.

"One box of Band-Aids, please," she repeated.

"How many Band-Aids, madam?"

Jorja looked confused. He produced a box of Band-Aids, put them on the counter and asked again, "How many, madam?"

She iterated that she wanted the entire box. He informed her that Band-Aids were sold individually and not by the box. Opting for three, the patient man counted them and placed them gently into a small, white paper bag.

Abassi, an occasional smoker, stopped at the tobacconist in a miniscule kiosk, wedged between two shops, with space for one salesperson. An elderly man, older than Abassi, was serving. "How many?" he asked Abassi. The cook answered that he wished to buy three filtered cigarettes. Jorja assumed he meant three packets of cigarettes, but the salesman counted out one, two, three cigarettes and placed them in a small, white paper bag. Clutching their purchases in paper bags, Abassi and Jorja returned to the office.

The last of the day's light had faded as Jorja worked in her room. Humidity hung in the air like a cloud. When she entered the bathroom to freshen up, lightning lit up the sky. She ran downstairs calling for Abassi. She ran into the kitchen. He had been there recently because it reeked of cigarettes. An ashtray on the bench was full of stubs. She ran into the office. No Abassi. Outside, she ran behind the house to his room and knocked forcefully. No answer. "Abassi, Abassi," she shouted. No answer. Jorja ran along the driveway and saw him at the iron gate talking to the security guard. "Abassi, Abassi," she called and ran toward him.

Tossing away his cigarette, he answered, "What's wrong, Miss Jorja? What's wrong? Why are you so fearful? Are you scared of lightning?" His white shalwar kameez shone brightly under the iridescent flashes.

"I'm fine Abassi, but I need more toilet paper. I've run out and can't find any."

Abassi grabbed her wrist as he led her toward the house. "Miss Jorja," he said in a firm voice. "You scared me. You scared me silly. I thought it was an emergency. You come running out of the house naked in the night and so I think it must be an emergency. Why didn't you use the intercom? That's what it's for. There's a number for the security guard. Why do you come running outside like this?" He shook his head when he spoke. Inside the house, he led Jorja to the larder.

"Naked? I'm not naked. What are you talking about?"

"Look at your feet. Bare feet! You come running outside with bare feet. It's unladylike. Next time, cover your nakedness," he insisted gruffly. "Now, let's see to this emergency. Come with me to the pantry."

"Abassi, running out of toilet paper *is* an emergency to a for-eign woman. Believe me!" she implored. She had never heard the cook talk with such authority before. Defending her actions was futile. He clicked his tongue indignantly and handed her a roll of toilet paper. "Excuse me, Abassi, I think I need more," she said apologetically.

"More? How many, Miss Jorja? How many does a woman need for this emergency?"

"Three. Three's a good number." Jorja was prepared for any future contingencies.

The cook returned to his conversation with the security guard while Jorja bounded up the stairs and dumped the rolls of toilet paper on her bed. She returned to the front garden and sat on the bench facing the gate. The moonlight danced on the leaves and cast eerie shadows. Like a camera flash, lightning lit up the yard. She watched Abassi and the guard share a cigarette; their backs to her, ignoring her presence.

A car tooted to signal the guard to open the gate. Both the guard and Abassi held the gate wide open and the white vehicle entered. Jamshid's colleague, Shareef Zardini, whom she met in Muzaffarabad, slammed the door closed and approached Jorja.

When she stood, he kissed her lightly on each cheek. She explained that Jamshid was in Peshawar.

"Good, then I can keep you company." Jorja and Shareef walked inside, arm in arm, while Abassi shared another cigarette with the night guard.

CHAPTER 55

SHAREEF'S COMPANY

Shareef and Jorja sat side by side on the divan watching the news.

"The short-sleeved kameez suits you. Perhaps it's because blue reflects the color of your eyes: blue for desolation. I'm so sorry at your loss," Shareef said as he touched Jorja's bare arm.

"Thank you, Shareef. It was sad enough to lose my uncle, but then Denny, my lover, too. It's difficult to accept."

"Your uncle? And Denny, your lover? I meant Gadi. I didn't know you had lost so much. Please, please my dear, tell me what's in your heart." His dark, hirsute hand squeezed hers and remained wrapped around her fingers.

"I'm so sorry. I was thinking of myself and not poor, poor Gadi. It was horrid to see his body lying on the stones. There were so many bruises on his face. It was horrible. What a terrible, terrible tragedy that he died so young. It happened only a few days after the news of my uncle's death in Mumbai."

"What! The Indians killed him. The bastards!"

"No, no, no. It was nothing like that. He died of a heart attack at the airport when he was leaving India. He liked spending time there with his wife. It was just one of those things. It was his time, I suppose, his destiny. But it was such a sad fate, and so sudden. No one expected it. And talk of the unexpected when I arrived in Islamabad, I received an e-mail from my lover in Australia. He's no longer my lover. It's over. It's all over. He's with another woman."

"The bastard!"

"Yes, the bastard! How right you are!"

"All gone in a week. Darling Jorja, how are you coping with these three tragic losses? How are you coping?" He leaned forward and kissed her on the forehead, then held her in his arms.

Jorja's blood rushed to the surface with excitement, savoring his tenderness and warmth. She could feel his breath on her cheek and ear. She could feel his chest inhale and exhale, slowly, steadily, calmly. Wrapping her arms around him, she held on tight; so tight she thought she heard her ribs crack.

The garish chandelier seemed unusually low as if it were descending upon her. She could see the dust on the red-hot phallic-shaped bulbs. The television announced a train derailment in New Delhi. Women screamed in desperation as they searched for their loved ones. The coarse fabric of the three-seat divan prickled against the skin of her arms. The surroundings were practical and uncomfortable.

With a light brush of his tongue, he moistened his lips, angled his head, closed his eyes, and ever so gently pecked Jorja on her closed mouth. Jorja gave him no resistance, and he did it again, holding her head in his hands. Simultaneously, their lips parted, as they nibbled each other gently. His kisses increased in frequency and urgency, pushing his tongue to meet hers.

"Jorja, Jorja. I want to kiss you forever," but she pulled away and he kissed her forehead. His firm hand caressed her temples and toyed with her hair. He kissed her with gentleness along the side of her face, first the left side, then the right. His technique, a sophisticated balance of symmetry, left no side neglected or numb with unilateral attention.

Kissing was not Denny's forte. He did not linger, nor did it ever feel as if his mind was totally consumed by the experience. It was as if he shielded himself from intimacy and commitment.

Shareef's finger skimmed her lips as he guided her mouth to his. "Jorja, may I make love to you?"

Caught off guard, she pulled away slightly and said, "Sex? You're asking for sex? But, your religion, it ..." Jorja's nape tingled, her nipples stiffened, and in the half-dark, she could feel his enlarged organ pressing against her. In her imagination, a mad frenzy of sexual entanglement was about to ensue. "Do you have a condom?"

"A condom?" he asked.

"It prevents sexual diseases."

Alarm froze his face. "Do you think I'm diseased?"

"No, no, no." Doubt clouded her feelings and she felt like a champion of abstinence.

"I feel something. It's heart-pounding, fabulous, warm, and wonderful. . ."

"It's what, Shareef?"

"It's love."

Raja, Jahmal, and Shareef expressed love in a way that Denny never did. It came from the heart, spontaneously, freely, and without inhibition. Jorja looked longingly at Shareef, wanting him to know she reciprocated the feeling, but in her mind she questioned her emotions. Her head ruled her heart and she hesitated. "Shareef, you are so, you mean a lot to me, and ..."

He sat bolt upright and pushed Jorja at arm's length. "Someone's coming. It'll be Abassi," he said.

Abassi entered the room with a pot of aromatic tea. He announced he was retiring for the evening, turned the television down, closed the windows, and drew the curtains. "Would you like me to walk you to your car, Mr. Zardini? Miss Jorja, do you need any water in your bedroom? Anything at all? No? Shall I turn the television off then or shall I leave it on while you have your tea? Perhaps I can take the tea to your room, Miss Jorja?"

Jorja nodded and looked at Shareef who waited in the doorway. "Call in any time. I'm not sure when I'm leaving Islamabad, but it will probably be soon."

"As always, take care, dearest Jorja. I'll see you before you leave Pakistan." He rubbed her bare arm and kissed her quickly on her forehead.

Abassi picked up Jorja's dupatta from the divan and wrapped it around her shoulder. "I'll walk Mr. Zardini to his car first and then I'll bring the tea to your room. What a wonderful man he is, don't you agree, Miss Jorja?"

She smiled at Shareef and placed an arm around the seventy-three-year-old Murree man, "Almost as wonderful as you, Abassi."

CHAPTER 56

IN CONTROL

"Noor, I'd like to have lunch somewhere else today. In a restaurant. Could you drive me to the Serena Hotel please?"

He frowned. "Does Abassi know? He'll be cross if he cooks and you don't eat it."

"I promise to tell Abassi."

The frown deepened. "It's not good for a woman to eat alone in a strange hotel. She will look, well. . .you know."

Jorja sighed. "Noor, please! I really want to go. You can join me for lunch and I'll pay."

Alarmed, he shook his head vigorously. "No, no, no! I cannot. No, no, no!"

"Please, please, please!"

Noor sighed, weary of listening to her pleading, and reluctantly relented.

Khaki-clothed soldiers lined the streets at sporadic intervals and congregated at intersections. Noor turned right into a street parallel to a park dotted with jacaranda trees. Sirens whirred, and one, two, three, four motorcycles whizzed by.

"Musharraf's convoy," Noor explained. Black cars followed. Splitting the convoy, a white van cut across the intersecting street without stopping and veered in front of Noor. The leading black car engaged its brakes, causing the others to skid wildly over the street. Jorja winced and braced for impact as the screech of brakes rose to a crescendo. They were going to be hit by either the white van or part of the convoy. It seemed inevitable.

"Turn left, hard! Left, left, left," Jorja shouted, but quick-thinking Noor was a step ahead of her. Already turning the steering wheel, he slammed on the accelerator, avoiding the van. Their car lifted into the air and landed on the footpath. Pumping the brakes, Noor maintained control until it came to a halt, rocking on its shock absorbers. An explosion boomed to the right where a bridge arched across a sickly, polluted stream. For a brief moment, a numbing silence followed before the air was shattered by a chaotic confusion of noises. Pops of machine gun fire spat out: pop, pop, pop, pop, pop.

"Head down, madam!" The driver reversed, spinning the wheels, off the footpath and into a residential driveway. "Head down, please, please, madam!" Jorja ducked and put her hands over her head. Noor flicked the steering wheel, turning it rapidly to undertake a one-eighty turn. Lifting her head, Jorja peeked over the seat. Behind her, the charred metallic carcass of the white van lay on its side, spewing smoke. Soldiers, with Kalashnikov's raised, fingers on triggers, weaved in and out of halted cars, into the park, and over fences. The convoy was nowhere in sight, having escaped the fracas. A peculiar orange glow filled the sky.

Out of danger, Noor calmly said, "Are you fine?"

"I'm fine."

"No lunch for you today."

Jorja laughed as they drove, without further incident, back to the office.

"Noor, is someone trying to kill me?"

"No madam. You aren't famous. People are trying to kill Musharraf. Do not worry. Everyone likes you."

"Everyone?"

"Yes, madam."

"Everyone in the whole wide world?"

"I'm not sure, madam. My neighborhood is not that big." Noor honked the horn to alert the guard, who opened the gate to the office.

Abassi was smoking in the garden. He opened the car door and before he could ask, Jorja said, "I changed my mind. Can you make me a sandwich, Abassi?"

Ignoring her, he said to Noor, "You drove Miss Jorja in that dirty car? Shame! Clean it!" Noor and Jorja looked at each other in surprise and noticed the sooty film streaking the vehicle's enamel. Tufts of grass were wedged behind the wheel guards and mud had splashed patterns onto the car's side. Noor looked at Jorja with disdain. Escaping his glare, she walked upstairs to the dining room, turned on the television, and flicked through the channels searching for news of the incident.

She had almost finished her sandwich by the time a news bulletin aired. An explosive-laden van had missed careening into the President's convoy. Musharraf announced that he had escaped an assassination attempt. "It was certainly a terrorist act and certainly it was me who was targeted, but let me say with confidence I am used to such incidents. It has happened before and one does not get bothered," he said. "It is the militants, extremists, terrorists, and fundamentalists who are out to not only damage our nation, but also bring a bad name to our great religion. God is great and one has to trust in God. There is no problem. Life continues normally. God is the savior."

CHAPTER 57

THE REFERENDUM QUESTION

Musharraf formally announced a date for a controversial referendum before the October election. He intended to seek legitimacy for a longer term in office. It was his insurance against any election outcome.

The referendum's question was as follows: *Do the people of Pakistan want General Pervez Musharraf with them in a seat of power for a further period of five years?* It was a simple question.

Jamshid and Jorja were discussing the referendum over dinner on his return from Peshawar when Shareef arrived.

"Oh, Jamshid, you're back. I, er, I came over in the … er, in the off-chance that you'd be in. How lucky I am that you're back from Peshawar."

He took both of Jorja's hands in his, kissed her on the forehead, and said quite loudly, "How lovely it is to see you again.

This time we are in the freedom of Islamabad." With his cheek brushing hers, he whispered, "Sorry, I thought you'd be alone."

After kissing Jamshid on each cheek, he made himself comfortable and poured himself a cup of milky tea. "Talking about the referendum? Who isn't? Did you know, Jorja, General Musharraf, President of the mighty military nation of Pakistan, is generally known as Big Khaki Chief?" He laughed. "Big Khaki Chief, true! His word is law. Everyone already thinks he'll win the referendum by a large margin. If he wins, he'll remain the head of state for another five years. This is in violation of the Constitution, isn't it Jamshid?"

The Constitution stated that if a president wanted to extend their term of office, without being an election candidate, an electoral committee consisting of members of the Federal Parliament and the four provincial assemblies must vote on the issue. The Constitution also stated that a person already holding an office of profit in the Government of Pakistan could not contest a presidential election. Musharraf, knowing that he could not offer himself as an election candidate, proposed the referendum for May. This contravened the Constitution.

"Most political parties are criticizing Musharraf and rejecting the referendum," Shareef continued. "The mainstream parties, such as the Pakistan People's Party and the Pakistan Muslim League, are the most vocal. They despise Musharraf's suggestion to keep Benazir Bhutto and Nawaz Sharif out of politics. But what can they do? The official machinery has already started the campaign for Musharraf. I think the polling attendance will be low."

"If the official machinery doesn't buy voters or take them to the polling stations, that is," added Jamshid. He shook his head in disgust.

"Musharraf will get a 'Yes' vote in the referendum. There's no doubt that he's extremely popular. People generally like his policies, especially those relating to the aftermath of 9/11 and the assault on religious militancy."

"True, but this isn't an issue of popularity," said Jamshid. "It's about providing the country with political stability and protecting the economic and political reforms by constitutional means. The 1973 Constitution in its original form gave powers to the prime minister. President Ziaul Haq weakened the Constitution with arbitrary amendments and made the president all-powerful, not the prime minister. He also introduced the, some say, 'vicious' clause that gave him powers to dismiss an elected national assembly, as well as the prime minister. This, of course, trivializes the position of prime minister. After that, not a single prime minister was able to complete their term. The Nawaz Sharif government later abolished the clause. If Musharraf is going to change the clause like he says he will, it's going to be interesting."

"The general public hope," added Shareef, "that while amending the Constitution, Musharraf would consider Pakistan's history and be conscious of the harm done to the country by previous heads of state. People believe that in the past, non-elected men such Ghulam Mohammad, Iskander Mirza, Ayub Khan and Zial Haq, did more to create anarchy than the elected prime ministers." Both men nodded.

"And Musharraf is a non-elected person too. Only time will tell whether Musharraf's new vision will give stability to Pakistan and lead to a consolidation of democratic institutions or whether his political experiment will end in disappointment. Some people think that if things don't go Musharraf's way, he'll quit by force of circumstance," said Jamshid.

"You said that Pakistanis like Musharraf, but don't they see his views as unconstitutional or crazy?" Jorja asked Shareef.

"The majority of people think Musharraf is sound of mind. He's not a bigot and he's a strong proponent against corruption in any form. To the people it's unthinkable that he could be replaced by any of the current political representatives, many of whom are corrupt crooks. There appears to be no alternative but to vote 'Yes' in the referendum. While President Musharraf has American support no matter what he does, it's not a reliable source of strength. The best source is always people's goodwill. To achieve this, Musharraf should conduct the referendum fairly and transparently so that the exercise impresses the people of Pakistan."

Jamshid scoffed. "It is, and always has been, the intent of all Pakistani leaders to enforce *their* will and to tailor the Constitution to suit their own particular needs so that they can remain perpetually in power. This has been true since the early Seventies."

"You've got to admit though, Jamshid, the Constitution is in need of thorough rewriting. The issue everyone is talking about is Article Sixty-Two. It states that a person is deemed unqualified to be elected or chosen as a member of parliament unless he's sagacious, righteous, non-profligate, and honest." They joked that ninety-nine percent of people elected from 1988 were therefore manifestly unqualified to stand for election. "They are criminals," exploded Shareef, suddenly serious, spreading both arms wide in disgust.

"No, no, that's not true. Bhutto is not a criminal," said Jamshid quietly.

"Not yet, but she will be when she's convicted," said Shareef. "Nawaz Sharif was a convicted felon, released from prison on the basis of a plea bargain in which he agreed to remove himself and his family from Pakistan for a period of time. Benazir Bhutto hasn't yet been convicted, but she's an absconder. She'll be arrested and detained if she returns to Pakistan."

"On the backside," said Jamshid, "Musharraf could allow her to be free on bail and do her electioneering while defending herself in court. The government should accommodate Bhutto because her participation in the coming elections might be in the public interest." Abassi had entered the room unobtrusively to clear the dinner table.

"How so?" yelled Shareef. "That's rubbish. When Sharif was in his first term as prime minister, his government filed a number of charges against Bhutto and her husband."

"But, when she came to power the second time her government withdrew these charges and proceeded to file charges against Nawaz Sharif," rebutted Jamshid.

"And when Sharif returned to power, his government withdrew the court cases against him and filed cases against Bhutto and Asif Zardari which are still going on. It was a see-saw situation Jorja," said Shareef, touching Jorja's hand when he spoke. "Suppose Benazir contests the elections in October, wins a resounding victory, and becomes prime minister for a third time. What will happen to the cases against her? Should she be able to withdraw them? What if the courts, or Musharraf, say she can't? Will the government, of which she herself is the head, prosecute her in half a dozen or more criminal cases? It would be a messy, ugly, and unprecedented situation. See what a mess this country is in politically?" He shifted aggressively in his seat.

Jorja naively asked, "Jamshid, how is the public interest involved in all of this? You said that allowing Bhutto to electioneer would be in the public's interest."

"Might be," corrected Jamshid. "It *might* be in the public's interest. A very vocal school of opinion within Pakistan, and among the Pakistanis living in America, says that the October elections will not be regarded as free and fair unless Nawaz Sharif and Benazir Bhutto are allowed to contest without hindrance," he said calmly. "The assumption is that these two politicians are hugely popular, certainly more popular than any other in Pakistan. Secondly, their followers are unconcerned with the charges against them, either because they think the charges are bogus, or because they believe that a bit of criminal activity on the part of their leaders is acceptable so long as they do something for the people."

"Rubbish!" gesticulated Shareef wildly.

"Let the will of the people prevail even if that will is misguided," Jamshid continued. "Next door in India, not so long ago, the people heartily approved of Tamil Nadu even though she was a convicted criminal."

"There's another perspective on this issue," Shareef added. "Let bygones be bygones. Take care of the present and look to the future. Stop digging dirt for there is dirt in all back yards. In many cases, the quest for accountability has turned out to be nothing more than an exercise in futility. Nawaz Sharif's government spent many millions of rupees looking for evidence that would convict Bhutto and her husband. Cases against them have gone on in courts for years, but neither has been convicted of any crime. So then, stop this scandalous travesty of law enforcement."

Jorja shook her head. "There's more to democracy than the unquestioning obedience to the will of the people that, in effect, means the will of the majority."

"Miss Jorja," said Jamshid, "it's always been recognized that acting from passion and prejudice, or even ignorance, the majority of the people will sometimes be wrong. That's why wiser men than I have concluded, rightly, that no law may override and place other restraints on the majority's decisions. It's not entirely clear what the public will dictate with regard to Sharif's and Bhutto's participation in the October election. Something can be said for both sides. Public interest will obviously be well served if the elections give us a government that brings us a stable majority in Parliament."

"Does the army want such a result?" asked Shareef, more to himself than to Jamshid. "Regardless of the opinions of individual officers, the army should want this result if it values a democratic government. We do not require a government that is tottering all the time and is therefore ineffective."

"Okay, which party is the most likely to bring a stable government to Pakistan?" Jorja asked.

"Good question," said Jamshid, "No party won a clear majority of seats in the National Assembly in the previous three elections. Nor is any single party likely to win this kind of majority in October. We'll probably have to settle for a coalition government."

"Rubbish!" interjected Shareef again. "A coalition of a large number of little parties will neither be stable nor coherent. We should look for a party with a substantial number of assembly seats joining hands with one or, at the most two, others to form a government."

"Who can do this?" she asked again. "What about Imran Khan? I'd vote for him," she teased.

"Nonsense to Khan and the Khanates! He's a little party," scowled Shareef. The creases on his forehead looked menacing.

"Khanates? Shareef, what's that?" Jorja asked.

"It's the dominion or jurisdiction of a khan, of course!"

Jamshid continued the argument. "The Pakistan People's Party might turn out to be such a party, especially if Bhutto is able to lead its campaign. If this expectation were well founded, her participation in the election would be an important element in gaining public support. If she is personally offensive to Musharraf, he should set aside his own reservations in the public interest. She made a deal with army chief, General Aslam Beg and President Ghulam Ishaq Khan, giving them preeminence in certain policy areas before the government swore her in as prime minister in 1988. Surely, someone can make a deal giving Musharraf assurances about his own continuance in office. On the backside, it's also the public's interest to force our major parties to get away from dynastic leadership, learn to function without their leaders in exile, and become viable institutions. It does nobody any good if there's nothing to the PPP besides Bhutto or that the Pakistan Muslim League is nothing but a dummy without Nawaz Sharif. I can see both sides of the argument for their participation. The PML, led by Sharif or his brother Shabaz, expect to emerge from the election as a major force in the assembly. But Sharif's party has to contend with the fact that most of his leading members have defected. Can Sharif win without them or can he persuade them to disband their faction and return to stand under his banner?"

"There's not enough time for him to negotiate such a maneuver," scoffed Shareef. "But Sharif's former lieutenants may be reluctant to support him again. So Sharif's chances of a big electoral victory are not good. Even without Musharraf's support, Sharif will emerge as the second largest party in the assembly. If unpleasant memories of the previous conflicts are set aside, as they often are in politics, a coalition between this faction and the PPP might not be a bad idea. Both parties are pragmatic. Deep down, neither is committed to any particular ideology. It remains to be seen what they will actually do and what General Musharraf will let them do."

"Well, the argument has returned to the decision of Musharraf and what he'll let other parties do. No one seems to play fair. It's just not cricket, is it?" Jorja concluded.

"Ah, yes, Miss Jorja, you're a hundred percent correct," said Shareef, agreeing with her for the first time. "Politics is not a fair sport. Politics in this country is certainly not cricket! I must go, it's late."

"Before you go, Shareef, I have one more important question."

"If you must ask, Jorja."

"How are your marriage arrangements going?"

The men looked at each other. Jamshid answered. "He'll be married soon enough if he can decide on the woman. He didn't like the first one I recommended."

"The one in the bank?"

"Yes, he's now looking at a teacher. She is very pretty with good hips to bear many children." In his mid-thirties, Shareef was not unattractive and was an exceptionally astute businessman, having amassed a considerable nest egg. He would be an excellent prospective husband for any woman.

"Have you spoken to her yet?" she asked Shareef.

"Oh, no! I've just looked at her. Jamshid pointed her out to me."

"He's too shy to talk to her," said Jamshid. "No wonder he's not married. He hasn't even kissed a woman before. Passionately I mean; on the mouth."

Shareef mockingly bowed his head and looked sheepish. "It's true. I'm too shy."

"You've never *ever* kissed anyone?" Jorja looked Shareef in the eye.

"He's never ever done it," said Jamshid. "He's a virgin."

Shareef covered his face. "I'm so embarrassed now, Jamshid. I'm a good Muslim and I don't believe in sex before marriage. There's nothing wrong with that. Besides, I'm shy."

"I don't believe you're shy for a minute, Shareef. You aren't shy around me."

"You're not his prospective wife," said Jamshid.

She wanted to shout—*what about me?* "Do you love her?"

"Jorja, I haven't met her yet, but love will grow," he said as he cast his eyes to the floor.

"Love will grow? How can you be so sure?"

"Jorja, it is what it is."

"Absolutely," said Jamshid. "My friend is right. Love will grow. Love will grow quickly. When you are only on the second date with a man Shareef will be wed. You would have to be dating a man now to beat Shareef to the altar. " Both men laughed. Jorja did not.

As Shareef moved to leave, he put his arm around her and squeezed tightly. He made no acknowledgement of their intimacy. "As soon as I'm married, I'll become your uncle and I'll start looking for a man for you. Jamshid, you're interested in taking a second wife, aren't you?"

Amid peals of laughter, Jamshid called out, "I can't afford it. A wife in Karachi and a wife in Australia. Oh my, oh my! I'll have no rupees left. Now get out of here so I can ring my wife or she'll kill me."

"I'm going, I'm going. Don't tell me I have a nagging wife to look forward to when I'm married. You're scaring me!"

CHAPTER 58

THE ROAD HOME

I'm on my way home. That was all Jorja wrote to Denny. She didn't know what else to write. Denny had another lover.

Flights out of Islamabad were heavily booked so she accompanied Noor and Jamshid by car to Lahore. Minhas had arranged a flight from Lahore to Australia for her. Jamshid had business in Lahore and afterwards was flying to Karachi to be with his family. "The job is a good one and pays well so I work in Islamabad. It won't be for long. One day I'll get work in Karachi. I don't like being away from my wife and two children, but that's just the way things are in Pakistan." In some way, Jorja understood how he felt.

"I'd like to say farewell to Shareef, Jamshid. Can we stop at his office?"

"No time, no time," dismissed her colleague.

Jorja sunk into the seat. With some effort, she could've fallen in love with Jamshid's friend. He was younger than her, but with a demeanor of confidence and wherewithal.

It was exceptionally hot weather. Five hours along the La- hore-Islamabad Motorway in temperatures as high as forty degrees Celsius was draining. The air-conditioning in the car worked for the first hour until the strain of operating forced it to halt suddenly. Jamshid was distressed in the heat and to relieve the suffering, he slept.

They made two brief stops. One was by choice. Gently veer- ing onto the side of the motorway, Noor stopped the car on a low rise overlooking the plains. While Noor found a place to relieve himself, Jorja pressed her thighs against the cold steel barricade and stared into the distance across the flat plains of Pakistan. There was nothing to see. She could see no end, no destiny, and no future.

Three highway police officers instigated the second stop. Seemingly, in the middle of nowhere, the policemen patrolled the motorway, checking the license and legitimacy of drivers. Noor's license was in order and he was motioned on his way.

The traffic police had an easy job. For the entire duration of the journey there were few cars sharing the concrete lanes to La- hore. Jorja marveled at the motorway. It was an impressive feat of five years of construction. Built in the Nineties, it was three hundred and forty kilometers of a six-lane divided controlled-ac- cess motorway with seventy-one bridges, a hundred and five un- derpasses and six interchanges. Traversing the agricultural belt of the province of Punjab, the motorway passed briefly through a hilly region that relieved the otherwise monotonous flatness. For such a grand motorway, it was rarely used. It was, therefore, a long and lonely drive.

Noor had difficulty finding the Lahore International Airport. A pedestrian inadvertently gave him instructions to the newly built terminal. It was a remarkable sight. The five-storey building had separate departure and arrivals tiers, five passenger-board- ing bridges and a bridge to the departure area. In progress was the construction of a parking lot, aircraft hangars, and a state-of-the-art fire, crash and rescue facility.

A lone guard stopped the car before Noor reached the new terminal. Noor stepped out of the car, exchanged words with him, and shared a cigarette. Neither was in a hurry. Tossing the stub away, Noor continued to locate the old terminal while relaying information gained from the security guard. The new terminal would also include climate control, passenger boarding bridges, lifts and escalators, security systems, check-in and baggage-handling facilities, as well as heating, ventilation, air conditioning and flight-information displays. The construction would cost an estimated two hundred million American dollars.

"You mean it'll be a real airport?" said Jorja.

Noor understood the joke. 'I'm so sorry that the new airport is not open yet. Next time you'll be able to use it."

"Yes, next time."

Jamshid woke when Noor braked to a halt in a parking bay at the old terminal. Groggy from the heat and sudden wakening, he chose to wish Jorja good luck by the car instead of walking with her into the terminal. "You are welcome back any time, Jorja," he said and gingerly hugged her.

Noor assisted her with her luggage, as far as officials permitted him, where they said a sad farewell. The international waiting lounge was decidedly more comfortable than the domestic lounge, with rows of seating, larger restrooms, refreshment kiosks, and a limited number of shops. Jorja waited, relieved that there was air conditioning. Evening approached. Rumbling thunder blanketed the noise of the terminal and lightning pierced the purple sky illuminating the airport runways.

A thunderous roar shook the terminal and the power went out. For a split second, the waiting passengers sat in darkness before a generator chugged into action and the emergency lights came on. The air conditioning remained off. A strident voice through the loudspeaker announced a delay for all flights. Jorja waited. She waited in the dim, oppressive airport, wondering whether her flight would prevail. Prevail it did, three hours late. She almost missed it. A woman gently touched her arm and calmly said, "I think this is our flight. I hope lightning doesn't strike us. I hope that it's not our destiny." She was young, beautiful, and graceful. Elegant in a shimmering copper shalwar kameez, she smiled as she led Jorja, willingly, gratefully, in a heat daze, to her destiny.

Lightning struck twice. The first was soon after the flight departed Lahore. The announcement throughout the airplane calmed passengers, notifying them that the pilot was rerouting around the storm. The second lightning strike was before Jorja's flight from Sydney to Canberra, as the plane sat in its parking bay. It was a strange day with unusual winter warmth, squalling winds, hailstones, and sheets of rain. Airline staff delayed its departure to ensure that there was no damage to the airplane. Twenty-eight hours after leaving Islamabad, Jorja arrived home.

PART THREE

MAY 2002

CHAPTER 59

A WIN AND A LOSS FOR PAKISTAN

Rejection, for Jorja, was always difficult to understand. Nevertheless, she could understand Denny's decision. Denny was not the cause of her pain. Pain came from her initial resistance to accept the situation. Back in Australia, although closer to Denny physically, she did not pursue him. She wrote a brief e-mail saying she was home. When she telephoned him, Jorja left a cheery message on his answering machine. That was all.

Instead, she found comfort in her friends and in exercise. Running through the hills and bushland of home was more peaceful and exhilarating than ever before. Admiring the native trees, she ran through a grove of Scribbly Gums, the iconic Australian eucalyptus; their smooth, pale trunks etched with brown wriggly marks caused by larvae burrowing close to the surface. The Drooping She-oaks, with their branches resembling cassowary quills, formed an arch over the track. Her feet missed the Narrow Leaf Bitter Pea and the Golden Everlasting Daisy, not yet in bloom. She had the freedom to run for kilometers dressed in attire that would make a Kashmiri blush. After the mangy donkeys, dogs, and cats of Muzaffarabad, it was a delight to see again kangaroos and rabbits, parrots and finches.

The simple experience of dining with friends in the evening, without the noise of gunfire or the fear of kidnapping, was precious and uplifting. No one ordered Jorja to wait and no one told her not to worry. No one said, "As you wish, madam." Blessed with a feeling of expansion, Jorja felt as if she were receiving life's most vibrant gifts. It was no more than normal life, but she no longer took it for granted.

Each morning, as Jorja viewed herself in the mirror, she could see Pakistan's legacy although she knew it would disappear with time. Actually, it was Abassi's legacy. He had cut her hair too short. Worse than that, a missing chunk had left a triangular gap clearly visible above the bridge of her nose. Hair grows she mused and shrugged off the mishap. When a friend asked what had happened to her hair, she merely said, "Pakistani style."

As May began, General Pervez Musharraf gained an overwhelming referendum victory giving him another five years in office. It was a controversial win. Higher than expected polling numbers had given the vote legitimacy. No one could dispute the landslide win with Musharraf attracting ninety-eight percent of public support and over thirty-six million votes. Only 625,891 voters opposed him.

Lufti e-mailed Jorja the news:

Jorja
As you know, I must be quick on the e-mail. I rarely use it now because it's so tedious. I think Jamshid told you how successful the workshops were. Everyone missed you and all hope you are well and glad to be home.

Musharraf was victorious in the referendum, as we knew he would be. The voting was orderly. No untoward incident was reported from any part of the country. Those who opposed the referendum preferred to stay home and didn't create any problems. His supporters praised him for backing the American war on terrorism, promoting economic stability, and fighting corruption. Now they will expect continued action against corruption and terrorism. His detractors said the referendum was illegal and a contravention of the Constitution. They think Musharraf won't be able to meet his expectations. Time will tell, Jorja.

May peace and happiness be with you,
Lufti

Musharraf spent his early childhood in Turkey and migrated to Karachi in the same year Pakistan adopted its Constitution in 1956. After a long career in Pakistan's military forces since 1964, Musharraf achieved the rank of General in 1998. In October of the following year, he seized power in a bloodless military coup appointing himself president two years later while advocating democracy and peace.

Despite being the head of Pakistan's powerful military, he campaigned like a politician. Global leaders, while conscious of the controversial manner in which Musharraf called the referendum, strongly supported him and his democratic ideals and moderate Muslim approach.

A week after the referendum, a suicide bomber struck in the streets of Karachi. Eleven French nationals and two Pakistanis were killed outside the Sheraton Hotel in the volatile southern city where they were staying while working on a government submarine project.

The bombing shocked and angered the southern hemisphere. Australia and New Zealand, two great sporting nations, were drawn inextricably into the events of the suicide bombing. The touring New Zealand cricket team was staying at the adjacent

Pearl Continental Hotel. It was not clear whether the insurgents were also targeting the cricketers along with the French submarine workers. Nevertheless, New Zealand cricket authorities immediately cancelled the Test Tour of Pakistan. They were not taking any chances.

Jamshid e-mailed Jorja to express his horror at the event in his hometown and the disappointment of Pakistanis who reveled in the game of cricket.

Jorja

The news of the Karachi bombing is horrendous. I'm disgusted at the actions of these terrorists. They've done so much damage to our country. Airlines have suspended international flights to Karachi and Lahore because of security concerns. No one wants to come to Pakistan any more. If they did, there are not many airlines that will bring them here. We are going to the dogs.

Now there will be no cricket matches against New Zealand. Karachi has fourteen million people and I think all of them wanted to watch the cricket. It's the only thing we are thankful for from the British Rule. Depriving Pakistan of cricket is a cruel fate for the nation. There is talk that the terrorists are against General Musharraf's support of America's fight against al-Qaeda and the Taliban in Afghanistan. It's not really an attack on internationals, but an attack on Musharraf's ideologies. I wish you could tell the New Zealand cricket team that and make them come back to Pakistan.

India and Pakistan have resumed their fight at the border in Kashmir. Indian troops started the fighting across the Line of Control and Pakistani troops fought back. Fortunately, this fighting is sixty kilometers away. There are many civilian losses and much panic. Three people died yesterday in the upper Neelum Valley northeast of Muzaffarabad. One was a woman. India blames Pakistani militants and yesterday ordered Pakistan to withdraw its high commissioner in New Delhi. This is not good news. It will make the tensions worse. Our government has demanded an impartial investigation of the attack. India is asking for another war.

Jorja, the world is not a good place. You are lucky to be in Australia.

I hope to see you again in Pakistan. I will show you the beautiful sights of Karachi and Lahore.

Jamshid S Mohammad

CHAPTER 60

INCREASING TENSIONS

By the end of May, Denny had still not contacted Jorja. She came to expect that he wouldn't.

In that time, Pakistan had called for increased international efforts to make India "see reason" and begin negotiations as war clouds gathered over the two countries. Pakistan's foreign ministry spokesman, Aziz Ahmed Khan, when asked at a news conference whether he thought war was imminent with India, said that he was not in the business of "fortune telling." Strangely, Jorja felt the same way when friends asked her whether she thought Denny would ever contact her. The forecast, however, did not look favorable, for Pakistan, Kashmir and Jorja.

India blamed Pakistani militants for the Jammu massacre that led to them ordering Pakistan to withdraw its high commissioner from New Delhi. Pakistan denied the charge and denied that it armed or funded Islamic militants in Kashmir. Pakistan, however, acknowledged that it provided moral and diplomatic support to what it described as an "indigenous freedom struggle." Jamshid suggested that the United States should be more involved in resolving the issue through dialogue as a third party.

Jorja

It's getting worse in Pakistan. We are close to war. There is too much blame. The Indian government blames Pakistan and we blame them. It's like brothers fighting. The father should stop this. America should scold the two brothers and make them talk to each other.

The fighting is more intense now. If India starts more fighting at the border, our officials said it would provoke retaliation. Any raids into Pakistani territory or Azad Kashmir will be met with full force. The Indian government responded that it was determined to launch strikes on militant camps in Azad Kashmir. The fear is that if the Indian government did launch the strikes, the tension would initiate another full-scale war.

Troops of both countries are already at the border, waiting for trouble. They have been like this since December 2001, but now there are more troops. Both countries don't want to look weak. The Indians cannot afford not to take action after having amassed troops for six months and the Pakistanis cannot afford to back down from their repeated threat of meeting any aggression with full force. Everyone is crystal balling, but no one can be certain of the outcome. War between Pakistan and India has happened in the past and the current tensions are pushing everyone to the brink. Full-scale war is a definite possibility, Jorja.

Jamshid S Mohammad

Reading Jamshid's account of his country's situation, Jorja was thankful that she wasn't arguing with Denny. They each had a separate circle of friends so there was no likelihood of seeing him and hence no possibility of friction. Silence was probably no better. Jamshid had made no mention of the prospect of peace between Pakistan and India. By all accounts, the possible union of the two countries seemed an improbability in the near future. Likewise, the possibility of a reunion with Denny was sure to be fraught with failure.

CHAPTER 61

PREPARING FOR WAR

"Has he contacted you yet?" asked Marie Stevenson, Jorja's friend, a previous work colleague.

"No."

"Why don't you ring him? Why don't you leave him a rude e-mail?"

"What's the point? It's over. I'm over it, so why don't you get over it? Just let things be."

"He owes you an explanation." Marie's angry voice rose above the restaurant noise.

Jorja abhorred conflict. "He doesn't owe me anything. We weren't married. We weren't in a long relationship. I'm not even sure now that we were in any kind of relationship at all, other than exceptional friendship."

"What poppycock! You were drooling over him before you went to Pakistan. You were in a fucking relationship!"

Jorja laughed. Marie's phrase reminded her of Mr. Kaliq and his quest for a fucking relationship.

"What's so funny? This is serious. Dennis, Denny, or whatever you call him, owes you an explanation. Confront him! Make him talk to you. Keep ringing him. You rang once. Once! You're an idiot. And what have you got? Nothing but silence! You deserve more than that."

Marie intervened regardless of Jorja's protests. She adopted the role of Jorja's Defense Secretary, much to her annoyance. Marie's extensive network of contacts led her to a friend of Denny's and eventually to Denny himself. The confrontation occurred at a party.

"I went straight up to him and looked him in the eye. I must say, his green eyes almost stopped me in my tracks. What a knockout guy. I pulled myself together and asked if he knew you. He said that the two of you were friends. Well, I just fumed, didn't I? 'Friends?' I screamed. 'Friends? You aren't even talking to her.' I let fly with a mouthful. He just stood there. All he said was 'I've been busy.' That set me off again. 'Busy? Busy?' I yelled at him. After I launched an attack, he bit back, saying I was an interfering busybody intent on causing friction. He said I was a battleship looking for a war."

Visualizing the cat-woman unleashed on Denny made Jorja cringe. "Marie, I'm embarrassed. You should've just let this be. Now he'll never want to come anywhere near me because he'll be scared witless my friends will attack him. You've made the situation worse."

"But don't you want to hear the rest?" Her brown eyes widened in amazement.

"No! Give it up."

Marie continued. "Sorry, but do you know what he did? He just walked away. He just walked away. From me! What does that mean? Eh? You should confront him! Get him to talk to you. Confront him Jorja! It's the only way." Less aggressively, she added, "Anyway, I found out he's not with anyone at the moment. He's footloose. I bet he'll contact you now. Do you think he will?"

"Clearly, Marie, he will not."

***

The possibility of a full-scale Pakistan-India war was gaining momentum. On the twenty-second day of May, India's prime minister visited his soldiers on the Kashmir frontier, telling them to prepare for a "decisive battle" against Pakistan-supported Islamic insurgents.

> *Jorja*
>
> *I think full-scale war is coming. Hundreds of Indian soldiers in bullet-proof vests are patrolling the mountain roads at the border. Prime Minister, Atal Bihari Vajpayee, asked his soldiers to be ready for sacrifice. He said the Indians will write a new chapter and it will end with victory. He has also sent extra warships to the Arabian Sea. Soon after Mr. Vajpayee arrived in Kashmir, masked gunmen assassinated Abdul Ghani Lone, a Kashmiri peace advocate. Abdul was a quiet, seventy-year-old Muslim leader, a moderate, who sought dialogue with India to bring self-determination for Kashmiris. Now he's dead. Things are going to get drastically worse from now on. The Indian prime minister is inciting trouble. Kashmiris are protesting against the killing of Abdul and Mr. Vajpayee's visit. Before his death, Abdul said Indian authorities had tried to kill him and that an Islamic militant group fighting to separate Kashmir from India had threatened his life. His son, Sajjad Lone, said Pakistanis killed his father, but later took back his comments. The murder of Abdul is yet another incident in the continuing terror in this country and in Kashmir. We are close to war. We must bring sanity where there is total insanity. The*

Australian Embassy in Pakistan has warned its people that Indian troops could strike soon and that they could be the targets of terrorist attacks. They have been told to leave Pakistan. If you were here, you would have to go home. It's a good thing that you aren't here. If there is war, no one will win. We will both be losers.
Jamshid S Mohammad
PS: Shareef is married to a dressmaker. Are you married yet?

Jamshid expressed what Jorja felt. Marie's suggestion that Jorja confront Denny for an explanation was ludicrous. Confrontation would only make them both losers. She thought of Shareef Zardini fleetingly. There was no point dwelling on what might have been.

Pakistan conducted two missile tests in two days. The country was preparing for war. The first missile test was to trial the short-range Hatf-111 Ghaznavi missile for the first time. With a range of almost three hundred kilometers, the new surface-to-surface missile could hit border regions of India. The second test was to trial Pakistan's medium-range Ghauri ballistic missile. Both the Ghauri and Ghaznavi missiles were capable of carrying conventional and nuclear warheads. The Ghauri missile with a range of one thousand and five hundred kilometers could strike deep into India.

As tensions escalated, residents on both sides of the disputed border fled for their safety. The Government of Pakistan said the tests had nothing to do with the current situation. India said it was not worried.

As the world scrambled to avert a war that could escalate into a nuclear conflagration on the Asian subcontinent, Russian President Vladimir Putin invited the leaders of India and Pakistan to Kazakhstan for one-on-one talks to prevent future conflict. Pakistan said it was ready to talk. India wanted Pakistan to end cross-border incursions by Islamic militants, demanding either outright independence for the divided Himalayan State or union with Islamic Pakistan. India indicated that action on Pakistan's part was preferable to constant high-level discussions.

The precariousness of their relationship was an ongoing issue. Neither of them wanted to discuss peace. Neither of them wanted to back down. Yet, neither of them wanted to initiate the first act of aggression that would invariably and inevitably lead to full-scale war. Pakistan reacted to the escalating tension by test firing, for the third time, a short-range missile capable of carrying nuclear warheads: the Hatf II missile, the Abdali. Pakistan defended the tests as routine, "as routine as India's similar missile tests in January," said Musharraf.

In his much-awaited televised address to the nation, General Musharraf said Pakistan would not initiate war, but it would defend itself. Musharraf said the same people were responsible for the terrorist assaults in India in December 2001, a Protestant international church in Islamabad in March, and a bus carrying French engineers in Karachi in May. He concluded by saying there had been many arrests, therefore ending militant infiltration into Indian-controlled Kashmir.

Militants were outraged at Musharraf's speech, believing he had stabbed them in the back and abandoned them in the same way Pakistan had disassociated itself from the Taliban. A jihad, or holy war, was the only solution to the Kashmir issue, said the militants.

Indian foreign minister, Jaswant Singh, said Musharraf's speech was "disappointing" and "dangerous" because tensions had increased, not reduced. As May ended, India's foreign minister attended a conference with British Foreign Secretary Jack Straw telling the world Pakistan must take urgent steps to halt cross-border terrorism and Islamic insurgents in Kashmir, an act vital for peace. Meanwhile, cross-border firing continued.

Jorja kept track of the news by reading the online version of *Dawn*. One Neelum Valley villager who arrived in Muzaffarabad said: *I walked away to save my life. There is no fixed time for firing, it can happen anytime, whenever India wants to. The Indian army announces on loudspeakers that you should leave the area and vacate your houses. We are so close to the border that even small arms fire can hit us. We stay up all night shaking with fear.*

Denny was not wired for battle. He was a pacifist with an instinctive knack for calming hysterical people. Even if hurt, he could not strike back. Perhaps if an argument caught him unaware, he may lash out in confusion, although it was more his tendency to simply agree in order to end the dispute. He fought best by walking away. More to the point, Denny was not a person of action. He would not deliberately instigate a fight, but neither would he consciously initiate peace. This was an emotional stalemate, and one best put behind them, Jorja thought.

CHAPTER 62

HOPES RISE

Osama bin Laden had not been found. Operation Anaconda had been terminated. The Americans had failed to root him out of the mountains of Afghanistan. Peter Bergen's novel, *Holy War, Inc: Inside the Secret World of Bin Laden* was a *New York Times* bestseller, translated into eighteen languages. Bergen continued to report on terrorism for the CNN. Every time Jorja saw him on television, she imagined him with a beard, a long thinning peppery beard. She imagined him with drooping eyelids and thicker lips. She imagined him with a dark turban. She imagined him offering her aromatic tea in the mountains of Kashmir. She even imagined marrying him and setting off into the sunset on a crusade to hunt for the real Osama bin Laden. It seemed fanciful to everyone, except Jorja.

It was the tenth day of June, and a night with a new moon. The easing of tensions between India and Pakistan eventuated after a senior United States peace envoy said he expected India to take steps to cool the conflict within the next few days. India announced it would resume cricket matches with Pakistan. The sport-loving people of both nations cheered the good news. Imran Khan applauded the move, saying it was a positive step from India to revive the sport because cricket could help in the peace process.

The crisis was not over, however. Pakistan announced it shot down an Indian spy plane with no personnel on board. India said a reconnaissance plane went missing after a routine flight, but gave no further details.

During discussions, a veteran of Kashmir's independence struggle warned India and Pakistan not to carve up the Himalayan region, arguing that independence remained the only solution. Kashmiris now feared deals would cement the current division of their land between the two armies, separating families forever. The chairman of the Jammu Kashmir Liberation Front, the organization that launched the armed struggle against Indian Rule in Kashmir in 1988, said both India and Pakistan were denying Kashmiris the right to self-determination, believing they were only interested in the land for tourist and strategic reasons.

Indian Prime Minister Atal Bihari Vajpayee hoped for peace when asked by a reporter about "war clouds." *Dawn* reported Mr. Vajpayee's response: *The sky is clear. But sometimes lightning strikes even in clear skies. We hope lightning will not strike.* Soon after Mr. Vajpayee left Kashmir, militants lobbed a grenade at a paramilitary post in Srinagar. Mr. Vajpayee then moved five warships closer to Pakistan and ordered hundreds of soldiers on the Kashmir border to prepare for war.

Restraint prevailed on both sides. Discussions continued. All was not lost. Pakistan and India were talking. Denny and Jorja were not.

Jorja had ceased her approaches to Denny. Denny had not conceded a millimeter. It was no longer a stalemate, but rather a decisive ending to an embryonic relationship. Although they had only been together for a few months, the time was intimate and memorable. Denny often appeared aloof and brooding in public,

but when he was with Jorja, he was warm-hearted and romantic. His humor could dissipate her tensions and, under his touch,
she felt the world was no longer a lonely place. She adored the
quirkiness and individuality of her sensitive and creative lover.
Any woman who had loved Denny seldom hated him afterwards.
She wished for the sweet days and months that had vanished.

* * *

Six weeks after leaving Kashmir, hopes were increasing for
the de-escalation in conflict between Pakistan and India, but
without a clear resolution for Kashmir. Again, Kashmir was the
pawn in the relationship. Six weeks after leaving Kashmir, Denny telephoned. It was unexpected. He was conciliatory, offering
a reunion, a renewal of friendship. All was not lost.

*Jorja, you know I didn't mean to hurt you. You were there,
I was here. You might have been in Pakistan for eight months.
What was I to do? I don't like being alone.*

It's okay. I understand.

*Can we talk? Can I tell you how much I miss you? Can we
go back to our discussions about capitalism versus communism?
Can I come to your place this Friday – after work?*

Sure. Bring flowers.

*Thanks, I'll bring our favorite Italian wine too. Thanks so
much, Jorja. See you soon.*

Jorja hung up the receiver and stood on the eastern balcony looking across at Mt. Ainslie, a mound compared to the
mountains of the Himalaya. Kashmir had forced her to balance her own conflicting and divergent emotions, often precariously, but always with an impact of profound proportions.
Her time in Kashmir was one of dominance and subservience,
of love and loneliness.

Jorja shivered on the balcony when the wind whipped
through her sweater. She watched a wisp of fluffy white flakes
waft in front of her, followed by another and another. Snow was
falling. It was a rare occurrence in the city. Before a layer could

form on the ground, it melted. Lasting a brief half an hour, the snow had merely lined the city with a hint of white dust. Nevertheless, in its brevity, it caused a great deal of excitement.

AUTHOR'S NOTE

This is a fictional work based upon my experience in Kashmir and Pakistan in 2002. Articles by staff reporters of the Pakistan newspapers, *News International* and *Dawn,* supplemented my information and knowledge of the region. In particular, I referred to the following *Dawn* articles: *A bumpy road to literacy* by Ghizala Kazi, *Why poor people continue to stay poor?* by Tasneem Siddiqui, and political references by Kunwar Idris, Anwar Syed, and Ardeshir Cowasjee. The *Dawn* Supplement of March 23, 2002 was the source of information on Pakistan Day and the Quaid-i-Azam Mohammed Ali Jinnah. Contributors to the Supplement included Professor Ziauddin Ahmad, Ghayoor Ahmed, Sharif al Mujahid, Hussein Ferhan Zafar, Dr. Muhammad Ali Siddiqui, Dr. Mahmudur Rahman, Bahre Karam Khan, Pervez Tahir, Dr. Safdar Mahmood, Dr. Hasan Askari Rizvi, and I.A. Rehman. I referred to *The Canberra Times* for political issues on Pakistan, especially articles by staff reporters Lincoln Wright and Simon Grose. Other sources included various websites on Madam Noor Jehan. For information on pit latrines, I referred to the World Health Organization, *Medecins Sans Frontieres*, and World Vision.

Lightning Source UK Ltd.
Milton Keynes UK
UKOW051931040112

184747UK00001B/90/P